A
Harlequin
JANET
DAILEY
Collector's Edition

Harlequin
JANET
DAILEY
Collector's Editions

A Harlequin

JANET
DAILEY

Collector's Edition

Harlequin Books

TORONTO • NEW YORK • LONDON
AMSTERDAM • PARIS • SYDNEY • HAMBURG
STOCKHOLM • ATHENS • TOKYO • MILAN

These books by Janet Dailey were originally published as
follows:

SWEET PROMISE
Copyright © 1976 by Janet Dailey
First published by Mills & Boon Limited in 1976
Harlequin Presents edition (#308) published
September 1979

TIDEWATER LOVER
Copyright © 1978 by Janet Dailey
First published by Mills & Boon Limited in 1978
Harlequin Presents edition (#292) published
June 1979

ISBN 0-373-80610-8
First edition May 1984
The Harlequin trademark, consisting of the word
HARLEQUIN and the portrayal of a Harlequin,
is registered in the United States Patent and Trademark
Office and in the Canada Trade Marks Office.

PRINTED IN U.S.A.

CONTENTS

SWEET PROMISE

"DO YOU THINK YOU OWN ME, RAFAEL?"

His fiercely possessive glance answered her. "Yes, I suppose you do," she continued brokenly. "Marrying you was like selling myself to the devil."

"Perhaps our marriage was made in hell," he jeered. "But our union was legal and binding. You will never be free of my touch or my name!" He pulled her roughly against him, claiming her mouth with a savage sweetness that met bitter denial. A question burned in his eyes as he released her.

"I am in love with another man," Erica said huskily. "I want a divorce, Rafael."

His silence frightened her. Then he laughed, a cold, harsh sound that sent ice through her veins. "There will be no divorce," he said hoarsely. "And you shall pay for your foolishness."

CHAPTER ONE

THE MUSIC WAS a slow, sentimental ballad, spinning its love theme for the few couples on the floor. The subdued lighting added to the magic of the moment, creating another romantic spell.

A happy sigh slid through Erica's lips as she felt the caressing touch of Forest's chin against her dark hair. Her fingers curled tighter around his neck while she lightly rubbed the side of her head along his chin and jawline in a feline gesture, smiling when she felt his mouth against her hair.

Tilting her head back she gazed into his tanned face, admiring again his striking looks; the commanding strength in repose signified by the square jaw and the cleft in his chin, the sensual line of his mouth, and the velvet touch of his brown eyes as they possessively examined her face.

To speak in a normal voice might break the spell, so Erica whispered softly instead. "Would it sound very corny and silly if I said that I could do this all night?"

"With me or with anyone?" Forest murmured. An eyebrow, the same light brown shade as his hair, arched to tease her.

"That's another thing I like about you. You never take me for granted." Her soft voice trembled with the depth of her emotion and Erica buried her head in his shoulder, knowing her violet eyes were much too expressive of her thoughts.

"What else do you like about me?" His lips were moving against the silken length of her hair again, igniting warm fires in her veins.

"Conceited?" she taunted him, but with a catch in her husky voice.

"Where you are concerned I need all the assurance I can get." The arm around her waist tightened, holding her closer to his muscular body as if he expected her to slip away. "Tell me." His growling order was a mock threat, but one Erica was only too happy to obey.

Hesitant to reveal how deeply she cared for this man who was noted for his careless and carefree association with women, she adopted a light-hearted air.

"For starters, you don't make all those affirmative noises when daddy is around. You're independent and very secure about your own ability. You're much too handsome for a girl's peace of mind. Elusive, always managing to escape being led down to the altar and all the while making a girl believe she's the only one in your life." Erica raised her head from his shoulder and encountered the smoldering light in his eyes. With her lashes, she shielded the answering light in her own eyes. "A girl wants to forget everything her parents taught her when she's with you."

"Not all girls." His hand cupped her chin, lifting it so he could gaze thoughtfully into her face. "Certainly not you. That first night I took you out,

I was ready to agree that all those rumors about your being an ice maiden were true. To be perfectly honest, Erica, in the beginning you were a challenge." White teeth flashed as his mouth curved in a rueful smile. "I don't believe anyone has said no to me as many times as you have."

Determinedly she forced herself to breathe evenly. "Do you mean all those times you invited me to your apartment, it wasn't to see your art collection?" she teased, her eyes widening with false surprise.

"Only the one in my bedroom." The laughter left his face as he studied her solemnly. "Every time I touch you or kiss you, I sense that you're holding back. I know you're Vance Wakefield's daughter and many men have taken you out not only because of your looks but because of his wealth and influence. Surely you know me well enough by now to realize that I'm not the least bit interested in who your father is."

"I know that." Their steps had nearly ceased as they absently swayed in tempo with the music.

"Not that I haven't taken into account that you're his daughter to the extent that he is your father and very important in your life," Forest added. "That's the way it should be, even though I know he doesn't totally approve of me."

"It's not you he disapproves of, but your reputation." Erica shrugged weakly.

"And that I may in some way sully yours." He nodded understandingly.

"Daddy isn't an ogre," she said, smiling humorlessly. "He sees me as an adult and realizes

11

that my relationships with other people are on an adult level."

There was no need to add that if Vance Wakefield felt his daughter was being used, he would fall upon the offender with all the weight his power and money could bring to bear. Yet that was not a comforting thought for Erica. In the almost twenty-two years of her life, she had tried very hard to become close to her father. He was a strong, indomitable, ruthless man who despised weakness of any sort. She seriously doubted if he had ever mourned the loss of his wife, her mother, but rather cursed her inability to survive the birth of a child, Erica.

In her early years she had fought for his love, always terrified that her handsome father would marry again and she would have to compete with a new wife and possibly another child for the attention she wanted so desperately. No other woman entered his household, but he became married to his business, a more jealous and demanding rival than Erica could compete against and win. Still she fought and struggled for every ounce of attention that she could steal, using every weapon from open rebellion and stormy scenes to smothering love.

It had taken her nearly twenty years to realize that in his own way he loved her. As strong as the bonds were, she was still a female, hence weak. And Erica concealed any exploit that would point out her vulnerability and lower his esteem of her.

"If it's not your father's wrath you fear, why have you refused me?" A frown of puzzlement drew Forest's brows together. "You aren't an ice maiden—I've discovered that. There have been times when I've held you in my arms that I've been certain I touched a core of passion inside you. Don't you want me as much as I want you? Or don't you trust me?"

"Oh, no, I don't trust myself," she corrected quickly. She could feel the glowing heat of previous shame rising in her cheeks and murmured a silent prayer of thanks for the dimness of the room that concealed it.

"And you've been afraid to do something in the heat of the moment that you would regret in the cold light of day," he finished for her, a gentle and satisfied smile curving the strong line of his mouth.

"Yes, that's what I have been afraid of," Erica admitted. It was a fear that had very firm foundation.

The last note of the song was tapering into silence. For a second, Forest retained his hold, keeping her pressed against his long length, and Erica wondered if he had caught the qualifying statement she had just made. She had been afraid, but she wasn't any longer.

Two months wasn't a very long time in which to know a man. Still, Erica was positive that what she felt toward Forest was not simply physical attraction or even sexual attraction, but a deeper emotion called love, however futile it might be.

A musician in the small combo announced they would be taking a short break and all the couples had left the dance floor by the time Forest guided

Erica back to their table. His arm retained a possessive hold on her waist, relinquishing it only when they were seated, their chairs drawn closely together.

"I'm beginning to understand more things about you," Forest said softly, letting his arm curve over the back of her chair to caress her bare shoulders. "But I've been making even stranger discoveries about myself."

"About you? Such as?" prompted Erica, tucking a strand of shoulder-length dark hair behind her ear so it wouldn't interfere with her view of him.

"Such as—" His gaze wandered over her face, lingering on her lips "—I've fallen in love with you, irrevocably and irretrievably in love with you."

Her gasp was a mixture of disbelief and elation. She had never dared hope that he might care as much as she believed she did. The wonder of it darkened her eyes to a royal shade of purple heightened by a diamond mist of happy tears.

"I love you, too," Erica breathed. "I never believed . . . I never thought it was possible that you might love me."

"Only a man in love would take no for an answer as many times as I have." He smiled, and something in his smile confirmed the truth of his words.

She wanted to wind her arms around his neck and feel the warmth of his lips against hers, but just then laughter sounded from one of the tables near theirs and Erica was reminded that they were not alone.

"If you doubted my feelings," Forest murmured, his hand intimately caressing the curve of her neck, "can you imagine how I wondered about yours? I felt you were bound to mistrust me because of my reputation. I've heard some of the stories that have been circulated about me, and some were based on fact."

"It's never mattered to me what others have said about you," she insisted.

She wanted to explain that one of the things that had drawn her to him was his somewhat diehard bachelor attitude, but to do that would mean explaining her reasons and she hadn't the courage for that yet.

"Shall we drink a toast then, to each other?" he suggested. His fingers closed around the stem of his martini glass and Erica reached for her own glass. Compared to his strong drink, hers was an innocuous sherry. Over their glasses their eyes met, sending silent messages while the expensive crystal rang when their glasses touched.

"I think there's something in my martini," Forest declared, drawing the glass near the light after the first tentative sip to study it.

"Besides the olive?" Her tremulous smile was to cover the fluttering of her heart as she covertly studied his profile.

"Would you look at this?" His voice was amused and vaguely triumphant as he directed her gaze to the miniature plastic spear in his hand.

At the end of the spear was the olive with its stuffing of red pimento, but dangling in front of it was a ring. The muted candlelight touched the stone and reflected myriad colors.

"This must be yours." At his announcement, Erica swung her stunned look to him.

"No." Her head moved to deny it.

He had wiped it dry with his linen handkerchief and was now handing the ring to her. "I hope you're going to accept it," he said. "It might be poetic justice to have the first girl I've ever proposed to turn me down. But after all this time of saying no, now that I'm asking you to marry me, please say yes, darling."

Somehow she eluded his move to place the ring on her finger, taking it instead and clutching it between the fingers of both hands. The single diamond solitaire winked back at her, laughing at her until her head throbbed with pain as Erica fought to stem the hysteria that bubbled in her throat.

"Don't you like it?" He voice was low and controlled, but with a razor-sharp edge to it.

The face she turned to him was unnaturally pale and strained. "Oh, Forest, I love it," she gulped, tearing her gaze from the mocking ring to meet his, only to bounce back to the diamond when she was unable to meet the probing brown eyes. A tear slipped from her lashes to blaze a hot trail down her cheek, but she quickly wiped it away. "Please—may we leave here?"

"Of course."

Erica knew Forest would misinterpret her reasons for wanting to go, believing that she wanted a less public place for her tears of happiness. They were tears of happiness. The salty tang of them on her lips was what brought the bitterness and produced the misery of the moment.

With the ease of a man who knew his way about, Forest disposed of their check, produced the light shawl that matched the layered chiffon dress she wore, and had the car brought around to the front of the club.

Moments later he had turned the car onto a quiet San Antonio street and was switching off the engine. Not one word had he directed to her, and he didn't now as he drew her into his arms. Her lips hungrily sought his descending mouth, welcoming and returning the ardency of his touch while his hands arched her toward him. Her unbridled response unnerved both of them and it took some minutes before they were able to recover their powers of speech.

Forest's mouth was moving over her eyes and cheeks. "Will you marry me, darling?" His breath caressed her skin as he spoke. "Or do I have to carry you off into the night until you agree?"

"I want to marry you," Erica whispered, a throbbing ache in her voice. "More than anything else, I want you to believe that."

For all her fervid assurance, his searching kiss stopped, halted by the unspoken qualification in her statement. His tensed stiffness tore at her chest. The ring was still in her hand, burning its imprint in her sensitive palm.

"But I can't accept your ring." She added the

words Forest had instinctively braced himself to hear.

"Why?" The demand was combined with the tightening of his hold just before he thrust her away. "You do love me?"

"I love you, darling, honestly I do," vowed Erica, caressing the tanned cheek with her hand. "I simply can't accept your ring. At least not now, I can't."

There was a slightly imperious and bemused tilt of his head. "I've always known you were old-fashioned in some ways, but I never guessed that you would want me to speak to your father first."

"No, that's not what I meant!" Her cry was one of despair and panic.

"I don't understand," Forest sighed impatiently, wearily rubbing the back of his neck. "Do you want to marry me or not?"

"Yes, I want to—oh, please, Forest, I can't take your ring. It wouldn't be fair." She begged for his understanding, to have the touch of his hands become once more loving.

"Are you engaged to someone else?" An incredulous anger narrowed his gaze.

"No!" She pressed her fingers against the pounding pain between her eyes. "I can't explain and I beg you not to ask me. I swear it's true that I love you, but I need time."

He stared at her for a long moment, his expression carved and impenetrable before a slow smile broke the severe mold. "It is a big step, isn't it? I've had plenty of time to think it over, but I haven't given you much warning."

Time for a decision was not what Erica had meant, but she was very willing to take advantage of it. She opened her clenched hand and stared at the ring. The starlight streaming through the car windows cast a milky sheen on the many facets of the large diamond.

"It is a big step," she agreed, taking a deep breath. "Not something that's done on the spur of the moment." The only smile she could summon was somewhat twisted and wry, its ruefulness concealed by the dimness. "Marry in haste, repent at leisure. I don't want it to be that way with us, Forest."

"Neither do I. I want you to be as certain as I am," he stated.

Although she didn't look up, she could feel the caress of his eyes. The calm determination of his voice almost made her want to put the ring on her finger and damn the consequences, but she steeled herself against doing anything so foolish. Slowly she stretched out her hand to him, palm upward, the engagement ring in the center.

"Would you keep this for me?" she asked. As she met the controlled desire in his gaze, the pain at giving back his ring softened and she sought to reassure him. "I think I'll be wanting it shortly, so please don't give it to some other girl."

"I burned all my telephone numbers weeks ago. There is no other girl." His light brown hair gleamed golden in the pale light as he bent his head to retrieve his ring.

When the ring was safely in his pocket, his velvet brown eyes skittered over her face, its oval

19

perfection framed by the rich brown hair combed away from it. His searching glance came to a full stop on the curve of her lips.

"Don't make me wait too long, Erica." It wasn't a request because of the autocratic ring of his voice. Nor was it a threat, since passion throbbed beneath the surface.

"I won't." The starlight gilded her smooth complexion as she waited in anticipation of the moment when Forest would draw her firmly in his arms.

His hand trailed lightly over the hollow of her cheek back to the base of her neck, sliding under her hair as a thumb gently rubbed the pulsing vein in her neck.

"No woman has ever dangled me on a string before," he told her, his expression paradoxically tender and hard. "I don't like it." Erica started to initiate the movement that would bring her to the muscular chest, but his hand tightened around her neck to check it. Then he released her and turned to the front. "I'm taking you home. I haven't much patience left, so the sooner you make the decision, the better off I will be."

Erica was given no opportunity to argue as he started the car and drove it back onto the street. Part of her wanted the evening to last forever, not to go on torturing Forest as her lack of an answer was doing, but to postpone what she was going to be forced to do if she wanted to marry him. And Erica was certain that she did.

The closer they came to her home on the outskirts of the city, the more her thoughts became

20

preoccupied with her dilemma. When Forest walked her to the door, the kiss she gave him appeared natural enough on the surface, but underneath her nerves were becoming raw from the strain of her decision.

When she stepped inside the house, she discovered her legs were trembling. Their weakness had no basis in Forest's ardent kiss. Her widened eyes, like fully opened African violets, darted to the closed study door, almost the only room in the large, rambling house that her father used. In her mind's eye, Erica could visualize the freezing scorn and contempt that would pierce the blue depths of his eyes if she went to him with her problem.

It had never been his contempt that she had feared. There had been times in the past when she had deliberately provoked his wrath to gain his attention. Only once had her actions backfired on her, the very last time she had done it. Only afterward had she realized how very foolish her childish attempts had been.

But it had succeeded in forcing her to grow up. And Erica had finally realized that her father was incapable of loving her as much as she loved him. In many ways their temperaments were alike. She could be as bullheaded and stubborn as he and just as quick to anger. Yet Vance Wakefield was not able to give of himself and he had never been able to understand her need as a child to be constantly assured of his affection.

Her coming of age had opened her eyes to this one flaw of her father's. In the past almost two

21

years, Erica had stopped demanding more than he could give. Their relationship had reached a peak of casual companionship that she had never thought they could attain. To go to him now would destroy it.

Her teeth sank sharply into her lower lip to bite back the sob of despair. Casting a last furtive glance at the study, she hurried down the hallway to her bedroom. When the oak door was closed behind her, she leaned weakly against it, then pushed herself away to cross the Persian carpet of a richly patterned blue and gold. Her fingers closed tightly around the carved oak bedpost while her darkly clouded eyes stared at the brilliant sea of blue of the bedspread.

Her first impulse was to throw herself on the bed, to wallow in a pool of self-pity that she was ever foolish enough to get into such a situation. Instead Erica shook her head determinedly, banishing the impulse as a waste of energy. She tipped her head back and stared at the ceiling, breathing in deeply to calm her jumping nerves. Low, mocking laughter surged through the tight muscles of her throat, its echo taunting her as it sounded through the room.

"I've spent nearly two years hiding and dreading this day," she chided herself. "I kept stupidly believing that it would all work out on its own."

She buried her head in her hands, refusing to cry as she forced her mind to search for a solution— any solution that would not involve going to her father. Lifting her head out of her hands and letting her fingers close over her throat, she sighed dispiritedly. If only she had someone to talk to, she thought dejectedly. Someone close who would understand what had prompted her to do such a stupid thing. She refused to take the chance of confiding in Forest and risk the loss of his love.

She had no close girl friends, at least, none she would trust with this kind of damaging information. As she was growing up, her father had insisted she attend private schools, snobbishly believing they offered a better and broader education. At the same time Erica had thought he was sending her to these expensive boarding schools because he didn't care about her. Only now could she see that he simply had not known what to do with a young child under his roof. The few friends she had made lived in other parts of the country and after more than four years of separation, correspondence between them had ceased except for annual Christmas cards.

Lawrence Darby, her father's secretary and Man Friday, had always been a sympathetic sounding board in the past, but Erica was totally aware that he automatically carried any major problem to Vance Wakefield, the very thing she wanted to avoid. Not that Lawrence would deliberately betray her; he would only be turning to the man he knew would have the connections and influence to solve her problem.

As for relatives, Erica only had aunts and uncles and cousins, none of whom were overly concerned about her personal problems or even whether she had any. She drew a sharp breath of hope.

"Uncle Jules," she murmured. "Oh, how stupid! Why didn't I think of him before?"

Jules Blackwell was not related to her at all, but he had grown up with Vance Wakefield and was one of her father's rare friends. When Erica was born, Jules Blackwell had appointed himself as her godparent and had taken an active interest in her life. His affection she had never doubted, in fact took for granted. His position and profession were independent of her father's and therefore Jules looked on her father as a man and not the powerful Vance Wakefield. And the man she had affectionately titled "uncle" was aware of the struggle she had made to win her father's love. He could be trusted not to race to her father.

Equally important as all the other reasons was the knowledge that Jules Blackwell was an attorney of some renown. For the first time in nearly two years, the yoke of shame and guilt seemed to ease its ponderous weight from her shoulders and Erica wanted to cry with relief. But the time for weeping was when success was in her grasp.

Dashing to the polished oak chest of drawers, she rummaged through the expensive lingerie until her fingers closed around the knotted handkerchief buried in one corner. Hot color raged over her skin at the touch of the heavy metal object penetrating the material. The red stain didn't leave her cheeks until the knotted handkerchief was buried again, this time in the bottom of her purse.

Sleep eluded her so that most of her rest came in fitful dozes. Still Erica tarried in bed as long as she could the next morning to avoid meeting her father. When she arrived in the sunny yellow breakfast room, only Lawrence was still seated.

"You're late this morning." He smiled, his eyes crinkling behind wire-rimmed glasses. He was only two years older than Forest, yet his receding hairline and thinness added at least ten years.

"I overslept," Erica fibbed, helping herself to toast and marmalade before pouring a cup of coffee for herself.

"Vance has already eaten, but he asked me to pass a message on to you."

"What's that?" Subconsciously she was holding her breath as she took a chair opposite Lawrence.

"The first part was to remind you about the dinner tonight at the Mendelsens' and the second was to suggest that you invite Mr. Granger to accompany you."

Her surprised glance took in the rather smug expression. Her father's suggestions were virtually royal commands, and never before had he even hinted one of her dates should be included in an invitation extended to them.

"Did you have any part in his suggestion, Lawrence?" A knowing smile played with the corners of her mouth.

"No one makes decisions for your father." But there was a twinkle in the pale blue eyes that indicated he had undoubtedly introduced Forest's name into the conversation. "I think Vance is beginning to realize there might be something serious developing between you two."

It was a probing remark designed to inspire confidence, but Erica knew her reply would be passed on to her father. It was his indirect way of remaining involved in her life without taking the time to inquire for himself.

"It's a bit soon to be certain, but it could be serious." It was serious, but Erica didn't want to admit that until she had her other problem solved. "I'll call Forest when I get to the boutique and find out if he's free this evening."

"How is business?" Lawrence inquired.

"I believe daddy is going to be very surprised when he receives my monthly report," she declared, raising a complacent brow as she sipped her coffee.

More than a year ago Erica had persuaded her father that she needed an outside interest, some reason for getting up in the morning. It was beneath his dignity to allow her to be employed by someone. She was Vance Wakefield's daughter. Erica doubted that her father had actually believed she was serious. To humor her, he had financed the setting up of a small boutique along the landscaped riverwalk.

Along with some of his other traits, Erica had also inherited his business acumen. At the end of her first year in business, the exclusive dress shop had broken even. Now, partly due to nearly flawless taste in fashions and her keen management, it was beginning to show a profit.

Being responsible for its success or failure had also made Erica appreciate more the endless demands her father's multiple interests placed upon him.

The instant Lawrence left the breakfast nook, all conscious thought of the boutique vanished. The haste that made Erica leave her toast and coffee half-finished was due to a desire to arrive at the shop and call Jules Blackwell in privacy where there was no risk that her father or Lawrence could accidentally overhear.

The boutique, appropriately called Erica, was already open when Erica arrived. As she locked the doors of her sports car, she said a silent prayer of thanks that she had acquired a clerk as trustworthy and conscientious as Donna Kemper, a petite attractive blonde in her early thirties, divorced and with two little school-age girls. With Donna and a teenage girl named Mary who helped part-time after school, Erica had discovered the shop could survive without her constant supervision.

There was only one customer in the store when she walked in. Smiling a hello to the woman, Erica murmured a friendly greeting to Donna.

"The shipment has arrived from Logan's," Donna informed her.

Erica's head bobbed in wry acknowledgment. "I have some calls to make, then I'll be out to give you a hand."

A wide smile of understanding spread across the fair woman's face. "We've waited this long to receive it. Another few hours before it's on the rack won't make much difference."

Then the customer required Donna's attention and Erica walked to the back of the store to the small alcove hidden in the storage section. After she dialed Jules's office number, she sifted through the mail Donna had placed on the desk, schooling her hammering heart to slow down. It was several minutes before his secretary was able to connect her with Jules. He was plainly delighted and surprised that she had called. The open affection in his voice made her wish she had done it earlier and not have to seek him out now when she had a problem.

"I was calling to see if you would be free around lunchtime, Uncle Jules." Erica explained in answer to his question.

"Are you asking me out to lunch, young lady?" His teasing laughter lifted her spirits. "Because if you are, I'm accepting."

"Actually, I am," she smiled at the beige-colored receiver, visualizing the rotund, ever smiling face on the opposite end.

"Good. Where would you like me to meet you?"

Erica hesitated. "I . . . I was hoping I could see you for a few minutes at your office."

Her statement was followed by a small silence before he spoke again, the laughter giving way to solemnness. "Are you and Vance having problems again?"

"No, not exactly," she hedged.

He must have sensed her unwillingness to

discuss it over the telephone. "All right. I'll expect you here at eleven-thirty. How's that?"

"Thank you." She sighed.

"Don't worry. Uncle Jules will fix it, whatever it is."

When Erica replaced the receiver, a tentative smile was gleaming in her eyes. With her burden lightened, she telephoned Forest, who very willingly accepted the invitation her father had extended.

CHAPTER TWO

PROMPTLY AT ELEVEN-THIRTY, Erica entered the spacious reception area of the Blackwell & Todd law firm. The receptionist-secretary glanced up, her keen look appraising the fairly tall, curvaceously slender girl in the simple, elegant dress of vivid blue flowers against a background of white.

"Good morning, Miss Wakefield," she greeted Erica. "Mr. Blackwell said for me to send you right in the minute you arrived."

Erica nodded her thanks, her fingers tightening nervously on the strap of her white purse. Between unpacking the shipment of new fashions that had arrived and waiting on customers, there had been little time to mentally prepare for her meeting with Jules. She would have welcomed a few minutes' delay.

The door to his office was open and a moderately heavyset man was sitting behind the desk, his dark hair liberally peppered with gray as he bent over some papers on his desk. At her light rap, his head raised, the stern expression of concentration replaced by a jovial smile that seemed to better fit his features.

"Hello, Uncle Jules," she smiled, stepping into the room as he pushed himself out of the large leather chair.

"Close the door." His hand wagged in the air in

accompaniment of his order. By the time Erica had complied, he was standing in front of her, only an inch or two taller than she was. "I don't want to make my associates jealous when they see me kissing a beautiful young girl," he declared with a broad wink. After he had placed an affectionate kiss on her proffered cheek, his arm circled her shoulders as he drew her toward a large chair near his desk. "It's been two months—no, three months—since I last saw you. That's much too long, Erica."

The mild reproof changed her smile to one of rueful apology. "I'm sorry, Uncle Jules. It doesn't seem that long, but what with one thing or another, time has a way of slipping by."

"From all I've heard, your dress shop is doing well," he said with a nod, forsaking the chair behind his desk for one next to Erica's while he retained possesion of one of her hands. "I've also heard you've been seeing a great deal of Forest Granger," he added with a twinkle. "If he's lasted this long, you must be more than just fond of him."

Erica had forgotten how easy it was to confide in Jules. "I am," she admitted, glancing down at the stubby fingers holding her hand. "As a matter of fact, I'm in love with him." She tossed her head back, sending her long brunette hair away from her shoulders and down her back. "Last night, Forest asked me to marry him."

"Mmmm." A thoughtfully serious look crept into his otherwise smiling expression. "And Forest Granger has been something of a playboy, loving them and leaving them. Which means his

31

reputation has preceded him in your father's eye. Is that what you wanted to see me about? So I could use my charm to convince Vance that he's the right man for you?"

"No, I . . . I don't think daddy is bothered by that." Now that it was time to tell Jules why she was here, Erica found herself faltering. "Daddy isn't going to be a problem."

"But something else is," he prodded gently.

The deep breath she had taken was exhaled slowly so that her affirmative "yes" came out as a sigh. "Do you remember—it will be two years ago this January—when I insisted that daddy and I take a vacation together?"

"To Acapulco? Yes, I remember," Jules smiled. "As I recall, you came to me then to enlist my persuasion in that effort. Considering the improvement in the relationship between the two of you after you came back, I think spending time alone together was the best thing that could have happened. It's unfortunate that you didn't take a vacation together before."

"The whole thing was a fiasco, a terrible disaster," Erica declared in a trembling voice.

She stared sightless at shelves of law books behind his desk, no longer trying to stop the flood of vivid memories. Her voice was flat and unemotional as she related the events that had taken place. It was a censored version dealing only with facts, but in her mind, Erica relived every moment.

The idea for the vacation had developed from an obsessive need to be the sole object of her father's attention. Only by separating him from his business could she succeed. There were many times in her growing years that Vance Wakefield had hired a female companion and sent Erica off in her company to some exclusive resort. Never once in all her years could she remember her father taking any vacation, any respite from his work.

Enlisting the aid of everyone around him, Erica had forced a reluctant agreement from her father that he should take a vacation. Her first clue that her plans were not going the way she had intended was when her father made reservations for three, explaining that Lawrence had not had any vacation in the four years he had worked for him.

Not until they had stepped from the plane and were registered and shown to the expensive suite of rooms in one of the luxurious hotels in Acapulco did Erica fully realize that a vacation to Vance Wakefield meant conducting business long distance. Her first reaction had been anger, then a complete denial that she wanted his company at all as she commandeered Lawrence with her father's permission.

Lawrence tagged faithfully after her that first afternoon when Erica fled the hotel for the sun-kissed beaches of Acapulco. Anger tempered with self-pity seethed just below the surface as she realized that Lawrence was to be her companion-bodyguard, a male babysitter not much different from the women chaperones her father had forced on her in the past. As the toes of her sandals dug into the golden sand, she knew her father was probably congratulating himself over his twofold usage of Lawrence: a secretary when he needed him; and a suitable companion to show Erica the sights. And at the same time he was providing Lawrence with a paid vacation in a luxury resort. Vance Wakefield was capable of such a callously insensitive thought.

"Poor Lawrence," she murmured aloud, staring at the vast expanse of blue water, broken only by curling whitecaps, the occasional boat and the heads of swimmers.

"Why, poor me?" he asked quietly, stopping beside her, his tan jacket thrown over one shoulder with his tie sticking out of its pocket. The whiteness of his shirt, opened at the throat, accented his pale skin.

"As long and as hard as you've worked for daddy, this is some kind of repayment—being constantly at his beck and call and forced to put up with me," sighed Erica, feeling almost as sorry for him as she did for herself.

"I don't mind." Lawrence shrugged, his light blue eyes gazing back at her through the wire frames.

"Well, you should mind!" The stamping of her feet was negated by the soft sand. "Why should you be responsible for Vance Wakefield's daughter? And I am his daughter, whether he likes it or not!" A diamond mist shimmered over her violet blue eyes as outrage gave way to despair. "Oh, Lawrie, why can't he be like other parents? Is it so much to ask to have him spend two weeks with me? Am I not entitled to two weeks out of twenty years?"

"He isn't like other parents, Erica, because he's Vance Wakefield," Lawrence returned calmly, very accustomed to Erica's swift changes from anger to tears. "You have to see him the way he is, and not the way you want him to be."

"In other words, enjoy the sun and fun of Acapulco but don't make waves," Erica mocked him scathingly. "Forget that I have any rights to his time."

"In his own way, he cares very much about you."

"I'm not giving up." Her voice was low with determination and her chin was tilted at a defiant angle. "Daddy is not going to be able to ignore me for two weeks!"

"Don't do anything foolish," Lawrence cautioned.

Erica didn't answer, but there was a mischievous and challenging glint in her eyes as she hooked her arm around his elbow. "Let's walk down by the water," she commanded.

"We can't go far," he said, leading her toward the gentle waves rolling onto the beach. "Your father will be expecting us back."

"So what?" Erica taunted. "I've waited for him long enough. Let him wait for me for a change!"

Her rebellious mood brought a worried frown to his thin face, but Erica ignored it. She deliberately focused her attention on her surroundings, absently enjoying the warmth of the sun on her shoulders, glad she had changed out of her heavier traveling suit to the gold sundress with white polka dots. The salty breeze from the Pacific fanned her cheeks, lifting long strands of her hair so it could reach her neck.

Her gaze skipped over the scanty attire of the swimmers and sunbathers, noting instead the thatched, open shelters on the beach to provide places for shaded afternoon siestas. Behind them were the gently swaying palm trees while rows of high-rise hotels formed a necklace for the bay. Beyond them were the mountains, gray, craggy sentinels guarding the golden sand and the sapphire blue sea.

"It reminds me a bit of Hawaii," she commented idly. A laugh bubbled from her throat. "Remember that silly old maid daddy hired the last time, Lawrie? Prudence Mulier, her name was. She used to get so outraged if anyone tried to flirt with me, but you could tell she was dying for them to look at her."

"Was that the one with the good figure and blond hair that was black at the roots?" he chuckled.

"That's Prudence!" Erica grinned as Lawrence pulled her out of reach of an adventurous wave, its watery fingers stroking the golden sand in front of them. She turned to him eagerly. "Let's wade in the ocean."

"Not me." He shook his head, reaching up to smooth back the hair the breeze had ruffled, revealing his receding hairline. "Go ahead, if you want to."

Before the words were out of his mouth, Erica had slipped her sandals off and was walking toward the waterline. The smooth sand beneath her toes was warmed by the sun, as were the waves that curled around her ankles. Wading was an ageless sport and she pitied Lawrence who was too staid and self-conscious to take part.

Twenty feet or more in front and to the ocean's side of Erica, a swimmer broke water, rising majestically to stand hip-deep before he began to wade ashore. The lean yet very muscular torso gleamed bronze gold in the sun and a medallion winked at Erica from the cloud of jet black hair covering his chest. Almost in spite of herself, her gaze raised to the man's face. Black—his hair, his eyes, his brows, all were black, glistening and shining from the wetness of the ocean, but no other shade than black.

As that physical impact receded, she was struck by the aloof arrogance etched in the patrician features, a ruthlessly molded jaw and chin, high cheekbones, nobility stamped in the forehead and nose. As Erica waded closer, their paths intersecting, she was conscious of his height. She was five foot six inches, and few men towered above her, but this one did.

His glance flicked dismissively over her as he strode by. Erica was accustomed to a more thorough appraisal by men. This arrogant rejection stung. She jerked her gaze to Lawrence, who was strolling out of reach of the waves, but parallel to her. Her joy in wading in the warm salt water was gone, somehow disrupted by the dark stranger. This dissatisfaction carried her to Lawrence's side, using his arm as a support while she slipped on her sandals.

Yet the pull of the bronze shoulders tapering down to narrow waist and hips magnetically drew her gaze. There was something very compelling about the man. He was handsome, yet not in the same wholesomely open way of the American men Erica knew. His looks were foreign, ultimately male, striking some primitive chord of attraction inside Erica and creating an impression of underlying steel.

Erica was not aware that Lawrence had noticed the direction of her gaze until he spoke. "He's quite something, isn't he? Lord of all he surveys."

"Yes," she agreed absently, watching the stranger approach one of the thatched shelters nearest them. At the same instant a golden arm reached for a crisply white towel and she saw the woman reclining there.

Even at this distance, Erica could tell that the woman was no longer youthful. Her first instinct was that the woman was a relative until she saw the blond hair beneath the sunhat. There was a flash of white as the man smiled at some comment the woman made. Erica glanced at Lawrence, curious what his opinion was.

"Who do you suppose she is?" asked Erica.

"I don't know what the modern terminology is, but at a guess, I would say he's the woman's lover—for a small fee, of course," Lawrence replied.

"Are you serious?"

"It's a fairly common occupation in resorts like this," he chided her open-mouthed amazement. "A lot of wealthy women come here. I would guess they would be quite anxious to have an escort who looked like that."

Silently Erica agreed, knowing there were some women who would adore that arrogant, lordly air, just as others were drawn to the titles of impoverished counts and dukes. Her back stiffened in anger at the dismissive glance he had given her. She was so anxious to be out of sight of the despicable stranger that she raised no objections when Lawrence directed her back to their hotel.

The following morning Lawrence rented a car. The plans made the evening before were that all three of them, Lawrence, Erica and her father, would take a trip to the colorful open-air market. At breakfast, Vance Wakefield changed the plans, insisting that he had to remain at the hotel because he was expecting an important telephone call.

Resentment smoldered, destroying Lawrence's obvious attempts to lighten the atmosphere and Erica's usual enjoyment of the extensive display of handcrafted items. The only satisfaction she obtained was by flagrantly spending every cent of the money her father had given her. Nearly everything she purchased was designed to anger him.

It was nearly two o'clock in the afternoon when Lawrence drove up to the hotel entrance and patiently unloaded the innumerable packages.

"Do you suppose you can get one of the bellboys to carry all this up to our rooms?" Lawrence asked with a teasing smile, as he wiped the perspiration from his brow. "I'll go and park the car."

Erica nodded reluctantly, feeling suddenly hot, sticky and irritable, and wishing she hadn't given in to such a childish impulse that resulted in the mound of sacks and boxes. Glancing toward the hotel entrance, she searched for the usually ever-present, uniformed bellhops, but oddly there were none in sight. As she pivoted toward the car to send Lawrence into the lobby, it pulled away from the curb. An exasperated sigh hissed through her clenched teeth. It would be foolish for her to leave all these packages unattended while she went in search of assistance.

An impatient movement of her head brought a tall figure into view, lithe strides bringing him closer to Erica. A vengefully haughty expression swept across her face as she recognized the stranger from yesterday. The white tropical suit he was wearing enhanced his dark attraction even as he retained that savagely noble look.

Her hand raised in an imperious gesture to summon his attention. When the glitter of her purple gaze locked with the blackness of his, it was Erica who came away with the feeling of being bruised.

"You wish something, *señorita*?" The condescension of his inquiry scraped at her already irritated nerves so that she missed the flawless English and the seductive pitch of his voice. Her chin raised a fraction of an inch higher.

"I would like you to carry these packages into the hotel for me." But it was spoken not as a request, but as a command. Erica noticed with satisfaction the hardening of his gaze and the arrogantly arched brow.

"I do not work for the hotel," he informed her icily.

The rapier thrust of his gaze sent the adrenalin pumping through her system, heightening her senses as she extracted some of her own money from her purse. The man obviously had an inflated idea of his own importance.

"That doesn't concern me," retorted Erica, extending a handful of bills toward him. When he failed to accept it, her head tilted loftily to one side. "Aren't you accustomed to accepting money from a woman?"

Her question was put forth with the unmistakable certainty that the answer was yes. His gaze traveled with insolent slowness over the length of her body until it stopped once again on her face. A mirthless smile curved the hard line of his mouth at the red flags that had run up her cheeks.

A Mexican of shorter stature and a more swarthy complexion appeared at her side, wearing the uniform of the hotel. "Would you like me to take your packages, *señorita*?" he asked in heavily accented English.

Her hand still held the folded bills. Erica looked directly at the taller man. "This man will carry my things," she said to dismiss the hotel employee and thus succeed in putting the stranger in his place, but she wasn't prepared for the torrent of protest.

"Oh, no, *señorita!*" the hotel bellhop declared in a horrified voice. A stream of rapid Spanish followed the outburst while he darted wary looks at the man now regarding Erica with smug amusement.

When the incomprehensible flood stopped, the stranger replied in the same tongue, no doubt guessing by the blank look on Erica's face that she had not understood a word that had been said. Whatever was said seemed to satisfy the bellhop, but the only words Erica was able to distinguish were *turista* and American. She felt their usage had not been complimentary.

Aristocratic fingers took the money from Erica's hand and gave it to the uniformed Mexican. Her mouth opened to make her own protest, but the arrogant stranger forestalled her.

"It is his job, *señorita.*" The chiseled mask of his face was inclined graciously toward her. A caustic smile edged his mouth, black lashes veiling the bold mockery of his gaze at the mutinous set of her chin. "Or would you have me take money from the mouths of his hungry family?"

His gaze flicked distastefully over the ill assortment of purchases, arrogantly reminding her that not everyone had an abundance of wealth at her fingertips as she undoubtedly had. And Erica was shamed.

In a sense she had been spoiled since her father had never deprived her of anything money could buy, but she had never flaunted her wealth. And she wasn't about to explain to this stranger the reason for her flagrant extravagance this time, which even she recognized as being childish and in bad taste.

She didn't bother to reply to his taunting question as she pivoted sharply and marched toward the hotel doors with the laden bellhop following in her wake.

ON THE FIFTH DAY in Acapulco, Erica rose early in the morning. Restless and thwarted in her attempts to spend time with her father, she wandered onto the beach, peacefully silent and empty at that hour of the morning. The temperature was mildly warm, although the wind blowing off the ocean was unusually strong. She hoped that an early-morning swim might soothe her restlessness and put her in a better mood before she met her father and Lawrence at the breakfast table.

Slipping off the decorative lace beach jacket, she laid it beside her towel and sandals on the sand. She took her time wading into the warm water, absently watching the soaring gulls. Not until she was almost hip-deep did she realize she had forgotten to put on her bathing cap.

With an irritated sigh, she turned back to the shore. Walking into the waves, she had not noticed the force as they broke around her. Her thoughts had been preoccupied with her father and not on the slight choppiness of the normally calm sea.

Her foot slipped off a seashell at the same moment that a strong wave struck the back of her knees. Already off balance as she was, the wave swept her feet from beneath her, and her cry of surprise was cut off as she was suddenly submerged in salt water. Erica struggled for the surface, trying to get her feet beneath her again. A toe touched bottom. She gulped for air and another wave covered her, its following outward flow dragging her into deeper water.

An iron grip closed over one of her arms, then another hand was taking the opposite shoulder and drawing her to the surface. Instinctively she reached out to cling to her rescuer, coughing out the water she had involuntarily swallowed. Her hands closed around the muscular upper portion of his arms and her legs were weakly supporting her.

"There is another wave coming, *señorita*. Brace yourself against me," a familiar voice ordered succinctly.

In ready compliance, Erica slid her arms around his waist as she reclined her head on his chest. Through the watery spikes of her lashes, she saw the gold medallion in the curling black hairs of his chest.

At that moment the wave broke around them. Its force carried her against him, her motion stopped by the taut muscles in his thighs and legs. The severe constriction of her lungs, robbing her of breath, had no basis in the wave as the water molded her against his body.

When it receded, Erica reluctantly tilted back her head to gaze, rather frightened and bewildered, into his face. A hand left his waist to brush the wet hair from her eyes.

"Th . . . thank you." Her sincere words were met by an impassive look.

"Come." An arm was firmly around her waist and he was half dragging, half carrying her toward shore. "You can catch your breath in shallower water."

Her mind, her senses, her body were in a chaotic state. Her mind was insisting that she reject the gratitude that surged through her toward her rescuer, the stranger who had antagonized her. All the while her senses were reacting to his male virility and her body was still tingling from the burning warmth of his.

They didn't stop in the shallow water but continued all the way to the shore. His arm was no longer supporting her as Erica walked under her own power, his hand firmly resting on her back guiding her steps. When they reached her small pile of belongings, the pressure on her back was taken away, stealing some of the strength in her legs as it went. She sank gratefully to her knees, using the thick towel to rub her shivering skin, wondering how she could be cold when she felt so warm inside.

"It isn't wise to swim alone, *señorita*, especially when the beach is so deserted," he said curtly.

The stern reprimand jerked Erica's head up sharply. He towered above her, his hands resting on the band of his black swimming trunks. Her gaze swung away from the unnerving, masterful stance and searched the empty beach.

"You were," she pointed out crisply.

An eyebrow flicked upward, the small gesture

emphasizing Erica's impression that he was not accustomed to being questioned.

"I am familiar with the beach and the tides, *señorita*. You are not."

"No," Erica agreed dryly. "I am a tourist. An American tourist."

The eyebrow descended to its proper place and she sensed a softening in the hard lines of his face. "Who spends many dollars on the handiwork of my country." Amusement glittered behind the mask. "It is good that I saved you to spend more, no?"

"I . . ." Patches of red appeared in her face at his mention of her embarrassing spree, and Erica bent her head to let the wet hair cover the betraying flush as she reached for her lace jacket. "I'm grateful you were here." But her thanks didn't match the sincerity of her earlier words. "I honestly didn't believe anyone else was around."

"Then it is lucky I saw you as you came down to the beach and heard your cry."

Erica slipped on her jacket and scrambled to her feet, clutching her towel and sandals in front of her as if they were a shield, although her bikini was considerably more modest than some she had seen.

Again she was jolted by the sight of so much bronze skin. Seeing a man in bathing trunks had never disturbed her before. But there was a dangerous fascination to this man, pulling her, compelling her attention even as she reminded herself, in old-fashioned vernacular, that he was a gigolo, escorting wealthy, older women for the monetary favors they would bestow.

"You are not going to swim?" The lilting inflection of his low voice turned the sentence into a question.

Swallowing nervously under the intent regard of his eyes, Erica shook her head firmly. "No. I was only going to take a short swim before breakfast." Her hand self-consciously touched her dripping hair. "My father will be expecting me."

"Of course." He nodded.

"Thank you again," she added over her shoulder as she turned to leave.

"*De nada.*" But there was a vague smile of acceptance on his lips.

Erica wondered a bit breathlessly as she hurried away how devastating a genuine smile of his would be. Then she firmly pushed such conjecture from her mind and fervently hoped she never saw him again.

But she did the following day, although she was certain that he hadn't seen her. He had been with the blonde from the beach. Under the stranger's spell, the older woman had looked quite youthful and animated. Erica had been disgusted.

CHAPTER THREE

ERICA HESITATED ON THE EDGE of the hotel grounds. She wasn't in the mood for sunbathing or swimming and she felt if she had to spend one more afternoon staring at the replica of Columbus's ship, the *Niña*, which rested on the beach, she would scream.

They had been in Acapulco a full week. Apart from the marketplace, the hotel, the cliff divers and the beach, Erica had seen nothing. They could have easily been in Miami Beach instead of Mexico for all she had seen of the country.

Her father had even claimed Lawrence, admonishing Erica to enjoy the sunshine. She tucked her book deeper under her arm. It was an interesting and informative book on the history of Mexico that her father had given her. When she had left her father and Lawrence clustered over some figures, she had intended to find a secluded nook in the hotel gardens and read. Now that thought didn't appeal to her.

Sighing dejectedly, Erica turned down one of the garden walks. Her heartbeat quickened as she recognized the figure walking toward her. As yet the dark stranger hadn't seen her. Uncertain exactly why she wanted to avoid meeting him again, attracted and repelled at the same time, Erica tried to dodge behind a high bush and slip through the foliage to another walk that she knew was only a few feet away.

In her haste, she forgot the book tucked beneath her arm and it tumbled to the ground, landing with a resounding thud. For a split second, she froze behind the concealing leaves, staring at the book now lying in the center of the walk. That second's hesitation deprived her of the chance to slip away unseen as the purposeful footsteps slowed as he neared the book.

Silently cursing her ineptitude, Erica stepped into the walkway as he bent over to retrieve her book. "I'm afraid I dropped that," she said stiffly.

"*Señorita.*" He nodded in recognition. There was speculation in the glance that darted from her to the bush.

"I was taking a shortcut to the other path." The defensive thrust of her chin dared him to ask why.

But the glitter of amusement in his dark eyes said he had guessed. His gaze traveled down to the book in his hand before he held it out to her.

"It is a pity to read about Mexico when you are here and can learn about it firsthand," he commented.

His observation was an exact echo of her own sentiments. Her fingers tightened convulsively on the book.

"The way things are going, I'm going to have to be satisfied with this." Anger and self-pity made her voice tremble as it was drawn through clenched teeth. "My father is much too busy for sight-seeing." She darted him a sideways look that didn't quite reach his face, although she was all too aware of the attractive contrast of his white polo shirt and the deep blue trousers tautly molding his thighs. "Thank you for giving me back my book, *señor*." She started to turn away.

"*Señorita.*" The authoritative ring of his voice halted her, only to become mellow when he spoke again. "I would be pleased to show you around this afternoon if you are free."

"No, thank you." Her denial was vigorous, causing her sable brown hair to dance about her shoulders. Erica didn't care to be exposed to the potent sexual attraction that threatened to captivate her whenever she saw him.

"Why not?" Again there was that impression of arrogance, of a man who was not accustomed to having his invitations refused.

The amethyst pupils of her eyes darkened to plum by her scorn. "I wouldn't like to make your ... your lady friend jealous and deprive you of what must be very hard-earned money," Erica stated.

"My lady friend?" His lips thinned as her arrow found its target.

"Yes." Her expression was smugly sarcastic. "The blonde. I've seen you with her several times, on the beach and other places."

"Ah, you mean Helen." He nodded, mocking amusement glittering in his eyes.

"I really wouldn't know what her name is." Erica shrugged. "I simply noticed that the tan she's so keen to acquire only makes her look older."

"I would think someone as young and beautiful as you are could afford to be sympathetic to a woman who finds her beauty fading with each rising of the sun."

The gentle reproof made Erica avert her head. She did feel sorry for the woman, and at the same time contempt that she should attempt to capture her lost youth in this man's arms.

"Perhaps," was the only admission she made.

"Helen is visiting friends this afternoon, so you need not think that you are stealing me away from her by accepting my invitation," he mocked.

"It never occurred to me to try to steal you away." Her eyes widened with genuine innocence.

"Then if you are not burdened by guilt feelings of trespassing and you truly would like to see the city, there is no reason for you to refuse my offer."

His logical statement figuratively removed the ground beneath her feet. "I suppose not," she faltered.

"Then you do accept?" There was a patronizingly inquiring tilt of his head.

"I . . . I suppose so," she stammered uncertainly, trying to shake off the feeling that she had fallen into some trap he had set for her.

"If we are going to spend the afternoon together, I cannot keep calling you *señorita*." A faint smile edged the corners of his mouth. "What is your name?"

"Erica—" Then she stopped. Even in Acapulco, she had discovered that the name of Wakefield was known. This man already saw her as a rich tourist and she would rather he didn't know how rich. "My name is Erica."

"Erica." His pronunciation lightly rolled the

"r", the foreign inflection giving her name a very caressive sound. "My name is Rafael."

Like Erica he added no more than that. Unlike him, she didn't test the sound of it on her lips. The unusual name was too much like its owner, smooth and commanding like satin covering steel, and arrogant.

"Do you wish to notify your father where you are going?" Rafael inquired.

"As long as I am back by five, he won't care where I am," Erica sighed.

Vance Wakefield was too involved in some pending crisis and was too confident of her ability to take care of herself, his trust a compliment if Erica had chosen to look at it that way

Rafael didn't seem surprised by her remark as he stepped to the side, his hand extended for Erica to precede him in the direction from which he had just come.

"My car is parked over here," he told her.

The car was a very expensive European sports car, its color a highly polished silver gray, the luxurious interior upholstery a blend of black and silver.

"Is this your car or ... Helen's?" Erica questioned when Rafael slid into the driver's seat beside her.

The sleek elegance matched the driver, who glanced at her casually before turning the ignition key that sprang the powerful engine to life.

"Do you think I could afford such a model?" answering her question with a question.

"No, I guess not," she agreed with a rueful shake of her head.

The beginning of their drive took them along the familiar bayfront as Rafael identified the small rocky island as La Roqueta, suggesting that Erica take the glass-bottom boat to see the submerged shrine of Our Lady of Guadalupe near the island. When she expressed curiosity about some of the yachts sailing in the harbor, he took her to the docks where many were moored.

He pointed out a mammoth vessel and said, "That is—where I am staying."

Erica glanced at him in surprise. "I thought you stayed at the hotel."

"No, it is only a popular place." Rafael shrugged.

She looked back at the yacht, its name indecipherable at this distance. "Helen must be very rich," she mused.

"I believe she is." He changed gears and turned the car away from the water.

From the yacht club, they went to the San Diego Fort overlooking the bay. Rafael took her through the museum housed in the reconstructed star-shaped fort, the original buildings destroyed by an earthquake. Erica was surprised to discover that Rafael was quite knowledgeable about the history of the area and knew that on her own she wouldn't have found the tour as enjoyable or interesting.

Their next stop was the Plaza de Toros. Erica needed no one to translate the sign. This was the place of the bullfights. She glanced sharply at Rafael.

"I really don't care to go here," she said firmly.

"You don't like bullfights?" The question was asked with the certain knowledge that her answer would be negative.

Erica didn't disappoint him. "No, I don't like bullfights."

"They are only held on Sundays and holidays, and today is neither." A whisper of amusement was in his expression. "I thought you might like to see the inside of a bullring, however empty it might be. Wait here while I get permission to take you in," he instructed.

A few minutes later he returned and guided Erica into the Plaza de Toros, admitted by an elderly Mexican who nodded deferentially to both of them. Erica listened with half an ear while Rafael explained the ritual of the contest, the parts played by the mounted picadors, the banderillos who enabled the matador to observe the fighting characteristics of the bull, and the matador himself who is obligated to execute difficult passes to prove his skill to the crowd.

Mostly Erica was caught up in the eerie atmosphere of the empty stadium, the blood-red color of the wooden barrier that separated the crowd from the ring, the sawdust and sand arena. She had only to close her eyes to hear the cries of the crowd and visualize the black bull charging the magenta cape of a gold-bedecked matador. In spite of herself she shuddered.

"You find the thought of the contest revolting?" Rafael's quiet voice asked.

"I'm afraid I would be rooting for the bull," Erica stated. He was standing beside her, a complacently amused smile on his face. "Have you ever fought a bull?"

"I would guess that all of my countrymen have, if not in reality then in their mind," he replied smoothly, turning his dark gaze on her.

"But you actually did, didn't you?" she guessed correctly. "Why? To prove that man is superior to beast? Or did you simply want to find out how you would react at—what do they call that—the moment of truth?"

"Some consider it a test of manhood," Rafael said sardonically. An enigmatic light in the depths of his eyes held her captive. "But I have found there are much more difficult moments of truth to be faced in a man's life than the one containing a fighting bull. Ones in which a man's future and his happiness hang in the balance."

A spell seemed to be cast on her and it was she who was dangling in the air while Rafael controlled the strings. His words held some portent for her that Erica couldn't understand. Then there was a glimmer of white as he smiled and took her arm.

"Have you seen enough? Shall we go back to the car to continue your tour?"

"Yes, yes, of course," Erica replied, fighting the odd breathlessness that paralyzed her lungs.

The silver car climbed the mountains guarding the city, hugging the switchback curves as it climbed higher and higher. Erica was still inwardly analyzing that moment in the Plaza de

Toros while absently responding to Rafael's questions.

Not until they were nearly to the top did she realize that her answers had dealt mainly with her childhood and her relationship with her father. Some defense mechanism in her mind had prevented her from answering in specifics, but thinking back she realized her replies had given him a very accurate picture of her life. She was not normally so open with strangers and she resented his ability to penetrate her reserve.

"And you are twenty years old, you said." His gaze left the road long enough to see her affirmative nod.

"How old are you?" Erica asked quickly.

"Almost twelve years older than you are," Rafael replied, switching down to a lower gear as he braked and eased the car into a wide turnout. "This is what I wanted to show you."

As the car rolled slowly to a stop, Erica stared at the panoramic view before her, barely conscious of the brakes being set and the engine switched off. When Rafael opened her car door, she stepped eagerly onto the gravel.

The vividly blue water of the bay below them was ringed by the golden beach. The multistoried hotels looked more like miniature blocks while the boats on the water resembled grayish white dots. Beyond the city were mountains and beyond the mountains was another range of mountains. The sky was as blue as the sea, its brilliant color only disrupted by thin tails of high filmy clouds.

"At night the view is equally beautiful," he told her.

"I can believe it," Erica breathed, walking forward to expand her nearly limitless view.

"Careful!" His voice rang out sharply at the same instant his fingers closed over her arm, drawing her away from the edge.

The suddenness with which he drew her back made her lose her balance so that she fell heavily against him and his other hand gripped her waist to steady her. Her palms felt the burning warmth of the hard chest beneath his shirt.

"The edge is sometimes undermined," he explained.

Erica's heart was racing, the closeness of his lithe, muscular body erasing any other thought. She tilted her head back to gaze into his face so tantalizingly near her own. His dark eyes were focused on her parted lips, the sensual line of his mouth only inches away.

Erica was consumed by an overwhelming desire for Rafael to kiss her and for a split second she was positive that he would. Then his gaze flicked to the ardent glow in her eyes and he firmly set her apart from him.

She stared at him for a long moment. "Why didn't you kiss me?" she asked, fighting the pangs of rejection.

An expression of amazed amusement lifted one corner of his mouth. "The women of your country are always this forthright, aren't they? They boldly seek out the answers."

The hint of criticism brought a faint tinge of

pink to her cheekbones, but Erica wasn't deterred. "If you don't ask, you don't learn," she answered calmly.

"Since you wish to speak candidly, Erica, why did you want to kiss me?" Aloofly he studied her sudden increase of color. "Did you wish to discover if this mystique about Latin lovers was true? A little experiment to brighten your holiday, perhaps?"

Erica averted her head, nervously brushing her hair away from her face. "Frankly, I didn't give your nationality a thought at the time," she answered truthfully.

It was his overpowering maleness that seemed to make her gravitate toward him. She glanced at him from beneath her lashes and saw the faint glitter of doubt.

"It's the truth," she asserted curtly, "although I wouldn't be surprised if your experience puts you in the class of a Don Juan."

"Do you believe the mark of a great lover is the number of women he possesses?" he asked, watching her reaction intently.

"Don't you?" Erica snapped.

"I think the test of a lover is keeping one woman happy for her entire life," Rafael stated, his seductively quiet voice vibrating with firm conviction.

"That—" Shivers raced down her spine at his words. She paused to swallow the sudden catch in her voice before answering boldly. "That still doesn't answer why you didn't kiss me. You said before that I was beautiful."

"A man does not seek outward beauty. That can be found in abundance. It is inner beauty that is rare."

"What about me?" The question was reluctantly asked as she proudly lifted her chin.

"I think," Rafael answered slowly, "that inside you are a bit selfish." He ignored her gasp of anger. "You claim to have deep affection for your father, yet you try to separate him from his work, which gives him great pride and pleasure. If you truly love someone, you want their happiness above yours."

"That's a terrible thing to say!" There was a betraying quiver of her chin. Her hand raised to wipe the vaguely superior expression from his face, but his own lightning quick movement stopped her, her wrist held in a vise grip.

"I was about to add," Rafael continued calmly, a wicked glitter of laughter in his eyes, "that you are very sensitive and would not knowingly hurt anyone."

"Let me go!" Erica tried to twist her wrist free without succeeding. "I don't want you to touch me!"

"A moment ago you wanted me to kiss you." His other hand slipped beneath her hair to cup the back of her head. "Or are you trying to prove you aren't hurt by pretending that you don't care?"

"It's called pride," she said, breathing heavily with anger and frustration. "You should know what that is. You seem to have an overabundance of it."

"I did not kiss you because I don't like being

59

used. And I could not be certain that you regarded me as a man or as a Mexican," he stated.

Erica blinked in disbelief. "How could any woman not be aware of you as a man?" It was a thought she hadn't realized she had spoken until she saw the arrogant satisfaction in his eyes.

There was a fleeting sensation of danger, of being drawn to the edge of a deep abyss and catapulted into its dark depths. The sensual expertise of the mouth that covered hers banished her hold on reality. She should protest, struggle free from his kiss, her mind told her, but with a shuddering sigh she clung to him. Some latent instinct arched her body closer to his, a gesture of surrender.

Immediately his hold on her tightened with crushing suffocation, choking off her breath and strength. And his kiss hardened into possession, ruthlessly staking an ownership that Erica couldn't deny and didn't want to deny.

Then Rafael was firmly untangling the hands she had wound around his neck and placing them at her side. Erica still trembled from her total, elemental awareness of him. The roundness of her eyes gazed into the impersonal mask, her skin tingling with the electric shock of his possession.

"It is growing late," he said tautly, a hand descending firmly on her shoulder and pointing her weakened limbs in the direction of the car. "I will take you back to your hotel."

At that moment his hold over her was so complete that Erica would have jumped off the cliff had he asked. Blinded by the dizzying heights his kiss had taken her to, she found it temporarily impossible to regard him as a paid escort, a fortune hunter, but his distant air when he helped her into the car forced her to do so.

The pangs of humiliation set in as Erica realized the embarrassing position she had placed herself in. She turned her face toward the window to hide the burning surge of heat in her face.

They were halfway down the mountain before Rafael broke the silence. "You should not kiss a man in that way, Erica."

Pride surfaced in a rush of spirit. "Isn't that the way your women usually kiss you?" Keeping her head turned, she made certain she didn't flinch under the obsidian glitter of his swift and thoughtful regard.

"You are not experienced in the fires of passion that can flame between a man and a woman or you would not flirt with them so dangerously," he observed.

"Kissing you doesn't mean I want to go to bed with you," Erica retorted sharply.

"Ah, but when you kiss a man that way, it is he who wants his possession to be complete."

An awkward silence crackled in the air between them as his disturbing statement robbed Erica of any witty reply. Her own response to him was much too vividly recalled and Rafael was not a man to be challenged or bluffed by girlish lies to the contrary.

When he stopped the car in front of the hotel entrance, Erica wanted to dash through the double doors, but she schooled herself to remain in the passenger seat as he walked around the car to open her door. The sun was warm, yet Erica shivered when he politely took her elbow and guided her to the doors. His dark vitality was much too overpowering and his sensual virility made her feel all too vulnerable and young.

Rafael graciously inclined his head toward the doorman who held the gold-enscrolled glass doors. The naturalness of the arrogantly superior movement curled her fingers and she stepped a few yards inside the entrance.

"There's no need for you to accompany me any farther," she told him curtly.

His arrogant demeanor didn't change as he turned to her, his head back, his eyes narrowing into black diamond chips. "I hope you found most of the afternoon enjoyable, *señorita*."

A brow lifted in anger at his sudden reversion to the impersonal term of address. Out of the corner of her eye, Erica saw her father and Lawrence Darby entering the lobby and the sharp questioning look she received when Vance Wakefield saw her with Rafael.

"It was very informative. Thank you." Her nod was condescendingly dismissive.

His gaze centered for a brief moment on her mouth, mocking the coldness that came from the lips that had trembled beneath his.

"*Adios*." Then Rafael was lithely striding away from her.

Erica hesitated for a second, drawing an audible breath to calm the wild beating of her heart. With a determinedly bright smile, she turned toward her father and Lawrence.

It was unlikely that Lawrence had forgotten that first afternoon when they had seen Rafael with the aging blonde. The polar-blue color of her father's eyes as they met hers told Erica that Lawrence had passed on the information. Refusing to be daunted by his displeasure, she lightly brushed a kiss across her father's cheek.

"If you two will give me a few minutes to change, I'll join you for cocktails before dinner," she said, making her request airy and gay so they wouldn't guess anything was wrong.

"What were you doing with that man?" her father demanded with his usual facility of getting straight to the point.

"Who? Rafael?" Erica inquired with false innocence. "He took me on a tour of the city this afternoon."

"Do you mean you hired him?" Vance Wakefield questioned sharply.

"Yes," she fibbed, adding with an expressive shrug to give credence to her lie, "you and Lawrence were busy this afternoon and I didn't feel like sitting around the hotel."

Vance Wakefield was not an easy man to fool. As he inclined his leonine head toward her, his expression was doubting and laced with penetrating concern.

"You do know what kind of man he is. He's an adventurer, a fortune hunter, living like a parasite off rich women." The undertone of his low voice was warning her in no uncertain terms.

"I know what he is, daddy," Erica replied calmly.

Lawrence glanced at her apologetically and she smiled in return. To his way of thinking he had only been doing what he thought was best. It would never have occurred to Lawrence to say nothing of their having seen Rafael on the beach.

"That type of man is completely mercenary and without morals," her father continued. "I will not have a daughter of mine getting mixed up with the likes of him. Do you hear me, Erica?"

"Yes, daddy," she responded patiently.

"I've put up with a lot of your shenanigans in the past, but this is one thing I won't tolerate. Now go and change and we'll meet you in the lounge."

CHAPTER FOUR

VANCE WAKEFIELD NEVER gave warnings lightly and he never saw the need to repeat them. If he ever found out that Erica was attracted to Rafael, however much she fought against it, she would hate to suffer the consequences.

When she had rejoined her father and Lawrence for cocktails, his earlier displeasure must have been placated by her explanation. As if to reward her supposed good sense, he agreed to attend the performance of a locally renowned singer appearing in a nearby lounge the following evening—a concession that surprised Erica since she had tried many times to persuade him to go without success.

The next day, Erica credited her tolerance toward the demands of her father's business to this concession. Her attitude had not been swayed by Rafael's statement that she was selfish; of this she was certain.

The evening of the performance, Erica took special care in choosing what she would wear. Her father had agreed to this evening without any coercion from her and she wanted him to be proud of her. She fingered the cream silk of her long gown and smiled. The silk molded her curvaceous figure, highlighting the darkness of her hair and the violet hue of her eyes.

Picking up her matching evening bag studded with cultured pearls, Erica moved softly toward the connecting door of the suite, rapped once and walked in. Her father was restlessly pacing the room and Lawrence was at the round table, surrounded by papers, with a calculator in front of him.

"You aren't even dressed yet, daddy?" she scolded lightly.

He halted his pacing, pushed back the cuff of his long-sleeved shirt, then shook his head ruefully. "I didn't realize it was that late," Vance Wakefield replied after glancing at his gold watch.

"Well, it is," Erica smiled good naturedly. "Do you want me to lay out your clothes while you shower?"

"I'm afraid I'm not going to be able to make it tonight, honey," he said as he walked over to take her hands in his.

The absently placating gesture added to the chill that was already shivering over her. For a moment Erica could only stare at him in frozen silence.

"What do you mean?" she demanded hoarsely.

"That Houston deal looks as if it's going to blow up in my face." His sigh accented the lines of strain in his face, but they evoked no sympathy from Erica. "We're going to be lucky if we can salvage it."

"What has that got to do with tonight?" She jerked her hands free. "Houston is more than a thousand miles away."

"I'm expecting some phone calls."

66

"So? Tell the hotel switchboard where they can locate us or have them take a message!"

"With all the figures and information in the hotel room?" he scoffed. "That wouldn't even be sensible, Erica. We'll simply have to call off tonight, that's all."

"That's all!" Her voice rose shrilly. "I don't know why you bothered to come to Acapulco at all! You haven't even stepped outside this hotel since we came. All you think about is business, business, business! What about me? I'm your daughter! Don't I deserve some of your time?"

"For God's sake, will you listen to reason? This is a million-dollar deal. I didn't just dream up this crisis to avoid taking you somewhere." His own quick temper was beginning to surface.

"Didn't you?" Erica jeered.

"If this silly performance is so important to you," he growled, "I imagine I can spare Lawrence to take you."

"Oh, no." She backed away, her hand rigidly raising in protest. "There isn't any need for you to provide me with an escort. That has always been your solution, but not this time. I'm quite capable of entertaining myself. There isn't any need for you to pay someone to do that. From now on that's going to be my choice!"

"Damn your insolence! You'll be sorry for this," her father declared, trembling with rage.

"I'm not the one who'll be sorry, daddy. You will be."

And Erica stormed from the room, the telephone ringing just as she slammed the door. Her anger-driven steps didn't slow up until they had carried her through the gardened pool area onto the beach. She paused briefly on the water-packed sand, then turned away from the ghost ship *Niña* and walked up the beach.

A copper moon floated among the stars, a giant gold balloon in the heavens. Its light gilded the whispering ocean waves with silver, their iridescent sheen adding to the magic of the warm night. Only rarely did the breeze generate enough motion to stir the spiked leaves of the palm trees.

Gradually her steps slowed to a meandering pace. But frustration still burned inside with a vengeful fire. Her heart cried bitterly at the unfairness of the situation. Erica stared at the gentle waves rolling onto shore, bringing its treasures to lay on the golden sand.

A long shadow fell along her side. "I hope you aren't thinking of taking a swim at this hour of the night."

Tension thundered through her pulse as Erica slowly turned to face Rafael, bracing herself against the force of his compelling attraction. The tip of her tongue moistened her lips as a fantastic thought entered her mind. She shook the dark mane of her hair and willed her body to relax.

"Actually I was only admiring the beauty of the evening," she lied, letting her mouth spread into an alluring smile.

"It is a tropical night," Rafael observed, not taking his gaze from her moonlit face. "Warm and languid and tantalizing."

Her heart thumped violently against her ribs.

She felt certain the wild thoughts running through her mind were visible in her face. What she was contemplating was risky, even supposing she could succeed. Abruptly she turned away from him, momentarily frightened by what she was going to do.

"Is something wrong?" Rafael immediately moved nearer as she perhaps subconsciously guessed he would.

A strange combination of excitement consumed her as her senses reacted to his vital maleness and her mind whirled with fantastic revenge. There was light contact of his hand against her shoulder and Erica leaned against it. The warmth of his skin through the tan jacket burned away the last chill of apprehension. Her neck curved sideways so she could gaze into his face.

"Rafael," her voice vibrated huskily. "Will you marry me?"

The dark glow of concern was immediately withdrawn from his gaze and she sensed the freezing aloofness that crept into his shadowed face. Erica turned fully into his now indifferent touch, her eyes roundly innocent and apologetic.

"Have I shocked you?" she whispered.

"The boldness of the women of your country always shocks me. In Mexico, it is the man who is the aggressor." The arrogant flare of his nostrils revealed his displeasure.

Her head was bent in a gesture of contrition. "Yes, I know," she sighed. "It was foolish of me to think you would take my proposal seriously."

Silence throbbed loudly for several seconds

before a lean finger touched her chin to raise it.

"Do you truly wish to marry me even though you know—what type of man I am?" Rafael demanded, thick dark lashes further veiling the unreadable expression in his eyes.

Erica blinked back the exultant gleam that leaped into her eyes. "That doesn't matter to me at all," she assured him fervently. Her hand raised in a natural movement to let her fingertips caress his lean cheek. "I only want to marry you, now, tonight."

A muscle in his jaw tightened beneath her intimate touch. "What about your family . . . and mine?" There was a mocking flash of white teeth at her startled expression. "Didn't you think I had a family?"

"Of course." Her breathing was becoming uneven under his shadowed but intent regard. Erica searched his face in desperation, trying to discern the reason for his reticence. A frightening thought struck her. "Rafael, you aren't planning to marry Helen, are you?"

"Since she is already married, it is unlikely," he answered smoothly. A dark brow arched at her stunned look. "You didn't know that. Perhaps you no longer wish to marry me?"

"No. I mean—no, it doesn't matter," she added hastily, her cheeks taking on a rosy hue. "I want to marry you."

"Tonight? With none of our families present? That is a very selfish request."

"Is it so wrong to be selfish?" Erica whispered, edging closer to him and feeling the touch of his

70

hands on her waist. "Is it so wrong to want this night for ourselves alone? To not want to share this moment with anyone?"

There was a peculiar ring of truth in her voice that even Erica didn't understand. Yet it existed. A marveling light sparkled in her eyes as her heartbeat shamelessly quickened when Rafael's hands tightened about her waist.

Willingly, eagerly, she slid into the hard circle of his arms, burying her head in the hollow of his throat and inhaling the intoxicating scent of his maleness. The firm pressure of his thighs sent scorching fires racing through her blood, leaving her limbs weak and yielding. His low, seductive voice spoke softly in his native tongue, his warm breath stirring her hair.

"Oh, Rafael," Erica moaned. "Please, I don't want to be alone any more."

Again his hand captured her chin, forcing her to look into the unfathomable blackness of his gaze. "Then you must marry me, Erica." Her name rolled caressively from his mouth. "It is I who ask you."

"Yes," she whispered her agreement, wondering at the strange catch in her voice.

There was an ominous sensation that things were not going the way she had planned. She seemed caught in the wake of his dark virility, swept along by forces she couldn't control. Yet this was what she wanted, what she had planned. The risks had all been calculated in that moment when she had formulated the idea. The first obstacle, Rafael's agreement, was behind her. Everything else would occur the way she intended it should. Or so Erica kept telling herself.

WITH A HEART that was light and untroubled, she waited in the foyer of an old but well-furnished building that Rafael had brought her to while he made arrangements for their wedding. This blithe unconcern lasted through much of the ceremony, conducted entirely in Spanish, another reason that made her feel so detached from the proceedings. Rafael's gentle promptings ensured that she made the proper responses to the solemn-faced official.

Then he removed the gold ring from his little finger and slipped it onto her ring finger. Its heaviness, still retaining the warmth of his hand, brought the gravity of her actions to the front. Her gaze tore itself away from the silver eagle with its double head on the face of the ring to look helplessly into his impenetrable eyes. Nervously she moistened her dry lips and swallowed the lump of fear in her throat.

The official's voice had stopped its flow of rhythmic Spanish. Temporarily paralyzed, Erica could only watch as Rafael bent toward her. Her heartbeat fluctuated wildly when his mouth touched hers, breathing warm fires of life into the ice-encrusted regions of her heart. As he drew away, she clung to his arm, nodding in numbed shock at the smiling official and the woman witness at his side.

Distantly she heard Rafael accepting their congratulations while the realization set in that she was married to him. For a moment she was terrified by the swiftness with which it had happened, before she consoled herself that a divorce could be just as quickly achieved. Still her legs trembled beneath her as Rafael led her to the car and her face was paper white. The interior light switched on automatically when he opened the door. His observant gaze immediately noted her pallor, narrowing on it when he slid behind the wheel.

"Are you not well?" His eyes lingered on her trembling lips that still held the sweet taste of his.

Erica ran a quivering hand over her cheek to her hair, half in defense of his regard. "I feel a bit giddy," she admitted, cutting off the hysterical laugh that accompanied her words. "I just realized I haven't eaten since breakfast."

"Then we must remedy that with a wedding dinner, no?" The devastating effect of his smile made her empty stomach churn all the more violently.

"Yes," Erica agreed readily. A full stomach would combat the weakness flowing through her body.

Later she watched as a waiter prepared their steaks on a cooking trolley beside their table. The restaurant had an authentic Mexican air and most of the well-dressed customers were nationals instead of the usual tourists that frequented the hotels. Beautifully scrolled wrought iron separated the dining area from the lounge, allowing the strumming notes of a flamenco guitarist to serenade both sections.

The entire mood of the place allowed Erica to relax and enjoy her meal without any twinge of anxiety. When the dishes were cleared, she picked up her wine glass to finish the last of the sangria. The signet ring on her finger clinked loudly against the crystal, reminding her sharply of her new status. Over the rim of her glass, she glanced at Rafael composedly leaning back against his chair, a thin cheroot between his fingers. Yet there was something very watchful about him. Erica replaced her glass and smiled as naturally as she could.

"Would you excuse me" she asked lightly as she reached for her evening bag, "while I freshen my makeup?"

As she rose to her feet, Rafael was there holding her chair, his gaze flicking over her face as if to decry her need for artifice, but he made no protest. Her pulse beat rapidly in her throat. Erica had to force herself to walk slowly in the direction of the powder room.

By a stroke of luck, a telephone was located near it. In her extremely limited, phrase-book Spanish, she succeeded in having the operator connect her with the hotel. In a nervous, breathless voice, she asked for Vance Wakefield's room.

Triumph glittered in her eyes as she imagined her father's anger when he discovered she had married a fortune hunter. Any thought of his supposedly vital business deal would be vanished at the news. In the blink of an eye he would have the marriage annulled. No doubt there would be a violent scene in which he would vent his wrath on her for doing such a stupid thing, but her father wouldn't be able to ignore her. This time his business would take a second place to Erica!

"Señor Wakefield is not here," the operator's voice informed her.

Icy fingers of panic gripped her throat. "What do you mean, he isn't there? Have him paged," she ordered. "This is his daughter and it's imperative that I reach him."

"One moment, *por favor*," was the reply.

Her fingers curled tightly over the black receiver as the seconds dragged by. He had to be in the hotel, she told herself.

Another voice came on the telephone, this time a male's. "Señorita Wakefield?"

"Yes, this is she. Where is my father?" she demanded, hysteria edging her voice.

"Señor Wakefield has returned to the States—"

"That's impossible!" Erica broke in. "There isn't a flight back at this hour!"

"I believe he chartered a jet, *señorita*," the man replied patiently. "He has made reservations for you to return tomorrow and has left a message at the desk for you. Would you like me to read it?"

"No," she answered numbly, more to protest the truth of what was being said. "No, that won't be necessary."

"I believe it was an emergency, *señorita*."

"Yes." A bitter laugh stopped in her throat. "A business deal. Thank you. Thank you very much."

Her mouth was twisted in a grimace of irony as she replaced the telephone. His business had won and she had lost. Erica stared at the ring on her

75

finger. She was married and her father wasn't here to rescue her. What was she going to do? What could she do?

Her first instinct was to flee. To get as far away from Rafael as she could, as soon as she could. She could send him a message explaining that it was all a mistake. She hadn't much money in her personal account, but to a man like him, it would be a great deal. But how would she go about getting a divorce? She pressed her hands to her temples, fighting the panic that threatened to surface. She desperately needed time to think. But Rafael was waiting in the dining room for her to rejoin him.

With the same impulsiveness that had got her into this situation, Erica decided to leave a message for Rafael that she was returning to her hotel. The manager could summon a cab for her. In the sanctity of her room, she would come up with a solution. As she turned to carry out her decision Rafael appeared before her.

The color drained from her face at the sight of the compelling figure. Her eyes noted the hard line of his mouth that was momentarily softened by a smile of concern. Cowardice reigned supreme inside her. There was something very indomitable about his personality. Her father might be a match for Rafael, but she wasn't.

"Did you think I wasn't coming back?" she asked with forced gaiety as she glided toward him.

"Should I have thought that?" he returned, thoughtfully watching her swift change from pallor to high color.

"Well—" Erica's smile was tremulous as she answered as truthfully as she dared "—I admit to a few jittery nerves like any ordinary bride!"

His regard switched to one of indolence, wicked glimmers of arrogant amusement behind the lazily veiled dark lashes. The firm touch of his fingers on her elbow seemed to enforce his right of possession as he led her into the restaurant proper.

"Those nerves I will allow," he stated. "Do you wish to leave or would you like a drink in the lounge?"

"May we go to the lounge?" Erica requested, stalling for time to cope with this new problem.

The flamenco guitarist was still performing, his agile fingers caressing the strings. The throbbing notes coming from the instrument matched the wild song in her heart. Erica restively held the *marguerita*, a tequila cocktail that Rafael had ordered for her, taking quick sips of the tart liquor, hoping the alcohol would have a calming effect on her jumbled nerves. Her attention was determinedly centered on the musician to avoid the wide shoulders only inches from her own.

"Do you enjoy the music?" Rafael inquired.

"Yes, he's very good." Her gaze bounced away from his face. The aristocratic lines were thrown into sharp relief by the dimness of the room.

"Would you like another drink?"

Erica glanced in surprise at her empty glass and quickly agreed. Time elapsed with unnerving slowness. She consumed the second cocktail and a third, yet she was no nearer a solution than when they had entered the lounge. She didn't dare have another drink since her head was already swimming with the potency of the others. There was no alternative except for her to agree when Rafael suggested they leave.

The freshness of the night air increased the effects of the alcohol. Her nerves were now too relaxed and her mind refused to function properly. Her muteness was traitorous evidence of her cowardice. She sat silently as Rafael started the car and drove away from the restaurant. The bright lights of the hotel row beckoned them, but he was not heading toward them.

"Aren't we going to the hotel?" Erica murmured. A lightning thought occurred to her and she seized upon it immediately. "My things are there. I'll need them."

Once at the hotel, she would be safe. It was suddenly essential that Rafael take her there. In her room she would be able to assert her father's authority. If Rafael should dare to attempt to force his way into her room, she had only to notify management.

"Not yet," Rafael replied, glancing swiftly at the oncoming traffic as he turned down a street. "I thought I would take you to the yacht. Have you ever been aboard one?"

"None of that size," she admitted, her heart sinking as she realized that short of ordering him to take her to the hotel, she had no alternative but to agree. "Isn't Helen there?" she asked hopefully.

"One of the engines is being overhauled, so she is staying with friends," he explained, amusement

78

glittering in the upward curl of his lips at her hesitant question.

"I see," Erica murmured. If Helen had been there, she would have had grounds for refusing to go to the yacht. As it was, she had to resign herself to taking a tour of the ship.

Minutes later they were at the yacht basin and Rafael was switching off the ignition. Erica waited nervously as his tall figure walked around the silver nose of the car to open her door. Again his hand was firmly holding her arm, guiding her along the dock past the silent ships toward the majestic monolith at the far end.

The heel of her satin slipper caught on the ridge of the ship's gangplank, causing her to stumble. Instantly Rafael's arm was around her as he swung her off her feet and carried her the few steps on to the polished deck. It all happened so swiftly that Erica didn't have time to protest, the unexpected contact with his steel-strong frame depriving her of the power of speech. The power of his attraction was never more formidable than at that moment. When he set her on her feet, she leaned weakly against him, her head curved back over his arm.

"Welcome aboard, Señora—" Rafael murmured caressively, his dark head inclining toward her, but his sentence was incomplete as brisk footsteps approached them and he straightened.

"*Buenos noches, señor.*"

Erica blinked rather bewilderedly in the direction of the voice that had granted her a reprieve. A man in a gleaming white uniform stood in front of them, obviously one of the yacht's crew. In spite of the deferential attitude, Erica sensed the curiosity when the man's gaze shifted from Rafael to her.

"*Buenos noches*, Pedro," Rafael replied. The rest of his swift Spanish Erica couldn't follow, but she thought she guessed accurately that he was explaining who she was and his purpose in bringing her aboard.

Rafael introduced the man as a crew member, Pedro—and the rest of the name escaped Erica in the fluent roll of his Spanish. Unbidden, the thought came to her that she was going to have to learn Spanish since she was married to a Mexican. There was a moment of horror as she realized how permanent she was making the marriage sound. When the man nodded respectfully toward her, she was incapable of speech and her head inclined stiffly in answer.

Sobering instantly, Erica succumbed readily to the pressure of Rafael's hands at her back, eager to complete the tour of the yacht and be taken ashore to her hotel. The change in her manner brought his quizzically watchful gaze to bear on her. She attempted to conceal her haste as he led her into the main salon.

"What is the name of the ship?" she asked, the barest tremor of nerves in her voice.

"She is called *Mañana*—tomorrow." His enigmatic dark gaze held hers. "A suggestion of sweet promise, no?"

There was something suggestive in his statement. Her skin stretched with white tautness over her knuckles as her viselike grip on the pearl evening bag increased. It seemed to her that tomorrow would never come and not with any promise of sweetness.

Turning away from him, she made a show of studying the salon, admiring, in spite of herself, the bold clean lines, the Spanish decor that was elegant and bright. She would never have associated the vivid colors with Rafael's blond mistress. The bold background would not be complementary at all, she decided with some satisfaction.

There was a desire to linger in the tastefully furnished room, but Erica resolutely denied it, and her feet led her into the dining room. She kept her comments to a minimum as Rafael showed her the lounge, the well-equipped galley, and pointed out the direction of the crew's quarters. Her interest was aroused by the book-lined study, but she forced herself to glance around with indifference.

"Lastly, the staterooms," Rafael announced.

Erica paused in the carpeted passageway, her gaze sliding away from his lean, aristocratic features. "I don't want to see . . . hers." The admission came out tautly, a strange anger burning in her chest.

"As you wish." Amusement lurked in the mocking edges of his voice.

Rafael opened the doors of two guestrooms for her to see, pointedly ignored a third and fourth door and led her to the last one in the passageway.

"These are my quarters," he told her as he opened the door.

Female curiosity pushed her inside, but the startling decor took her a step farther into the spacious room. The abundant use of rich browns and blacks was arresting, their darkness relieved by a shade of muted gold. There was nothing dreary about it as the atmosphere it generated was luxurious, sensuous and masculine.

Erica pivoted sharply, needing to escape before some mystical spell was weaved. Rafael was standing behind her, his wide shoulders blocking her view of the door. Undercurrents of emotion vibrated the air between them to rivet her feet to the floor. The unwavering gaze pinned to her face, the tapering length of his build, the expensive material of his tan slacks stretched over muscular thighs, the raven blackness of his hair and eyes, the aura of regal arrogance kept her motionless. The air was so charged that Erica hardly dared to breathe.

With slow, deliberate movements, Rafael's hand reached out to touch her cheek, his thumb caressing the bone. His touch released a torrent of desires and her lashes fluttered down to conceal them, steeling herself not to react, not to melt in his arms as she had done before and as Helen had undoubtedly done many times before in the same room. Unexpected pain pressed her lips tightly together.

"No one has been in this room except myself and the crew, Erica."

His uncanny perception of her thoughts opened her lash-shuttered eyes in surprise. The look in his bronzed face Erica couldn't define, but it sent her heart pounding like a trip-hammer. His thumb moved down to the corner of her mouth and traced the outline of its feminine softness. When his hand moved to the side of her neck, her lips trembled in unwilling protest to its departure.

The descent of his dark head was unhurried, her lips parting in anticipation of the moment when Rafael would claim them. His kiss was a lick of flame, igniting her already kindled desire. Possession was immediate with no tender, probing search for a response by Rafael.

A swirling mist of lascivious weakness swayed Erica against him. Her shoulders were seized as she was pulled to the rock wall of his chest. The mastery of his embrace was a seduction of the senses. The total exploration by his mouth of her face and neck and shoulder was beyond her power to halt had she wanted it to stop. He alternately gave and took, demanded, received and returned her ardency.

In a moment, she would be lost beyond recall, absorbed by a personality more forceful than any with which she had come in contact. It was this fear that enabled her to whirl away from him when every other warning had been swept aside.

Her freedom of his touch was only for an instant as her hair was brushed aside and his mouth sent tongues of wildfire along the sensitive cord of her neck. Erica gulped for life-giving air, her trembling fingers closing over the lean hands spreading across her stomach, drawing her back against his rising male hardness. One hand allowed itself to be pushed away. Her success was met by failure when Erica felt the nearly silent sound of the zipper sliding open down her back. She ached to feel his touch against the nakedness of her flesh. The intoxicating desire to submit was overpowering.

She turned back toward him, her hands clutching the bodice of the cream silk gown that threatened to slip away. Her face reddened as she saw his gaze lingering on the tantalizing shadow between her breasts. Mutely she beseeched him with her luminous eyes.

"Do not be ashamed." His seductively soft voice caressed her. "You are my wife, Erica." Again the smoldering light in his eyes swept over her breasts, the intimacy of the look causing her to draw a deep breath that only made the light burn brighter when it returned to her face. "Every inch of you is beautiful to me. Don't be frightened, *querida*."

Strangely Erica wasn't frightened. Her arms willingly wound themselves around his neck as he carried her to the bed, setting her on her feet beside it. She was his wife, he had said. A delicious sensation of bliss washed over her. It was right that he had such power over her.

His jacket was off, his shirt unbuttoned and being tugged free of his trousers. The sight of the golden tan chest, the naked skin being revealed as he removed the shirt, brought the last vestige of resistance. Her fingers tightened convulsively on her loosened gown.

"I . . . I have to go back to the hotel . . . now," she said huskily.

Rafael looked at her for a long moment, his arms gently circling her. "If that is what you wish, *querida*, I will take you there," he murmured. "Speak now or let us speak no more."

But the fruit of temptation was there before her and the age-old desire to bite into its sweetness was supreme. Her hands slipped around his waist as she tilted her head to receive his kiss.

Later Rafael kissed the blood from her lips inflicted by her teeth when she attempted to bite back her cry of pain. He cradled her in his arms, murmuring reassuring words in Spanish that she didn't understand. Tenderly, patiently, he waited for the agony to subside before he initiated her to the dizzying rapture a man and woman can attain. When the last sigh of ecstasy shuddered through her, he possessively held her against his own chest, pressing her head to the uneven beat of his own heart.

"*Esta mañana, querida,*" he whispered softly.

CHAPTER FIVE

ERICA STIRRED RESTLESSLY beneath the leaden band
that held her down. The pressure eased slightly
and she shifted into a more comfortable position
on her side. In a state of near-wakefulness, she became conscious of an alien warmth against her
breast. Instantly all her senses were alert, her skin
tingling where the hand possessively cupped the
rounded firmness of her breast. Then the rest of
her body became aware of Rafael lying beside her.

Gently she rolled away from his unresisting
hand, hugging the edge of the bed in case she had
awakened him. Her mind raced in panic as she
stared at the shadow-darkened form in the bed.
What had she done? Horror and shame ate at her
insides. How could she have been so permissive as
to go to bed with this man, this virtual stranger,
simply because some Mexican official had mumbled a few legal words that she hadn't understood?

This man who had erased her innocence forever
was an adventurer, a fortune hunter! How could
she have allowed herself to be seduced by him?
Her father would have forgiven her for marrying
him if he had arrived in time. But now, once he
learned how weak she had been, Vance Wakefield
would never forgive her.

Erica backed away from the bed in terror.

Frantically she grabbed at her gown lying on the floor and the rest of her garments scattered nearby. Keeping an eye on the still figure in the bed, she dressed with fear-driven swiftness. Her muscles were stiff and resisting. Guilt turned her stomach with sickening movements at the cause for the soreness.

Carrying her shoes and evening bag in her hand, she tiptoed into the hallway, quietly closing the door of the stateroom behind her and listening for any sign that Rafael might have heard her leave. The only sound in the entire yacht was the waves licking the sides of the structure. Pausing in the doorway to the deck, Erica glanced furtively around, afraid of running into one of the members of the crew. Nothing. She hurried as quickly as she dared to the gangplank and didn't stop running until she was ashore.

The sky was pitch black. By the time she was able to wave down a cab and arrive at her hotel, the first glimmers of dawn were lighting the sky in the east. The night life of Acapulco ran from dusk till dawn, so there were few glances from the hotel staff at her early morning return.

Once in her room, Erica walked directly to the shower, discarding her gown in the wastebasket and willing the sharp spray of water to banish the licentious memories that burned so vividly. It was futile. They were seared there beyond recall.

As she reentered her room, the door to the connecting suite opened. For a split second, she froze in terror, half expecting to see Rafael standing in the doorway. Instead it was Lawrence, a maroon robe tied around his waist, his fingers raking his thinning hair.

"I thought I heard someone stirring in here." A yawn punctuated his sentence. "What are you doing up at this hour?"

Erica was between Lawrence and the bed. Chances were he hadn't seen that it hadn't been slept in and he obviously believed she had come in much earlier. She was too ashamed and humiliated by her own conduct to tell him what had happened.

"I'm getting ready to leave," she replied tautly.

"Vance had a maid pack most of your things." A sleepy smile crooked the corners of his thin mouth. "He left me behind to see that you made the plane—which, by the way, doesn't leave for hours."

Something told Erica that if she didn't leave the hotel within the hour, Rafael would be here to get her and the whole sordid story would be out.

"We're leaving now," she declared.

Lawrence frowned. "There aren't any scheduled flights at this hour of the morning."

"Then we'll charter a plane like daddy did!" A strange mixture of torture and temper stormed in her eyes. "But we're leaving now!"

There was a wry shake of his head as if he gave up trying to understand what caused her mercurial moods. "I'll meet you downstairs in twenty minutes."

Only after Lawrence had left the room did Erica notice she was still wearing Rafael's ring on her finger. She hurriedly stuffed it in the bottom of one of her suitcases and got dressed. Three-quarters of an hour later, their chartered plane was leaving the runway with not a sign of Rafael anywhere.

They didn't return to San Antonio but flew to Houston where Vance Wakefield had gone. He was too involved in negotiations to notice Erica's agitated behavior. The rare moments he spent in her company were too short for her to confide in him had she gathered the courage. It was nearly three weeks later that they returned to their home in San Antonio.

"So I NEVER TOLD DADDY," Erica sighed as she finished telling her story to Jules Blackwell. "I've never told anyone until today."

"And you say the marriage was consummated?"

"Yes," she nodded, not trying to hide the scarlet shame in her face.

"Now, now," he said, patting her hand affectionately. "Don't start chastising yourself again. It seems to me that you've punished yourself enough."

Erica smiled at him ruefully. "Thank you for not telling me how foolish I was for getting myself into this mess."

"Hindsight isn't going to get you out of it." His round figure was pulled out of the chair beside her as he walked around to his desk. "You haven't seen this fellow since you left Acapulco, have you?"

"No, I haven't."

But she remembered those first months of fear

when she had waited out those long days not knowing if she was pregnant and wondering which day Rafael would appear, to blackmail her. And there had been the anxiety that her unprincipled response to his advances meant she was promiscuous. Her subsequent severely controlled behavior with other men had since earned her the nickname of ice maiden that Forest had teased her about.

"Do you know where this man lives? Is his home in Acapulco?" Jules asked.

"I don't know." Erica shook her head.

"What is his full name?"

She looked into his gently inquiring gaze, a bubble of hysterical laughter escaping her throat before she could stop it. "I don't know. San Antonio has always been my home, but I grew up in boarding schools. I never learned basic Spanish other than good morning and thank you until last year. I took private lessons so I could converse with some of the customers in my boutique. But then—" she shrugged "—in Acapulco, I couldn't follow the pronunciation. Isn't it funny, Uncle Jules? I'm married and I don't even know what my name is."

"What about the marriage certificate?" he asked, not giving her a chance to dwell on another example of her stupidity.

"Rafael must have it. I vaguely recall signing my name. I suppose he put it in his pocket."

"It's a legal document, so it will be on file. I can get a copy of it," he assured her as he removed the ring from the handkerchief Erica had given him. The silver eagle with two heads stamped on the face of the ring stared back at him. "This signet ring could be a family crest, but it's unlikely."

Erica watched the attorney anxiously. "How much do you think I'll have to pay Rafael for the divorce?"

"It depends on how wealthy he thinks you are and whether he has discovered you're Vance Wakefield's daughter," Jules answered. The look he gave her was sincerely apologetic. "I'm sorry, Erica, but your husband—"

"Don't call him that!" her tempestuous pride made her snap.

He smiled understandingly, silently glad to see her stoical regret had not completely replaced her spirit. "Very well, this man is obviously mercenary. I doubt if he'll settle for a small sum."

"I don't have a great deal of money, Uncle Jules, outside of the allowance daddy gives me. You know how the trust fund is tied up." Her teeth nibbled at her lower lip. "Daddy will ask all sorts of questions if I have to ask him for a large amount. He would probe until he found out why I wanted it. We get along so well now." The last sentence was a despairing sigh.

"I know."

A mirthless smile lifted the corners of her mouth. "If I'd had an affair with Rafael, daddy could have forgiven that. But to marry him! And keep it a secret all this time. I simply can't let him find out no matter how much money Rafael demands. I'll have to find a way of raising it on my own."

"You're worrying about a bridge we haven't

reached, my dear," Jules scolded. "There's time enough for that later when I've located this man." He held out his hand to her. "Are you going to take me to lunch or not?"

His gruff tone was meant to cajole her out of her worry. Erica laughed easily and reached out to take his hand. "Of course!"

After lunch, they paused outside the riverwalk restaurant. Jules's jovial expression was converted to professional reassurance.

"I'll make a few discreet inquiries when I get back to the office," he promised. "I'll let you know as soon as I find out anything."

"It would be better if you contacted me at the boutique. I don't want daddy getting suspicious," Erica returned. She hesitated for a second. "When you do find Rafael, I . . . I don't want to see him."

His wink said he would take care of that. "Give Vance my regards."

"I will, Uncle Jules, and thank you."

He waved aside her thanks as they parted. Following the meandering San Antonio River to her shop, Erica discovered she wasn't as relieved as she had thought she would be. Her burden had been lightened and she was confident that Jules Blackwell would be able to find Rafael and arrange the divorce. Yet she was restless, curiously on edge, as if there was something she hadn't taken into account.

The ominous gray cloud was still hovering on the horizon when she dressed for dinner that night. The vibrantly yellow cocktail dress she wore was chosen especially to chase it away. Erica tried to derive satisfaction at the calm way her father included Forest in the conversation en route to the Mendelsens' home. Vance Wakefield could be quite cutting if he didn't like or approve of a particular person. But her inner preoccupation made her gaiety forced, although no one appeared to notice it except herself.

John Mendelsen greeted the trio at the door of his Spanish-style home. He was a distinguished-looking man, a contemporary of Vance Wakefield's and a sometimes business associate, friend and golfing partner. His pale blond hair had long ago lightened to silver and the leather tan of his skin contrasted sharply with it and the ice blue of his eyes.

"Where's that dark-eyed wife of yours?" Vance demanded in a laughing voice.

"Luisa is on the patio with the rest of our guests. You're the last to arrive, as usual, Vance, but there is still plenty of time for a couple of drinks before dinner," John assured him. "I'm certain Luisa will stop flitting among our distinguished guests long enough to see that your thirst is satisfied."

"Luisa is much too aristocratic to flit," her father corrected.

Erica smiled a silent agreement. John Mendelsen's wife was a petite but imposing woman, a member of an old and respected Mexican-American family, innately proud and regal.

"Who has your philanthropic wife invited this time?" Vance asked as John began leading them through the cool hallways. "Should I have brushed up on my Spanish?"

"We have our usual group—George and Mary

93

Saunders, the Cliftons, the Mateos and their daughter, and Reina Cruz." Their host shrugged. "If Luisa seems to be preening a bit, it's because she succeeded in persuading Torres to come this evening. He's the head of an old Mexican family and an authority on Latin-American history. He's in San Antonio to oversee a new exhibit at the Mexican Cultural Institute. Have no fear, though. He speaks perfect English."

Erica and Forest were walking a few steps behind her father and John Mendelsen. With the two older men deep in conversation, Forest leaned slightly toward Erica.

"Have I told you how stunning you look?" he murmured in a low, growling undertone as his eyes ravaged her face.

She darted him a sparkling, flirtatious smile. "No, tell me."

His hand tightened around her waist. "If we were alone, I'd do more than tell you."

Erica glanced up to his face, noting the ardent light in his warm brown eyes. Only for a second her imagination played tricks on her and she saw smoldering black eyes. Her stomach constricted painfully before she could blink away the tantalizing image and she was once more seeing the square jaw and dimpled chin belonging to Forest.

"Have you mentioned us yet to your father?" Forest asked.

"I haven't said yes to you yet," she whispered with forced lightness. In her heart, she knew she couldn't give him an answer until the arrangements had been made for her divorce from Rafael.

94

"But you will say yes. If I wasn't positive of that, I . . ." They had arrived at the patio and Forest was unable to complete his sentence.

Erica understood the urgency in his voice. In a lesser way she felt the same. Since that long-ago night with Rafael, she had learned that she was neither permissive nor promiscuous. Her laxity that night had been caused by a combination of circumstances.

The first of the guests to notice their arrival on the patio and to step forward to greet them was Reina Cruz, an attractive vivacious widow in her late thirties. Her smile encompassed all of them, but Erica thought it lingered a little longer on her father. In the past if any woman had singled her father out for attention, she would have disliked her on the spot. But her recently acquired, mature attitude toward her father no longer dictated such a reaction. She liked and admired Reina and even wished her good luck should the woman choose to pursue her father.

"I have heard a great deal about you, Forest." Reina smiled after Erica had introduced him. "I am glad to meet you. Erica is very lucky."

"I hope to make her luckier some time soon," Forest replied, flicking a possessive glance to the dark-haired girl at his side.

"So you've arrived, Vance." Their hostess moved gracefully to the quartet.

"You know I wouldn't miss one of your dinner parties, Luisa," her father declared in his typically diplomatic and offhand way.

"Erica, you look lovely." The still-dark-haired

95

woman brushed her cheek with a kiss that was composedly affectionate without being overly so. Just as graciously, she turned to Forest. "And I'm so glad you were able to come, Forest."

"It was thoughtful of you to invite me," he nodded.

Luisa's dark eyes sparkled at Erica. "It seemed the best way to ensure that Erica could join us."

She felt her father's eyes rest on her thoughtfully, but Erica made no reply to the leading comment except to smile calmly. Luisa Mendelsen linked her arm with Vance's.

"Come, all of you. I want you to meet my guest of honor," she said.

Luisa was very active in civic organizations and projects dealing with the Spanish-American heritage of Texas and San Antonio in particular. Her dinner parties usually included a Latin-American dignitary, cultural, political, or artistic, so Erica was not surprised that one was here this evening. She glanced idly ahead of her father and their hostess to see the elderly historian from Mexico.

Among the familiar faces of the other guests was the foreign visitor—tall, bronzed, hair and eyes of pitch black. Erica's knees almost buckled beneath her. Her vision blurred and for a second she thought she was going to faint. Briefly she leaned against Forest before her sight cleared and blood flowed again to her limbs.

Controlled by a numb sense of inevitability, Erica let Forest escort her to Rafael, bracing herself for the moment when he would see her. As if from a great distance, she heard Luisa's voice call to him and the dark, arrogant face that she knew so well turned in answer. The aloof gaze swept the group. Erica couldn't be certain, but it seemed as if his gaze narrowed for a lightning second on her before it stopped on Luisa. A polite smile lifted the firm line of his mouth, firmer than Erica remembered.

"I would like you all to meet Don Rafael Alejandro de la Torres," introduced Luisa.

Erica dug her fingernails into the palm of her hand. She glanced anxiously at her father as he was presented to Rafael. There was no recognition in his face. Any second she expected Rafael to blurt out that he was Vance's son-in-law, then gradually she realized he wasn't going to.

"This is Vance's daughter, Erica Wakefield."

Luisa's voice directed Rafael's gaze to her. The lean, chiseled mask was molded by courteous lines while the rapier thrust of his gaze stripped what little color remained in Erica's face. There was a jeering arch in one black brow.

"You are not married, Miss Wakefield?" Rafael asked dryly as he offered his hand in greeting.

Her hand trembled as she forced it to touch his, remembering the way those lean fingers had caressed her body with erotic intimacy. That same heat seemed to scorch every inch of her.

"No, I'm not married," she denied. Her quivering chin lifted proudly.

Then her hand was released and Rafael was turning toward Forest as Luisa made the introduction again, adding in explanation that he was Erica's friend. There was no reaction by Rafael to that statement. A servant arrived with a tray of drinks. Instantly the other guests, friends of long standing, moved forward to greet them and Erica was able to slip away from the circle that included Rafael.

Yet the abandon with which she threw herself into the conversation with the new group didn't make Erica any less conscious of Rafael's presence. Never once did she look in his direction, but she saw the way the other women's eyes gravitated toward him. At times, she could hear his low-timbred voice, and icy chills of apprehension danced along her spine.

Had he come here to find her? Was the exhibit at the Mexican Cultural Institute just a pose? Or was he an impostor? In Acapulco he had admitted to being a fortune hunter. Erica herself had seen him with a woman many years his senior. He had remained silent about their mariage. Did that mean he intended to blackmail her? There was no question any more that he knew who her father was.

Erica knew she had to find out where he was staying so she could let her Uncle Jules know. Yet she shrank from inquiring directly, and asking the others at the party would only arouse curiosity. Forest, what would he think? Her head pounded with the multitude of her questions. She hadn't wanted to see or speak to Rafael again, but the choice had been taken out of her hands.

If Rafael's plans were to blackmail her, then to run, to avoid seeing him would show cowardice and increase his hold over her. Perhaps the best thing would be to seek him out, apart from the others, and let him realize that she wasn't afraid of him. But it was inconceivable that such an occasion would arise. His being, his personality were too compelling for him to be alone in a group of people unless he chose it. A despairing cloud darkened her eyes to a royal shade.

Dinner was announced. Erica discovered her father was seated opposite Rafael, who was on the hostess's right, while she was down the table and across from him, a position that promised that any time his gaze looked down the table it would include her. Even Forest was separated from her so that she could no longer use him as a shield.

The carefully prepared meal was tasteless. Erica spent most of her time pushing the food around her plate and making sure her eyes didn't stray to Rafael. Tension was beginning to etch tight lines around her smile when the dessert dishes were cleared and Luisa suggested they move to the living room.

Forest started toward her, only to be waylaid by George Saunders. Rafael was talking to her father a few steps away and Erica glanced desperately around for a haven. With a smile of relief, she saw Julie Mateo, only a year younger than herself, just entering the living room.

"What have you been doing lately, Julie?" Erica asked brightly to draw the girl to her side.

"Very little, actually. Helping out at the hospital part-time." She was a quiet, unassuming girl with auburn hair and pleasing features. It had only been in the past few months that Erica had got to know her very well. "I like your dress. Is it from your shop?"

"As a matter of fact, it is," Erica admitted with a self-consciously proud smile.

"That's an excellent way to advertise your boutique." Julie grinned.

"Do you own a boutique, Miss Wakefield?" There was a knowing gleam in Rafael's eyes as he watched the startled turn of Erica's head.

"It's a joint venture between my father and myself." In spite of her efforts to reply calmly, her voice sounded cool.

Vance Wakefield smiled at her indulgently. "I have to admit my daughter has a sound business head. She picked out the location on the riverwalk and except for a little advice from me, she has operated it all by herself."

The raven-black head tilted patronizingly toward her. "Your shop on the riverwalk, is it called Erica's?"

"Yes, yes, it is," she answered defensively. "Not very original, I admit."

"What a coincidence!" One corner of his mouth moved in a mocking smile. "I stopped there today, close to noon, to buy a gift for my sister. I'm quite sure I would have remembered if I had seen you there, Miss Wakefield."

"I believe I was out to lunch at that time," she said, her expression freezing as the irony of the situation struck her. The very hour she had been discussing her elopement with him to Jules Blackwell, Rafael had been in the boutique. "I hope Donna was able to find a gift suitable for your sister."

"She did." The instant the reply had been made, Rafael turned to her father, a suggestion of boredom in his features both with Erica and the subject of the conversation.

"What do you think of San Antonio, Don Rafael?" her father inquired. "Have you been here before?"

"Not for some time," he replied, answering the last question first. "San Antonio is like an aging dowager, really proud of her rich heritage and culture, and futuristic in her outlook. Yet she has never lost the grace and old-world charm she was born to possess. She truly deserves to be one of the four unique cities in the United States."

Erica stared at him in silence, stunned by the way he had put her feelings toward the city into words. She had forgotten how very charming Rafael could be. How she hated him at that moment! It took all her willpower to prevent her from telling the entire gathering what a despicable person he was. He had married her for her money and he was here to collect some of it.

Her rage seethed like a cancer inside her as she watched the way his presence dominated the room. The center of interest was always where Rafael was. Erica stood on the fringes of satellite groups, not trusting herself to speak for fear she would be pronouncing her own death sentence as well as Rafael's. And the subjects of the other guests' discussions never seemed to stray far away from Rafael.

When the small group she was standing with began to gravitate toward him, Erica pretended an interest in a statue of Aztec origin. Forest was on the far side of the room leading some discussion with Matt Clifton and Ed Mateo. Both were nodding agreement to what he was saying. She tried to be glad that Forest was mingling so well with her peers, but she wanted to be gone from this house and Rafael, to feel the comfort of Forest's arms around her. From past experience, she knew the party would drag on for another hour or more.

"The statue is an excellent example of early Aztec art." Erica's back stiffened as her head jerked sideways to see Rafael standing negligently by her side. His black gaze ridiculed the impotency of the anger in her expression. "I'm afraid this will have to do," he murmured mysteriously.

A confused look entered her eyes as she regarded him haughtily. "I don't know what you mean."

"I believe you wished to speak to me privately. This is as private as we can get, unless you wish to cause comment by leaving the room in my company," he mocked.

"What are you doing here?" Erica hissed, staring at the statue and wishing she could throw it at him.

"Didn't our hosts explain? I am here with an exhibit from Mexico," he answered in an amused voice.

"Don't play games!" she snapped, whirling about to face him. "You know very well what I'm talking about!"

Her anger seemed to amuse him more. "Do you truly wish to discuss it here, *mia esposa*?" Erica caught her breath sharply as his eyes seemed to physically touch the upper portion of her body, traveling with unnerving slowness. "You are my wife, Erica de la Torres, by word and by deed."

Coloring furiously at his unnecessary reminder, she glared her resentment. "No, we won't discuss it here," she admitted grudgingly.

His superior nod of acknowledgment indicated that he had known very well that it could be no other way. "I am staying at Palacio del Rio," and he gave her his room number. "May I expect you there at noon tomorrow?"

"Yes," she snapped.

"I shall look forward to the pleasure of your company," he said as the sensual line of his mouth curled tauntingly.

The only satisfaction Erica could acknowledge was the fact that Jules Blackwell and not she would meet Rafael tomorrow. At least, she would be spared another disturbing encounter with him.

As Erica predicted earlier, all the guests lingered for better than an hour. Rafael was standing with Luisa and John Mendelsen as the others bade them goodbye. Forest was standing behind her, his arm loosely circling her waist so she rested lightly against him. There was a sense of protection in his casual embrace as they waited for her father to finish speaking to his host.

"I didn't truly expect to enjoy myself tonight," Forest murmured near her ear. "Your father's friends aren't nearly as stuffy as I expected them to be."

Erica bent her head back and to the side to gaze into his ruggedly handsome face. "I would have much rather been somewhere else," she said decisively.

"Damn, but you're beautiful!" Fire leaped into his brown eyes as his lips possessively touched hers, unmindful of watching eyes.

Erica held his ardent gaze a second longer, his tender caress touching her deeply, before she turned to see if her father was ready to leave. Her softly luminous eyes were pinned by the ominous blackness of Rafael's, his nostrils flaring in arrogant disapproval. Erica's heart catapulted in fear at the ruthless lines etched in the handsome, bronze mask. Then he turned away and she was free, but she wondered how long it would be before she was truly free.

Later, in her own home, Vance Wakefield discreetly made himself scarce so Erica and Forest could say their good-nights in private. Erica went eagerly into his arms, responding with forced ardor to his kisses. Yet she found she couldn't block out the events that had taken place.

Worse, she discovered herself trying to compare her reaction to Forest with the way she had felt with Rafael. Even when she had disliked Rafael in Acapulco, she had admitted that she was sexually attracted to him. But a comparison was foolish. Sensations aroused by the first time that a man awakened a woman to her inner physical desires would never be as stunning or overwhelming again.

CHAPTER SIX

ERICA PRESSED A HAND to her churning stomach, then pulled open the door to the hotel's riverwalk entrance. She had telephoned Jules the instant she had arrived at the boutique that morning. The receptionist had informed her that he was out of the city and not expected back until Tuesday or Wednesday of the following week.

A half a dozen times during the morning, Erica had walked to the telephone to cancel her appointment with Rafael. As reluctant as she was to see him again, she was also aware that she desperately needed to know what his demands were so that she would have time to raise the money. The sooner she found out how difficult a task it was going to be, the sooner she could find a way of accomplishing it. Besides, she wasn't certain she could put Rafael off until Jules came back. It was conceivable that he might try to contact her at the boutique or at home.

There was no sign of Rafael in the restaurant on the river level and none in the lobby's cocktail lounge. Her watch showed exactly twelve noon. With her heart beating unevenly, Erica walked to the house phone and dialed his suite. Her hand nervously clutched the white receiver.

"Yes?" His rich voice flowed smoothly in her ear.

"Th-this is Erica." She faltered momentarily. "Shall I meet you in the lounge?"

A mirthless chuckle sounded on the other end of the receiver. "You indicated that you wanted a private discussion, then you pick a public gathering place to have it. Do you not wish to speak to me where no one can overhear?"

"Yes—"

"Then come to my suite," Rafael commanded, and the line was disconnected.

Erica held the phone to her ear for a long moment, her throat choked by the words of refusal she hadn't had the opportunity to say. Mutely she rebelled against the conspiracy that continued to give Rafael control.

Replacing the receiver, she walked self-consciously toward the elevators, glancing furtively around her in case someone she knew saw her. It was one thing to pretend that she had accidentally bumped into Rafael in the crowded lobby and it was another to be seen going into or coming out of his room.

Luck was, for once, on her side as the doors yawned to admit her to an empty elevator. There was no one around on Rafael's floor, either, and Erica walked swiftly to his room, praying that he wouldn't make her wait too long in the hallway before opening the door.

When it opened, she quickly darted in, not drawing a secure breath until she heard the door close behind her. Then she swung to face Rafael. The upheaval going on within caused her considerable consternation as she tried not to notice how effectively the azure blue suit complemented his dark coloring and increased his attraction. His hand made a politely mocking gesture toward the burnt-orange cushions of a small settee. Erica walked stiltedly toward it, trying to calm her chaotic thoughts and emotions.

"Sherry?" Rafael offered a stemmed glass of the amber liquid to her.

She accepted it, more to have something to occupy her hands to ease their nervous trembling. The last thing she wanted was drink to cloud her thinking. This was the moment that she needed all her faculties alert.

Hitching his trousers, he sat down in a bulky-styled Mediterranean chair next to the settee. His manner reminded Erica of a lord dutifully about to listen to the problems of one of his lowly subjects. Indignantly her lips tightened.

"You wished to discuss our marriage," Rafael prompted with infuriating calm.

"I wish to discuss our divorce," she corrected him curtly.

"Why have you waited a year and a half to make your wishes known that you want our marriage to end?" His voice sounded disinterested, but his unreadable dark eyes had grown blacker.

Erica glanced down to her glass. "I didn't know how to reach you or where you lived."

"And you made no effort to find out," he stated.

"No." She refused to be intimidated as she lashed back sarcastically, "I was simply glad to get away from a fortune hunter like you!"

"Ah—" a mockingly complacent smile widened

his mouth "—but you learned last night that my profession was not what you imagined it to be."

"If you are who you say you are," she answered coldly, then shrugged. "Either way, it's immaterial. I want a divorce."

"Last night I heard talk that you and this Forest Granger are in love." The soft jeer sliced out at Erica. "Perhaps he is the reason for your sudden decision."

Her chin raised to a defiant angle. "We are in love with each other. Now, will you give me a divorce?"

Rafael lifted his sherry glass to the light. "I am Rafael Alejandro de la Torres." A black brow arched derisively toward her. "I realize the name means nothing to you, but in my country, it is synonymous with pride, honor and influence. I am the eldest male of my immediate family, thus the one in command. The traditions and religious beliefs of my family will not permit a divorce—on any grounds."

Ice ran through her blood, sending shivers of terror to every extremity. Erica stared at him blankly, refusing to believe that she had heard what he said. Somehow it was imperative for him to realize her position.

"I don't think you understand." Her voice was small and weak. "I don't love you. I'm in love with Forest!"

The shining dark head inclined arrogantly toward her. "Are you asking my permission to take him as a lover?"

"No!" Her protest was unmistakably shocked and indignant.

"That is good, because I would not permit you to disgrace my family's name."

"You would not permit me!" Erica's cry was one of outrage. "No one dictates to me! I do as I please!"

"You are Erica de la Torres and you do as *I* please," Rafael informed her tersely.

Her anger was nearly beyond control as she rose on shaking legs, her hands doubled into fists at her side. Rigidly she stared down at him, fighting to check her temper.

"I am not one of your meekly submissive countrymen. I will not be at the beck and call of a domineering male, ever!" she declared tightly.

A cold anger spread over the lean features. He pushed himself out of the chair to tower in front of her. "Have I ever given you any reason to believe that I would mistreat you?" he demanded.

"No." Erica faltered slightly under his menacing gaze. "But it wouldn't frighten me into cowering in front of you if you did. I will not allow you to try to dominate me!"

His expression immediately altered into one of mocking amusement. "If a person is domineering, *querida*, he uses physical force to have his wishes carried out. Domination uses superior intelligence and knowledge. It would be wise to differentiate between the two in future."

"Don't twist words," she protested, spinning away from him. Anger evaporated as hopelessness drained its source. In a last gambit to persuade him to change his unyielding stand, she turned over her last card. "I'll pay you anything you ask."

"Money will not buy me a legitimate son of my blood," Rafael stated.

"A son?" gasped Erica, whirling around to search his aloof, arrogant face.

"Does the thought of bearing my child offend you?" His head was thrown proudly back as he intently watched her reaction.

His child, a miniature version of the man before her. Erica's mind reeled at the thought, yet not with distaste. She shook her head to chase away the image.

"I find it offensive to be your wife," she said instead.

His hand touched her shoulder. Impulses of disturbing awareness tingled down her neck. She pivoted sharply away from his hand.

"You did not always find my touch repulsive," Rafael murmured, his eyes narrowing at her apprehensive expression.

"I was young and inexperienced, but you changed all that," Erica retorted.

"You are my wife. That hasn't changed."

"Then change it! Divorce me!" she demanded vigorously.

"I have already explained that it is impossible," he stated.

"If you don't willingly grant me a divorce, I shall sue for it," she threatened. "I will not be married to a man I don't love!"

Rafael's lean jaw was tightly clenched, a muscle

in the side rebelling against the iron control. The fury in his darkened eyes reminded Erica too late that he was of Spanish descent. The blood of cruelty ran in his veins. The fine suit he wore was merely a cloak of civilization to conceal the primitive savagery she had noted before.

"That is something you should have considered before you married me," he snapped harshly.

"I did consider it." The fear that nearly paralyzed the workings of her lungs was masked by a show of bravado. "I never intended the marriage to last more than an hour. The only reason I married you was to get back at my father for always putting his business ahead of me. I knew he would have our marriage annulled that same evening."

"But your plan backfired, no?" Rafael smiled.

Erica turned away from that complacently arrogant expression. "Yes, he had flown back to the States—on *business*," she admitted bitterly.

"Why did you not tell me of this that night?" he asked with ominous quiet.

"I was afraid of you then," she tossed over her shoulder. "I was no match for you. I thought if I could go back to the hotel I would be safe. Only you didn't take me back to the hotel."

Rafael studied her thoughtfully. "Was it cowardice that dictated your submission to me?"

Erica swallowed nervously. The memory of his fiery caresses brought a disturbing ache to the lower areas of her stomach. Tongues of shame licked her cheeks as she remembered the way she had welcomed his intimate touch.

111

"Of course," she breathed. "That's why I ran at the first opportunity." It took all of her pride to look into his face without faltering. "How can you possibly want to remain married to me when you know why I did it? When you know I love someone else?"

"What I want and what I must accept are two very different things, Erica," Rafael stated grimly.

"I won't accept it!" Her cry rang angrily through the room. "I'll have my attorney start the divorce proceedings immediately."

"I shall fight you, Erica," he told her coldly. "The newspapers will sell many copies with the names of Wakefield and Torres emblazoned on the front page. And you do not want that kind of divorce. You want a quiet one so that your father will never find out what you have done. It would be interesting to discover what your boyfriend's reaction would be when you are involved in the scandal I would create."

"You wouldn't," Erica whispered. Her rounded eyes searched his ruthlessly set face for some indication of compassion.

"I would."

Trembling fingers touched her pale cheeks as she took two shaky steps away from him. She believed that he would do everything he said.

"I can't just simply announce that I'm married to you," she murmured.

"I will be in San Antonio for several weeks—with the exhibition. We will go through the motions of a courtship. People have fallen in love

112

in less than a few weeks. Another wedding ceremony can be arranged for the benefit of your father and you can return with me when I leave for Mexico," Rafael stated.

"But I'm not in love with you," Erica repeated again. "I love Forest."

"In time you will forget him," he declared arrogantly. "This is not the type of marriage I would prefer, either, but we must deal with reality. Perhaps one day we both may derive some measure of satisfaction from it."

"No," she protested weakly. He was asking her to commit herself to a life sentence with him. Blackmailing her not for money, but for her life, her happiness.

"There is no alternative, Erica. If you are so foolish as to fight me in this, I will go to your father and tell him of our marriage. I do not think he will understand your motives for marrying me nor your actions on our wedding night. A messy divorce would not be to his liking, I think."

Erica knew her father too well not to admit that much of what Rafael said was true. Yet surely there must be another way. She hugged her arms about her to ward off the cold chill of inevitability.

"I can hear your mind racing," Rafael mocked. "I don't ask you to agree with me today. I will give you a week to think over what I have said. You will see that to become my wife is the only amiable solution."

"I must have sold my soul to the devil when I married you," Erica murmured hoarsely. "Or else I married the devil."

"Perhaps it is a marriage made in hell." His derisive jeer disturbed the bronze mask. "But it is no less legal and binding. That is what you must remember."

His words echoed in her mind all the way back to the boutique. Erica had escaped from him once, but it had never really been an escape, merely a postponement. If she ran this time, Rafael would unhesitatingly go to her father and they would both hunt her down. Her anger had not moved him. Her appeals for his understanding, his pity, or his mercy had not touched him. Rafael wanted her as his wife to keep his family tradition unblemished and to bear him a child. He did not care that she didn't love him. Her wishes or desires mattered not at all to him.

As she pushed open the shop door, Erica knew she would never be able to get through the afternoon pretending that nothing was wrong. The throbbing pain in her temples was nearly blinding her. Her statement to Donna that she wasn't feeling well was barely out of her mouth before her assistant was agreeing with her.

"Go on home, Erica. I didn't think you were feeling well this morning. Now there's hardly any color at all in your face. I'll take care of everything."

For the rest of the afternoon and all of Sunday, Erica shut herself in her room, using the pretense of illness to break her date with Forest. Each passing hour made her realize there were only two choices, as Rafael had said. And she rebelled against both of them.

She alternately pounded her pillow in anger and sobbed into it from frustration. Restlessly she paced the floor like a frightened and disoriented caged animal. Her only choice was which of the two evils would she choose. Did her father's love and respect matter more to her than her own future? A messy divorce might even lose her Forest's love and hence her future. His career was only now bringing him fame and success. The publicity and notoriety that Rafael promised would accompany any divorce action she started could destroy Forest's career should he stay involved with her. How long would Forest love her when he saw every one of his ambitions dashed to the ground because of her?

Yet Erica couldn't conceive of actually becoming Rafael's wife. Undoubtedly he was handsome and obviously the head of a very respectable family. But she had always wanted her husband to cherish and adore her, to give her all the affection that her father had not been able to demonstrate. Was she fated to spend the rest of her life never feeling loved? Rafael did not love her. He wanted a wife. It wouldn't have made any difference if he had loved her. She still loved someone else.

Monday morning arrived and she was no closer to a decision. But Erica knew she couldn't keep hiding in her room. Besides, Rafael had given her a week to make up her mind. Perhaps a miracle would happen. Maybe her uncle Jules would have a suggestion to make when he returned. With that slightly encouraging thought, Erica allowed herself to become absorbed in the work at the boutique.

Forest had a meeting to attend on Monday evening, so it wasn't until Tuesday noon that she saw him. He took her to lunch at one of the sidewalk cafés on the riverwalk. They sat in the shade of an umbrella, a tenderly possessive light in his eyes whenever he looked at her.

Erica toyed with the guacamole salad she had ordered. "Are you very ambitious, Forest?" she asked lightly.

"Of course I am," he replied. His gaze was speculating as it touched her downcast face. "There was something behind that question, wasn't there?"

She tried to shrug it off, wishing she hadn't tried to find out what his reaction would be. But Forest didn't accept her easy dismissal of the subject.

"Honey, are you afraid I'm marrying you because I think your father can further my career?" he asked softly, a teasing note of reproof in his voice.

"No," Erica assured him quickly, gazing into the ruggedly attractive square-jawed face. "I know how very much it means to you that you've achieved the success you have because of your own ability."

"Then why the question?" An amused frown creased his brow.

"I was . . . only wondering how important your work was to you," she hedged.

"A man's work is his life." There was still a puzzled gleam in his velvet brown eyes. "I know how much you resented the demands your father's empire made on him. You aren't asking me to give up my career, are you?"

"Would you if I did?" Erica tried to make it sound like a joke, as if his answer didn't matter.

"No," Forest stated unequivocally. "I love you very much, but you'll have to marry me the way I am."

"Oh, darling, I do love you the way you are," she whispered, sorry she had ever made him doubt it.

The dimple on his chin deepened as he smiled. "Then you'd better hurry up and say yes so I can put that ring on your finger."

A noncommittal statement sprang to her mouth, but it never got beyond her parted lips. An ashen pallor stole over her face as she saw Rafael approaching their table in the company of another man.

"What a pleasant surprise to see the two of you again!" he greeted them when Forest glanced away from Erica's face.

"Don Rafael," Forest acknowledged, rising to his feet.

Rafael's eyes were mockingly amused when he saw Erica hide her shaking hands beneath the table.

"I'd like you to meet Señor Esteban Rivera, a noted archaeologist of my country," he said, introducing the man standing beside him. His identification of Erica and Forest to Señor Rivera was done in Spanish.

"*Buenos dias, señorita, señor.*" The man nodded graciously to them both.

"It's a pleasure, Señor Rivera," Forest said, smiling.

Accustomed now to conversing with Mexican-American customers in her shop, Erica automatically replied in the man's native language, adding that she hoped he was enjoying the beauties of San Antonio. She thought nothing of it until she encountered the piercing intentness of Rafael's gaze.

In deliberately rapid Spanish, he demanded, "How long have you been fluent in my language?"

Erica glanced hesitantly at Forest, whose grasp of Spanish was very limited. He was quite plainly curious at what was said and a little suspicious of the tone.

"I have only recently learned Spanish," she answered Rafael in English, her tone stiff and defiant. "It is useful in my shop."

"Of course." Rafael nodded.

"Would you care to join us for coffee?" Forest offered.

"I'm sorry. Señor Rivera and I have another engagement. Perhaps another time," he replied, deferring the invitation with a patronizing tilt of his black head.

"Why do you suppose he stopped?" Forest mused thoughtfully after the two men had disappeared.

Erica shifted uncomfortably. "I imagine he was just being polite."

"Maybe." But Forest wasn't convinced and neither was Erica.

Jules Blackwell called her at the boutique the

following morning, before she had an opportunity to see if he had returned from his trip.

"I have made some discoveries, Erica. Some of them may surprise you," he told her, continuing before she had a chance to tell him of Rafael's presence in San Antonio. "Your husband is not a fortune hunter. Far from it. My dear girl, you married into a very old Mexican family that has holdings in Central and South America."

"I know. Uncle Jules, he's here—in San Antonio," she said.

There was a moment of startled silence. "Have you talked to him?"

Erica sighed heavily and proceeded to tell Jules of what had transpired while he was gone. When she concluded, it was he who sighed.

"This puts an entirely different complexion on things, doesn't it?" Erica could visualize the frown of concentration. "I guess I could go to see him at his hotel. At this point, it certainly can't do any harm."

"Would you, Uncle Jules?" Emotion choked her throat.

"We can't give up without a fight, can we?" he asked, back to his usual jovial voice. "I'll call you right after I see him."

Then he hung up.

"YOU'RE AWFULLY QUIET tonight, Erica," Forest commented, trailing his fingertip over the pensive line around her mouth. "Is something troubling you?"

119

"I was thinking." Erica breathed in deeply and glanced about the intimate lounge.

"About me, I hope." He smiled and his arm tightened affectionately around her shoulder.

"Actually about the shop," she laughed. In truth, it had been about her conversation with Jules Blackwell. He had called back the following afternoon after having met Rafael. He had been unable to persuade Rafael to revise his stand. When she had asked his advice, Jules had hesitated, then insisted that this was a decision only she could make. He refused to advise her one way or the other.

"Having problems at the boutique?" Forest asked.

"Nothing important." Erica shrugged.

"Then let's talk about us instead of the shop," he murmured.

"N-not yet." She swallowed nervously, knowing there was no way she could tell him that there might never be an "us."

He sighed impatiently and moved away from her, darting her an angry glance that couldn't be mistaken even in the dim light of the room.

"I'm sorry, Forest," Erica apologized. "I don't have an answer for you and it isn't fair to lead you on. I'm trying to be honest with you." As honest as she could in the circumstances.

"Thanks." Caustic bitterness ate into the edges of the word. He stared at his drink for an uncomfortable moment. Then his gaze slid to her face. "You didn't deserve that. It's my turn to apologize, honey."

"I understand," she said, nodding.

"Well, well, well. Will you look at who just walked in?" he murmured cynically. "I wonder if it's another coincidence."

Erica glanced toward the entrance and immediately averted her head when she recognized the tall dark figure just entering the lounge. Her heart skittered wildly along her ribs. Nervously she clutched her glass, wishing she could make herself small so that Rafael wouldn't see her.

"Is he coming here?" she asked tautly.

"He's with some other people," Forest replied, watching with undisguised speculation. "They're taking a table on the other side. I don't think he's even seen us. I guess I was wrong."

A nervous laugh of relief bubbled from her throat. "What ever made you think Don Rafael was following us in the first place?" she chided.

"I don't know." He shrugged, glancing at Erica, then back to the table where Rafael was seated. "I had a hazy impression at the dinner party the other night that he was interested in you. He always seemed to know where you were and who was with you."

Her cheeks flushed hotly. "You must have been mistaken. I didn't notice that he paid any special attention to me," she protested with false lightness.

"It was just an impression. I didn't say it was right." He smiled a crooked smile. "Tell me, did you notice him?"

"Oh, Forest!" Erica tilted her head to one side in

simulated amusement while her mouth felt unnaturally parched. "He's an imposing man. A woman would have to be blind not to notice him, and even then she would probably pick up his vibrations."

"Do you know, I've never been jealous before?" He chuckled. "Dance with me, Erica. I have this terrible need to hold you in my arms."

His arms held sweet torment. She felt that she had to savor every moment they were together in case it was their last. She might never again be able to know this sense of security and well-being. The song ended much too soon, forcing her to open her eyes and move away from Forest's broad chest.

Her gaze focused immediately on Rafael sitting at a table on the edge of the dance floor. Sardonic amusement etched the blackness of his eyes as they shifted their glance to Forest. It was impossible for her not to acknowledge his presence without being blatantly rude. She tried to force polite words of greeting from her trembling mouth, but Forest was already filling the void.

"We meet again, Don Rafael," he said politely.

Rafael rose and extended a hand to Forest in greeting, leaving him with no choice except to cross the few feet to accept it. Introductions were quickly made of the two couples accompanying Rafael before he insisted that Forest and Erica allow him to buy them a drink.

Erica silently raged at the way Rafael was maneuvering events. She had wanted this evening with Forest to be special. She wished she could have had the courage to persuade Forest to leave when Rafael had arrived at the club, but she hadn't wanted to arouse his curiosity. Now she was seated between Rafael and Forest, feeling stiff and uncomfortable, knowing that Rafael had arranged it this way deliberately.

Her skin went hot as Forest rested his arm along the back of her chair as if staking his proprietorial rights to her. Her violet eyes darkened with resentment that she couldn't respond as she wanted to Forest's touch. Rafael's presence was an all-too-potent reminder that she wasn't free. As if feeling her censure, Rafael glanced at her, a mocking awareness of her thoughts in his eyes.

The conversation had been following an impersonal line until Forest suddenly asked, "I don't believe you have mentioned whether you were married or not, Don Rafael?"

The color drained with sickening rapidity from Erica's face. One corner of Rafael's mouth lifted in a humorless smile as he pointedly stared at her.

"The woman I have chosen has not yet consented to be my wife," he stated ambiguously, letting his indolent gaze slide back to Forest's tightened jaw. "But I have no doubt that she will soon make her decision."

Forest glanced quickly at Erica, a suspicious jealousy darkening his usually soft brown eyes. Her hands were rigidly clasped in her lap, as she tried to ignore the crackling electricity in the air.

"Perhaps, Don Rafael," she murmured in an even voice, "she needs more time." Deliberately she looked at Forest. "Marriage requires the commitment of the rest of a girl's life."

"I agree, Miss Wakefield," his seductive voice mocked her. "To leap into it hastily could have disastrous results. A life of repentance would not be pleasant for either party."

One of the other members of his group spoke up and the subject was gratefully changed. Erica knew that she had sidetracked Forest's suspicions by looking at him when she had made her comment to Rafael, but she despised herself for tricking him that way, just as she despised Rafael for putting her in the position where she was forced to do it. She wondered what form of retribution he would extract, then his next words to Forest left her in no doubt.

"Do I have your permission to claim this dance with Miss Wakefield?" he asked.

To refuse would make Forest appear churlish. In the next instant, Erica found herself accepting Rafael's guiding hand as he led her onto the dance floor.

When he turned her into his arms, Erica wondered how she could have forgotten how very powerful his physical attraction was. Her senses vibrated with the provocative nearness of his thighs and the spread of his lean fingers on her back. She hated this awareness of a man she didn't love.

"Why can't you leave me alone?" she whispered tautly, staring at the whiteness of his shirt collar and idly wondering if he still wore the gold medallion.

"I thought women liked to have their husbands pay attention to them," Rafael mocked.

"You may not be my husband for long," was her tart reply.

He laughed softly, his warm breath stirring the hair near her face. "Your threat does not convince me, Erica. Your tongue has the boldness of a hawk, but your heart belongs to the dove," he murmured. "With your tongue, you start tempests while your heart seeks the tranquillity of the storm's eye. I know you better than you know yourself."

"You can't be sure I'll agree to be your wife," Erica declared with stiff defiance.

"Can't I?" His mouth curved into a cruel smile. "If your sensitive heart did not seek peace at any cost, our marriage would not be a secret today."

She closed her eyes against the frightening truth of his words. When Rafael returned her to Forest at the end of the song, his eyes taunted her with his knowledge. And Erica was still searching for a way to deny it when Forest took her home. She tried to find it in his embrace and failed.

CHAPTER SEVEN

ERICA SNAPPED OPEN her evening bag to make certain she had transferred the house key from her other handbag. The gold key winked reassuringly back at her. She glanced at her petite watch as she stepped into the hallway from her room. Forest would be arriving at any minute.

"Another date with that Granger fellow?" her father's vaguely interested voice asked.

"Yes, the symphony orchestra is giving a concert tonight," she said, smiling.

"I don't think he's going to hear much of it," Vance Wakefield commented, his gaze running admiringly over the gauzy length of lavender- and blue-flowered chiffon that covered her azure blue evening gown.

"That's the idea, daddy," Erica replied, widening her violet eyes with provocative mischief.

He laughed softly and walked into his study. The corners of her mouth straightened, knowing that as he shut the door, her father also shut out his thoughts of her. Not callously, but simply because there was no reason for him to worry about her.

The doorbell rang and Erica pushed her self-pity aside. She meant to enjoy herself tonight. It might possibly be the last time that she would. Tilting her head at a happy angle, she opened the front door.

"You!" she breathed in astonishment.

Rafael studied her with mocking thoroughness. The black turtleneck beneath his leisure suit emphasized his darkness.

"Yes, Erica, it is I," he replied, thinning his lips into a mirthless smile. "Aren't you going to invite me in?"

Her fingers tightened on the edge of the door, but she didn't step aside to admit him. The paralysis of fear didn't allow any movement.

"What are you doing here?" Her demand came out in an anxious whisper.

"You are going out this evening?"

It was a rhetorical question that required no response, but she gave it anyway. "Yes, I'm going to a concert," she murmured self-consciously, glancing behind him in anticipation of Forest's arrival. "You . . . you haven't answered my question. What are you doing here?"

His black eyes mocked her persistence, his dark head arrogantly tilted back. "Your week has passed," Rafael stated.

"I have tonight," Erica whispered desperately, bands of fear constricting her throat. Her eyes searched for some sign of compassion in the derisive bronze mask. "Is that why you are here? For my answer?"

"I am here to see your father," he replied with a complacent lift of his brow. "There is something I wish to discuss with him."

"Have you come to tell him a-about us?" Panic

removed any pretense of demand from her question.

"Should I?" he parried, the blackness of his gaze burning holes in her despairing hope.

A car door slammed and Erica saw Forest walking swiftly along the stonewalk to the door. Rafael glanced over his shoulder at the approaching man, then brought his gaze back to her face, amusement glittering vibrantly at the dilemma mirrored on Erica's face.

"You won't tell daddy," she pleaded in a whisper. He stared at her and smiled. "Please, Rafael, don't!"

A strange light flickered in his eyes while his lips twisted in irony. "I will await your decision, Erica," he said harshly.

With Forest only a few steps away, she was forced to open the door and admit both men. Rafael's statement should have reassured her, but it didn't. Forest greeted him naturally enough, but with curious suspicion in his eyes.

"I'll . . . let daddy know you're here, Señor Torres," Erica mumbled, turning awkwardly away from his jeering glance.

Her father evinced no surprise when she announced from his study door that Rafael was here to see him. Deliberately she ignored Rafael's mocking countenance as he walked by her into the study.

"What does he want?" Forest asked grimly, taking her arm.

Erica glanced apprehensively toward the closed study door. "To talk business with daddy, I guess," she murmured, but she didn't believe that.

There was only one subject that Rafael and Vance Wakefield had in common, and that was herself. Rafael hadn't exactly said that he wouldn't tell him, but the implication had been there that he would keep silent. Yet she didn't trust him.

The evening was ruined before it had even begun. Halfway through the performance, Erica knew that she had to return home. At this very moment, Rafael might be relating the entire sordid tale to her father. The complete absence of color in her face and the tightly drawn lines of strain around her mouth convinced Forest more than her words that she wasn't feeling well. His tenderly solicitous concern made her feel guilty, but not so guilty that she didn't take advantage of it.

With the lingering gentleness of Forest's goodnight kiss still on her lips, Erica rapped lightly on the study door and entered. Angry sparks flashed in her eyes when she saw Rafael sitting in a chair opposite her father, casual lordly grace in every line of his form. She had seen his car parked in the driveway, but her expression was one of feigned surprise at seeing Rafael still there.

"Is the concert over already?" Her father frowned as he glanced at the heavy gold watch on his wrist.

"No. Forest received an important phone call that required his immediate attention," Erica lied. "I decided to come home rather than sit through the concert alone."

"A business call at this hour?" Vance questioned.

"You know how that goes, daddy." She shrugged, trying to read through the pensive, brooding lines on her father's face to discern what he and Rafael had been discussing. "I've become used to it."

"What a pity," Rafael drawled, "to become accustomed to such a thing."

His sardonic expression was openly laughing at her and Erica knew he had guessed why she had returned. He was not at all surprised by her sudden arrival. She sensed that he had anticipated it.

"I've learned to accept it, *señor*," she murmured tautly, putting sarcastic emphasis on the latter word.

There was a satanic lift of a jet-black eyebrow. Then, aloofly, Rafael turned away from her. "It is growing late, Señor Wakefield, and I have taken up too much of your time."

"Not at all, not at all." Her father rose to his feet when Rafael did, waving aside the arrogantly worded apology. "I—" he cast an oblique glance at Erica "—I enjoyed our discussion."

"I will see Don Rafael to the door, daddy," she offered quickly as her father started around his desk.

The absently thoughtful look in his blue eyes frightened her a little. Their discussion had to have concerned her or her father wouldn't be looking at her so strangely.

"Yes, you do that, Erica," he agreed soberly, and wished Rafael a hasty good night.

Erica didn't trust herself to look at Rafael until

130

the study door was closed behind them. Then she whirled around, the delicately flowered chiffon net billowing about her.

"What did you tell him?" she hissed angrily.

"What do you think I told him?" Rafael countered, his gaze insolently sweeping her face.

"You told him something about us, didn't you?" Erica accused, hating his air of detachment that her anger couldn't touch.

"I said I would await your decision," he reminded her coolly.

"I know what you said," she whispered contemptuously. "I didn't believe you then and I don't now!"

"Do not push me, Erica." The warning was echoed in the clenched line of his lean jaw.

"I want to know what you told him," she repeated. "What devious and evil thing did you say to prejudice him against me?"

His gaze narrowed on her upturned face. "Your father has his own rigid code that he lives by and expects others to live by. I doubt that anyone could influence that code, least of all a stranger."

"Do you honestly expect me to believe that you said nothing about us?" Erica snapped.

Her shoulders were seized in a violent grip. The icy glitter in Rafael's eyes took her breath away as she was vividly reminded of the ruthlessness she associated with him.

"Do you dare to question my integrity when your lips are still warm from another man's kisses?" he demanded harshly, angry forks of lightning darting from the black thunderclouds of his eyes.

"Rafael!" she gasped, helplessly unable to free herself from his iron hold.

She was pulled roughly against his chest, her head snapping back at the abruptness with which she was crushed against him. The muscular hardness of his body drained what little strength she possessed.

"You use my name only when you want something," he growled. "But I will teach you not to be so careless with its use!"

"Y-you're hurting me!" Erica protested weakly, fighting the waves of awareness that flowed in her veins.

"What is it you seek?" His teeth flashed in a jeering smile. "The gentle touch of your lover? Is it his hands that you wish had touched your nakedness first instead of mine?"

His fingers dug even deeper into her soft flesh. "Rafael!" She moaned in pain, crystal tears shimmering in her eyes.

"You want to be free, no?" His nostrils were distended as he crushed her tighter. "You want to be free of my touch and my name." His silent laughter scorned the futility of such a wish. "But I will not let you go, Erica. You will pay for your foolishness."

Then his mouth claimed hers in a savage possession. Blackness swirled around her. She was incapable of resistance just as she was incapable of responding to his hard, fierce kiss. When he released her mouth, her emotions were as bruised and battered as her swollen lips. His fingers lessened their hold on her shoulders for a second, then let her go altogether. He stepped back, shedding the demon skin for one of arrogant reserve.

"I will pick you up tomorrow afternoon at two o'clock," he told her with autocratic command. "I will expect your answer then."

"Go to hell!" Erica whispered, pressing the back of her hand to her throbbing mouth.

A cynical smile twisted his mouth. "With you, I am condemned to that."

"Then why make this demand of me?" she protested.

"You are my wife," Rafael said simply, and turned away.

Erica hovered for uncertain moments in the hallway, her system recovering from the shock of his brutal touch. Then the door to her father's study opened and she spun around to gaze blankly at her father.

"Wh-what did Don Rafael want?" she asked, striving for an air of uninterested curiosity.

A thoughtful look spread across Vance Wakefield's stern face. "He came to see me about some property I own. At least, he said that was why he had come. He asked for my permission to see you, Erica."

"He did?" she breathed. Antagonism surfaced for a brief moment that Rafael should be so certain she would agree to be his wife. "What was your answer?"

"I told him . . . well . . . ." He hesitated, wryly shaking his head. "My first instinct was to laugh until I realized he was quite serious. Then I told him that you were seeing Forest Granger, but I

133

told him he had my permission to see you if you were willing."

"He asked me out for tomorrow," Erica told him.

"Did you accept?"

"Yes." She couldn't very well tell him that it had been an ultimatum.

"How serious are you about Granger?" It was the first time in her memory that Vance Wakefield had ever made a direct inquiry. Usually he had someone else do it for him and relay the answer.

"I'm not sure, daddy," Erica hedged.

"Do you know, I forget sometimes that I'm your father," he commented absently. The statement didn't surprise her, although it wasn't meant to be unkind. "I'm always too busy, aren't I?"

"I understand, daddy, I'm a big girl now." She smiled wistfully, wishing they were close enough that she could go into his arms and be hugged.

"Forest is a hard, independent and ambitious young man. He isn't intimidated by me, either," Vance Wakefield mused. "His career, his business, is vitally important to him."

"Isn't it to every man?" Erica returned, swallowing the bitterness in her throat.

"No," he sighed heavily. "With some men, the family comes first and will always come first. It's their tradition, their life-style."

A terrible stillness settled over her. "Are you referring to Don Rafael?"

"Not specifically, no," her father replied smoothly. "Although at a guess, I would say that family would have a priority with him."

A priority! Erica thought bitterly. Family and

134

tradition were so important to Rafael that he was determined to keep her as his wife whether she loved him or not. Even he admitted that life would be hell with her, but that didn't deter him.

"Maybe you should think about how much a family means to you before you make any commitment to Forest," Vance Wakefield suggested, running a hand through his thick mane.

Slow anger burned within her. "Did R— Did Don Rafael make that suggestion?" Erica accused.

"Of course not!" His reply was plainly astounded and offended. "Whatever made you think that?"

She shifted self-consciously under his piercing gaze. "You don't normally talk this way."

"No?" Once again the withdrawn look set in as his mind began to wander. "No, I suppose not. Good night, Erica."

He was already walking into his study and the door was swinging shut when she added her good night. She doubted that he had heard her. That moment of concern about her future had disappeared as rapidly and unexpectedly as it had come.

THE HOT OCTOBER SUN blazed down with the heat of a thousand hells. Erica's teeth grated as she accepted the hand Rafael extended to her as she stepped out of the air-conditioned coolness of his car. She had barely said five words to him since he had picked her up at the house promptly at two o'clock. The cynically amused tilt of his mouth indicated that her freezing tactics had not worked.

She had shown no interest in their destination and he had deliberately not enlightened her.

Defiantly tossing back her long hair, Erica glanced around the downtown section of San Antonio. The Tower of the Americas loomed benevolently above them. Its feet were firmly planted in the Hemisfair Plaza. Perhaps he intended taking her to the top and throwing her off, thus removing the obstacle of their marriage.

But it wasn't toward the Tower of the Americas or Hemisfair Plaza that Rafael led her. Instead he guided her to one of the many sets of steps leading from the street level of San Antonio down some twenty feet to the picturesque walkway along the river banks. He strolled leisurely by the quaint shops, sidewalk cafés and nightclubs in the commercial area of the riverwalk, indifferent to Erica's displeasure.

The cool serenity of the river, the lush tropical foliage of the gardens, and the age-old trees that shielded the walk from the direct rays of the burning sun soon had their effect on Erica. She had never been able to remain unmoved by the quiet splendor.

Rafael paused to light a thin cheroot, the aromatic blend of burning tobacco strangely fitting the atmosphere. Lean aristocratic fingers hooked themselves in the pocket of his finely tailored trousers as he resumed his leisurely pace.

"It is rare that a man's dreams come true," he commented idly as though voicing his thoughts aloud. For a second Erica thought he was speaking personally and her relaxed expression hardened. "To think that it was once proposed to cover this river with concrete and turn it into a sewer! That visionary architect and the conservationists who fought at his side are to be congratulated."

Erica smiled in silent agreement, wondering if the architect had ever dreamed back in the thirties and the forties that so many people would come to enjoy the graceful beauty of the arched footbridges and the luxuriant crush of greenery. The natural beauty was enhanced, never overpowered by man's touch.

Her glance at Rafael's profile was cool. "I hadn't realized you were familiar with San Antonio and its history."

"You have forgotten, Erica—" he smiled at her absently "—that I am a historian. And I think you have forgotten that most of the Southwest was once ruled first by Spain, then by Mexico."

"Does it bother you to be here in the city that possesses the 'Shrine of Texas Liberty'?" A malicious sparkle gleamed in her eyes.

His regard of her was one of a person overlooking the ineffectual barbs of a child. "You are, of course, referring to the thirteen-day siege by the dictator General Santa Ana of the Alamo."

"And the hundred and eighty-eight men who died there to be free," Erica tossed back.

"Are you asserting your right to freedom?" he inquired lazily. "In the background, do you hear the bugles sounding 'Deguello,' the song of no quarter? It was not only Americans who defended the Alamo till death, but Mexicans, as well. One of your more famous Texas patriots was José Antonio Navarro, who signed the Texas Declaration of Independence. Yet you prefer to look on me as Santa Ana."

"Then don't fight me," she cried angrily. "Let me be free!"

"I am not able to do that." His sardonicism was tinged with resignation. "I, too, must fight for what I believe."

Her hand lifted the heavy weight of her hair and massaged the tense cord in the back of her neck. She had known all along that his stand was adamant, but she had to try.

"Because I will not give in to you," Rafael stated with a note of impatience, "you look on me as ruthlessly cruel, my demands as unfeeling as those dictated by Santa Ana to the peoples of Texas before the rebellion. Look at the unending string of missions founded by the Spaniards throughout your country, Erica. The streak of cruelty is tempered by kindness and devotion. I will be kind to you. You will not be my slave, but my wife. I do not ask for your love in return, but your loyalty to the vows we took. That is the only demand I make of you."

Erica laughed shortly, without humor. "What choice have you given me? Why don't you simply put a gun to my head and shoot me?" Her voice lacked emotion, her hope slowly dying as she resigned herself to fate.

"You are not a lamb, Erica. Do not act like one!" he snapped.

Immediately her temper blazed. "No, I'm not a

138

lamb! All along you've known what my answer would be, the only answer I could give. Now you're going to hear me say it!" she burst out hotly. "I will be your wife. Not because I fear you. I am agreeing only because of my father."

Rafael's face was a study of implacability during her impassioned speech. When she drew a breath to continue, he raised a hand to silence her.

"I am aware that you don't come to me willingly, that I have coerced your agreement. I know you do not love me. There is no need to keep repeating these things. You would do well to direct your energies to convincing your father of your interest in me. I am certain you will share my wish not to maintain the pretense of starry-eyed romance any longer than is necessary." His clipped statement brought her abruptly back from the satisfying heat of her anger. Color receded sharply from her face.

"Must we do that?" she murmured, inwardly shivering at the thought of spending endless evenings in his company gazing rapturously at his face, enduring his touch, the incredible warmth his smile could convey. "Isn't there some other way?"

"So you still wish to run away from that which is unpleasant?" There was no mockery in his indulgently gentle voice. "Running only delays that moment when you must face the thing you find so difficult."

"I have already made the decision," Erica reminded him coldly. "I have agreed to become your wife."

"But you wish to avoid these weeks we must

spend in each other's company for the sake of your family and friends. You would prefer to elope with me and stay away until the furor of your actions subsided rather than face the awkward moment when you reject Forest for me."

Erica looked into the placid mask, wondering at his easy perception of her innermost thoughts. As much as she disliked Rafael, she had to admit that she felt the pull of his dark attraction, the lean, muscular body, the strikingly handsome face.

"I'm not a very good liar. I doubt that Forest will believe me if I tell him I'm in love with you and not him," she replied.

"When we are remarried, he will have no choice but to accept it," Rafael stated. "He has asked you to marry him, has he not?"

"How did you know?" Erica frowned, knowing she had never mentioned that.

"Your attorney Jules Blackwell told me, but I would have guessed it anyway. Had Forest suggested an affair instead of marriage, I don't believe you would have made such an instant demand for a divorce." He studied the glowing tip of the thin cigar.

"Forest knows I love him. I told him so." There was a defiant tilt of her head to remind Rafael how unwillingly she was agreeing to his demands.

"People fall out of love." He shrugged dismissively. "Many times the attraction to a member of the opposite sex is mistaken for love. You will need to convince him of that."

Rafael always had an answer, Erica thought dejectedly as she turned away from his unnerv-

140

ingly penetrating regard. At the same moment she counted herself lucky for recognizing that she only found Rafael sexually attractive and had not foolishly believed herself to be in love with him. A heavy sigh vibrated her shoulders. Now she wished she had been blind to the difference, since she was about to commit the rest of her life to him. A pair of rose-colored glasses would be welcome, however inaccurate their view.

"You have my decision. Can't we leave now?" she demanded tightly. "Or do you want to gloat a little longer over your triumph?"

An angry ejaculation was muttered behind her as Rafael spun her around to face him. Lightning currents emanated from the touch of his hands.

"At the moment, I feel no triumph!" he flashed. "If I did not believe that—" As suddenly as he had gripped her shoulders, he released her. "I think you derive satisfaction from igniting my temper." A muscle twitched convulsively in his jaw to indicate that his temper was not fully under control despite the evenness of his voice. "Come, I will take you back to your home."

His brooding silence during the return journey had Erica shifting uncomfortably in her seat. She tried unsuccessfully to block him out of her thoughts, to ignore him as completely as he was ignoring her, but his dark looks and primitive magnetism made that impossible. He was sleek and regally elegant like a jungle cat, and like a jungle cat, there was a strain of savageness that years of civilization hadn't entirely erased.

This man was her husband. She had just committed herself to spending the rest of her life with him—the full enormity of that decision didn't strike her until that moment. A sense of unease crowded around her at the thought of sharing all those intimate moments between a husband and wife with Rafael.

When the car stopped, it took Erica a full second to realize that they were in the private driveway of her home. Her color fluctuated alarmingly as she accepted Rafael's hand out of the car. It troubled her considerably to discover how susceptible she was to his touch. Instead of starting toward the house, he tightened his hand on hers to keep her beside the car. Erica glanced curiously at his slightly narrowed eyes.

"Fate has offered you an easy solution to let Forest know of your change of feelings. He is driving in now—no, don't look around," Rafael commanded as she started to turn in the direction of the approaching car. "All you have to do is kiss me, Erica. He will put his own construction on the rest."

She breathed in sharply, wanting to resist yet knowing that she doubted if she could convince Forest in words that it was Rafael she preferred. Her eyes pleaded with Rafael not to make her do this thing when she was still regretting her decision.

"Decide quickly, Erica," he murmured.

Slowly she moved nearer, drawn more by the seductive sound of his voice than a desire to show Forest her change of heart. The steady rhythm of Rafael's heartbeat was felt by the hands she rested against his chest as she tilted her head to receive his kiss. The gentle insistence of his mouth disarmed her and a pleasant warmth relaxed her tense muscles. A hunger that she had long denied parted her lips so that she was pliant to his touch.

The slam of the car door was unexpected. She sprang guiltily away from Rafael, forgetting completely that the scene had been staged for Forest's benefit. She colored profusely at her shameful lapse, hating that strange power that Rafael held for her physically.

"I couldn't believe it when Lawrence told me you were out with him!" Forest muttered hoarsely. His face was unnaturally pale with controlled rage.

The fierce pain in her heart throttled any words of denial she wanted to say as she gazed hopelessly at him.

"Erica is free to see whom she pleases. There is no understanding between you, is there?" Rafael's arrogantly confident voice inquired.

"I was stupid to believe there was," Forest growled, flicking a maligning glance at Erica. "You've given me your answer, haven't you? I never realized you were so cold-blooded. That must have been what they were talking about when the others called you an ice maiden."

When that last contemptuous sneer had been driven into Erica's midsection, Forest pivoted sharply and stalked back to his car. Her hand raised in a feeble attempt to call him back and explain.

"Forest—" her shaky voice murmured as she took a hesitant step toward his retreating form.

But Rafael reached out and stopped her. "Let him go, Erica," he said firmly. "Don't drag out his agony. Let the killing blow be swift and sure."

A tear glimmered in the corner of her eye, but the fiery light that blazed in the violet blue depths glittered only with resentment.

"You ask that I be merciful," she jeered, "when there isn't any mercy in your heart!"

"I do feel mercy," Rafael stated. "Although I spoke of it for Forest, I meant it for you. I do not want to torture your heart with a love you can never have with this man. Break cleanly from him now so he will not lie between us in the many nights of our lives that are ahead of us."

"How can you speak of such things?" Erica cried, drawing free of his hand in distaste.

"We are married, *mia esposa*. It is not as if we had never known each other in the Biblical way." A lazy smile of complacency curved his mouth. "And I know that Forest has never held you in his arms in the middle of the night, or he would know there is no ice in your veins—huh, *querida*?"

Her cheeks were scorched by the memory his words recalled. She spun angrily on her heel and raced for the house, wondering how many times in the future she would flee from him when she was left with no weapons to attack.

CHAPTER EIGHT

THERE WAS MANY AN EYEBROW raised over Erica's sudden break with Forest, and several more when she was seen repeatedly in Rafael's company during the next two weeks.

Their evenings together were always spent attending a concert, theater production or a similar function where there was little need for small talk between them. The distraction of having something to occupy her attention was welcome, although she was never able to completely ignore Rafael. He was much too masculine, and charming when he chose, for any woman to ignore. Yet Erica still refused to like him. How could she when he had blackmailed her into this charade?

All of her friends and acquaintances thought she was extremely lucky to have a man as devastatingly handsome as Rafael paying such marked attention to her. When her replies were less than enthusiastic, they laughed them off as a sign that she wasn't sure she could hold him. Considering the number of her female friends who wandered over during intervals on the pretense of saying hello to her, she tended to marvel at Rafael's seeming indifference to them.

The tinkling of the bell on the shop door announced the arrival of another customer.

Donna was in the back room, freshening up after her lunch break. Pushing a welcoming smile on her reluctant mouth, Erica stopped straightening the rack of new dresses to greet the customer. Only it wasn't a customer. It was Rafael.

His dark glance slid past her surprised expression to the back of the boutique, and the wide smile he gave her indicated that Donna must have stepped into view. She was always surprised at the way that smile could take her breath away.

There was only a slight hint of false happiness in her voice when she greeted him. "Rafael—I didn't expect to see you today."

"It is always the unexpected that gives the most pleasure." The caressing tone of his voice reached out to her. "I found myself with the afternoon free and only one person that I wanted to spend it with."

Those black eyes were regarding her with such sincerity that Erica almost believed him until she remembered Donna was listening. The corners of her mouth were tugged downward.

"I hope by that you mean me," she answered in a half-hearted tease.

The intensity of his gaze increased, his brows drawing together in a questioning frown. "Have you not learned that I have eyes for none other but you?" he asked softly. So softly that Erica doubted Donna had heard.

"I think you will have to convince me of that," she whispered, an unknown pain clouding her eyes.

"Erica." The use of her name was an impatient

146

sound that was quickly replaced by his low, cajoling voice. "First I will take you to lunch. You have not eaten, have you?" At the negative shake of her head, Rafael continued, "Then I have something I want to show you."

The last statement astounded her. In all their previous outings, there had been witnesses, crowds of people to insulate her. But Rafael was indicating something entirely different. Erica balked visibly at the prospect of being alone with him.

"Can't it wait for another time?" she blurted. "I really don't have time for more than a lunch break today."

"We're seldom busy on Tuesday." Donna spoke up. "I'm sure I can cope by myself for a few hours, Erica."

Erica pressed her lips tightly together to keep from crying out for Donna to be still. Rafael didn't make it any easier by looking at her with open mockery in his eyes.

"If that is all settled," he murmured complacently, "there can be no more objections, no?"

"No." She shot him a furious look. "I have to get my bag. I'll only be a moment."

A few minutes later they were walking out of the boutique with Donna smiling her goodbye with the enthusiasm of one who has done a good deed. Erica had become accustomed to the possessive touch of Rafael's hand on the back of her waist, but today she took exception to it.

"There isn't anyone watching us," she told him icily, "so there's no need for you to touch me."

"What is it that has made you angry? I do not believe it is my touch." He raised his dark eyebrows.

"I've never stopped being angry," Erica retorted, swinging her head defiantly in his direction. "I've never stopped resenting that you've forced me into this agreement."

They had reached a staircase leading from the riverwalk to street level. Erica was on the first step when Rafael made her turn around to face him. The one-step advantage brought her eyes level with the ebony blackness of his.

"I wonder which it is that you resent so much. The agreement? Or that I forced your acceptance?" he mused. His hands closed over her hipbones to keep her in place when she would have pulled away.

Her palms were moist and Erica found it difficult to speak clearly. "O-one is th-the same as the other." She was much too conscious of how very near those masculine hard lips were.

"If you say so." He shrugged, laughing silently at her refusal to differentiate. "Why do you hold yourself so rigidly, Erica?"

"I don't see any need to keep up this pretense of devotion in private," she replied quickly.

"How else will you learn to be natural with me? he mocked.

"I could never react naturally to you," she declared.

An exasperated sigh accompanied the release of

his hold. "Let us go and eat before my appetite is completely robbed by your stubbornness."

What little appetite Erica had was gone. Rafael, too, ate very little of his food, as the electrical currents charged the air between them.

"I would prefer to go back to the boutique now," Erica said crisply the minute they were outside the small restaurant.

"This side trip will only take a few minutes of your precious time," was his caustic response.

Often he mocked her, but rarely was he sarcastic. Erica discovered that his acid voice had the power to hurt. There was a sickening knot in the pit of her stomach that she didn't quite understand.

"Where are we going?" she asked hesitantly as he opened the car door for her.

He didn't bother to reply until he was seated behind the wheel and he had maneuvered the car into the traffic. Even then his response was indifferent as though he regretted insisting on this trip.

"A friend of mine bought a house here in San Antonio. It is in need of considerable repair." A sardonic light was in the brief glance he gave her. "Since neither my friend nor his wife is able to be here at this time, he asked if I knew of anyone— any woman who possessed good taste—who would look at the house from a woman's point of view and recommend any changes that might be necessary."

"That's why you're taking me to see it," Erica murmured.

"What did you think?" Rafael jeered softly. "That perhaps I was luring you off to some isolated place to demand my rights as a husband?"

"I didn't know what you had in mind—" she colored "—but I doubt that you would be so desperate as to take a woman you know would be unwilling."

"That cloak of another man's love that you wrap yourself in will not always protect you, Erica. Do not depend on it too greatly."

To that half-threatening statement, Erica chose not to reply, fearing that she might incite him to prove his point. And she had never had any doubt about his superior strength. She had felt the muscles in his arms and legs and knew they could be steel bands.

The large Mediterranean-style home Rafael parked in front of was bustling with activity. Three gardeners were clearing the months of neglect in the abundant foliage around the front of the house. Towering oaks gracefully arched over the cream yellow façade with its tile roof of chimney red. Other workmen were repairing the loosened mortar of the courtyard walls and replacing broken tiles on the roof.

Rafael led her through the ornate wrought-iron gate into the courtyard with its overgrown walkways and the nearly vine-covered gazebo and from there into the house. Again there were workmen, painters covering the walls with a fresh coat of oyster white and stripping the old varnish from the woodwork. New floors were being laid in other rooms.

In spite of all the commotion, Erica was drawn by the undefinably proud character of the old home. The enormous living room with its high ceilings and mammoth fireplace captured her imagination. She could visualize its elegant grandeur furnished with heavy carved sofas and tables of Spanish design. The breakfast area was surrounded by glass, the individual panes stacked from floor to ceiling.

"Are there any changes, additions that should be made?" Rafael asked her opinion for the first time since the tour had begun.

"I wouldn't change a thing," vowed Erica. In her mind's eye, she was picturing the glassed-in breakfast area abundantly dotted with green-house plants to increase the outdoor effect. "Not if you're referring to knocking out walls and altering the basic layout of the rooms," she hastened to add.

"Then you like it?"

"Yes." She looked to him, making no attempt to mask the glow that radiated from her smile. "Your friend is very lucky. This house is a treasure."

"I have told you a small lie, Erica." Rafael turned his enigmatic gaze to the garden beyond the stacked windows. "My friend does not own this house. It belongs to me—to us."

Erica stiffened indignantly. "You tricked me! Why?"

His head was tilted at an arrogant angle so that the impenetrable depths of his black eyes could

151

look down on her. "I believe that if I had told you before we came that it was ours you would have been prejudiced against the house."

She shifted uncomfortably away from his pinning gaze, unwilling to admit there might be any truth to his observation.

"You live in Mexico. Why did you bother to buy this?" she asked with cold scorn.

A savage imprecation was released from his curling lips as he roughly jerked her around to face him. "I do not know why I allow you to be so insolent," he muttered impatiently. "Yes, Mexico is my home just as Texas is yours. Foolishly I thought it would please you to have a home in San Antonio so that we might spend part of the year here where your family and friends live."

Erica took a deep breath, his thoughtfulness moving her even as she rejected it. He was trying to make her regard him less harshly, lull her into believing that he was really concerned about her happiness. Once she believed that, she would be lost. Rafael's only interest was in himself and getting his own way, and she realized how very expert he was in achieving it. For a moment she had nearly believed that his motive in buying the house had been an unselfish gesture for her.

"I'm sure you will understand that the prospect of sharing any home with you does not fill me with joy," she returned with slow and deliberate sarcasm.

His fingers tightened convulsively on her shoulders and his expression was ominously grim.

Erica's heart was beating at a frightening rate as she stared at the taut line of his mouth.

"If you are wise, you will leave without opening your mouth to speak again and wait for me in the car," he ordered harshly, shoving her away from him. "I will have a word with the workmen before I drive you back."

Erica hurried away, knowing her sharp tongue had pushed him too far. She felt sorry for the innocent workman who would bear the brunt of his anger.

That episode, although the house was never mentioned again, brought a decided change in their relationship. They still went out several evenings a week. Any onlooker would have still considered Rafael to be an attentive escort. Only Erica knew how cold and aloof the glitter in his gaze was when he directed it at her, and there was always something very distant in his smile.

Whenever she returned from an evening with Rafael, she was haunted by the specter of those first weeks. Perhaps it was piqued vanity that made her smiles and looks convey an undertone of intimacy as if to draw a similar response from Rafael. But her attempts to flirt with him had only been met by derisive mockery, in itself a sharp reminder that there was nothing between them except a bitter tomorrow with no promise of any sweetness.

The evening before, one of Erica's friends, Mary Ann Silver, had spent nearly the entire interval talking to Rafael about the exhibit he was supervising at the Mexican Cultural Institute.

Although a lean hand was possessively resting on the back of her waist, Rafael had not addressed a single remark to Erica. When Erica's patience had been stretched to the breaking point, Mary Ann had glanced at her with a superior smile.

"Have you seen the exhibit, Erica?" she had inquired.

Rafael's withdrawn smile had been aimed in her general direction as he replied before Erica had a chance. "No, I am taking her on a personally conducted tour tomorrow afternoon."

Erica had clamped her mouth tightly shut and smiled wanly, knowing the thought hadn't occurred to him until that moment. Yet at the same time he had managed to convey to Mary Ann that he was eager for Erica to discover more about his avocation.

A gentle breeze stirred the hair along Erica's neck as she and Rafael walked by the Aztec-designed gargoyles that marked the entrance and exit of the Mexican Plaza on the Hemisfair grounds. Exhaling softly, Erica managed to conceal her dispirited sigh. The exhibit could have been interesting, but Rafael's impersonal tour had taken away the fascination. She remembered wistfully his tour in Acapulco that had been so informative and entertaining.

"Where are we going now?" Erica asked as she repressed another sigh.

"Where would you wish to go?" Rafael countered disinterestedly.

"Oh, it doesn't matter," she declared harshly,

and increased her pace so that she was carried ahead of him.

If she had hoped he would catch up with her or reach out to slow her down, Erica was to be disappointed. Resolutely she refused to slacken her steps, needing to show him that his indifference was not equal to hers.

In the small square ahead there was a bustle of activity. Pretending a curiosity that she was far from feeling, she headed toward it. The defiant angle of her head indicated that Rafael could follow if he chose.

Then a smile shattered the strained lines around her mouth. Unconsciously she turned it to Rafael as she exclaimed, "Look! They must be going to have an armadillo race!"

As she reached the fringes of the group, she felt his hand on her back and realized he had followed her. But she was much too caught up in the excitement and gay laughter that surrounded her. In the center of the cleared circle was the starting point of the race. The owner-handlers of the armadillos were just entering the circle carrying the strange armor-plated mammals with their tiny ears and thin faces and long bony-plated tails.

"I missed the annual spring race," Erica commented as she glanced back at Rafael. "It's quite an event. There were over twenty-five thousand people there."

The handlers were kneeling down on the center, each holding the tail of his particular armadillo with one hand and cupping the hard breastplate with the other.

"Which one do you think will win?" she laughed gaily, too delighted by the impromptu event to notice the curiously enigmatic light in Rafael's eyes. "I pick the one on the right side. See how he's struggling to get away!"

"I'll pick the quiet one next to yours," Rafael decided in an indulgent tone. "He is wise not to waste his energies so soon."

"He's probably too frightened to move," Erica warned with an impish glance at him. "Mine will beat him easily!"

A half smile of doubt was on his lips when the order was given to release the armadillos. The one Erica had chosen scampered immediately away, only to stop within a few feet, while Rafael's raced directly into the crowd and won.

As Erica half turned to laughingly admit defeat, she found herself jostled against him by the crowd. The sudden contact with his hard and warm length drew a gasp of shock from her. His hands tightened in support, drawing her inches closer. The strange light in his eyes made it difficult for her to breathe.

"I have not heard you laugh so naturally for a long time, Erica," he murmured. Then gently he was setting her apart from him and firmly guiding her toward the car. "What happens to the armadillos now?" he inquired, diverting the conversation back to a less personal subject.

Erica fought off the magnetic pull that wanted to draw her back into his arms. "They make terrible pets, so they're turned loose at the place where they happened to be caught."

Rafael nodded and the aloofness set in again.

A STRANGE RESTLESSNESS had circled Erica in a cold hand for the past three days, but she couldn't put a finger on exactly what was troubling her. She had sent Donna home and locked up the boutique over an hour ago. There had been no need for her to go home since she had the evening free.

A purpling dusk had begun to settle over the city, adding to her strangely melancholy mood. Her wandering footsteps were drawing her near one of the sidewalk lounges. It was still too early for the night life along the river to begin and the tables were empty. Normally she avoided drinking except at social functions and she especially avoided drinking alone. Yet she found herself sitting down at one of the tables and ordering a glass of wine. She was idly fingering the stem of the untouched glass when a familiar voice sounded behind her.

"My, my, my, if it isn't Miss Wakefield! All alone and without her Latin Romeo," the sarcastic voice declared.

Her stomach tumbled sickeningly as she glanced around. "Forest!" His name came out in an achingly tormented sound.

"I wondered if you would even recognize me." His ruggedly handsome features were drawn with sardonic lines.

Erica had not seen Forest since that Sunday afternoon when he had rejected her, believing that she preferred Rafael to him. Tears pricked her eyes at the harshness that was in his usually warm velvet brown eyes.

"I thought the grand Don Rafael was occupying all of your time now," Forest jeered.

She hunched her shoulders at his stinging arrows. "Don't, please, Forest." She bent her head, her hair swinging down to cover the tear that slipped from her lashes.

He uttered a savage imprecation. In the next instant, she heard swift footsteps carrying him down the few flagstone steps to the riverwalk proper. Erica sprang to her feet and raced down the steps after him.

The pain hurt too badly for her to let him go this way and selfishly she knew she needed the reassurance that he cared, that somebody cared. Rafael's cold manipulations for the future were simply too heavy a weight to carry alone. Those carefree days with Forest seemed so uncomplicated compared to the twisted path of life she was walking now.

"Forest!" she called out breathlessly.

He hesitated, then turned around sharply. His forehead was creased with an entreating anger. "Erica, there isn't really anything more to say. And I damn sure don't need your pity!"

"I miss you," she whispered, standing in suspended motion before him.

For a second, a hungry light flashed in his eyes before his square jaw was clenched in a rejecting line. "You can't have both of us. You made your choice."

"But it wasn't the one I wanted to make." Her frank protest came out before she could stop it.

He stared at her in silence, then ran his hand through his thick brown hair. "You aren't making any sense," he growled, and started to turn away again.

Her fingers closed over his arm to stop him. "I know I'm not making any sense," she murmured. "I only wish I could explain to you."

The touch of her hand seemed to break the slim control he held. He spun around, taking her by the shoulders and pulling her into his arms. Roughly his mouth caressed her hair as he crushed her even closer to him.

"I must be insane," he murmured. "When I saw you sitting there, I should have walked away."

"I'm so glad you didn't," Erica sighed. The suffocating embrace was easing the cold ache in her heart.

"Why? Erica, why?" He cradled her face in his large hands and tilted it back so he could look into it freely.

Closing her eyes tightly against his beseechingly demanding voice, she shook her head slightly in a negative movement. Her courage failed when it actually came to the moment of explaining her decision.

"If I told you," she said in an aching whisper, "you would only hate me more than you do already."

"I *should* hate you. I actually believed that you loved me as much as I love you. I thought you were seriously considering marrying me. This last

159

month when everyone has so kindly made sure I knew every place you went with that—that—"

The touch of her fingers silenced the sarcastic flow from his mouth. Forest breathed in deeply to regain control.

"I'd almost convinced myself that I didn't care about you any more," he continued with a rueful sigh, "until today. And all the hurt came back."

"I thought it had eased, too." Erica couldn't keep the sadness out of her smile.

The sound of the tourist boat came from the hidden curve of the river and Forest slackened his hold. Reluctantly Erica moved away, wishing they were alone so he could hold her so tightly that she would forget Rafael. Silently Forest held out his hand to her.

"Shall we walk?" he asked quietly.

"I—I don't think we'd better." Erica shook her head.

He looked away grimly. "A minute ago I was holding you in my arms. Now you are saying that you won't even walk with me? For God's sake, are you trying to drive me out of my mind?"

"I don't know what I'm doing," she admitted wryly. Her mind was in a jumbled state of confusion. Her commitment was to Rafael. Seeing Forest again hadn't changed that, nor the circumstances that had prompted her commitment.

"Then explain to me what's going on," Forest said crisply. "Do you find yourself attracted to this—Don Rafael? Is that it? Were you testing to make sure that our love was genuine? That would be ironic, wouldn't it?" He laughed bitterly. "I never even gave you a chance to explain that day. Why didn't you come to me and tell me what a fool I was?"

"Because you weren't a fool," Erica protested.

"What does that mean? You can't be in love with both of us."

"Please, don't ask questions that I can't answer."

"They're simple questions," Forest snapped. "Are you in love with me?"

"Yes, but . . . ." That strange restless confusion returned, leaving her uncertain and apprehensive.

"Are you in love with Don Rafael?"

"No!" Her response came out sharper than she intended and Erica experienced a pang of guilt she couldn't identify. It was silly, because she couldn't possibly care for Rafael.

"Then what's going on?" he demanded. "If you're not in love with the guy, why are you letting everyone, including me, think that you are?"

"I can't tell you." Her voice was choked with frustration.

"Is your father behind this?"

"Whatever made you think that?" she asked in an astonished tone.

"Because this isn't like you at all, Erica. Is he making you see this man to further some business deal he's got in the works?" His voice had become threateningly soft.

Erica's response was immediate and indignant. "Of course not! How could you accuse my father of

161

such a thing? Daddy is insensitive at times, but never to that extent!"

Forest shook his head, trying to shake free of the wall of bewilderment she had erected. "I get this feeling that you're afraid of something. You imply that all this is happening against your will. The only one who's ever been able to make you do anything that you didn't want to is your father, yet you tell me he has nothing to do with it."

"He hasn't." She took a hasty step backward, regretting the impulse that had prompted her to speak to Forest when he would have willingly left her. Rafael had been right. She should have kept the break clean and not let herself become entangled with Forest again.

"Erica, let me help you. I love you," he said earnestly. "I don't begin to understand what's going on, but whatever it is we can face it together."

"You don't know what you're saying." She retreated again. "I think I'd better go."

"Don't you think I would protect you from whatever it is that's frightened you?" Forest demanded.

"I h-have to work it out by myself," Erica refused, knowing how dangerously easy it would be to confide in Forest right now. "I can't involve you."

"I love you," he said quietly. "I am involved."

"Stop—saying that," she breathed. Her palm was raised to ward off the temptation.

"We'll go somewhere else and start over again,"

he suggested as he saw the slight weakening of her stand. "If—"

"No!"

The second after the strident cry of denial was sounded Erica was running away from him. Her chest heaved with sobs of pain, but fortunately Forest didn't pursue. As much as she tried to shut them out, his last words kept echoing in her mind. Perhaps she had misjudged the depth of his love after all. Maybe he wouldn't desert her if there was a scandalous divorce from Rafael. Her father would be violently angry, but if Forest was there to support her, she might be able to deal with Vance Wakefield.

Then anger and resentment began to build against Rafael. Undoubtedly he had guessed that Forest was the weak link in his plans. He had probably congratulated himself very profusely for getting Forest out of the way so early. Alone, Erica had been vulnerable to his threats and malleable to his proposal. She brushed the tears from her eyes, another impulsive plan taking shape, a plan that could bring her the happiness she had believed was impossible.

In the past her impulsiveness had got her into considerable trouble, including this hated marriage to Rafael. This time she would think it over very carefully, and weigh the risks and advantages before leaping in.

CHAPTER NINE

ERICA PROWLED RESTLESSLY about her bedroom, casting impatient glances out the window at the snail-slow movements of the rising sun. The oval clock on her dressing table indicated only half-past six. With an angry movement, she grabbed her bag and bolted from the room.

She had been up half the night making her decision. Even now there were frightened butterflies in her stomach. Rafael had been right when he told her that she had spent nearly all her life trying to run from the things she found unpleasant. He had used that streak of cowardice to his own advantage just as he had done everything else. Only he had cleverly made her believe that remaining married to him and becoming his wife in fact was the way to live up to the obligations and decisions she found distasteful.

His reasoning was about to backfire. Agreeing to his plan had simply been another way of running. She hadn't wanted to face her father's anger or feel his condemnation. She hadn't wanted to take the chance that she would lose Forest's love. Foolishly Erica had accepted martyrdom, telling herself that she was sacrificing her happiness for those whom she loved. But she had only been taking the path that offered her the least resistance.

Elation swelled like a giant balloon inside her as she imagined the consternation on Rafael's face when she told him that she had seen through his devious plot. She was even beginning to doubt that he would oppose a suit for divorce. After all, his family name was important to him. He would hardly want it dragged through the scandal he had threatened her with if she attempted any legal proceedings.

It frightened her to think how long it might have taken her to discover this if she hadn't seen Forest. Perhaps the whole thing might still blow up in her face. Her father could, at least figuratively, disown her. Forest might not want anything to do with her once he discovered the lie she had been living, but she would be free of the tangled web she had weaved.

The traffic was heavy with people on their way to work. It was seven o'clock before Erica had parked her car and hurried into the hotel where Rafael was staying. The light of certain victory was in her eyes as she started for the elevator doors. Then she changed her mind. She would ring Rafael's suite first and let him wonder why she had come to see him at this hour of the morning. She wanted him to feel the uncomfortable prickles of apprehension before she had the satisfaction of telling him how completely his plan had failed.

She picked up the white house phone, and a wide smile brightened her face as she remembered how childishly frightened she had been the first time she had gone to his room. This time it would be entirely different. She would be the one issuing ultimatums, not Rafael.

On the other end the unanswered ring sounded again and again. Erica nibbled impatiently on her lower lip. She hadn't imagined that Rafael would not be in his room. With a sigh of exasperation, she hung up and dialed the front desk.

"Would you please page Don Rafael de la Torres?" she requested. "I didn't get any response when I dialed his room."

"One moment, please," the courteous voice on the other end replied.

Seconds later she heard his name called over the public address system. Interminable minutes later, the operator came back on the line.

"I'm sorry, he doesn't answer the page."

"Would you try his room again for me?" Erica asked testily.

"What room, please?"

Quickly she gave the operator the number of Rafael's suite. There was a slight pause before the voice responded. "I'm sorry, that suite is not occupied."

Erica frowned. "But I know he's staying here."

There was another request for her to wait and more seconds ticked by slowly. "Señor de la Torres checked out a week ago, miss," the operator told her.

"Checked out? That's impossible!"

"He left a forwarding address here in the city," Erica was informed.

"May I have it, please?" she asked as she

166

rummaged hurriedly through her bag for a paper and pen.

With the address in hand, it wasn't until Erica was back in her car that she realized the address the hotel had given her would take her to the house Rafael had purchased. He had obviously been living there for the past week and she wondered rather curiously why he hadn't mentioned it. Of course, she hadn't evinced the slightest bit of interest in what he did, so she supposed he simply hadn't bothered to tell her.

When she parked her car in front of the house, she was surprised at the transformation that had taken place in such a short time. The riotous foliage was still tropically abundant in front of the house, only now there was a semblance of control. The stone fountain had been scrubbed clean of the grimy moss and ensnarling vines so that water sparkled clearly in its basin.

The scrolled iron gate had a fresh coat of black paint and the thick walls of the courtyard were firmly solid once more. The shaded walkways of the courtyards were no longer losing the battle with the foliage and the view of the freshly painted gazebo wasn't obscured by the previous overgrowth. With an excited quickness to her step, Erica hurried toward the door, eager to see what had been accomplished with the interior of the stately house.

Only when she rang the doorbell did she remember that her reason for coming had nothing to do with the renovation of the house. In fact it didn't concern her at all since she would never be living here. As footsteps approached the door from the other side, she tilted her head to its haughtiest angle.

This forthcoming moment was one she was going to enjoy tremendously. Rafael had been too arrogantly sure of himself. What satisfaction there was going to be in putting him in his place!

A cool smile teased her lips as the door swung open and she was surveyed by a curious pair of dark eyes belonging to an unknown Mexican-American. She guessed that he was a servant of some type, although he wasn't in uniform.

"I would like to see Don Rafael. Is he in?" she asked, making her voice deceptively pleasant.

"Yes, he is in, but—" the man hesitated "—I don't believe he is seeing anyone yet this morning."

"I'm Erica Wakefield. Would you tell Don Rafael that I'd like to see him?"

Her clipped request brought an expressive lift of the man's shoulders that seemed to doubt her name would impress Rafael, but he nodded. "*Si*, I will tell him."

There was another instant of hesitation when the man debated whether to let her wait outside or invite her into the foyer. He evidently decided that she might be someone of importance and politely asked her to step inside.

While Erica waited in the entryway, she listened to the click of the man's heels on the polished tile floors as he carried her message to Rafael. Her view of the other rooms of the house was limited, but she could see it was now sparsely furnished.

168

The Mediterranean style was the one she would have chosen to match the house's character. She longed for a peep at the breakfast nook, but her curiosity was set aside as she heard the footsteps approaching the entryway.

She stepped forward expectantly as the man reappeared. His dark head inclined graciously toward her, then he smiled with decided apology.

"I am sorry, *señorita*. Don Rafael is unable to see you. He asks that you return in an hour."

Her eyes snapped with amethyst sparks. "The arrogance of that man!" she muttered beneath her breath. She checked her temper, saving it for Rafael. "I will not return in an hour," she said firmly. "You will go back and tell Don Rafael that I want to see him now!"

The man's head tilted to the side as if he was about to refuse, then he decided against it. Again he left her standing in the foyer and disappeared down the cool hallway. His eyes were dancing with secret amusement when he returned a few minutes later. Furiously Erica wondered what Rafael had said.

"Don Rafael will see you now. This way, please," the man invited with only a suggestion of a smile.

The servant walked rapidly back the way he had come and Erica had to hurry her steps to keep up. They passed the living room and the library, and Erica couldn't help blinking in surprise when the man started up the staircase to the second floor.

When Rafael had shown her the house, the staircase was being repaired and she hadn't been able to go through the rooms above. He had said at the time that there were only bedrooms on the second floor. She realized it was early, but she hadn't dreamed that Rafael would not be up. The anger that had built receded rather sharply at this possibility.

As the servant opened one of the doors at the top of the stairs, she found herself nervously clutching the strap of her bag as though it were a weapon. She almost wished she had waited the hour Rafael had suggested, especially when she saw the ornately carved wooden bed that was still unmade. Thank goodness it was empty.

Her heart was thumping unevenly as she stepped farther into the room. The French doors to the balcony were standing open and the aroma of freshly brewed coffee was in the air. It was in the direction of the balcony that the man was leading her.

Rafael glanced up as she hovered between the French doors. "Bring Miss Wakefield a chair and some coffee, Carlos," he instructed calmly.

A large wicker chair was immediately pushed up to the round table where Rafael was seated. Erica was uncomfortably aware of the black dressing robe that Rafael wore, tied at the waist, and revealing the bareness of his legs. As she walked toward the empty chair, she caught the scent of soap and shaving lotion. Her gaze bounced off the glistening wetness of his black hair as she realized that Rafael must have only recently stepped from the shower.

A plate of sweet bread sat in the center of the

table and a bowl of fresh chunked pineapple was in front of Rafael. Erica shifted uneasily in the cushions of the winged wicker chair. The man called Carlos reappeared with a steaming cup of coffee and set it in front of her.

"Would you like something to eat, Erica?" Rafael inquired.

She had difficulty looking into the smoothly bland mask, so she addressed her denial to Carlos. "No, thank you," she refused. Out of the corner of her eyes, she saw the nod of dismissal that Rafael gave Carlos.

At the soft click of the closing bedroom door, she felt the penetrating darkness of Rafael's gaze directed at her. He always succeeded in putting her off balance. Her chin lifted in challenge, determined that it wouldn't happen this time.

"You will forgive me, Erica. I have not yet had my breakfast and I am ravenous." There was little apology in his low voice. "This discussion must be quite serious if it brings you here at this hour of the day. I hope you don't object if we postpone it until after my meal."

She exhaled an angry breath. He seemed not the least bit concerned about what she wanted to discuss, she thought savagely. He was probably quite certain there was no way out for her.

"I don't object," she assured him, thinking silently that he was entitled to his last meal.

Yet it was she who seemed to feel the prickles of apprehension and not Rafael. In an effort toward composure, Erica concentrated on her coffee, trying to ignore the white teeth biting into the

171

juicy pineapple. It was difficult to shake off the sensation of intimacy that sitting across the breakfast table with Rafael created. The gold medallion winked mockingly at her from the vee of his robe.

Finally the pineapple was gone and Rafael seemed disinclined to have more sweet bread. Her teeth were on edge as he refilled her cup, then his, from the coffee server on the table. Leaning back in his chair, he took a slender cigar from the gold case on the table, placed it in his mouth and snapped a flame to it before he glanced at Erica again.

"Would you care to begin?" he murmured.

Erica glared at him, hating the fact that it was he who was so casually relaxed while she sat on the edge of her chair. She folded her trembling hands in her lap.

"I'm not going to go through with your proposal," she replied in a voice that was coldly emphatic.

A dark brow registered amusement instead of surprise. "You're not?"

"No, I am not!" she declared. "I'm going to start the divorce proceedings at once!"

"I see," Rafael replied calmly.

Lazily he rose from the wicker chair and walked over to the balcony railing. Beyond the Spanish lace grillwork was the courtyard, the golden light of the morning sun just beginning to pick its way into the shadows. Erica stared at him in amazement, searching for any sign of anger, any small gesture that would indicate she had thwarted him.

He glanced over his shoulder. "The courtyard is beautiful once again, isn't it?"

Erica pushed herself out of her chair. He was deliberately ignoring her announcement as if it were some child's protest.

"You haven't believed a word I've said," she accused.

Again his gaze swung indolently over her, then returned to the profusion of green below. "Of course I believe you. I don't think you would say what you don't mean." He shrugged, his manner indicating that the matter was unimportant to him. "The gardener has suggested planting climbing roses along the wall. What is your opinion?"

Erica's mouth opened in disbelief. A confused frown crossed her forehead as she walked the few steps to the iron railing.

"I did not come here to discuss gardening, Rafael," she said hotly.

"No?" His bland gaze studied her through the wispy smoke from his cigar. "Is there some uncertainty regarding your decision to file for the divorce?"

"None at all," she avowed, lifting her chin defiantly.

Again there was the expressive lift of his shoulders. "Then what is there to discuss? Why are you here?"

A short, confused laugh came from her throat. She had expected anger, threats, but certainly not

173

indifference, a much more difficult thing to combat.

"I came to tell you I was calling your bluff. Your blackmail isn't going to work. I'm not going to be forced to become your wife," she declared, bewilderedly wondering why she was explaining her reasons.

"That's what you said earlier. But why come here to tell me?"

"I wanted you to know." Her hands raised in confusion.

"Why?" Rafael countered.

"I . . . ." His question baffled her and she groped for an answer. "I suppose I thought it was fair."

There was a complacent lift of his brow. "But according to you, I am a blackmailer as well as your husband. Why should you be fair?"

"I don't know!" Erica murmured angrily. "This isn't making any sense."

"I agree." He smiled lazily. "But I doubt if you have guessed why." He turned slightly to face her. "May I ask what prompted your decision?"

This was firmer ground and Erica tilted her head with defiant arrogance. "I saw Forest last night."

A mocking light entered the dark eyes. "And you discovered you couldn't live without him?"

"No, I discovered that I couldn't live with you!" she retorted sharply. "I don't care how much you threaten me. I don't care if daddy throws me out of the house. And if Forest finds he doesn't want to risk his career, that doesn't matter, either. I'm simply not going to be your wife any longer!" Her violet eyes narrowed shrewdly. "Besides, I don't think you'll want your precious family name dragged through the mud of a messy divorce."

"I believe, Erica, that you have finally grown up," Rafael murmured.

She looked at him blankly. His calm acceptance was simply too startling to believe. In a daze, she turned toward the courtyard, her fingers closing over the railing as she tried to fathom the reason for his attitude. The smoke of his cigar drifted closer to her.

"Have you spoken to your father and Forest of our marriage?" Rafael was standing beside her, the blackness of his robe visible out of the corner or her eye.

"Not yet," she sighed, then glanced at him sharply. "Why? Do you think you can still talk me out of it?"

He snubbed the cigar out in the gold pottery ashtray that stood beside her. "I can't do that, can I?" he replied with that same casualness that she couldn't understand. "It is a pity, though. Our children would have been beautiful and intelligent, although perhaps too impulsive, no?" He smiled.

His comment brought an unaccountable flush to her cheeks. "And too arrogant," she added.

"*Si*, everyone has faults," he agreed with a mocking grin. "But even in my arrogance I know that I cannot talk you out of your decision. The only way I could persuade you to change your mind was if you loved me. And of course you don't, do you?"

"No," Erica breathed. A tremor raced down her spine, vibrating her nerve ends as she realized how very close Rafael was to her.

"Have you ever wondered what might have happened if you hadn't fled from my yacht that night?" he asked quietly.

"Your yacht?" She turned in surprise.

"You do not still believe it was Helen's?" Rafael chuckled. "It amused me at the time to let you believe that. However, Helen, who happens to be my uncle's wife, was actually staying at your hotel. She had decided against accompanying him to South America on family business. He joined her there a few days after you left. A very happy reunion it was, too."

"But she was an—"

"An American, yes," he supplied. "It isn't uncommon for the Torres family to marry outside their country. My maternal grandmother was French."

"I know very little about you," Erica mused.

"Véry little," Rafael nodded, his gaze running lightly over her upturned face. "I know a great deal more about you, yet there are times when you have puzzled me. For instance, I know that you married me to spite your father." The breeze had tossed a lock of her hair across her face and Rafael reached out and tucked it behind her ear, letting his fingers trail down her neck. "Why did you not have me take you back to the hotel when I said that I would?"

Quickly she lowered her gaze from his face, shifting nervously beneath the touch that vividly

176

reminded her of his caresses. She felt shame and embarrassment toward the permissive curiosity that had directed her actions on their wedding night.

"Please, I . . . I don't want to discuss that."

His fingers stopped on her exposed collarbone. "I did not mean to hurt you, Erica." The sincere tenderness in his voice brought an aching throb to her chest.

"You didn't. I mean, you did, but . . . ." Embarrassment took over again as she found she couldn't speak of their intimacy with any degree of objectivity.

Gently he lifted her chin. "In the morning, I intended to tell you that you were a very passionate and satisfying lover. I never guessed that you would run from me after we had shared so much."

"Rafael, please!" A weakness descended through her limbs.

"You use my name again." A wry smile curled his mouth, the hard tantalizing mouth that riveted Erica's gaze. "What is it you want of me this time?"

"I don't know," she whispered, her lashes closing on the chaotic thoughts in her mind.

"Do you remember the time in Acapulco when you asked why I didn't kiss you? Where is your boldness now?" he chided.

Desperately Erica reached out for it. "Why aren't you angry? I'm going to divorce you."

"I know." His voice remained softly gentle and subtly seductive. "How can I feel anger over that?

Perhaps if I believed that you were leaving me for another man, I would." Erica gasped sharply, her eyes opening in time to see the half smile. "It is your freedom you want, not Forest."

"What makes you think that?" she demanded in protest.

"Have you not yet learned that it isn't the same when he touches you? The same as it was with us?" Rafael countered. "His caress is pleasant, but not the same."

"I don't know what you mean," she denied vigorously. "The only reason it's different is because I was inexperienced before. I do love Forest."

"A false cloak of love will not protect you."

The vague warning was no sooner spoken than Erica felt the touch of his mouth against hers. Lightly he explored her lips, warming them with the kindled flame of his kiss. Desperately she tried to be analytical in her comparison of his embrace and Forest's, but the strange leaping of her senses made it impossible. His arms curled down her back and gently arched her toward him while her hands encountered the nakedness of his chest.

In a blinding flash, she knew that her responses to Forest had been in answer to his ardency and not aroused by it as was the case with Rafael. Of their own volition, her arms had slipped inside his robe to wrap around his waist. Now she pulled them free and pressed her palms against his chest.

But she didn't have to struggle as Rafael gently let her step back, his hands supporting her trembling frame for a minute before he released her completely. The intensity of his gaze was too disturbing and her pulse was already behaving much too erratically.

"I—I think I'd better leave," Erica whispered after she had taken a deep breath to restore air to her lungs.

"It's a pity you could not love me." His eyes studied the high color in her face. "This thing between us could have been beautiful."

"It would have been the perfect answer for you, wouldn't it?" she agreed dryly. "Now you'll simply have to find some other woman to bear your children and carry on your precious family name."

His lips thinned. "No other woman will bear my name or my children. You may have your freedom, but I will still be bound by my own chains."

"Aren't you going to contest the divorce?" she frowned.

"The only condition that I make to your freedom is that you tell your father and Forest the truth." The gentleness that had softened his face in the previous moments was replaced by the mask of arrogant aloofness. "Not such a terrible price to pay, since it is one you would have paid if I fought the dissolving of our marriage."

"I don't understand. Why are you giving in?" She shook her head in confusion.

"I never intended to force you to honor our vows," he replied, turning away from her and walking to the table to light another cigar.

"I don't believe you," Erica murmured, watching him warily and wondering what new ploy he was intending to use. "You simply thought you could succeed in bullying me into agreeing. You threatened me with scandal and made me break off with Forest. Why did you go through the deception of taking me out this last month if you didn't intend to marry me in public?"

"Foolishly I thought you might begin to care for me as a person," he said grimly. "I would rather sleep alone for the rest of my life than have a woman who resents my presence in the bed."

He meant every word he said. For the first time Erica knew that Rafael had been deadly serious when he said that he would not marry again. There was a tight knot of guilt in her stomach that she could treat their marriage vows so lightly. She didn't really. She wanted her marriage to be forever, but with a man who loved her, who needed her.

"Rafael, you must marry again," she whispered.

"Do not pity me!" he snapped. "I was aware of the risks I took when I married you. And like you, I will pay the price."

"I wish there was something I could do." Pain snatched at her heart.

"There is," he sighed bitterly. "You can stay my wife."

Erica pivoted sharply away, rueing the damage she had done to both their lives. There was a muffled imprecation from Rafael, then silence. She glanced hesitantly behind her, only to find that she was the sole occupant of the balcony. The sound of impatient movements came from the bedroom and she walked slowly through the open French doors. Rafael was viciously yanking a shirt from a wire hanger as she entered. "What are you doing?" The question sprang from her lips unexpectedly.

"I am getting dressed," he replied coldly, pulling a pair of slacks from the closet.

She stood motionless until she saw him unknotting the cord tie of his robe. Then she quickly turned around, his laughter mocking her movement.

"You are still shy, Erica," Rafael commented unkindly.

"I'd better leave," she murmured nervously, and started for the door.

"Wait," he commanded, catching her by the arm before she reached the door. "Give me a moment and I will go with you." There was no request in his ordering tone.

From the corner of her eye, she could see he had his trousers on, but his bronze chest was still bare. "I'm going home," she said curtly.

"I'm going with you."

"Why?" Her demand held accusation for his motives.

His eyes narrowed into black diamonds, hard and cutting. "Because I want to be there when you tell your father about us."

"Don't you think I'll keep my word?" she demanded in a choked voice, hurt by his lack of trust.

His fingers tightened for a fraction of a second before he let her arm go. "I have no doubt you will tell him," he answered tautly. "I realize you believe that I have no mercy, but it is my place to be there to deflect some of his anger."

181

"Because you're my husband?" Erica taunted, tears stinging her eyes at his unexpected gesture.

"Yes, because I am your husband. Do you think I would make you face it alone?" He turned away from her in disgust.

"Rafael?" she said his name hesitantly.

"What?" he snapped as he roughly put on his shirt, showing a blatant disregard for the expensive material.

"Thank you," she whispered.

He glanced at her over his shoulder, the rigidity leaving his expression. "You are welcome," he nodded, an enigmatic light burning in his eyes.

CHAPTER TEN

AFTER RAFAEL WAS DRESSED, he asked Erica's indulgence for a few minutes so that he could make the telephone calls that were necessary to postpone his appointments for that morning. Then he followed in his own car as she drove back to her home.

Parking her car in front of the garage, Erica waited nervously on the flagstone walk for Rafael to join her. As she watched the lean, dark figure approaching her, so composed and controlled, she was suddenly grateful for that underlying steel she had always sensed beneath his strikingly handsome face. Before when it had surfaced, she had fought it as an unruly, frightened horse would fight the commanding hand on the reins.

No one, not even Forest, had ever guessed at her hidden desire to be protected. Independence had been thrust on her and Erica's headstrong willfulness had seized it as a shield to hide her weakness. Yet Rafael knew instinctively that she cringed from her father's displeasure even when she deliberately incurred it. New emotions raced to the front as she viewed Rafael in this fresh light. He was no longer threatening her happiness but promising to guard it in some indefinable way.

Her hand reached out for his physical support, strength flowing from his firm grasp of her cold, shaking fingers. She tried to conceal her dependence on his presence with a false smile of bravado.

"Shall we go in?" she suggested brightly.

Rafael touched the edge of her mouth where the tremors of fear were betraying the lack of genuineness in her smile. "Do not be frightened, *querida*."

She wanted to tell him how safe she felt with him at her side, but the admission wouldn't come out. It was as if, if she acknowledged the security she felt, she would have to confess something else.

A firmness straightened the masculine line of his mouth as Rafael released her hand, letting his arm curve around the back of her waist. The guidance of his touch propelled her along the walk to the front of the house.

A car pulled into the driveway as they neared the entrance. With a halt of surprise, Erica recognized the driver as Forest almost instantly. He parked the car and walked stiffly toward them.

"What are you doing here, Forest?" she asked, glancing hesitantly at Rafael's unrevealing expression.

"I thought for a minute I was going to be treated to another exhibition," Forest answered grimly, flashing a look of open dislike at Rafael. "I received a telephone call at my office to come here immediately. What's going on, Erica?"

"I . . . ." Her head moved uncertainly toward Rafael.

"I left the message," Rafael stated, ignoring Forest's obvious challenge to explain quietly to

Erica. "I believed it would be best if you only had to tell your story once."

She pressed her lips tightly together, moved by his gentle understanding. She had never expected to find security in his embrace, but now she found she wanted to seek it in his arms. Before, the chemistry between them had only been the potent combination of male and female. Only this minute did she realize that his presence offered something more than sexual attraction.

"Thank you," she whispered.

Rafael stared at the brightness of her violet eyes for a long moment, a curious intensity in his dark gaze, then he abruptly swung his attention from her face.

"Shall we go in?" he suggested curtly, the words directed at Forest.

"By all means," Forest jeered.

Suddenly, in Erica's eyes, Forest turned into a stranger, someone she barely knew at all, and she found herself edging closer to Rafael. It was difficult to remember that she had despised him and his trickery only a few hours ago.

Lawrence was in the hallway outside her father's study as the trio entered the house. There was undisguised speculation in the look he darted at the three of them, but his voice was professionally calm when he spoke.

"Mr. Wakefield is expecting you if you would like to go right in," he said, motioning in the direction of the closed study door.

Rafael had evidently contacted her father at the same time as Forest, Erica decided, experiencing a sense of relief that they weren't barging in totally unexpected. The reassuring pressure of the hand on her back was removed as Rafael stepped forward to open the door. It wasn't replaced as he allowed Erica and Forest to precede him into the room. Vance Wakefield seemed to be in an amicable mood as he rose from his desk to greet the two men and his daughter.

The smile on his face didn't cover the sharpness in his blue eyes when he turned to her. "I see I've evidently been chosen as a mediator in this lovers' triangle."

Erica was perched on the edge of a leather chair. Her gaze skittered across the room to where Rafael was relaxing in the large leather armchair and on to Forest who was sitting nearest her in a watchful silence.

"You're not exactly a mediator, daddy," she responded quietly, twisting her fingers together on her lap. She breathed in deeply, searching her mind for a place to begin. "I don't know of any way to start without sounding melodramatic." She smiled weakly at the ice-blue regard. Her gaze darted immediately to Rafael and clung to the vague reassurance she saw in his eyes. "You see, daddy, Rafael and I are married."

"Married?" The expected explosion came from Forest instead of her father. "Do you mean you had me come over here just to learn that you'd married him? You cold-blooded little female!" he shouted as he pushed himself out of the chair.

"Sit down, Señor Granger," came Rafael's

clipped order. "You will hear my wife out before you leap to condemn!"

Forest glowered at him, then sat back in his chair. Erica turned away from the disgust in Forest's expression, her heart leaping at Rafael's quick defense.

"This was a bit sudden, wasn't it, Erica?" Her father said quietly with an underlying hint of disapproval. "Not that I have any objections to Don Rafael."

"Actually—" she stared at her tightly clenched fingers "—I met him almost two years ago when we were in Acapulco. I didn't know who he was at the time—that is, I thought I knew." The red of embarrassment stained her cheeks as she raised her head. "I believed he was a fortune hunter. I married him the night you flew to Houston, daddy."

An uncompromising coldness entered her father's face. "Are you saying that you've been married to him for nearly two years?" he demanded.

She nodded, squarely meeting the anger building in his eyes. "I did it to spite you. I know it sounds childishly stupid now, but then I only wanted to make you sorry for ignoring me when it was supposed to be our vacation. When I found out you'd left, I was too frightened to tell you what I had done."

Vance Wakefield made no comment. He simply looked at her with icy displeasure as if saying that he wasn't surprised that she had behaved so foolishly. She was a willful female without an ounce of sense.

"I suppose he's been blackmailing you all this time," Forest muttered, glancing at Vance Wakefield. "We only have his word that he is who he says he is."

There was a thread of finely honed steel in Rafael's voice as he responded to Forest's implication. "Señor Wakefield has already made discreet inquiries of the local Mexican Consul to verify my identity."

"That's true. I did," her father replied without any apology.

"And he's why you didn't accept my proposal, isn't he?" Forest said grimly.

"I couldn't very well agree to marry you when I was already married to Rafael." Erica laughed bitterly.

"At least you were sensible about that," her father murmured dryly. "I suppose I should be grateful that you didn't get yourself into a bigger mess."

"Your criticism of Erica is unwarranted," Rafael inserted smoothly as Erica flinched at her father's cutting remark. "Everyone is capable of mistakes."

"My daughter has a penchant for trouble," Vance Wakefield bristled, "and then expects me to get her out of it. I don't think I would be wrong if I said that she's made this confession today in order for me to arrange an annulment so that she'll be free to marry Forest."

"An annulment isn't possible." A stunned

silence followed Rafael's softly spoken voice, and Erica flushed under Forest's accusing glare. "It is true that Erica ran away after we were married, but not until the morning after our wedding."

Forest cursed beneath his breath, while her father's eyes narrowed into ice chips of polar blue. Erica couldn't bear their joint censure and bounded to her feet, turning her back to them and hugging her arms about her churning stomach.

"If your intention was to divorce him, why have you been seeing him constantly this past month?" Forest demanded.

Erica glanced over her shoulder at Rafael, strangely unwilling to tell of the way he had forced her to see him. He returned her look steadily and answered the question for her.

"Because my wife believed that I would not grant her a divorce. I told her if she did not break off with you and begin seeing me, I would go to her father and tell him of our marriage, knowing how highly she valued his opinion of her. Erica came to me this morning and told me she was going to tell her father the whole truth and face the consequences."

"I would like to know why you married my daughter and kept silent about it." Her father's sharp gaze swung from Erica to Rafael.

But Rafael was immune to his disapproval as he studied Erica's face before replying. "I married your daughter because I loved her, and for no other reason."

"That's not true," Erica gasped. "You only married me so you could have children!"

"You never asked why I married you," Rafael reminded her cynically. "You have never considered what my reasons might have been. Yes, I want children, but there were any number of women who would have married me and given me children. I guessed that you didn't love me the night I married you, or at least, not as fully as I loved you. But in my arrogance—" he smiled in self-mockery "—I believed you would come to return my love in time. I never expected to find you gone in the morning."

Erica stared at him in wordless amazement, the knowledge that he loved her jolting through her like an electric current.

"As you once pointed out, *querida*," Rafael continued, "I have a vast quantity of pride. When I found you in San Antonio, you demanded a divorce and claimed to be in love with another man. I could hardly fall to my knees and declare my love for you under those circumstances."

"If you knew she loved me," Forest inserted, "why didn't you do the decent thing and set her free?"

Rafael's aloof gaze swung arrogantly to Forest. "Because I knew you could never make her happy. Oh, perhaps for a little while." His hand moved in a short dismissive gesture. "But you are too much like her father. A few months after your marriage, you would begin taking her for granted, pushing her aside to further your career. You might have one or two children to occupy her time, but the love for a child can never take the place of the love that a man and woman share. I had hoped that Erica

190

might begin to care for me in this past month, but she has not. So I have agreed to her request for a divorce and will not contest it."

He rose lightly to his feet and turned to her father. "Do not be harsh with Erica. The sensitivity you see as a weakness, I see as strength. She accepts your affection and returns it tenfold. Not many parents can say that of their children." His glance encompassed Erica and Forest. "There is no more of the story that needs to be told. My presence is no longer required. *Buenos dias.*"

Silently, almost in a daze, Erica watched him walk past her to the door, with no more than a gracious nod in her direction. When the door closed behind him, she knew that she would never see him again. There was no elation, no sense of relief, no feeling of victory that she had finally achieved her freedom, in word if not yet in deed. There was only a frightening emptiness, a void as if some precious part of her had walked out the door, as well.

"I'll call Jules," her father said gruffly. "He can start drawing up the papers for the divorce."

"No!" The denial was spontaneous and firm. "No, there will be no divorce," Erica declared.

"Don't be idiotic!" Forest cried angrily. "The man is giving you your freedom. We can be married."

"I don't want to marry you." She looked into the strong square-jawed face, seeing beyond the rugged exterior for the first time. "I don't love you, Forest. I'm sorry, but you're just a shadow of my father. You're so very like him that I'm surprised I didn't see it before. I love my father, but I don't want to be married to him."

"You certainly don't think you're in love with Rafael, do you?" Forest laughed shortly in scornful disbelief.

Erica said nothing for a second before she replied slowly and with increasing sureness. "Yes, yes, I think I am."

"Don't make another mistake, Erica," her father cautioned, but there was nothing dictatorial in his voice.

But Erica was already racing out of the house and around to the side where Rafael had parked his car. The door was open and he was about to step in when he saw her. She stopped, then hesitantly walked toward him, trying to fathom the aloof mask for some sign that she wasn't too late. The words that would be said between them in these next few moments would determine the outcome of her future.

"Rafael." His name came from her parched mouth in a croaking whisper and she wished for the courage of the matador when he faced the black bull in the ring.

"Yes. There is something more you require?" Impatience edged his low voice.

Erica moistened her lips nervously. "I don't want a divorce, Rafael."

If anything, his expression hardened. "I do not need your pity. Leave me to seek what peace I can find."

"I don't pity you, Rafael," she insisted. "I pity

myself for perhaps finding out too late that I really love you. I know there's nothing I can say to make you believe me, but it's true all the same. I do love you."

"You are only grateful," he corrected harshly, "grateful that I shouldered some of the blame for our stupidity and blunted your father's anger. Do not hide your gratitude in words of love."

"I don't know when I began to love you. I only know I realized it a few moments ago when you walked out of the study and part of me went with you." Erica refused to give up. "It was as if a fog lifted and I understood why you had this strange power over me every time you touched me. Don't you see, Rafael? I could never let myself love you before because I thought you'd married me for my money. I pretended that I let you make love to me because you were so physically attractive. Then I was terrified that I was promiscuous. Only I found out that no other man made me feel the way you do, not even Forest. When you came here and I discovered you weren't a fortune hunter, you backed me in a corner and demanded that the marriage become a reality. But I believed you wanted it to save your family from the shame of a divorce and so you could have children, not because you cared for me."

His attitude remained unreachable and she clapped a hand to her mouth as a bitter laugh of discovery ripped her throat. Tears scalded her eyes and trickled from her lashes down her cheeks as she turned swiftly away from him.

"What a fool I am!" she exclaimed. "That was

all just a ruse in there with my father, wasn't it? You only said you loved me to save my pride. You never expected me to take you seriously, but I don't care!" she declared wildly. "You wanted a wife and children. Well, I'm your wife and I will give you children. But I love—"

"Stop it!" Savagely Rafael grabbed her by the shoulders and spun her around. The iron control was gone and an inverted anger was in its place. Despite the vicious shake he gave her, the tears didn't stop as she gazed at him with the full futility of her love in her eyes. "You are giving in to an impulse. You do not know what you are saying," he snapped.

"And you're too arrogant to believe me!" she cried.

In the next instant, the arms that had so rigidly held her away crushed her against the hardness of his chest, locking her in an embrace that was exquisite punishment. Hungrily his mouth probed hers until she throbbed with a feverish ache for him. Even when he later untwined her arms from around his neck, she was blissfully aware of his reluctance.

"I do love you, Erica, *mia esposa*," Rafael declared huskily, and the burning fire in his gaze convinced her beyond all doubt.

"Why did you wait so long to come for me?" she whispered, touching the face that she now had a right to caress.

"So long?" He laughed softly. "Ah, my love, when I found you were not on board the yacht, then later discovered you had checked out of the hotel, I flew to San Antonio immediately. No one could or would tell me where you were. I waited here for nearly two weeks before I received word that my father had suffered a stroke. I had to return to Mexico. Circumstances have kept me there all this time."

"And your father?" Erica prompted.

Pain flickered for a moment in his eyes. "He died this last spring."

"Oh, darling, I'm sorry." Her lips trembled in sympathy. "I wish I'd been there with you."

"You did not love me then." Rafael kissed her mouth lightly so she would know he meant to inflict no pain with those words.

"You do believe that I love you," Erica sighed, resting her head contentedly against his shoulder as his arms tightened around her.

"You must tell me that tomorrow and every tomorrow after that." The husky command was muffled by the soft skin of her throat.

"I promise I will," she whispered as she felt the melting of her bones beneath his fiery caress.

"Every morning that I woke without you in my arms made the night that we shared so bittersweet," Rafael murmured. "Several times I have thought you were about to discover you loved me. Then I gave up hope. When you were with me, you seemed to become more unhappy and I knew I must set you free."

"I don't deserve you. You were right when you said I was selfish." She gazed sadly into his face.

"I hope you cannot bear to let me out of your sight," he vowed. "It has been sweet torment to be so near to you and not touch you or show you the way I cared. If you had learned Spanish before, you would have known how much I loved you on our wedding night aboard the yacht."

"Where is the yacht?" asked Erica, now cherishing the memories of that night.

"In Acapulco, waiting for you to return," he answered.

"*Mañana*," she murmured the name of the yacht. "Let's go there."

"We will spend our honeymoon on board after we fly to my home tomorrow so my family can meet you," he declared.

"Do they know about me?"

"Yes," Rafael smiled tenderly. "Not that you are my wife, but I have spoken of you and of my intentions to make you my wife. My pride would not let them think ill of you nor pity me that I had lost you. We will have another small wedding at the church in the village near my home. You do not mind?"

"No, I'd like to say our vows again. But, Rafael—" a shy pink heightened her face as the desire to feel his touch swept over her "—must we wait?"

He drew in his breath sharply. "You are my wife." From his pocket, he removed the signet ring and slipped it on her finger. "Your friend Jules Blackwell returned it to me. I told him I loved you and would not leave until this was on your finger again."

TIDEWATER LOVER

"WHAT ABOUT WHAT YOU DO TO ME, LACEY?"

Cole laughed without humor and continued. "Do you know what it's like going to bed each night and imagining you in the next room?"

Lacey knew she was a breath away from surrendering to his attraction. "Then leave! Move out," she challenged in desperation rather than let her senses lead her down the path of temptation.

"And worry about you being here by yourself at the mercy of vandals and burglars?" Cole argued. "I'd be trading cold showers for ulcers."

"I suppose you want me to move out, then," she said stiffly.

"It would solve things." Cole sighed heavily.

"Well, I'm not moving out," Lacey declared, even though every ounce of logic in her mind cried out that's what she ought to do.

CHAPTER ONE

THE RING of the telephone checked the step Lacey Andrews had taken away from her desk. The light was blinking on the interoffice line. Shifting the stack of file folders to her left arm, Lacey reached across the desk to answer it. The movement swung her silky brown hair forward. She tucked it behind her right ear before lifting the receiver to the same ear.

"Lacey speaking," she identified herself automatically.

"You have a call from a Margo Richards on line three," was the reply.

A dark eyebrow flicked upward in surprise at her cousin's name. "Thanks, Jane." And Lacey pressed the plastic button of the third line, wondering with faint cynicism why Margo was phoning her. "Hello, Margo." Her brown eyes glanced toward the ceiling. Lacey knew this would not be a short conversation. Her cousin could spend an hour just saying what time it was.

"I'm sorry to call you at work, Lacey," the melodic voice rushed on, hardly a trace of sincere apology in her tone. "I don't mean to get you into any trouble with your boss, but I simply couldn't wait until tonight to talk to you."

"You aren't getting me into trouble. There are no

restrictions against receiving personal calls," Lacey explained with amused patience. "What is it that's so urgent?"

"I wanted to let you know that Bob and I are leaving tomorrow to fly to Florida to visit his parents. From there we'll be taking a two-week cruise in the Caribbean."

"Sounds marvelous!" Not for anything would Lacey permit even the tiniest suggestion of envy to creep into her voice. She adjusted a box pleat on her plaid skirt and settled down for a long dissertation from her cousin.

"It is exciting, isn't it?" Margo gushed. "It all happened so quickly, too. I mentioned in passing to Bob how romantic a cruise like that would be—and you know how Bob is. If I liked the moon, he'd try to buy it."

Poor man, Lacey thought. She hoped he would learn to say no to Margo before she spent all his money. Lacey was certain that Margo truly loved Bob, but she doubted if her love would ever mature as long as her slightest whim was indulged as if she were still a child.

"I've been dashing around madly ever since he told me," Margo continued. "Half of my summer wardrobe was so sadly dated that I would have been embarrassed if I'd worn it. Oh, Lacey, I wish you could see this gorgeous gown I bought! It's so daring I don't know if Bob will let me wear it. And there's this stunning pair of satin evening pajamas in a shimmering blue that's pos—"

"Margo, I'd love to hear all about your new clothes," Lacey interrupted, knowing that if she didn't stop her cousin now, she wouldn't. Margo's conversation was threatening to run longer than normal. Next she would be hearing the entertainment schedule of the cruise ship. A strong sense of loyalty to her job demanded that Lacey not spend an hour on a private phone call. "But I'm fairly busy at the moment. Maybe you should call me tonight."

"But that's just it. Bob and I are invited to a dinner party tonight—that's why I'm calling you now." There was an incredulous note in Margo's voice, as if she couldn't understand why Lacey was so stupid as not to have reasoned it out by herself.

Lacey gritted her teeth and smiled rigidly at the receiver. "Well, I really appreciate your letting me know you're going to be leaving." What else could she say?

"Oh, but that isn't why I called. I thought I told you." Lacey could imagine Margo's wide-eyed look of innocence.

"No, Margo, you didn't," she replied, concealing an impatient sigh. "Exactly why have you phoned?"

"I ran into Sally Drummond yesterday. Quite by accident," Margo assured her as she identified a close friend of Lacey's. "I was on my way to the car with an armful of packages when she came out of a restaurant."

Lacey sat down on the edge of her desk. She had absolutely no idea what Sally had to do with this phone call, but she would learn. There was simply no way to speed up Margo's explanation. It was an irritating fact, but unchangeable.

"I stopped to say hello," Margo went on. "Then we got to gossiping a bit—you know how that goes. Anyway, one subject led to another until finally we were talking about you."

"Really?" Lacey murmured dryly.

"Nothing bad or anything like that," Margo laughed. "Sally mentioned that you were going on vacation next week for two weeks, but she wasn't sure if you'd made any specific plans. Is that right?"

"Yes," Lacey admitted grudgingly. Her little excursions would pale in comparison to Margo's cruise.

"You aren't going away anywhere?"

"I thought I'd spend a couple of days with the folks, but outside of that, I'm just going to relax and do nothing."

"That's great!" Margo declared enthusiastically.

Lacey didn't think she would go as far as to say that, but it would be a refreshing change from the hectic pace of the office. Still, it was doubtful if Margo had had that reasoning in mind when she made her comment.

The truth was Lacey couldn't afford to leave the Tidewater area of Virginia to go anywhere on her vacation. A variety of unforeseen expenses, the largest being some major repairs to her car, had drained Lacey's savings account almost dry, but she was too proud to volunteer that information to her cousin.

"Why do you ask?" She tried to hurry Margo to the point of this conversation.

"I've been worried about our house and all our beautiful things," Margo stated. "Situated the way we are on the beach, virtually isolated from any close neighbors, you just never know what might happen. Especially with all the summer tourists that are showing up now. Someone could break into the house and steal everything we have the instant they noticed it was vacant. I've been in an absolute quandary as to what to do about it. You know what beautiful things we have, Lacey."

"Yes," Lacey agreed. Over a month ago Margo had taken her on a tour of the place, to show off—no other term could fit more perfectly—her home. She hated to admit to being envious, but she had fallen in love with her cousin's home.

"I was sitting here this morning, worrying myself half sick with what might happen while Bob and I are on the ship. Then I remembered Sally telling me that you were going on vacation and I knew I had the perfect solution. You could babysit the house while we're gone!"

Lacey hesitated. "I suppose... I could."

As she ran the idea over in her mind, it sounded like the perfect plan. A vacation spent in luxurious surroundings with the ocean and beach at her doorstep. It was something she wouldn't have been able to afford at twice her salary.

"I just knew you'd help me out!" Margo exclaimed.

"It will be my pleasure," Lacey returned sincerely, already picturing lazy days in the sun. Maybe she would even splurge on a new swimsuit.

"There is one thing," Margo paused. "I told you we were leaving tomorrow. Well, I just hate the thought of the house being empty for an hour. Could you... would you stay here tomorrow night?"

Breathing in deeply, Lacey wondered if her cousin knew what she was asking. Commuting from Virginia Beach to Newport News during rush hour traffic would practically mean rising with the sun. But tomorrow was Thursday. If she could arrange to have Saturday morning off, it would mean only having to make the round trip once.

"Sure," Lacey agreed finally. "I'll pack and drive out after work tomorrow."

"I'll be eternally grateful for this," Margo vowed effusively. "Now there's plenty of food, et cetera, in the house and I'll leave the front door key in the flowerpot near the door."

"Okay."

"You just make yourself at home, Lacey. Listen, I really have to run—I still have oodles of packing to do. See you when we get back from the Caribbean. Bye!"

"Bye." But Lacey's response was given to the dial tone buzzing in her ear.

Shrugging, she replaced the receiver on its cradle. It was typical of Margo. Once her objective was achieved she lost interest. But Lacey didn't bear any grudge. Thanks to Margo, her two weeks' vacation had suddenly taken on a new perspective.

Of course, she still had to talk to Mike Bowman, her employer, about Saturday morning. Straightening from the desk, Lacey walked to the twin set of metal cabinets in her office and deposited the folders on top. As she opened a drawer to begin the filing, the door to her office opened and Mike Bowman, who was one of the chief engineers for the construction company, walked in.

"Hello, Lacey," he greeted her absently, frowning as he paused beside her desk to go through the stack of messages waiting for him.

Brushing aside the sleek brown hair that curved across one side of her forehead, Lacey studied him for an instant. Mike was in his late thirties, a peppering of gray showing up in his dark hair; a confirmed bachelor—so he claimed.

Even with her limited experience, Lacey knew she could search a long time and never find an easier person to work for, nor one more fun on a date. They had dated occasionally in the last few months, although neither had spread the fact around to the others in the office. Mike was good-looking in a strong, dependable kind of way.

"Judging by your expression, I won't ask how your meeting went," Lacey offered with a sympathetic gleam in her brown eyes.

"Please don't." The corners of his mouth were pulled grimly down. "It was an exercise in frustration trying to explain to the big bosses the combination of circumstances that's put the Whitfield project so far behind schedule. Sometimes I think if they'd get out of their offices and out on the job sites, they might get a better understanding of what I'm up against."

"Maybe you should have suggested that," Lacey smiled.

"No, it's not their job." Mike sighed heavily in resignation. "They don't want to hear excuses, they want solutions. And they're right. I have to start coming up with solutions before the problems I have create more problems in and of themselves."

"Speaking of problems, I don't know if you remember or not, but my vacation starts next week."

"Don't remind me of that," Mike grimaced. "I don't want to remember it until Monday morning."

"Sorry, but I was hoping you might give me Saturday

morning off." There was a flash of even white teeth as Lacey smiled sympathetically.

"Why? I thought you said you weren't going anywhere on your vacation." He frowned, his hazel eyes confused as he met her gaze.

"My plans have changed slightly," she acknowledged. "My cousin called to ask me if I'd stay at her house in Virginia Beach while she and her husband are away on an impromptu vacation. They leave tomorrow, which means I'll move in tomorrow night. I'll have to commute on Friday—and Saturday, as well, unless you let me have the day off."

"Why not?" Mike shrugged.

"Thanks. I'll work late for you Friday to make up for it," Lacey promised.

"You'd better get out of this madhouse at five on the dot Friday or I might change my mind and postpone your vacation," he declared in a mock threat. "Then your cousin or whoever it was would have to find some other house-sitter. By the way, who's going to take your place here?"

"Donna is." Lacey knew the reaction that announcement would produce. Donna was not one of Mike's favorite people.

There was a skeptical glint in his eye at the name of Lacey's replacement. "You'd better leave the address and phone number of your cousin's house with Jane, just in case 'dumb Donna' gets things all loused up here or discovers she can't find something. Where did you say you'd be? Virginia Beach?"

"Yes. The house is right on the ocean. And so help me, Mike, if you call me to work on my vacation, I'll—"

Lacey never got a chance to finish her warning vow.

"On the beach, you say? Hell," he chuckled, "I just might take my vacation and join you. It sounds like paradise. You know what the travel brochures say—Virginia is for lovers. Maybe we should both take the next two weeks to prove they're right. I could stand to get away from the office myself." Both of them knew he was only dreaming. There wasn't a chance of Mike's having any time off.

"If you aren't doing anything Sunday, why don't you come over?" she suggested, knowing it was wishful thinking Mike was indulging in, but extending the invitation as consolation.

"It's a date," Mike replied without any hesitation, settling for a day instead of two weeks. "I'll bring a couple of steaks and we'll cook outside."

"Terrific," Lacey agreed.

The interoffice line rang and Lacey walked to her desk to answer it. Jane, the receptionist, responded immediately, "Didn't I see Mr. Bowman come in, Lacey?"

"Yes."

"Good. Mr. Whitfield is on line one. He's called a half a dozen times." She didn't bother to add that by this time Mr. Whitfield was a very impatient man. The tone of her voice was riddled with the statement.

"Thanks, Jane." Lacey replaced the receiver and glanced hesitantly at Mike. "Whitfield is on line one," she informed him.

He bared his teeth in a grimace. "I've just been through one frustrating series of explanations. See if you can use that soothing voice of yours and put him off for a while."

Sitting down in her chair, Lacey accepted the challenge. After all, in a sense it was part of her job to shield Mike from unwanted phone calls. Mike stood expectantly beside her desk, watching her intently as she picked up the phone and pushed the button for the first line.

"Mr. Bowman's office. May I help you?" she inquired in her most pleasant manner.

"Yes," came the crisp male voice. "I would like to speak to Mr. Bowman."

It was a command, not a request, and Lacey could tell the difference. Still she persisted. "I'm terribly sorry, but Mr. Bowman is on another line at the moment. May I take a message, please?"

"He's on another line, is he?" There was no mistaking the sarcastic skepticism in the response.

"Yes. May I have him call you back when he's through?" Lacey offered.

"No, you may not!" the voice snapped in her ear. She flinched slightly at the coldly raised voice and held the receiver away from her ear. "No doubt Bowman is standing beside you to see if you're going to succeed in stalling me off. But I assure you, miss, that you will not."

Whether it was the accuracy of his accusation or her temper reacting to his acid tone, Lacey didn't know, but she abandoned her attempt to be pleasant, resorting to the sarcasm he had used.

"I assure you, Mr. Whitfield, that Mr. Bowman is on another line. However, since your call seems to be so urgent that you feel the necessity to be rude, I shall see if I can interrupt him. Please hold the line." Without giving him a chance to respond, she pushed the hold button, shutting him off. Fiery lights burned in her brown eyes as she glanced at Mike, anger in the tight-lipped line of her mouth.

"I'm sorry I asked you to speak to him, Lacey," Mike said immediately. "I'll take the call in my office."

"I wish you could tell him to go take a flying leap into a dry lake," she fumed.

"Believe me, it's a temptation," he sighed. "But it is his time and money I'm spending every day that project falls further behind schedule. He has a right to know what's going on."

"He doesn't have any right to be such a...a...."

"Careful," Mike warned with a teasing wink. "Ladies aren't supposed to use the word you're searching for!"

"I don't feel very much like a lady at this moment," Lacey muttered, glaring at the blinking light that indicated that Mr. Whitfield was still holding.

"Just think about the two weeks you're going to spend away from all this," Mike suggested in an attempt to calm her anger as he started toward his private office.

As quickly as her temper had flared, it died. "And I'll occasionally spend a moment or two feeling sorry for you back at the office slogging away while I bask on the sand," laughed Lacey.

Minutes after Mike had entered his office, the light stopped blinking and held steady. Lacey felt sorry for him. Considering the vituperative mood Whitfield was in, it wouldn't be easy for Mike to explain about the new delays on Whitfield's construction project. He was in for a tongue-lashing, but she knew Mike would handle the unpleasant situation in his usual calm way.

With a sigh, Lacey walked back to the metal cabinets to resume her filing of the folders she had placed on top. The door to her office opened. Lacey glanced over her shoulder and smiled as she recognized the girl who had entered.

"Hi, Maryann," she greeted the girl who was one of her best friends. "What are you doing?" It was purely a rhetorical question.

"I am escaping," Maryann Carver declared and sank into the spare, straight-backed chair at Lacey's desk. She had the air of a person who had been pushed to the limit. "A word of advice, Lacey. Don't ever take a job as a payroll clerk. No, two words of advice," she corrected herself. "Don't ever put off going to the dentist."

"Is your tooth bothering you again?" Lacey sympathized.

"Yes. Have you got any aspirin for a suffering fool? I forgot to bring any with me this morning and this tooth is killing me." Maryann combed her fingers through hair that couldn't make up its mind whether it was brown or blond.

"I think there is a bottle of aspirin in the middle drawer of my desk. Help yourself." Lacey slipped a folder into its proper place in the file. "You really should see a dentist."

"I am, at four this afternoon. All I have to do is survive till then." The desk drawer was opened and pills rattled in their plastic bottle. "He's only going to fix this one tooth. I have to go back in a couple of weeks for a regular checkup. You know, that's one good thing about mothers. They always make sure you have your regular checkups when you live at home. Of course, I'll never tell my mother there are advantages to living at home. She'd have me back in my old room before I could say no.''

"So would my mother." Lacey closed the file drawer and returned to her desk, that task finished.

"Hey, I just remembered!" With pills in her hand, Maryann paused on her way to the water cooler. "You start your vacation on Monday. Are you still planning to visit your parents in Richmond?"

"Just for a weekend. My cousin Margo called a few minutes ago. She's going off on a cruise with her husband and asked me to stay in their beach house while they are away."

"Beach house? How lucky can you get? Are you staying there by yourself? Or would you like a roommate?"

"But that roommate—" Lacey knew Maryann was suggesting herself "—would have to commute back and forth to work every day."

Maryann grimaced. "You only brought that up because you want the place to yourself."

Lacey smiled away the remark. "It's certainly going to be a better vacation than I had planned. Imagine, two weeks with the ocean at my doorstep and an uncrowded beach." Each time she thought about it, it sounded more idyllic. As she set the bottle of aspirin back into the middle drawer, Lacey noticed the light had gone off on the first line of the telephone. "Poor Mike. I wonder if he needs an aspirin."

"Why should he? Don't tell me he has a toothache,

211

too?'' Maryann filled a paper cup with water and downed the aspirin in her hand.

"No, but I bet he has a headache." Lacey motioned toward the telephone. "He just finished talking to the sarcastic Mr. Whitfield. That man is the cause of many a headache."

"Who is Mr. Whitfield?"

"A very rude and obnoxious person. Doubly so because the complex we're building for him is way behind schedule. He's a real pain. I wish Mike would punch him in the mouth some day. After the job is done, of course," she added.

"Tut, tut, Lacey. The customer is always right." There was a definite twinkle of laughter in Maryann's eyes. "Look, I'd love to sit and exchange miseries all day, but we both have a lot of work to do. We'll have lunch tomorrow and you can tell me all about the beach house and your sarcastic Mr. Whitfield. I suppose the house is fabulous and I'll be green with envy. You'll leave when? Sunday?"

"No, tomorrow night. I'll have to commute on Friday, but Mike gave me Saturday off."

"Lucky you," Maryann sighed. "I wish I had him to work for instead of that crochety old pruneface."

Lacey merely laughed. "Hope your tooth gets better," she offered in goodbye as her friend opened the outer door.

"So do I. See you tomorrow."

On Thursday evening, with her small hatchback loaded with suitcases and odds and ends, Lacey drove into the driveway of Margo Richards's home. Her brown eyes roved over the elegantly simple lines of the beach house, painted a cream white that matched the foamy whitecaps of the ocean breaking beyond the dunes.

Only a fool would deny that she was looking forward to having the beautiful home all to herself for the next two weeks, and Lacey was not a fool. A faint smile curved her lips, which bore little traces of strawberry gloss.

Grabbing her cosmetic case and one of the smaller pieces of luggage from the rear seat of the car, Lacey stepped out and walked buoyantly to the front door. Intent on reaching the flowerpot where Margo had said she would leave the key, Lacey didn't pay attention to what was beneath her feet.

The toe of her sandal hooked the roughly textured mat in front of the door, catapulting her forward. The cosmetic case flew from her hand, the lock failing to hold so that the lid snapped open to scatter her cosmetics onto the concrete slab. Fortunately Lacey managed to regain her balance a stumbling second before she joined the case.

"Why don't you pay attention to where you're going, Lacey?" she scolded herself, then stooped to pick up the items scattered before her.

A gleam of metal winked at her near the edge of the mat. Curious, she reached for it, pushing the mat aside to reveal a shiny key. She studied it for a second, then tried in in the door lock. It opened with the first attempt.

"How typical of Margo," she murmured aloud, leaving the door open while she refastened her cosmetic case. "She forgot where she told me she'd put the key and chose the most likely place."

Inside the entrance foyer of the two-story house, Lacey paused. From her previous single visit to the house, she remembered that the rooms on the ground floor consisted of a study, a rec room and a utility room. The rest was taken up by a garage.

The main living area of the house was at the top of the stairs to her left. Looking up the staircase, Lacey admired again the tall built-in cabinet stretching from the landing of the open stairwell to the ceiling of the top floor. The carved moldings of its white-painted wood were etched with a darkly brilliant blue. Through the panes of glass in its tall doors, assorted vases and figurines of complementing blues were deftly scattered among a collection of books.

With cosmetic case and suitcase in hand, Lacey mounted the steps. A large potted tree stood near the white railing at the head of the steps. All was silent. The click of her shoes on the hardwood floor of the second story sounded loud to her own ears, but she resisted the impulse to tiptoe.

The decor of the stairwell was an introduction to the white and blue world of the living room. Matching cream white sofas with throw pillows of peacock blue occupied the large area rug, predominantly patterned in blue, in front of the white brick fireplace. Again, the assorted statues and figurines carried the theme of blue, accented by the hanging plants and potted plants that abounded in the room.

The dining room and kitchen were an extension of the living room with no walls to divide them. A mixture of white rattan and white wicker furniture in the dining room added an informal touch, with the emphasis

214

subtly changing from blue to green, mostly by the usage of plants.

Setting her cases down, Lacey walked to the large picture windows fronting the ocean. The blue drapes were pulled open to reveal an expansive view of the sea and the beckoning sandy beach. She turned away. There was time enough to explore the outdoors later.

An investigation of the kitchen with its countered bar to the dining room indicated that there was an ample supply of canned goods on hand and three or four days' worth of food in the refrigerator. She would fix her evening meal later. First on the agenda was to unpack and get settled in.

The bedrooms branched off the hallway to the left of the living room. Lacey only glanced into the master bedroom. The two guest rooms were smaller but still comfortably large. She chose the one with a view of the ocean. The guest rooms shared a bath that had its entrance from the hall.

Pastel yellow joined with the predominant theme of blue in the room's decor, giving a cheery impression of sunshine and ocean. Lacey glanced admiringly at the furnishings before catching her reflection in the mirror.

"I could grow to like this style of living." She winked at the mirror. The dark-eyed girl in the mirror, her seal-brown hair styled in a boyish cut that made her look ultrafeminine, winked back.

An hour later she had brought in all her luggage from the car, which she had parked inside the garage. A few of Margo's winter clothes were in the closet, but there was still plenty of room for Lacey's belongings. Fixing a plate of cheese, cold meat and fruit, she ate alone at the

215

dining table, facing the ocean. She lingered there, listening to the symphony of the surf, gentle waves breaking on the sandy beach. The music of the ocean was soothing and she hated to leave it, but there were other things to be done.

The picture-perfect house seemed to demand tidiness. Lacey washed the few dishes and put them away, effectively eradicating any trace of her presence. Then, and only then, did she submit to the call of the sea and the beckoning of the empty stretch of sand she could see from the windows.

The setting sun was turning the sand into molten gold when she finally retraced her steps to the house, tired yet oddly refreshed by the salt air. After showering and setting the alarm, she crawled into bed, falling asleep almost as soon as her head touched the pillow.

She stirred once in the night, waking long enough to identify her surroundings before slipping immediately back into a sound sleep. The infuriating buzz of the alarm wakened her as the morning sun was crowning the ocean's horizon. Her groping hand found the shut-off knob and quickly silenced it.

The long drive ahead of her in the morning traffic made her groan, "I'm glad I only have to do this once!"

Stumbling out of bed, she walked bleary-eyed into the kitchen, wearing only her long silky pajamas. A pitcher of orange juice was in the refrigerator. Filling a glass from the cupboard, she downed the wake-up juice quickly before putting water on to boil for instant coffee.

She wasted little time in the bathroom with washing and applying the little makeup she used. Back in her bedroom, she donned a plaid skirt and matching satiny textured blouse in mint green. Her return to the kitchen coincided with the first rising bubbles of the water.

With a cup of instant coffee in her hand, Lacey stifled a yawn and walked to the glass-paned door in the dining room. It led to the balcony overlooking the ocean. The breeze blowing from the sea was brisk and invigorating—exactly what she needed to chase the cobwebs of sleep from her head.

Leaning against a rail, she watched the incoming tide, mesmerized by the waves rushing one after another in to shore. For a while she lost all track of time, sipping at the steaming coffee until the cup was drained.

The sound of a car engine broke the spell of the waves, and she turned with a frown. The ocean breeze made it difficult to tell where the sound was coming from, but it seemed very near. Probably an early-morning fisherman, she decided and reentered the house.

In the kitchen, she started to rinse her cup and spoon under the tap. Her dark eyes rounded in surprise at the orange juice glass sitting on the counter.

"You're losing your grip, gal," she mocked herself as she picked up the dirtied glass. "These early-morning hours must be affecting your memory. You obviously didn't wash the glass as you thought you had."

Quickly wiping the cup, glass and spoon, she put them in their proper places in the cupboards. A glance at her watch told her she was running behind schedule. She quickly gathered her purse from the bedroom and sped down the stairs to the garage and her car.

The morning traffic through Norfolk was as heavy as

217

she had thought it would be at that hour. And the congestion at the tunnel under the ship channel to Hampton Road and Newport News lost her a lot of time. She arrived at the office twenty minutes late and spent all morning trying to make up for the lost time.

Coming back from her lunch break at a crowded café, which was hardly guaranteed to aid the digestion nor calm the nerves, Lacey stopped by the receptionist. One look at Jane's flustered and anxious expression told her that office gossip was not on the girl's mind.

"That Mr. Whitfield is calling again, Lacey. And he's very upset," Jane burst out. "I told him to call back at one-thirty. I thought Mr. Bowman would be back in his office by then, but he just called to say he was tied up at another job site. Mr. Whitfield is going to be furious when he finds out Mr. Bowman isn't here."

Lacey's first impulse was to say "Tough!" But she had felt the steel edge of Mr. Whitfield's tongue before and knew why Jane dreaded his call. Using a smile to hide her gritted teeth, she said, "Put the call from Mr. Whitfield through to me. I'll explain."

She was barely seated behind her desk, her bag stowed in one of the lower drawers, when the interoffice line buzzed. It was Jane, relaying the message that Mr. Whitfield was holding on line two. Lacey murmured a wry thanks at the message.

"Don't lose your temper," she cautioned herself with a personal pep talk. "Stay calm and pleasant regardless of what he says. Don't do anything that would make matters worse for Mike."

The advice was excellent, she knew, but just before she took the call she stuck her tongue out at the blinking light. It was a true expression of her feelings at the moment, combined with relief that tomorrow she would be away from Mr. Whitfield and the office for two glorious weeks.

"Mr. Bowman's office." When she spoke there was enough honey in her voice to fill a hive.

"Put me through to Bowman." Impatience crackled in the male voice.

"I'm sorry, but Mr. Bowman isn't in. I don't expect him until later this afternoon. May I help you?" Lacey kept the saccharine quality in her words and waited for the explosion. It came.

"I was told—" he began with cold anger.

"Yes, I know what you were told, Mr. Whitfield," she interrupted sweetly. "He was expected back at one-thirty, but he was unavoidably detained at one of the job sites."

"So you're claiming that he's not there?" came the taunt.

"I am not claiming it. I am stating it." It was a delight to hear the smiling confidence in her own voice.

"I don't know at which job site Bowman is, but I can assure you, Miss—"

"—Andrews," Lacey supplied.

"—Miss Andrews, that it isn't mine. Yesterday Bowman promised me a full complement of trades. I've been to the job site, Miss Andrews—" his rich voice was ominously low and freezing in its anger "—and a skeleton could rattle through the building and not find anyone to scare. You tell Bowman when he gets back to his office that I expect to hear from him—immediately!"

If, as Jane had indicated, there were problems on one

of the other job sites, Mike would not be in any mood to contact Mr. Whitfield when he returned. Taking a deep breath, Lacey plunged into her mission of mercy. It was the least she could do after Mike had given her Saturday morning off.

"I'm familiar with your project, Mr. Whitfield," she volunteered, "and the circumstances that have interfered with its completion. Perhaps I could explain."

"You?" The taunt was not so much skepticism as it was mocking contempt.

Lacey bristled, but steadfastly refused to take the bait of replying in kind. "Yes, Mr. Whitfield, me. I'm aware of what's happening on the various projects, including yours."

"Which is precisely nothing."

"For a very good reason," Lacey insisted, her composure cracking for an instant.

"All right." He accepted her offer to explain with a decided challenge. "Tell me why there aren't any painters on the job?"

"The painters aren't there because the bulk of the work left for them is in the various washrooms, work that they can't do until the tile setters are finished. The tile setters aren't there because the plumber isn't finished. You see, Mr. Whitfield, it's a vicious circle."

"Why aren't the plumbers on the job?" he demanded diffidently. "The story you've just told me isn't new. Miss Andrews. I've heard it all from Bowman, along with a promise that the plumbers would be out there today without fail."

"At the time that Mr. Bowman told you that, he fully believed it would happen. The problem is that the shipment of bathroom fixtures hasn't arrived. Yesterday the plumber misinformed him that it had come in. Late this morning, Mi—Mr. Bowman found out differently. I know he regrets the delay as much as you do," Lacey added with honey-coated politeness.

But Whitfield completely ignored the last comment. "Where is the shipment of fixtures?"

"I don't know, sir. I do know they were shipped several weeks ago from the manufacturer, but they haven't arrived."

"In other words, they're lost en route and you're saying, 'Too bad,' " he jeered.

"Of course not," Lacey protested.

"Then what freight company were they shipped by?"

"I . . . I don't know."

"What about the manifest numbers, points of origin? Do you know any of that, Miss Andrews?" Whitfield continued his biting questions.

"No, I don't." She was becoming flustered, color warming her cheeks.

"Do you know if anyone has put a tracer on the shipment?"

"No, I don't know if it's been done," she admitted stiffly.

"Has Bowman or the plumbing contractor looked into alternate suppliers for the fixtures, or are they intending to wait for the day when they show up?" he snapped.

"I'm sure they don't intend to—"

"I damned well hope not!"

"Really, Mr. Whitfield." Her lips were compressed in a tight line. "I—"

"Really, Miss Andrews," he interrupted caustically, "it seems to me if human skill and persistence can put a man on the moon, then it should also be possible to find a lost shipment of toilets, don't you think?"

"Yes, of course—"

"Then may I suggest that since you are supposed to be a secretary, you should use your time to see what can be done about finding the shipment!" And the line went dead.

Lacey sputtered uselessly into the mouthpiece before slamming the receiver on its cradle. His clear-thinking logic made her feel like a bumbling idiot.

A tracer should have been put out on the shipment several days ago, but it galled that Whitfield had been the one to point out the oversight. Picking up the telephone again, Lacey made the first step to rectify the mistake.

CHAPTER TWO

IT WAS CRAZY, Lacey acknowledged to herself as she stretched lazily like a cat. Here it was a mild summer night and she had all the windows open and a fire burning in the fireplace. But it seemed to somehow fit her mood, with the breeze off the ocean carrying a tangy salt scent; the gentle sound of the breakers rushing in to the beach; and the crackling of flames dancing to the soft music on the stereo.

After the hectic last day at the office, with the irritating phone call from that Whitfield man, and the long drive through evening traffic to Margo's house, Lacey had virtually collapsed on Friday night, sleeping until nearly noon this morning. An afternoon swim had been the only exertion she had allowed herself, outside of cooking a high-calorie Italian dinner all for herself.

Now, with the moonlight silvering the ocean and the yellow flames lighting the blackened hearth, Lacey's sole desire was to curl up on the sofa and read. Kicking off her gold mules, she carried out her wish.

The filmy baby-doll pajamas were decidedly brief, she realized as she tucked her legs beneath her, but she shrugged unconcernedly. There weren't any neighbors close by and a peeping Tom would have to be a giant to see in the second-story windows. Here in the flat country of Virginia's Tidewater basin along the coast, there wasn't such a thing as a hill or a mountain.

The blue-bottomed lamp beside the sofa cast a small pool of light on the pages of the book in Lacey's hand. Reclining against the fluffy pillows, she found her place and began reading. Soon her head began nodding lethargically until finally the book slipped from her fingers and she dozed.

An hour later something wakened her. Tiredly she glanced around, deciding it had been a log cracking in the fireplace. Closing the book, she set it on the chrome and white stand beside the lamp and switched off the light.

As sleepy as she was, she knew she should go to bed, but it was so pleasant and comfortable in front of the fire. Snuggling deeper into the pillows, she gazed at the yellow flames licking the nearly disintegrated wood in the fireplace.

From the bottom of the entrance stairs she heard the rattle of the doorknob, and the remnants of sleep fled as every nerve screamed in alertness. Some burglar was breaking in! And she was there all alone with no neighbors near enough to hear her cries.

Her bare feet didn't make a sound on the patterned rug as she darted to the telephone beside the other sofa. But the line was dead when she picked up the receiver. Panic raced through her veins.

It was too late to run. The front door had already been opened and there was the quiet even tread of footsteps on the stairs. Instinct sent Lacey racing madly to the fireplace. There was a brief clang of metal against metal as she grabbed the poker from its rack.

The footsteps on the stairs paused for an instant and

she froze a foot or two in front of the fireplace. Both of her shaking hands were clutching the poker, holding it like a baseball bat in front of her.

The steps resumed their climb. With only the flickering, dying flames of the fire to provide light in the darkened house, the stairwell was encased in shadows. Yet from these shadows emerged a darker figure, halting immobile at the head of the steps.

Breathing became painful for Lacey. She swallowed, trying to ease the paralysis in her throat.

The figure moved nearer, into the half light cast by the fire. Dark trousers gave way to a lighter-colored top, a knit of some sort, Lacey guessed unconsciously, judging by the way it outlined the breadth of his chest and shoulders. The man's face was all angles and planes, the firelight casting more shadows than it revealed. Yet the rough contours of his face gave her the impression that he was regarding her with curious—if not amused—surprise.

He took another step nearer and her heart jumped into her throat, blocking any bravado words of challenge. The shadows dissipated and she found herself staring into a pair of blue eyes, dark as indigo.

They began to make a slow, assessing sweep of her, traveling down the long column of her throat, over the jutting curves of her breast, noticing the slimness of her waist and hips, and following the length of bare legs to her bare toes, then reversed the order.

Lacey wasn't aware that the firelight flickering behind her made the filmy pajamas virtually transparent. Her only sensation was the way his eyes seemed to burn through her, increasing her feelings of danger.

225

When the unnerving pair of blue eyes leisurely made their return to her face, they skimmed over the fine bones and the sophisticated short cut of her silky brown hair. Lacey trembled when his gaze finally ensnared hers, her knuckles whitening as she gripped the poker tighter.

"Bob told me I would find everything I want here, but I didn't realize he meant it literally," the intruder mused, his tone riddled with suggestion.

Lacey brandished the poker. "Get out of here!" Her voice was a croaking whisper, making a mockery out of her attempt to threaten him.

She heard his throaty chuckle and wanted to run, but her legs were trembling. She had never been so terrified in her life as she was at that moment. There were so many things that could happen to her and she was trying desperately not to visualize any of them.

"You'd better get out of here," she warned again, this time with a steadier voice, "or I'll. . . I'll call the police."

She glanced at the telephone, inching closer toward it. She knew it was dead, but she was taking the chance that he had nothing to do with it.

"Sorry—" there was laughter in his voice, rich and low "—but the telephone has been temporarily disconnected."

As she breathed in quickly in despair, a tiny sob of panic made itself heard. She saw the male contour of his mouth curve into a smile that was oddly gentle, if mockingly indulgent.

"Why don't you tell me who you are and what you're doing here?" he suggested.

His question struck her as being so absurd that she was speechless. It became obvious that her presence

226

wasn't going to intimidate him into leaving. She would have to think of something else.

"I'm not here alone, you know," lied Lacey. "My husband has gone to the store and he'll be back any minute. You'd better leave before he comes."

"Is he now?" The intruder merely smiled. "That's good. Maybe when he gets here, you'll put down that poker and start explaining a few things."

He took another step forward and Lacey raised the poker to strike. Her heart was hammering against her ribs, her stomach churning with fear.

"Don't come any closer," she threatened shakily, "or I'll bash your head in!"

He stopped, the lazy smile still curving his mouth. His stance was indolent, but Lacey wasn't deceived. There wasn't any spare flesh on his muscular frame and a man that physically fit could react in a split second, like a predatory animal.

"I believe you would try," he acknowledged, but in his acknowledgment he was implying that she would be no match for him even with the poker.

Behind Lacey a log in the fireplace popped loudly. The explosive sound startled her to the point that, for a scant second, she thought she was being attacked from the rear.

Before she could assimilate that the sound had been caused by the innocuous popping of a burning log, the steel teeth of a trap had closed around her right wrist, the hand with the major responsibility of holding the poker.

A strangled "No!" was torn from her throat as the weapon was ripped from her grasp.

227

Adrenalin surged through her system. Where once her limbs had been shaky and weak with fright, they now throbbed with new strength. She struck out at her attacker, arms and legs flailing at anything solid. And there was a great deal that was solid.

At first he was satisfied to merely hold her arm and ward off the bulk of her blows, but as her accuracy improved, he changed his tactics. Lacey felt herself being bodily twisted onto the sofa. Primitive alarm raced through her frantic heartbeats when she felt the force of his weight following to press her against the cushions.

With panicked breaths, she strained to rid herself of the crushing weight of his chest—to no avail. His sheer maleness was awakening all sorts of danger signals and she reacted all the more wildly. The bruising fingers pinning her shoulders to the sofa and thwarting the ineffectual hammering of her fists easily kept her his captive.

As she made a superhuman attempt to twist away, she felt the delicate strap of her pajama top tearing beneath his fingers. It was an inadvertent happening, but the touch of his hand against her now bare skin made her blood run cold with terror.

His body heat had already burned its male imprint on her. She heard him curse softly when she muffled a sob of fear by sinking her teeth into her lip. She detected a trace of liquor—Scotch—in the warm breath that fanned her cheek.

"Will you stop struggling?" he demanded roughly. "I don't want to hurt you."

His assertion flashed through her brain. Immediately Lacey recalled some professional advice she had either read or heard that suggested a woman should not do anything to incite an attacker into further violence.

Gradually she stopped fighting his hold, although her muscles remained tense, waiting for his next move and the slimmest chance of escape. Her breathing was labored and deep.

"That's better," he said in approval, and shifted to one side, easing the weight from on top of her while retaining a firm hold, as if knowing she would run at the first opportunity.

"Let me go!" Lacey flashed in a hoarse voice. She knew he wouldn't, but needed to make the demand so he would realize she wasn't totally submissive.

"Not yet."

In the dim light she caught the brief glimmer of white teeth and knew he was smiling—laughing at her. It stung that she was so helpless in the face of his superior strength.

He seemed to move toward her and she cringed into the cushions. But his arm reached above her head to switch on the lamp beside the sofa.

Lacey blinked warily in the blinding light, calming under the inspection by the dark blue eyes. She couldn't hold his gaze for long. It was too strangely disturbing, oddly making her feel guilty, and the sensation rattled her.

"Now for some explanations," he stated, eyeing her steadily. "What are you doing in this house?"

"I'm...I'm living here." Lacey frowned in confusion.

Doubt flickered sardonically in his narrowed gaze. "You own the house?" he queried.

"Well, no, not exactly." She wondered why his question made her feel so uncomfortable. She had a perfectly legitimate right to be in the house.

Her left hand was free and she raised it to brush a glistening brown strand of hair from the corner of her eye. His narrowed gaze followed the movement, as if anticipating that she might be intending to strike out at him again.

"Not exactly?" He repeated her phrase. In the blink of an eye, her left hand was caught by his. "And what about your husband? You said he'd be here any minute. Yet your ring finger is bare and there's no sign that you've ever worn a ring on that finger."

Lacey had been caught in her lie and she felt as guilty as she had when she was a child. "It becomes obvious that you weren't expecting your husband, despite your provocative garb."

His gaze flicked to the filmy yellow pajamas more or less covering her breasts, the torn strap resting in her cleavage. Lacey was hotly reminded of the little clothing she had on—and the firm outline of his male length beside her on the narrow sofa.

"I don't think," he continued, "you're expecting anyone."

"You can't be sure of that," she retorted.

"Can't I?" he countered smoothly. "Women invariably cake themselves with makeup and dab perfume in erotic places when they plan to entertain their lovers. Your face is scrubbed clean and—" he turned her left hand and lifted the inside of her wrist closer to his face, catching the clean fragrance of soap instead of expensive perfume "—you aren't wearing Chanel No. 5."

"So what!" Lacey jerked her hand away. "None of

this is any of your business and I don't have to explain to you. You're the one who broke into the house and accosted me. You...." She stopped short, realizing she shouldn't have reminded him of his reason for being there nor that she could easily identify him to the police.

The metallic glitter in his eyes reinforced the thought. "I broke into the house?" He repeated her words with a steely coldness that rang a familiar note in her memory, but Lacey was too caught up in the present to dwell on it. "You have an uncanny knack for telling tales."

"Telling tales...?" she began indignantly.

"Yes, tales." His hand moved. In the next instant he was holding a key in front of her face. "I used a key to get into the house. You are the one who broke in."

Lacey stared at it open-mouthed. "That's impossible!" she exclaimed finally. "Just because you say that's a key to the door, that doesn't mean it is."

"Believe me, it is." He smiled lazily, folding his fingers around the key and placing it back in his pocket. "So it's time for you to cut the innocent act."

"Act?"

He ignored her look of outrage. "You have two choices. Either get dressed and get out—I presume you do have some other clothes—or if you're desperately in need of a place to sleep tonight, I can recommend my bed." His finger traced the hollow of her collarbone, sending fiery tingles over her skin. "The last couple of nights I've found it to be quite comfortable, if slightly empty."

"The last couple of nights!" Lacey burst out angrily.

"I think this house has developed an echo," he chuckled.

"You accuse me of telling tales! You have to be the

231

absolute tops," she sputtered. "You're nothing but a liar! Trying to con me into thinking you have any right to be in this house. Well, you just got caught in your own snare. I'll have you know that I've been sleeping in this house for the last two nights, as well, and I certainly haven't seen you."

"You don't give up, do you?" he declared with an exasperated sigh, and swung his feet to the floor to stand up.

"No, I don't," Lacey retorted, her brown eyes snapping. "And since you've so magnanimously given me the choice of staying here with you or going, I'll leave!"

"Good." His mouth had thinned into a grim line. "And pass on the word to any of your friends who were thinking this house might be vacant and available for a few nights' free lodging that it isn't."

Lacey was on her feet, halfway across the living room headed toward her bedroom, when he finished his comment. She stopped, glaring at him over her shoulder.

"I'll pass the word along," she promised impulsively. "As soon as I'm dressed, I'm going to get into my car and drive straight to the police." Turning away, she muttered aloud, "Margo was right to worry about leaving this place empty while they were away."

Long strides cleaved the distance between them. The soft flesh of her arm was grabbed to spin her around. She clutched at the drooping side of her pajama top, feeling the inherent intimidation of his looming height. But she faced him boldly.

"What did you say just now?" he demanded.

"I said I was going straight to the police," she returned coolly.

232

"Not that." He frowned impatiently, not relaxing his biting hold of her arm. "The last part that you muttered under your breath."

"About Margo?" Lacey questioned with surprise.

His gaze sharpened. "Who's she?"

"The owner of the house, of course. Didn't you know that?" she asked sarcastically.

"I knew it," he answered, nodding. "I'm just wondering how you found out. I suppose you've been snooping around the house this evening."

Lacey counted to ten swiftly. "Margo Richards happens to be my cousin."

"Really?" he said with jeering skepticism.

"Yes, really." She forced a smile.

"Then where is your cousin now?"

"She and her husband flew to Florida to visit his family before leaving on a Caribbean cruise. That's why I'm here, so the house won't be standing vacant while they're gone," Lacey said with all of the righteousness of the wronged. "You're the trespasser, not I."

"And Margo asked you to stay here?" he repeated, drawing his head back to study her as he let go of her arm.

"Yes."

"Her husband Bob asked me to stay," he told her.

"What?" Lacey was taken aback for a minute by his statement, then she shrugged it away. "You don't honestly expect me to believe that."

"Believe it or not, it's the truth." He reached into the pocket of his khaki-colored top and took out a pack of cigarettes, calmly lighting one while Lacey stared at him with disbelief. "I don't know your cousin Margo very

233

well—" he blew a thin trail of smoke into the air "—but Bob's family and mine have been friends for years."

"Can you prove that?" she challenged. "Bob should be with his parents now. Why don't you call him?"

"I've already explained that the telephone is dead. They had their service interrupted while they're on vacation. That's the main reason I agreed to stay here—to get away from the telephone."

"Then you can't prove you know Bob," Lacey concluded.

He studied the glowing tip of his cigarette. "Do you know where they went on their honeymoon?"

"Yes," Lacey admitted, but she wasn't about to be trapped. "Do you?"

"To Hawaii. The first day there Bob stayed out in the sun too long and spent the next two days of their honeymoon in the hospital with sunstroke."

"He did ask you to stay in the house!" she exclaimed in a breathy voice.

"That's what I've been telling you."

"And you claim you've been staying here since Thursday night?" Lacey frowned.

"Not claim. I have been staying here—in the guest bedroom," he replied.

"But so have I." She ran her fingers through the thickness of her short hair. "Oh." Pieces of the puzzle started to fall into place. "Oh!" They began fitting together rapidly.

"Oh, my gosh," she whispered, and turned the full force of her brown gaze on him. "Did Bob give you the key to the front door in person?"

"No, he left it for me."

234

"Where? Exactly where did he say it would be?" Lacey persisted.

"He said it would be under the mat, but I—"

"You found it in the flowerpot, right?" She finished the sentence for him.

"Yes." It was his turn to frown. "How did you know?"

"Because that's where Margo said she would leave me the key, only I tripped over the mat and saw the key underneath it, so I didn't bother to look in the flowerpot," she explained.

There were other things she remembered, too, that backed up his claim that he had been in the house since Thursday. "It must have been your car I heard leaving on Friday morning," she murmured aloud.

"I left around six-thirty, quarter to seven," he admitted.

"And it was your orange juice glass I washed," she went on.

"I was late." She could see by the absent look in his eyes that he was recalling the events of that Friday morning, too. "I had orange juice and didn't bother with coffee until I reached my office. But I didn't see you here."

"I was out on the balcony having my morning coffee. It's all so incredible!" Lacey declared, moving blindly back to one of the sofas and sinking on to its cushions. "I went to bed early both nights and slept like a log."

"It was nearly midnight Thursday and Friday before I came in," he added.

"And when you came in tonight I thought you were a burglar." She laughed briefly.

"And I thought you were some college girl sleeping in the first empty house you found," he chuckled in return.

"What a mix-up!" Lacey shook her head. "I wonder if Bob and Margo have discovered yet that they each asked somebody to stay in the house."

"I doubt it." He walked to the fireplace, flicking the ash of his cigarette into the smoldering remains of the fire.

"I guess it doesn't matter," she sighed, smiling at the humor she could now see in the situation. "They're in Florida anyway. There isn't much they can do to put it right now. It's up to us to straighten it out."

"It's too late to do anything about it tonight." Picking up the poker, he put it back in its stand. "Tomorrow is plenty of time for you to pack."

"Me?" Lacey squeaked in astonishment.

"Naturally you." He glanced over his shoulder, seemingly surprised that Lacey didn't agree.

"Why 'naturally me?' " she demanded.

"If I'd been a burglar tonight, exactly what could you have done?" he reasoned. "There isn't a neighbor close enough to hear you scream."

"I don't care," Lacey insisted stubbornly. "I'm on vacation. This is a perfect spot and I'm not leaving."

"If it's a vacation on the beach you want, go and check into a hotel." He regarded her with infuriating calm, his roughly hewn features set in completely unrelenting lines.

"Presuming, of course, that I was able to get a reservation at this late date, I couldn't afford two weeks in a hotel," she retorted. "I'm staying here. You go."

236

"I'm not," he answered decisively. "Thanks to some incompetent. . . ." He cut off that sentence abruptly and started another. "Business demands are not going to permit me the luxury of a vacation. The most I can hope for is to get away for a few hours now and then where I can't be reached by telephone. This place is ideal."

The corner of his mouth then lifted in a wry smile. "I don't even know your name."

"Andrews. Lacey Andrews."

A wicked glint of laughter sparkled in his eyes. "You are the redoubtable Miss Andrews?"

"I beg your pardon?" She tipped her head to one side, staring at him in total confusion. Why had he put it that way?

"Where do you live?" he asked unexpectedly.

"I have a small apartment on the outskirts of Newport News. Why?" Except for that glittering light of amusement dancing in his blue eyes, his expression was impassive and enigmatic.

"Where do you work?"

What does that have to do with anything? Lacey thought crossly, but answered in the hope that he would eventually satisfy her curiosity.

"I'm a secretary to a construction engineer in Newport News."

The wicked glint became all the more pronounced. " 'I am not claiming Mr. Bowman is out. I am stating it,' " he mimicked unexpectedly.

237

CHAPTER THREE

LACEY'S MOUTH opened and closed. "You...you aren't Mr. Whitfield, are you?" she accused with breathless incredulity.

"Cole Whitfield." He identified himself with a mocking nod of his head. "At last we meet face to face instead of via a telephone."

Stunned, Lacey stared at the tall, broad-shouldered man standing in front of the fireplace. Strong, carved features carried the stamp of a man accustomed to having authority over others. Lacey recognized that now.

His hair was brown, darker than her own, an umber shade that bordered on black. Yet there was a decided virility about him, an aura of sheer maleness that Lacey would simply never have associated with Mr. Whitfield.

Over the telephone he had been as abrasive as rough-finished steel coated with a winter morning frost. Her mind's image of Mr. Whitfield did not resemble this vital, compelling man at all. Lacey was still gaping when his firmly molded mouth moved to speak.

"Don't I come up to your expectations?" he asked mockingly.

She found her voice long enough to croak, "Hardly."

"What did you think I would be? An ogre with three heads?" Cole Whitfield inquired, his voice husky with contained amusement. "I left the other two heads at the office."

"You are the rudest, most caustic man...." Lacey began, quite evenly, to describe the man she had known as Cole Whitfield.

"If you had as much money, mine and investors', tied up in that building as I do and had suffered the delays that I have, you'd be snapping at everyone, too," he interrupted without a trace of apology for his behavior.

"And that's your excuse?" she declared indignantly.

"No, it doesn't excuse my attitude, Lacey." Cole Whitfield used her Christian name with ease. "But it does explain why I'm in such desperate need for some peace and quiet before it becomes impossible for me to live with myself. By the way—" his deeply blue eyes were laughing again "—did you ever find those toilets?"

"I know quite a few places where they're not, but there's a tracer out on the shipment." A smile tugged at the corners of her mouth, but she refused to let it show. She hadn't completely forgiven him for his rudeness. "There should be a more definite word by Monday afternoon."

"But you're on vacation, so you won't be there." He tossed his cigarette into the fireplace, momentarily releasing Lacey from his vaguely disturbing gaze. "Which brings us back to our present impasse."

"Who stays and who goes." Her chin jutted forward to an angle of battle.

Cole Whitfield saw it and rested an elbow on the mantelpiece, an indolent gesture that seemed to indicate his own entrenchment.

"Since we're both prepared to be stubborn, I think the solution is for both of us to stay." Lacey arched an eyebrow, more in surprise than rejection of his proposal. "After all, we've already spent two nights together under the same roof," he reminded her.

There was one point she wanted clarified before she considered his suggestion seriously. "Are you rephrasing your invitation to share your empty bed?" she questioned frankly.

"You are alluding to my comment earlier, aren't you?" He smiled. "At the time, you struck me as being a slightly naive and frightened college girl, and propositioning you seemed the quickest way of making you take flight." There was a brief, negative shake of his head. "I'm not interested in sex. I'm here for the peace and quiet. Although—" his gaze skimmed over her scantily clad figure "—if you make a habit of wandering around in that state of near-undress, I might exercise a woman's prerogative and change my mind," he added with a mocking inflection in his voice.

His allusion to her sex sent an odd tremor quaking through her nerve ends. Hastily she raised the drooping neckline of her pajama top and tucked the torn strap under her arm, but there was nothing she could do about the brevity of her nightclothes or the bare expanse of shapely leg and thigh they revealed.

"Part of it's your fault," she retorted defensively, referring to the torn strap.

"Entirely by accident," he assured her. "Well, what do you say?"

"You just said you wanted peace and quiet. Why are you willing to have me stay here, too?" Lacey wanted to know.

240

"My previous encounters with you may have been brief, but they left me with a lasting impression. If I tried to insist that you leave, I'm certain you would fight to the last breath, and I've had all the fighting and arguing that I want. Besides, I'm tired," he admitted, and Lacey noticed the lines of strain around his mouth. "I would much rather come to an amicable arrangement that would suit both of us. We're civilized adults. You are an adult, aren't you?" he asked sarcastically.

"I'm twenty-four," she declared.

Again he gave her the once-over. "You look older."

"Thanks a lot!" A faintly angered astonishment ran through her voice. She was usually accused of not looking her age instead of the other way around.

"Probably wishful thinking on my part," he sighed tiredly, and looked away. "It's just that you look so damned seductive sitting there like that."

An uncomfortable flush warmed her cheeks. "I'll get a robe," she murmured, and started to scramble off the sofa, tightly clutching the bodice of her pajamas.

Cole Whitfield moved to block her path. "Don't bother."

Immediately his mouth thinned impatiently. "What I mean is—" he started to put his hands on her shoulders, then stiffly drew them back to his side "—if you agree with my solution, there's no reason why we can't turn in for the night. In separate rooms, of course," he joked tightly.

"I...." Lacey hesitated.

At close quarters, his inherent virility suddenly held a powerful attraction. And if, as he had implied, he had felt a similar reaction to her, wouldn't rooming together

241

under a supposedly platonic agreement prove to be volatile and unworkable?

"I know what you're thinking," he said quietly—and strangely Lacey believed that he did. "Things could only get sticky if we let them. I may be ill-tempered at times, but I still have control over my baser instincts. And so, I'm sure, do you."

He was right. A smile flickered over her lips as she found humor in her silly apprehensions. They were both adults. The situation couldn't get out of hand unless they permitted it.

"Does that smile mean yes, roommate?" The corners of his eyes crinkled, although the line of his mouth remained straight.

"Yes," she nodded.

"Fine. Then what do you say we bring this conversation to an end so I can get some sleep?" Cole Whitfield suggested lazily.

"Right." Lacey smiled. "Good night," she said, and moved past him to the hallway leading to her bedroom.

Three-quarters of an hour later she was lying in her bed, dead tired yet unable to fall asleep. She fought to lie still and not toss and turn with her restlessness.

The previous two nights, when she hadn't known Cole Whitfield was sleeping in the next room, she had slept like a baby. But now, knowing he was there, she discovered she wasn't quite as nonchalant about it as she had thought she would be. Good grief, she could even hear the squeak of his bedsprings when he moved.

You're being immature, she scolded herself silently, and forced her eyes to close.

242

IT WAS A LONG TIME before she was able to ignore his presence in the house and drift into sleep. In consequence it was past midmorning before she awakened, vaguely irritable from having slept too late.

Grabbing her cotton housecoat from the foot of the bed, she pulled it on as she hurried toward the bathroom. In the hall she stopped face to face with a bleary-eyed, tousle-haired Cole, also en route to the bathroom.

His dark blue eyes made a disgruntled sweep of her and she felt a moment's relief that she had changed into her long-legged silky pajamas of turquoise blue. He couldn't accuse her of not being substantially covered!

The same couldn't be said for him, she realized as she became rather painfully conscious that below that naked expanse of his tanned chest he was wearing a pair of jockey shorts. She had often seen her two older brothers similarly attired, yet it wasn't quite the same when the man was Cole Whitfield.

There was a sardonic twist of his mouth as he gestured toward the bathroom door. "Ladies first." Then he retreated unself-consciously into the second guest room.

Lacey darted into the bathroom, her cheeks burning like a schoolgirl's. Cold water from the tap was more effective than the silent chiding words she directed at herself. With her face washed, teeth brushed, and light makeup applied, she emerged from the bathroom.

A glance into Cole's room saw him sitting on the edge of the unmade bed, his dark head resting tiredly in his hands.

"I'm all through," Lacey told him, with considerably more poise regarding his state of dress. "It's yours now. I'm going to put some coffee on to perk."

"Good." He sighed deeply, rubbing his hands over his face before rising.

In the kitchen, she filled the coffee pot with water and spooned fresh grounds into the basket. Water was running in the shower when she plugged the electric percolator in. She had plenty of time to dress before Cole was finished in the bathroom, so she poured a glass of orange juice and climbed on to one of the tall stools at the counter to drink it.

As she finished the juice, she heard the water being turned off in the shower. Sighing, she slid from the stool and started to her room.

She was halfway across the living room when the front doorbell rang. Changing her direction to answer it, she shrugged. It was probably someone to see Margo and Bob.

Descending the steps, she paused at the front door to look out through the peephole. A man and a woman stood outside, but Lacey couldn't see enough of them to recognize them as anyone she knew. She opened the door a crack.

"Yes?" She smiled politely at the pair.

They were complete strangers to her. The woman had beautiful long wheat blond hair, and makeup precisely applied to her striking features. Her green eyes registered shock at the sight of Lacey standing on the other side of the door.

Her clothes were casual, white slacks with a vividly red print top. On the blonde they looked chic—the only adjective Lacey could find to describe her impression.

The man, taller with sandy blond hair, seemed first surprised to see Lacey, then amused. He was very good-

244

looking, but she suspected he was probably conceitedly aware of the fact.

She opened her mouth to explain that Bob and Margo were on vacation, but the woman spoke before she had the chance.

"We must have the wrong address, Vic," she declared in an icy tone. She would have turned to leave if the man hadn't taken hold of her elbow to keep her at the door.

Without glancing at the blonde, he directed his curious gaze at Lacey. "We're looking for Cole Whitfield. Is he here?"

Lacey became tense, suddenly aware of all the embarrassing connotations that could be read into her presence in the house alone with Cole all night. But what did it matter? She had done nothing to be ashamed of, so why act like it?

"He's here." She opened the door wide to let the couple in. "Follow me."

She started up the stairs with the unnaturally silent pair behind her. Just for a minute Lacey wished she had dressed instead of having orange juice, but it was too late now.

As they passed the landing, the attractive blonde asked with a somewhat superior air, "Are you the housekeeper?"

To any other question Lacey would have probably answered politely, with an explanation of the circumstances for her being in the house. But that one grated. She half turned on the stairs, a hand on her hip, and gave the woman a deliberately cool and amused look.

"Do I look like a housekeeper to you?"

Without waiting for a reply she started up the stairs again. She could feel the blonde's freezing anger as surely as if a cold north wind were blowing.

Behind her she heard the man murmur very quietly and with considerable mockery, "You were really reaching for straws with that question, Monica."

"Shut up!" was the hissing reply.

In the living room Lacey paused near the sofa. She was about to suggest that the pair take a seat while she went to tell Cole they were here. At that same instant, she heard the bathroom door open.

"Lacey!" There was a savage bite in the way Cole called her name. Her head jerked at the sound, hearing his strides carrying him toward the living room.

"Have you been using my razor?" he demanded angrily, rounding the hall to stop short at the sight of the three people staring at him.

A white terry cloth towel was wrapped around his waist. A smaller hand towel was draped around his neck. His hair was glistening darkly from the shower and shaving lather covered his tanned face, except for one small strip that had been shaved away, revealing a telltale dot of red to indicate he had nicked himself with the blade.

Despite his abrupt halt upon entering the living room, he made no other outward sign that the appearance of his visitors had upset him in any way. His blue gaze was only faintly narrowed as it flicked from the woman to the man to Lacey.

Lifting a corner of the towel around his neck, he pressed it to the nick near his jaw. He seemed to expect a response from Lacey to his initial question.

"If you used the razor that was lying on the shelf above the sink, it was mine," she answered smoothly. "Yours is in the cabinet."

Her reply appeared to snap the thin thread of control the blonde had on her temper. "Cole, I want to know who this woman is and what she's doing here!" Her voice trembled violently.

"And good morning to you, too, Monica. Yes, it is a lovely day." The smile curving Cole's mouth was faintly sarcastic. He removed the towel from around his neck and began wiping away the foamy lather drying on his face.

"I think you'd better excuse me," Lacey inserted, certain she was witnessing only the first eruption from the attractive and obviously volatile blonde.

"Is the coffee done?" Cole asked. "I could use a cup."

"I think so," Lacey admitted.

He had partially cut off her retreat with his request. She had thought he would want an opportunity to explain in private the reason she was there, but evidently he didn't.

"Hello, Vic. How have you been?" Cole directed his calmly conversational remark to the man with the blonde as Lacey walked to the kitchen.

"Not bad, Cole. Not bad," was the reply.

But Lacey could hear the underlying laughter in the man's voice. She had no idea what the relationship was between the blonde and her escort, but it was fairly plain that he found a great deal of humor in the situation.

As she started to pour the coffee, a sobering thought

247

occurred to her. Whoever the woman was, she believed she had a right to an explanation from Cole. And Lacey realized that she had no idea whether Cole was married or not.

Good lord! What if the woman was his wife? She nearly dropped the coffee pot, the color rushing from her face.

"You haven't answered my question, Cole," the blonde whom Cole had addressed as Monica reminded him in an icily enraged tone.

"I didn't think you really expected an answer," he replied in a deadly low voice. "I was certain you had it all worked out for yourself."

The cup clattered rather noisily in its saucer as Lacey carried it into the living room to Cole. Her complexion was unnaturally pale, her color not completely regained from the shocking possibility that had occurred to her.

The three were still standing, Cole and Monica eyeing each other with almost open hostility. Lacey came up to Cole's side, offering him the coffee she had poured. The cup ceased its rattling the instant he took it from her hand to set it on the nearest table.

"Aren't you going to introduce us, Cole?" the sandy-haired Vic prodded, gazing intently at Lacey.

A muscular arm curved lightly and possessively around the back of her waist, and she stiffened in resistance to Cole's touch. Her gaze flashed to his, meeting the bland glitter of his unusually dark blue eyes.

She heard the other woman's savagely indrawn breath, which resembled a cat's hiss, her green eyes glowing with hatred. And she realized that Cole was deliberately goading the woman, further incensing her

248

with his action rather than trying to smooth her ruffled fur.

"You haven't formally met my roommate, have you?" His steel blue gaze swung to the couple, his arm tightening around Lacey's waist when she would have drawn away.

He had referred to her as his roommate last night in a joking sense, but his use of it now was provoking and suggestive. He propelled her stiffly resisting figure a few steps forward.

"Lacey, I would like you to meet Monica Hamilton and her brother Vic Hamilton." He identified them only by name without any explanation as to his relationship to either of them. "This is Lacey Andrews."

Monica merely gave Lacey a green look of hatred, but her brother reached to shake her hand. "It's definitely a pleasure to meet you, Lacey," he murmured.

He retained his hold of her hand. The look he gave her made Lacey feel as if she were wearing a black negligee instead of being so fully covered by long pajamas and her housecoat.

"Back off, Vic," Cole ordered quietly.

Lacey's hand was released as Vic smiled mockingly from her to Cole. "I see, private property—no trespassing, is that it?"

"That's it," Cole agreed with a curt nod.

"Don't you think," Lacey suggested stiffly, "that you should explain to your friends the exact circumstances for my being here, Cole?" As far as she was concerned this farce had continued much too long already.

He glanced at her, seeing her rigid with anger. "I

don't think Monica is interested in learning how you came to be here, Lacey,'' he replied drolly. ''Nor a description of what happened between us last night. She's seen all the evidence with her own eyes and filled in all the sordid details with her imagination.''

''Tell her,'' Lacey insisted.

With a mild shrug of acquiescence, he swung his gaze to Monica. ''Despite the way it looks, this is all perfectly innocent,'' he told her. ''As a matter of fact, Lacey and I slept in separate beds.''

''Before or after?'' Monica snapped.

There was an I-told-you-so glint in his eyes when he glanced back at Lacey, and she acknowledged silently that Monica was beyond listening to any explanation at this time. And Cole was to blame for that.

There was a challenge in the set of his jaw when he again reverted his attention to Monica. ''You haven't mentioned why you're here.''

''We came to invite you to dinner and arrange an impromptu beach party for this afternoon,'' she replied caustically. ''Of course, I was under the impression that you were here alone with nothing to do all day.''

''Obviously you were wrong,'' Cole returned with a complacent smile.

His arm tightened unexpectedly around Lacey's waist, drawing her more fully against his side before she could make a move to stop him.

''Don't!'' she protested in a low angry whisper.

By the time his grip lessened, it was too late. Monica was already turning on her heel, her long blond hair swinging around her shoulders.

''We're going, Vic,'' she snapped.

"I'll see you, Cole," Vic shrugged, but it was Lacey he was looking at before he turned to follow his sister.

"Monica, do you remember what I told you the other day?" Cole's voice halted her at the top of the stairs, her attractive features haughty with pride. "I think you understand now that I meant it when I said, 'Don't call me, I'll call you.'"

Liquid green eyes shimmered briefly and resentfully at Lacey. Then Monica was descending the stairs with a faintly smiling Vic behind her. Neither Lacey nor Cole moved or spoke until they heard the front door shut.

"You shou—" Lacey began reprovingly.

But the deep, rich laughter coming from his throat stunned her into silence. The hand resting lightly on the back of her waist suddenly exerted pressure to sweep her against his chest.

"You're a godsend, Lacey!" he laughed.

In the next second, his mouth was swooping down to claim her lips in a hard, sure kiss that took her breath away. When he lifted his head to study her, her reaction was chaotic.

The firm imprint of his mouth still tingled on her lips, the scent of soap and shaving cream assailing her nose. Her heart was tripping over itself, unable to find its normal beat. Over all that, confusion reigned at his lightning change from sarcastic coldness with Monica to this warm, hearty amusement.

He locked his hands together at the small of her back. Lacey's own fingers were spread across his chest in mute protest, aware of the solidness of his naked flesh.

His wickedly glinting eyes looked deeply into hers,

251

crinkling at the corners while taking note of the confusion darkening her brown eyes.

"I've been trying to get that attractive crow off my back for several months," he explained. "I think the sight of you scared her off for good. For that, you possess my undying gratitude."

"Who is she?" Lacey frowned.

"A couple of years ago I briefly, and unwisely, made her my fiancée. I soon rectified that mistake, but Monica isn't the type to take rejection lightly. In fact, she's been trying to persuade me to change my mind ever since I broke our engagement." His face was disconcertingly near hers, the chiseled male contours shadowed by the overnight beard growth.

"So that's why you deliberately let her believe we'd spent the night together—in the intimate sense," Lacey said, half in accusation and half in conclusion.

"Exactly. She wouldn't have believed me if I'd tried to convince her otherwise," Cole insisted calmly. "Knowing the way her mind works, if there'd been a motion picture camera hidden in the house to film all that happened—or failed to happen—last night, she still would have been certain that I'd somehow messed up the film."

Lacey wriggled free of his unrestraining hold, finding his nearness just a little too disturbing, especially when he was only half-clothed. She moved a few feet away under his watchful yet mellow gaze.

"I am sorry, though," he added. "It wasn't really fair to involve you, not when you're an innocent bystander." A smile tugged at the edge of his mouth, deepening the cleft in his chin. "I hope you don't mind being unjustly branded as a scarlet woman."

"Spending a night with a man in today's society doesn't put a scarlet stain on a girl anymore," Lacey answered, adultly shrugging away the suggestion. "To be honest, I thought for a moment that she was your wife, and I was more worried about being named a correspondent in some divorce suit."

Cole winced mockingly. "Please don't remind me how close I came to having Monica for my wife. A man doesn't like to believe he was ever that much of a fool."

"She's very beautiful," Lacey commented absently, picturing the green-eyed blonde in her mind.

"If ever the saying 'Beauty is as beauty does' is true, it is when it's applied to Monica," Cole stated. Then he asked unexpectedly, "Can you cook?"

It took Lacey a second to follow his rapid change of the subject. "I'm about average—definitely not cordon bleu. Why?"

"I'm hungry and I was hoping I could persuade you to fix breakfast," he grinned.

"I think first I'll get dressed," she replied, adding silently to herself, *before any more visitors show up*.

Cole rubbed the stubble on his chin. "And I still have to shave. You said my razor was in the cabinet?"

Lacey nodded. "I noticed it there this morning."

She was only a step behind him as he started down the hallway. When he stopped at the bathroom door, she started to walk by him to her bedroom, but he laid a hand on her forearm to stop her.

"I want you to know that I didn't mean this to happen this morning," he told her, a serious frown drawing

253

his dark brows together. "When I made the suggestion last night that we both stay here, I had no plan whatsoever to use you to get rid of Monica."

"I believe that," she assured him. "It never occurred to me that you might have."

"I hope not." Cole paused for a second. "If I'd known she was coming over this morning, I would have insisted you leave rather than have you the subject of her vile suspicions."

"It doesn't matter." Lacey didn't want to dwell on Monica's suspicions. "Would you like bacon or sausage with your eggs?" she asked, using his tactic of changing the subject.

"Bacon—crisp," he smiled, aware of what she was doing. "And three poached eggs on a slice of dark toast."

"I was asking your preference, not taking your order," she sighed with mocking exasperation.

His smile deepened for a teasing minute before he walked into the bathroom and closed the door. Lacey stared at the white woodwork, then moved to her own bedroom.

Cole Whitfield. The man in person was vastly different from the ill-tempered voice on the telephone. This Cole Whitfield she could like.

CHAPTER FOUR

THE BACON WAS already fried and draining on a paper towel when Cole wandered into the kitchen-dining area. Lacey lifted the poached eggs onto the dark toast.

"Looks good." He reached across the counter bar to take the plate from her hand.

Lacey hoped the food tasted good, but she didn't say so. "The silverware, salt and pepper are already on the table. Coffee to drink or would you like something else?"

"Coffee is fine." He moved to the table where a place setting and a clean cup were laid. Lacey brought him the plate of bacon, as well as the coffee pot to fill his cup. He glanced around the table, then at her. "Aren't you eating?"

"Just a slice of toast." She walked back to the kitchen area for her coffee cup and the small plate with additional slices of toast on it, one for her and the rest for him.

"Are you watching your figure?" There was something mocking in the sweeping look he gave her as she turned to rejoin him. Lacey hoped it implied that there was nothing wrong with her shape.

"No," she said. "I thought I'd go for a swim, so I didn't want anything heavy in my stomach."

She had expected him to say he would come with her, but he only nodded at her statement. Lacey wondered what he planned to do but decided it was better not to pry. After all, nobody liked a nosy roommate.

The colored bamboo blinds at the dining-room windows were raised, letting in the morning sunlight. Lacey nibbled at her toast and gazed at the ocean view of sparkling waves and brilliant gold beaches.

"How long have you worked for Bowman?" Cole asked with apparent casualness.

"I've worked for the firm for almost five years and for M...Mr. Bowman the past two." Despite her unusual living arrangement with Cole, Lacey decided it was wiser if he wasn't aware Mike was a friend as well as her boss.

"You must have gone to work for the company straight out of school," he commented.

"Straight out of secretarial school," she said, qualifying his answer.

"Did you attend school here?"

"No, in Richmond. That's where I lived—where my family still lives." Lacey dunked the last bite of toast in her coffee.

"What made you decide to come here to work? There must have been plenty of openings in Richmond where you could be with your family and friends." He eyed her curiously.

"That age-old desire to leave home and be totally on my own." She shrugged and cupped a hand under the dripping piece of toast to carry it to her mouth.

It occurred to her that she had the perfect opening to ask him about his family and background. But by the time she was able to swallow the food in her mouth, it was too late to take advantage of it.

"You're a very good cook," Cole stated. "Remind me to recommend you if you ever decide to change your profession to chef."

"Thank you." Lacey was ridiculously pleased by his compliment and tried not to show it.

He pushed his plate to the side and leaned back in his chair. "Since you did the cooking, I guess it's only fair that I wash the dishes."

"I. . . ." She was about to insist that she would clean up, then decided she would fast turn into his maid if she wasn't careful. And that wasn't the way she intended to spend her vacation. "All right," she agreed.

"What? No protest?" Laughter danced in his deep blue eyes.

"No protest. I hate washing dishes." Lacey rose from the table before she succumbed to the old-fashioned notion that doing dishes wasn't man's work. "I'm going for my swim. Have fun."

In her room, Lacey stripped off her slacks and knit top down to the bathing suit beneath. The suit was the promised vacation present to herself. Its slick material gave its blue gray color a metallic sheen and molded itself to her slender figure like a second skin.

Draping a beach towel around her shoulders, she closed the door to her room behind her. Lacey avoided the kitchen, where she could hear water running in the sink, and slipped out through the glass-paneled balcony doors to the steps leading down to the beach.

The water was cool. Lacey had second thoughts about her swim, her skin shivering as she immersed herself in the waves. But after some vigorous strokes, striking a parallel line to the beach, she soon became acclimatized to the temperature of the water and relaxed to do a bit of body-surfing.

Floating buoyantly, Lacey let the wave carry her toward shore. Before she scraped bottom, she righted herself and started to wade back to deeper water. As she made her turn seaward, she saw Cole farther down the beach. In hip boots, he was casting a fishing line into the surf. At least she had her answer as to what he planned to do and why he hadn't mentioned joining her for a swim.

An hour later, she decided she'd had enough of the sun and sea for a while and waded onto the beach. Shaking the sand out of her towel, she dried herself off and glanced toward Cole. He lifted a hand in greeting and she waved back.

"Having any luck?" she called.

He shook his head and shouted back, "None!"

It wasn't a response that encouraged more conversation and Lacey walked back alone to the beach house. A shower washed away the ocean salt and shampoo cleaned her hair. Dressed in fresh clothes, Lacey rinsed out her swimsuit and hung it over a towel rack in the bathroom to dry.

She wandered onto the balcony, leaning a hip against the rail while she idly toweled her short hair damp-dry. After several minutes, she hung the towel over the rail. The afternoon sun could finish drying her hair, she decided, and haphazardly combed the strands into order with her fingers.

She could see, up the beach some distance away, Cole

still engrossed in his fishing, apparently in the same spot as before. She thought back to their extremely brief exchange when she ended her swim.

Of course, Lacey hadn't expected him to suddenly turn into her companion just because they were temporarily staying in the same house. It was just—she sighed inwardly—it would have been nice to sit and chat with him for a while.

But she also remembered his statement that he was there for the peace and quiet. That was why she hadn't forced her company upon him. It had just seemed right and proper that she should respect his wishes.

As she watched him, Lacey saw him pick up his pole and tackle box and start down the long stretch of beach toward the house. She darted into the house to the bathroom, where she quickly ran a comb through her nearly dry hair and added a touch of strawberry gloss to her lips.

Inwardly she was laughing at herself all the while she was doing it, because it was quite laughable to think she might want to impress Cole. She was just stepping onto the balcony again when the doorbell rang.

Her first thought was that it was Monica returning for some nefarious reason, and she glanced toward the beach to see Cole still a considerable distance away. Then, shrugging in resignation that she would have to face the green-eyed lioness alone, she walked unhurriedly into the house and down the stairs to answer the door.

But it was Mike Bowman who was standing outside when she opened the door, and her brown eyes widened in surprise at the sight of him. He gave her a crooked smile.

"It took you long enough to answer the door," he teased good-naturedly. "I was beginning to think either I had the wrong house or you'd gone somewhere."

"Hello, Mike," Lacey murmured, not fully recovered from the shock.

He waited patiently for her to invite him in. When she continued to stare at him, he tilted his head to one side in an inquiring fashion.

"You did invite me over this afternoon, or have you forgotten?" he prompted gently.

An embarrassed pink rouged her cheeks. "I didn't forget," she lied rather than admit it had completely slipped her mind that she had asked him over this afternoon. "I simply wasn't expecting you so soon." Glancing down at her beige checked shorts and the orange midriff top, she tried to pretend it was a concern for her dress that had caused her to look so uncomfortable. "I'm not dressed or anything." She lifted a hand to her shining crown of silky brown hair. "And my hair isn't even all the way dry."

"You look great to me," Mike insisted. "Are you going to invite me in or do you want me to wait in the car until you're ready?" he teased as she continued to block the doorway.

"Do you see how flustered you've made me?" Lacey forced a laugh. She swung the door wider and stepped away to let him in.

Actually, she knew exactly why she was so flustered. In a minute she would have to explain to him about Cole Whitfield's living in the same house with her.

The situation was bizarre enough to her. She wasn't certain how Mike would react to it or exactly how she

260

would go about telling him, considering the biting things she had said about Cole in Mike's company.

As she led the way up the steps, she was still trying to decide whether she should just blurt it out or make a joke out of it or what. One thing was certain—she had to make up her mind pretty soon or Cole would be walking in and the whole thing would be out in the open before she could prepare Mike for the news. The entire situation was becoming more complicated by the minute.

"This is quite a place," Mike declared as they reached the top of the stairs and entered the living room.

"It is beautiful," Lacey agreed absently, and began, "Mike, I—"

"It's custom-built, isn't it?" He surveyed the room, his gaze narrowing as he studied its construction.

"I believe so. I—"

"It shows," he nodded. "I don't see anything that looks at all slipshod. And that fireplace is a masterpiece." He smiled at her. "No wonder you so readily accepted your cousin's request to stay here while she was gone. Oh—" he suddenly remembered the sack he carried "—here're the steaks I promised to bring. I had the butcher cut them special. He promised they'd be so tender you could cut them with a fork. There's also a bottle of wine in here." He handed the sack to Lacey. "You'll probably want to open it so it can warm a bit before we eat."

"Yes, I will." She started toward the kitchen, certain that Mike was following her. "Mike, there's something I have to tell you."

Setting the sack on the counter, she waited for him to

ask what. But when she glanced around, he wasn't anywhere in sight.

"Mike?" She took the bottle of wine from the sack and opened it. Looking around again, she saw the door to the balcony standing open and hurried to it.

"This is some view," he commented, turning as he heard her approach.

"It is spectacular." Lacey rushed on before he could interrupt, "There's something I have to explain to you."

"Look!" He pointed out to sea. "See that ship way out there?"

Lacey glimpsed the silhouette of a large ocean-going vessel on the horizon. She saw it strictly by accident as she scanned the beach and the path to the house for Cole. He was nowhere in sight. She felt as if she were sitting on a time bomb with the seconds ticking away.

"This is impressive," Mike nodded, his gaze sliding to the beach. "You practically have this whole area to yourself."

"Not exactly," Lacey qualified. "I—"

"It's fairly isolated," he reminded her. "Does it bother you to be here alone?"

This was her opening. "Not a bit, because I'm not—"

"Lacey!" Cole's voice sliced off the end of her sentence. She froze as Mike jerked his gaze to the interior of the house. "I rummaged around the garage and found Bob's grill." His voice was coming steadily nearer to the balcony door. "I decided that since you fixed breakfast this morning, it's only fair that I cook dinner."

The time bomb had exploded. Lacey saw the shock

waves reverberating through Mike as Cole stepped onto the balcony carrying the charcoal grill.

Cole stopped, drawing his head back when he saw Mike. "Bowman," he identified him before his questioning blue eyes swung to Lacey.

"I invited him over for dinner." She didn't add that she had forgotten. It was written in the look she gave Cole.

Cole set the grill down. "I know the way this must look to you, Bowman, but, believe me, it's really quite innocent."

"Are you staying here, Whitfield?" Mike frowned, his voice lifting to a pitch of disbelief.

"I was going to tell you," Lacey inserted, trying desperately not to sound guilty.

"I see." He sounded grimly skeptical.

"I don't think you do," Cole joined in. "You see, there was a mix-up. Lacey's cousin asked her to stay in the house and her husband asked me. When Lacey and I discovered what had happened—" he fortunately didn't explain the circumstances of their discovery "—we couldn't decide which of us would leave. Finally we mutually agreed that we would both stay."

"Do you mean—" Mike's frown deepened "—you two are living in this house together?"

"I was trying to find a way to tell you," Lacey repeated, sensing his rising anger, "so that it wouldn't sound as if we'd come to some illicit arrangement."

"We're sharing the house, not the beds," Cole stated bluntly.

Mike turned away, rubbing the back of his neck. "I don't believe this," he muttered beneath his breath.

He glanced bewilderedly at Lacey. "You're actually living with the same man that just last week I heard you wish would take a flying leap into a dry lake?"

Her darting look at Cole saw his mouth twitch with amusement, a mocking glitter in his blue eyes. Even though she hadn't made any secret of her previous opinion of Cole, she wished Mike hadn't repeated her words.

"I think it will be better if the two of you talk this thing out on your own, so I'll make myself scarce." Cole nodded briefly to Lacey, a rueful smile of apology touching the firm line of his mouth.

Lacey nodded her agreement to his suggestion, but offered no words of goodbye. She couldn't very well say "I'll see you later"—not without aggravating the situation.

His departure left an uneasy silence in his wake. Below her, Lacey could hear the opening of the garage door, followed by the sound of Cole's car reversing into the driveway. She glanced at Mike's profile, determined not to apologize for this situation that was so completely innocent.

"I can't believe you've actually agreed to this," Mike declared, slapping his palm on the railing in a mixture of anger and confusion.

"Honestly, Mike," Lacey sighed, "you make it sound as though I've suddenly deserted to the enemy camp! It isn't like that at all."

"I know," he admitted grudgingly. "It was just such a shock, seeing Whitfield here with you, then finding out that the two of you are living together."

Lacey bridled at his continued use of that term to

264

describe their arrangement. "You wouldn't consider it living together if we were both living in the same apartment building or staying in the same hotel. This isn't any different."

"It doesn't matter how you put it, Lacey," Mike retorted, "sharing a house is not the same as living in the same building. Good God, you cooked breakfast for the man. You don't do that for someone who is only living under the same roof."

"That's not the way I see it."

"You're a fool," he muttered beneath his breath.

"Look, we can argue about this all night, but I'm not going to change my mind," Lacey flashed, her chin stubbornly thrust forward.

Mike turned from the rail to confront her. "What do you want me to do, Lacey? Do you want me to leave?" he challenged. "It's apparent that you forgot you invited me today, so if you'd rather forget about dinner, I'll go."

"I don't want to forget about dinner," she insisted, because she didn't want to give Mike the impression that she preferred Cole's company for the evening—a conclusion he would surely reach no matter how she tried to deny it. "I want you to stay for dinner—as long as you agree to drop this subject. After all, you don't have any right to criticize my behavior."

Breathing in deeply, he eyed her for several seconds. "All right," he agreed tautly. "No more discussion about this."

Pretending that something didn't exist didn't make it go away. It was like sweeping dirt under the rug: it couldn't be seen, but it was still there. Subsequently it

265

was one of the most miserable afternoons and evenings Lacey had ever spent. The atmosphere had crackled with Mike's disapproval, stringing Lacey's nerves to a fine tension.

They were both relieved when he left early. The time they had spent together had been uncomfortable rather than like the companionable good times they had previously known. Even after he had left, Lacey remained irritated with Mike for making her feel guilty about a situation that was completely innocent.

She walked the beach to try to rid herself of her inner agitation with no success. The rush of the surf did not soothe her nerves. There was no magic in the play of the moonlight on the ocean swells. The tangy salt breeze didn't change the sour taste in her mouth. Finally Lacey returned to the house, but the vision of the night's dinner haunted her. She chose to stare out the window at the empty beach.

Absently she heard the sound of a car driving into the garage, but it was Cole's footsteps on the stairs that finally broke her brooding stance in front of the windows facing the ocean.

She remembered too late that she had intended to be in bed before Cole returned. She glanced at the watch on her wrist. It was nearly eleven. She turned as Cole paused at the top of the stairs to glance around.

"Bowman's left?" he asked for her confirmation.

"A couple, three hours ago," acknowledged Lacey, unaware of the vaguely dejected note that had crept into her voice.

His gaze became fixed on her, the electric blue of his eyes so intent that she had to turn away, afraid of what he might be seeing. There was an uneasy feeling in the pit of her stomach. A nervous reaction to the night's tension, she told herself.

"It didn't go very well with Bowman, did it?" Cole observed, crossing the room to where Lacey stood.

She blinked at him in surprise, then had to look away again to avoid the disturbing study of his eyes. He was much too observant and astute. As he stood tall beside her, tanned and vital, she also had to admit that he was rather overpoweringly male.

"No, it didn't," she answered truthfully.

"Didn't he believe you?"

"Mike believed that the arrangement was all perfectly innocent all right." Lacey laughed shortly without humor. "He just doesn't approve."

"I suppose you argued and that's why he left so early?"

Lacey shook her head in denial. "We didn't argue."

Maybe it would have been better if they had, but it would have meant an open breach between them. After tonight, she guessed that they would just drift apart—be employer and employee and nothing more. In a way it was sad that it was going to turn out that way.

"I knew you worked for Bowman, but it never occurred to me that you were going with him," Cole mused.

Her sideways glance observed him gazing out to sea, a thoughtful expression on his bluntly carved features. The suggestion of grimness around his mouth made her want to reach out with her fingers and smooth it away. It reminded her too much of the autocratic Mr. Whitfield who had so often infuriated her over the telephone.

"It's nothing serious between Mike and me," she said, correcting his impression that she was going with Mike. "We've dated a few times, that's all. It isn't likely to develop into any more than that, either."

"Because of tonight?" Again the dark blue eyes were studying her profile, alert to any nuance in her expression.

"No, not really." Which was true. "Mike just naturally shies away from any relationship that starts to become serious. I think you can truly say he's a confirmed bachelor." Lacey smiled.

"And that doesn't bother you?" An eyebrow flicked upward in curiosity.

"No. I enjoy working with Mike and he's good company away from the office—no more than that." A breeze stirred the edge of the drawn curtain, briefly ruffling the hair curling near her ear.

Out of the corner of her eye, Lacey saw Cole stifling a yawn with the back of his hand. She felt a twinge of guilt. He had stayed away to give her and Mike some time alone. He had probably intended to have an early night after a quiet, relaxing day.

"You'd better get some sleep," she suggested. "You have to work tomorrow."

"Are you calling it a night?" he questioned, tiredly rubbing his neck.

"Mmm, I don't think so." A smile flitted across her lips. She wasn't sleepy. "I'm not the least bit tired, and since I'm on my vacation, I can sleep as late as I want in the morning. I think I'll go out on the balcony for a while and enjoy the night air."

Cole didn't move as she stepped past him to the glass-paned balcony door. She strolled to the railing, leaning both hands on it as she gazed at the moon-silvered rippling of the ocean's waves.

It was a warm, languid night spiced with the tang of salt air. A firm tread sounded on the board planks of the balcony and she glanced over her shoulder, momentarily surprised to see Cole join her at the railing. She had thought he was turning in for the night.

"What's the matter, Lacey?" he asked quietly.

"What's the matter?" she repeated blankly, and faked a laugh. "Nothing is wrong."

"Isn't it?" persisted Cole.

His dark eyes were as midnight blue as the sky, shimmering with mysterious, indistinguishable flecks of starlight. They seemed fathomless to Lacey, and disconcerting as they remained steadfastly focused on her face.

"I don't know what you mean." She stared straight ahead, fixing her attention on the gleaming path of moonlight on the water.

"Don't you?" His fingers caught her chin and turned her head toward his searching gaze.

"When I walked in tonight, I could tell something was bothering you. At first I thought it was because you and Bowman had argued, but you corrected that impression. So it must be something else that's troubling you, and I'd like to know what it is."

"It has nothing to do with you." Lacey tried to twist away from his fingers, but Cole increased the pressure to keep her facing him.

"I think it has something to do with me," he argued quietly. "Indirectly perhaps, but I'm guessing that it's about our arrangement. Am I right?"

269

Lacey sighed in defeat. She swore he could partially read her mind, and she didn't know whether she liked that or not.

"It's silly," she protested.

"Why don't you tell me about it?" Cole let his hand slide from her chin to rest casually on her shoulder.

"It's just that I'm slowly beginning to realize I'm not quite as liberal and freethinking as I thought I was," Lacey conceded. "I never thought other people's opinions would bother me as long as I believed that what I was doing was right. I'm finding out that I'm a bit more old-fashioned and traditional than I thought."

"Because of Monica's and Vic's reaction to our sharing the house. And Bowman's disapproval, as well," Cole concluded.

"More or less," she nodded, her dark brown hair catching and reflecting the sheen of the moonlight. "I mean, I know it's perfectly innocent," she insisted forcefully.

"So now you're having second thoughts about staying here," Cole finished.

"Oh, no, I'm not." Lacey laughed, a tremulous sound. "I bet you were hoping that's what I would say, then you could have that big fat moon all to yourself." She flicked a glance toward the silver globe hanging suspended above the ocean.

"Strangely enough—" a furrow made a vertical crease between his brows "—I think I would find the house empty if you left."

His statement hovered in the air, electrifying her. She had difficulty trying to breathe and there was an odd fluttering in the pit of her stomach.

The hand on her shoulder began, almost imperceptibly, to exert pressure to draw her closer as his gaze slid to her lips. Caught in his spell, it didn't occur to her to resist, although Cole gave her the opportunity. His boldly defined mouth slowly descended to hers.

With a firmness absent of demand, he explored every curve of her full, soft lips. His hand lay along the side of her neck, his thumb resting against the tiny pulse that was racing madly. The blood tingled through her veins, setting every nerve alert.

He lifted his head a fraction of an inch, the scent of tobacco in the warm breath that caressed her skin. "Strawberry, isn't it?" he murmured huskily.

"What?" Lacey opened her eyes weakly and was immediately overcome by the sensation that she could drown in his indigo eyes.

"Your lipstick. It's strawberry, isn't it?" Cole repeated softly, and tasted her trembling lower lip.

"Yes," she whispered, and unconsciously swayed toward him.

"I always did have a weakness for strawberry." It was an absent comment. Lacey doubted if Cole was aware that he had said it aloud.

Then his mouth opened moistly over hers, devouring its ripeness as his strong fingers curled into the back of her neck, tilting her head backward to more fully receive his burning kiss. His other arm reached for her waist and Lacey pliantly let herself be arched against his hard, muscled length.

With consumate skill, Cole demanded a response and she gave it quite naturally. Her fingers spread over his chest to slide around his neck into the thickness of his

271

dark hair. A melting sensuality seemed to flow through her limbs as his mouth faultlessly continued its task of arousal until her hunger became an exquisite pain.

The light breeze from the ocean cooled her heated skin, but it couldn't abate the molten fire spreading through her veins. His experience far outstripped hers and she gloried in it, finding a heady exultation in the heights of abandoned passion.

The embrace that had begun so slowly ended abruptly with Cole pushing her an arm's length away. Dazed by the unexpected rejection, Lacey looked at him with inviting, luminously brown eyes. She could hear his ragged breathing and quivered at the sound.

A pained yet wry smile crooked his mouth. "You'll have to forgive me for that, Lacey." His voice was low and roughly controlled.

"Yes. . . ." But it was more of a question than it was an answer.

"You're a potent little package and more vulnerable than I realized," he added, exhaling a long breath.

"So are you," she admitted shakily, still confused. "But I don't see why you should apologize for kissing me. I may have said I was old-fashioned, but I'm not a prude."

"I wish you were." Cole smiled ruefully.

"That's an odd thing to say," Lacey murmured. He wasn't making any sense to her.

"Is it?" He let go of her arms and she had to stand without his support. Her knees trembled for an instant before they found the necessary strength.

"I think it is," she insisted.

"Our agreement isn't even twenty-four hours old and

I was on the verge of breaking one of our first ground rules," Cole stated in a mocking tone. "No sex."

Crimson flamed through her cheeks and just as quickly burned itself out, leaving her complexion unnaturally pale as she acknowledged the truth of his observation. She had lost control of herself for a moment.

There was no telling for certain just how far she might have let Cole go before she came to her senses. It was a sobering discovery.

He watched her changing color for a silent minute before he smiled gently. "Good night, Lacey." Turning on his heel, he walked into the house.

"Good night," Lacey echoed him faintly, and doubted if her voice had been strong enough to carry into the house to him.

She pivoted back to the ocean view, shivering at the sudden chill that danced over her arms. The fires inside of her were slowly being brought under control.

She remembered Cole's saying that the situation between them wouldn't get out of hand unless they permitted it. They had both come dangerously close to it. Cole had been the first to realize it, but it was just hitting Lacey now.

CHAPTER FIVE

THE BUZZ of the alarm clock hammered at her eardrums, and with a groan, Lacey rolled onto her side. She must have set the clock last night out of habit.

Her fumbling hand reached out for the knob to switch it off, only to discover the alarm wasn't turned on. Still the buzzing sound continued to drone its wake-up call.

Frowning, Lacey forced her eyes open. It was several seconds before she realized that the sound was coming from Cole's bedroom. It was his alarm clock she was hearing. She grabbed the second pillow and crushed it over her ears, trying to drown out the sound, but it continued with monotonous persistence.

"Oh, why don't you wake up and turn that darn thing off?" she moaned into the pillow. But the buzzing didn't stop. "I'll never get back to sleep!"

Angrily she tossed the pillow away and stumbled out of bed. She walked over to pound on the bedroom wall, remembering too late that the bathroom was between the two guest rooms. Grabbing her housecoat, she shrugged into it as she stalked into the hallway to Cole's door.

She hammered on it with her fist. "Shut that alarm off!" It kept right on buzzing. "Cole!"

There was an answering squeak of the bedsprings, then blissful silence. Sighing, Lacey hurried back into her own room and crawled under the covers, housecoat and all. As she closed her eyes, she heard his door open and the firm padding of his bare feet in the hall.

The bathroom door opened and closed. A few seconds later the shower was turned on full force, the hammering of its spray sounding as loud and as nerve-racking as the alarm clock.

"I want to go to sleep," Lacey moaned in self-pity.

Within a few short minutes, another sound joined that of the rushing water in the shower. "Oh, no," she groaned, "he isn't!" She listened. "He *is*. He's singing in the shower. That does it!"

The bedclothes were thrown aside again. It was absolutely pointless to try to go back to sleep now. She stalked angrily into the kitchen, opening and slamming the refrigerator door to get some orange juice and repeating the procedure when she put it back.

While she sipped at her juice, she readied the percolator to make coffee, perversely hoping that when she filled the pot with cold water, Cole would get scalded with hot water in the shower. After plugging the pot in, she hopped onto the tall stool at the kitchen's counter bar.

A quarter of an hour later, the coffee pot was emitting its last sighing pop when Cole walked in from the living room. A cigarette was dangling from his mouth while his hands were completing the knot of his tie. He saw Lacey sitting at the counter and frowned.

"I thought you were going to sleep late this morning," he said. "What are you doing up?"

275

"It takes gall to ask that question," Lacey declared with an exasperated look.

Cole grimaced with mocking ruefulness. "My alarm clock woke you up, did it?"

"Your alarm clock, followed by the shower and your stunning serenade," she answered caustically, enumerating the causes.

He paused beside the counter to rest his cigarette in the ashtray. There was a roguish glint in his blue eyes. "The strawberry is green and tart this morning, isn't it?"

"You would be, too, if it were the other way around." But her tone was less sharp.

"Is there any juice?"

"In the refrigerator. And there's coffee made, too," Lacey added.

He glanced at her empty juice glass. "Shall I pour you a cup of coffee?" he asked as he walked around the counter.

"Might as well," she sighed. After all, she was already awake and the freshly perked coffee had a decidedly pleasing aroma.

First Cole poured himself a small glass of orange juice from the refrigerator and downed it before taking two cups from the cupboard. He filled them and set them side by side on the counter, then walked around it to join Lacey.

He fingered the knot of his tie and muttered, "It isn't straight, is it?"

"No," Lacey admitted. When he started to try to redo it by touch alone, she said, "Here, let me." Cole didn't argue.

When she was finished, he inspected it with his hand, his eyebrow twisting in surprised approval. "That's very good. Where did you learn that?"

"I have a father and two brothers," she answered. "And they're all thumbs when it comes to tying ties."

"No sisters?" Cole sipped at his coffee, seemingly impervious to its burning temperature.

"None. Your cigarette is in the ashtray," she reminded him as the smoke wafted into her eyes.

He reached over and snubbed it out. "I have two sisters, both married and each with her own brood of little ones." He took another drink of his coffee.

"Neither of my brothers is married yet." Lacey tried her coffee and decided to wait until it had cooled more.

"Your parents must be getting anxious for grandchildren."

"I don't know...." She smiled faintly. "My mother claims she's too young to be a grandmother. She certainly looks too young."

Cole glanced at the gold watch on his wrist and gulped down the rest of his coffee. "I'm late," he declared grimly.

Hesitating beside her stool, he crooked a finger under her chin. "I'm sorry for waking you up this morning."

The devastating smile he gave her was Lacey's undoing. She found she could not summon any anger at the way he had deprived her of a few extra hours' sleep. But she wouldn't go so far as to admit that.

"I suppose I shouldn't get into the habit of sleeping late anyway," she said instead.

Before she could guess his intention, he bent down

277

and kissed her firmly. "You know this could become a habit?" A dancing light twinkled in his eyes.

Lacey wished her heart would stop beating so erratically. "You're forgetting the ground rules," she pointed out tersely.

"Oh?" Cole said it as if he'd forgotten about them, but the gleam in his eyes said differently. "That's right, I had."

The house seemed empty when he left.

IT WAS EIGHT-THIRTY-ONE that evening when Cole's car drove into the garage. Lacey knew exactly because she had been glancing at the clock nearly every five minutes since seven. But she steeled herself to react calmly and casually when he entered the living room. He looked haggard and exhausted, his briefcase in hand.

"Rough day?" Lacey questioned with pretended idleness. She glanced up from the fashion magazine she was supposedly reading.

"More or less," he nodded, and sat down in the other sofa.

"Have you eaten?"

"What?" Cole looked at her blankly before her question registered. "Oh, yes, I stopped on the way."

Lacey thought of the dinner she had kept warming in the oven after having eaten her portion, but said nothing. Cole opened his briefcase and took out a sheaf of legal-looking documents.

It was on the tip of Lacey's tongue to suggest that he should relax instead of doing more work, but she bit it into silence with a firm reminder that it was none of her business if he worked himself to death.

278

For all the notice he paid to her the rest of the evening, she could have been another throw pillow on the sofa. She tried to convince herself that she didn't care, but she knew it wasn't true.

Finally, at half-past ten, she tossed the magazine onto the table and rose. Cole glanced up with a questioning frown.

"It's late. I'm going to turn in," she said stiffly. "Good night."

"Good night," he returned indifferently, and looked back at his papers.

Pressing her lips tightly together, Lacey pivoted sharply. Tears were stinging her eyes and there was a bitter taste in her mouth.

"Oh, by the way," Cole spoke up and she glanced quickly back to him, "the toilets showed up today."

"They did?"

"It seems they've been in the city for the last two weeks—at the wrong warehouse," he replied with thinly disguised impatience. "It's a pity no one bothered to check on them before."

Anger simmered near the surface as Lacey read implied criticism of her in the comment, but Cole's attention was again riveted to his papers. She checked her biting reply, wondering if he even remembered that she worked for Mike Bowman. Holding her head stiffly erect, she walked down the hallway to her bedroom.

THE NEXT TWO DAYS were a repeat of Monday, with Lacey waking at the buzz of Cole's alarm and Cole returning late in the evening to bury himself in paperwork. Except for the early mornings and late evenings,

279

Lacey could have been staying at the house by herself, since she was either alone or left alone.

In the mornings she filled her time swimming in the ocean and strolling on the beach. The afternoons she would relax on the shaded balcony and read. Meals were a haphazard affair. She didn't repeat the mistake of the first night by keeping food warm for Cole. Lacey tried not to admit it, but her days were spent waiting for Cole to return.

On Thursday evening she went to bed as usual some time after ten, leaving Cole in the living room with his papers. She fell asleep almost instantly, but it was a restless, fitful sleep that finally wakened her shortly after midnight.

Her mouth was all woolly and dry. She slid out of bed and padded sleepily to her door. As she opened it, the artificial light glared harshly to momentarily blind her.

Shielding her eyes with her hand, she started to grope for the switch to turn off the hall light that Cole had left burning, but the whisper of papers being shuffled in the living room halted her hand.

She walked into the living room, her bare feet making little sound, her eyes still squinting at the unaccustomed light. Cole was sitting on the sofa where she had left him hours ago, going over his papers and making voluminous notes on a long yellow tablet.

"Haven't you gone to bed yet?" she demanded accusingly in a voice husky with sleep. "It's after midnight."

Cole glanced up sharply, momentarily startled out of his concentrations. One eyebrow twisted into a frown as he looked from Lacey to the gold watch gleaming below the rolled-up cuff of his white sleeve. His mouth thinned briefly before he bent over his papers again.

"I'm almost done," he stated, then asked absently, "What are you doing up?"

"I was thirsty," she retorted, and resumed her path to the kitchen, doubting that he had even heard her answer.

As she passed by the sofa, Cole rubbed the back of his neck and arched his shoulders in a tired stretch. "Damn, but I'm tired," he murmured to no one in particular.

"You could go to bed," she called back to him as she entered the kitchen, walked to the sink, and turned on the cold water tap. Perversely, she didn't feel any sympathy for him. If he was tired, the solution was simple. Since he didn't choose to make it, she wasn't going to waste words feeling sorry for him.

"I have to get this done."

Opening the cupboard door, she took out a glass. "Didn't you ever read *Gone with the Wind*? 'Tomorrow is another day.'"

"I need to have this first thing in the morning," he answered curtly.

"I suppose the world will come to an end if you don't," Lacey taunted.

After filling the glass with water, she started to raise it to her lips and, turning slightly, discovered that Cole had followed her into the kitchen. The tiredly etched corners of his mouth twisted briefly into a smile at her gibe, but he made no reply to it.

"Is there any coffee?" he asked instead.

She glanced at the percolator, noticing the cord unplugged from the socket. "If there is, it's cold."

"We have instant coffee, don't we?" Cole opened the cupboard door nearest him.

"In here." She gestured to the cupboard above her head without offering to get it for him.

Lacey did move to one side to avoid getting banged in the head when he opened it. Sipping at her water, she watched him take the jar down and spoon some dark crystals into a cup.

She became fascinated by his hands, strong and tanned, and the scattering of bronze hair curling on the portion of his arm exposed by the rolled-up sleeve. Her pulse fluttered, faintly disturbed. She took a quick swallow of water in an effort to forget his unsettling nearness.

"Aren't you going to heat some water?" she chided, certain he had overlooked it in his tiredness.

"It would take too much time." He stepped around her to turn on the tap. "The hot water from the tap will be good enough."

He let the water run until steam was rising from the sink, then ran it in his cup to fill it. He leaned a hip against the counter near Lacey as if too tired to support himself. Brushing a hand over his mouth and chin, he reached for a spoon to stir his coffee, but it slipped out of his fingers and clattered to the tiled floor.

As she stooped quickly to retrieve it, Lacey's fingers touched the handle at the same time that Cole took hold of the curve of the spoon.

They straightened together, each holding onto the spoon, an elemental tension coursing through Lacey. There was a velvet quality to the midnight blue of his eyes that did little to slow the sudden acceleration of her pulse.

"That was clumsy of me," he chided himself, and Lacey released her hold on the spoon.

"You're tired." She forced an evenness into her voice. "You should come to bed."

"Is that an invitation?" Despite the husky amusement running through his voice, there was a thread of seriousness that rocketed Lacey's heart into her throat.

"You know what I meant." She swirled the water in her glass and took a quick swallow.

"Mmmm."

She didn't know whether that meant yes or no, and glanced at Cole for a clearer answer. There was an unnerving darkness in the look he was giving her. It roamed over her face, touching the sleek fur-brown cap of her hair, the wing of an eyebrow, the finely chiseled bone of her cheek and the soft curve of her lips.

His wandering gaze didn't stop there, but traveled leisurely down the slender column of her golden-tanned neck to dwell on the rounded curve of her breasts. They seemed to swell under the almost physical caress of his eyes, the rosy peaks thrusting against the silklike material of her pajamas.

The sensations he was arousing inside her were both sensuous and seductive. She was possessed by the dangerous urge to glide into his arms and mold her supple body against his hard, rangy length.

Alarm bells rang a warning inside her head as his gaze began to slide down her stomach, starting a delicious curling sensation in her loins.

"Cole, stop it!" she protested shakily.

His answer was to move in front of Lacey, an arm braced on the counter on either side of her, trapping

283

her. A traitorous weakness caused her knees to tremble. She felt giddily light-headed, a feeling that increased as the rippling muscles of his legs pressed against her thighs.

Bending his head, he sought the curve of her neck, teasing the sensitive skin with his mouth. And the caress carried a promise of something more. Lacey quivered in expectation. He nibbled moistly on her neck, his breath warm against her skin.

"I want you, Lacey," he murmured against her throat.

When he put into words what had only been a nebulous thought in her mind, she wakened to the danger of the moment. Regardless of how strong his attraction was, she wouldn't be any man's plaything—to be used and discarded when his amusement was over. And Cole was capable of that. Hadn't he virtually ignored her for the past four days?

One minute she was pliantly yielding to his touch and the next she was ducking under his arms and stepping quickly away. He turned slowly, almost in surprise, as if he hadn't realized she could slip away, nor that she would want to.

"You were forgetting the ground rules again, Cole," she reminded him, her voice breathless. "Besides, you have your paperwork to finish." She retreated a step under his direct stare. "And your coffee is getting cold, too."

Cole made no move toward her and she turned to hurry to her bedroom, tossing hastily over her shoulder, "Good night."

As she started to close her door, Cole's quiet voice

carried from the living room, taunting softly, "You were forgetting the ground rules, too, Lacey."

There wasn't any reply she could make to that.

YELLOW BEAMS OF SUNLIGHT peeped through the slit of the curtains. Lacey opened an eye, absently studying the dancing particles of dust caught in the sliver of light.

Lifting her head from the pillow, she glanced at the clock and groaned. It was six o'clock. Obviously she had wakened in anticipation of Cole's alarm going off. She covered her head with the pillow and waited for the customary buzz.

Ten minutes later there was still no sound of the alarm clock going off. Not that it mattered, she sighed. She couldn't go back to sleep even if Cole had decided to have a late morning after working so late last night.

Climbing out of bed, she put on her housecoat and walked out the door into the hall. The door to Cole's bedroom stood open, and automatically she glanced inside as she tiptoed by. The bed was made.

"That's a first!" Lacey murmured wryly. Usually she made his bed after he had left in the morning.

Either Cole had risen much earlier or else he hadn't bothered to go to bed at all. He had still been in the living room working when she had finally gone back to sleep. It was possible that when he finished, he had dressed and gone into the office early. Or....

Lacey tiptoed into the living room. There he was, half sitting and half lying on the sofa, fully dressed, with his papers and notes strewn on the cushions around him. He looked so tired that she disliked the thought of waking him. But he also looked very uncomfortable.

285

As quietly as she could, she gathered up the papers scattered around him and set them in neat stacks on the lid of his briefcase. She managed to slip one of the throw pillows beneath his head and was debating whether she could swing his legs onto the cushions without waking him.

He stirred and she became motionless. Sleepy dark blue eyes peered at her through a screen of dark spiky lashes. Cole shifted slightly and grimaced, as if cramped muscles were making their soreness known.

"What time is it?" he mumbled.

"About a quarter past six."

Groaning, he rubbed his forehead. "It can't be. I was only going to rest my eyes for a few minutes."

"From the looks of you, you could do with a few more minutes of 'rest,' " Lacey suggested dryly.

"I can't." He pushed himself into a sitting position, arching his back and watching. "I have a meeting first thing this morning. I have to get into the office."

There was no use arguing; he wouldn't listen to her anyway. "I'll put some coffee on," she said instead.

She did just that while Cole showered and changed. A glass of orange juice was sitting on the counter for him when he entered the kitchen. She assured herself that she had only done it because she felt sorry for him.

"That helped," he declared after downing the juice.

Maybe, Lacey conceded to herself, but the reviving effect of the juice would be short-lived. Even after showering and putting on fresh clothes, there were still lines of strain and weariness cracking the vital mask.

"You really should get more rest, Cole," she said impulsively. "Get some sleep instead of working all night."

"The work has to be done." He shrugged and walked to the sink counter to set down the glass and pour a cup of coffee.

"You should do it at your office and not bring so much home at night," Lacey retorted.

"I get ten times as much done here as I ever did at the office. There aren't any distractions or interruptions." Cole paused, glancing at her. "Or at least, there aren't as many distractions."

Lacey pretended not to understand that comment. "It's no skin off my nose if you work yourself to death," she retorted stepping down from the bar stool.

"Where are you going?" He eyed her curiously.

"To shower and dress." She started into the living room.

"Lacey?" She paused to look at him. "Thanks for waking me up," Cole said, smiling.

Returning his smile, Lacey nodded and quickened her steps to the hall. He was gone by the time she had finished showering.

The previous days of her vacation had seemed to pass swiftly, but today the hours were dragging. It was barely the middle of the afternoon and she felt completely at a loose end. She had lain in the sun for as long as she dared, then sought the shade of the balcony, stretching out on a lounge chair with a book. But it had failed to hold her interest.

Sighing, she slid a piece of paper between the pages to mark her place and set it down. She stood up and walked to the railing, lifting her face to the cooling breeze blowing from the ocean.

She was still wearing her shiny one-piece bathing suit,

287

an unusual blue gray color. Maybe she could change her clothes and drive into Virginia Beach to treat herself to a dinner out.

The ring of the doorbell resounded distantly through the house. She turned in surprise, wondering who would be calling at this hour of a Friday afternoon. All of her close friends were working. Of course, there was always the possibility that it was a salesman.

Any distraction was welcome, so she went to answer the door, hurrying into the house to glide swiftly down the stairs. She peered through the peephole and frowned. It looked like Mike standing outside. She opened the door and confirmed the identification.

"I was hoping you'd be here," he announced with a smile.

"You should be working!" It was almost an accusation.

"I should be," Mike agreed, stepping into the house as Lacey moved aside to admit him. "But it's been one long, hectic week and I told the bosses I was taking off early today. And if they didn't like it, they could shove it."

"It's been as bad as that, has it?" Lacey grinned, knowing that Mike would never have put it that bluntly in his request.

She had been uneasy about meeting Mike again after that disastrous dinner. But within seconds after opening the door, she found that his attitude allowed her to slip back into the comfortable relationship they had previously shared. It made her feel good that the breach between them had been repaired.

"Worse!" he exclaimed with mock exaggeration.

"How far will a cold beer go to making it worthwhile?" she teased.

"It sounds better than a paycheck right now," Mike laughed. "Just lead me to it."

"Follow me," said Lacey, ascending the steps. "I know there's at least a couple of cans in the refrigerator."

A few minutes later, ensconced in a lounge chair on the balcony with a cold beer in his hand, Mike declared with a long sigh of contentment, "Now, this is living. Peace and quiet and your own unobstructed view of the ocean. I kept thinking about this view all week."

"And all the while, I've been thinking you'd driven all the way out here to see me," Lacey sighed mockingly.

"Oh, I did," he assured her, settling deeper into his chair. "I never realized what a gem of a secretary I had until you went on vacation."

"How is Donna doing?"

"She's driving me up the wall—that's how she's doing," Mike grumbled.

"She really is a very competent secretary." Lacey defended her co-worker while offering a wry smile of understanding.

"She is, yes," he agreed. "But she chatters like a magpie all day long, saying the dumbest things. I can't make up my mind if all that naiveté is for real or if it's an act she puts on because she thinks it's cute."

"I'm afraid the bulk of it is genuine."

"Thank God it's only another week before you come back." Mike took a swig of his beer. "More than that and I think I'd hand in my resignation."

"Really?" A mischievous light twinkled in her brown eyes. "I was thinking of giving you a two-week notice and recommending Donna to take my place permanently."

She squealed with laughter as Mike came bounding out of his chair, catching her by the wrist. Gaining a firmer hold, he swept her into his arms and off her feet to hold her over the balcony railing.

"Put me down, Mike!" She was laughing so hard she could hardly talk, her fingers clinging to his arms instinctively rather than out of fear.

"Take back what you said or so help me, I'll drop you!" he threatened, but his dancing hazel eyes indicated that he had not the slightest intention of carrying it out.

CHAPTER SIX

"I TAKE IT BACK! I take it back!" Lacey promised between gasps of breathless laughter.

Mike swung her away from the railing, letting her feet slide to the floor. "Don't ever joke about a thing like that again," he warned with a broad grin.

"I won't, believe me," she declared, leaning a shoulder heavily against his chest as she struggled to catch her breath.

"You'd better—"

"Is this where you go, Bowman, when you tell your office that you're out on a job site?" Cole's biting question wiped the smiles from both their faces.

Lacey turned with a jerk to see him standing in the doorway, the knot of his tie loosened and the top button of his shirt unfastened. He looked as tired and irritable as he had sounded, and coldly angry.

"The office was aware that I was through for the day when I left there an hour ago," Mike replied with commendable calm.

"That isn't what your secretary said," Cole snapped, his eyes glinting with the metallic blue of finely honed steel.

"Donna again!" Mike muttered beneath his breath.

And Lacey guessed that her replacement had decided

it was more politic to tell a client that Mike was working than that he had left early.

"It was an unwise decision on the part of Mike's temporary secretary to tell you that instead of the truth," she stated in Mike's defense.

"So you're playing the dutiful secretary again, rushing in to defend your boss," Cole taunted.

The angle of her chin increased. "I'm merely trying to straighten out your facts!" she retorted.

"Are you?" His mouth twisted cynically.

"And while we are on the subject of working, what are you doing here, Cole? Why aren't you at your office?" Lacey demanded accusingly.

"In case you've forgotten," he snapped, "I was up practically all night working!"

"So you decided to leave early," she concluded, and tipped her head to challenge him. "Can you be sure your secretary is telling that to those who call for you? Or will she make up some other excuse for your absence, the way Mike's secretary did when you called?"

"It sounds very plausible." Cole's voice was riddled with skepticism.

"The truth generally does," Lacey flashed.

His wintry steel eyes raked her from head to toe, taking in the shiny bathing suit that so attractively showed off her curves. "But I can't help wondering how many times this past week Bowman has been here when he was supposedly at a job site." On the last word, Cole pivoted sharply and walked away.

The arrogant set of his wide shoulders was like a red cape to a bull, and Lacey started to charge blindly after him. Mike laid a restraining hand on her arm.

292

"Let it be, Lacey," he suggested, recognizing the warning signs that her temper was ready to let fly.

She jerked her arm away from his hand and stalked into the house after Cole, catching up with him in the living room. In the act of stripping the tie from around his neck, Cole glanced at her coolly.

Lacey unleashed her anger in a flurry of acid words. "It's none of your business how many times Mike has been here this last week, *if* he's been here at all! Furthermore, he's my guest and—"

"Perhaps," Cole interrupted sharply, "if you'd possessed the common courtesy to let me know you were going to entertain tonight, I could have made other arrangements to be elsewhere so the two of you could be alone."

"So now you're accusing me of a lack of courtesy?" Her hands rested on her hips, fury trembling in her voice. "What about yours?"

"Mine? Because I was rude to Bowman, I suppose?" he concluded with a contemptuous twist of his mouth.

"Among other things," Lacey agreed.

He drew his head back to study her arrogantly. "What other things?" he demanded.

"Every single day this week your alarm has woken me up while you slept right through it," she retorted.

Lacey knew she was being goaded into this argument by more than just the things Cole had said against Mike. Some sort of explosion had been building inside her all week. It had needed only a spark to ignite the fuse.

"I've apologized for that," Cole reminded her grimly.

"Apologies don't help me go back to sleep." Sarcasm licked her words.

293

"If you don't like our arrangement, why don't you move out?" he challenged.

"I am not moving out! You leave!" Lacey countered angrily.

"Why? So Bowman can move in? That would be cozy, wouldn't it?"

Lacey sputtered impotently for a second. "His company would certainly be preferable to yours!"

"I bet it would. No ground rules. No separate bedrooms. No separate beds." Cole snapped out the words almost savagely.

"Your mind is as dirty and vile as your words are!" Lacey flashed spitefully. "You should marry Monica. You're two of a kind!"

"I'm leaving," Mike declared from the balcony door. "I didn't come here to start a free-for-all."

Lacey turned with a start. For a few minutes she had forgotten Mike was even there. "Don't go, Mike. Cole was just leaving," she insisted tightly.

"Like hell I am!" he growled. "You can either do your entertaining while I'm in the house or go somewhere else. But I am not leaving."

"Fine." Lacey clipped out the word and glanced at Mike. "Give me a couple of minutes to get dressed and I'll go with you."

He gave her a brief nod of agreement and Lacey walked purposefully to her room. Stripping off her bathing suit, she hurriedly donned her undergarments and an apricot flowered sundress. A taut silence stretched from the living room, its oppressive stillness spreading through all the rooms.

Mike was waiting at the head of the stairs when she

reappeared. Skirting the grim-visaged Cole, she walked to the staircase to join Mike. He shifted uncomfortably as Lacey paused to cast a fiery look at Cole.

"The house is yours for the evening," she told him with a cloying smile. "You can have all the peace and quiet you've been wanting." The sweetness turned to venom as she added, "And I hope it smothers you!"

With a toss of her head, she swept past Mike down the steps to the front door. Outside, the staccato click of her sandal heels on the pavement indicated that her anger had not fully abated. Mike moved forward to walk beside her, lengthening his stride to keep up with her rapid pace.

"Considering the present circumstances, Lacey," he began hesitantly, "don't you think it would be better if you moved back to your apartment for the rest of your vacation?"

"And let that man win?" she flashed. "Not on your life! I wouldn't give him that satisfaction. I can make his life as miserable as he makes mine."

Stopping beside his car, she waited expectantly for him to open the door for her. When he didn't immediately, she glanced at him and noticed the rather pained expression on his face.

"What's wrong, Mike?" she demanded, the crispness of leftover anger still in her voice.

"I don't know how to tell you this," he murmured uncomfortably.

"Tell me what?" Her patience was in short supply.

His gaze ricocheted away from hers. "I have a date tonight," he announced flatly.

"You have a *what*?" Of all the ironies, that had to be

the tops! Lacey nearly chocked on a gurgle of bitter laughter.

"I'm sorry, Lacey," he offered grimly. "I thought I'd stop over for a couple of hours to relax and talk, then get out before Whitfield came."

And she had automatically assumed that he had arrived for the evening. That definitely had to be the height of self-conceit, whether she had been aware of it or not.

She glanced back at the house. She simply could not go back there, not until much later. Cole would never let her hear the end of it if he learned the truth.

"It's all right, Mike," she said finally. "It's just what I deserve."

"What are you going to do?"

"I'm not going back in there and have Cole start gloating, that's for sure," she declared emphatically. "I'll go somewhere. Would you mind waiting a couple of minutes while I get my car out of the garage?"

"Of course I'll wait," Mike promised, smiling that it was the least he could do after letting her down.

Lacey hoped it would look to Cole as if they were going somewhere together but in separate vehicles. As she backed her car out of the garage, she glanced up to the second-story window looking out from the living room and saw Cole gazing out of it.

A surge of anger washed through her and she reversed recklessly out of the driveway without looking for traffic. Immediately she shifted gears, and pressed the accelerator to the floor, the tires peeling rubber as the car shot forward, leaving Mike far behind.

At the major highway intersection, Mike finally

caught up with her. His honking horn made Lacey glance in her rearview mirror to see him motioning her onto the shoulder of the road. Grimly she pulled over. He parked behind her and climbed out of his car to walk to hers.

Mike bent down to peer in her open window. "Who the hell do you think you are? A race driver?"

"Is that why you stopped me? Just to criticize my driving?" Lacey challenged, in no mood for a lecture.

"No...although it's a damned good reason for stopping you." He didn't back down completely from his stand. "It's just that...I feel responsible for what happened back there. Your whole argument with Whitfield started because you were defending me, whether I asked you to or not."

"The argument was inevitable." Her fingers drummed the steering wheel. Lacey was impatient to be on her way, even if she didn't know where she was going.

"I put you in an awkward position. I should have told you when I first arrived that I had a date with someone else tonight." Mike gallantly took the blame for her present dilemma.

"It isn't your fault," Lacey denied. "I was the one who put my foot in my mouth. I didn't need help from anyone to do that."

"What are you going to do tonight?" His look was sympathetic and compassionate.

"I don't know." Her gaze skittered away from his face.

"I don't like the idea of your being alone. I could round up one of my friends and make a foursome," he suggested.

"I'd be rotten company for anyone, but thanks. Besides I wouldn't want to cramp your style.'' She attempted a smile, but it wasn't very successful.

''What are you going to do, Lacey? You can't just drive around all night.''

She hesitated before answering. ''Maybe I'll stop by to see Maryann.''

Her statement seemed to satisfy Mike. ''You do that. And drive carefully, will you, Lacey?''

''I promise.'' As Mike straightened, Lacey shifted her car into gear.

She checked for oncoming vehicles before pulling into the traffic lane, waving to Mike. Obeying the speed limits, she drove sensibly to the apartment complex where Maryann lived. She parked her car in the visitors' lot and walked up the steps to her friend's unit. Lacey rang the doorbell and waited.

The door, still secured by a chain latch, opened a crack. Through the narrow opening, Lacey glimpsed the washed-out brown hair, that peculiar dark blond shade, so distinctively Maryann's.

''Hi. It's me, Lacey,'' she identified herself to her cautious friend.

''Lacey, what are you doing here?'' The door closed a moment, then swung wide to admit her. ''I thought you'd be having your own private little clambake on the beach tonight.''

''My own clambake, huh?'' Lacey's smile was twisted. ''And I came to see if you had a hot dog to share.'' As she walked in, she noticed that her girl friend was wearing a housecoat. Only then did it occur to her that it was Friday night and it was very likely her friend had a date. ''I bet you're going out, aren't you?''

"No, it's just another Friday night for me and my cat to spend together. I was just changing out of the clothes I wore to work when you rang the doorbell. Both of us will be glad to have you for dinner," Maryann insisted as a pumpkin-colored cat sauntered from the kitchen to rub against his mistress's leg. "I don't have any hot dogs, but I do have some hamburger."

"That's fine." Lacey really didn't have any appetite.

Maryann closed the door, locked it and refastened the chain. "You never did say what you're doing here. Did it get too lonely out there in your luxurious beach house?"

"No, it wasn't lonely. Far from it," Lacey declared.

"What do you mean?" Maryann frowned. "I thought you didn't have any close neighbors."

"It's a long story," was the sighing answer.

"I have all night if you do." Her friend shrugged away that excuse.

"It isn't lonely because I'm not staying in the house by myself," announced Lacey.

"You're not staying in the house alone." Maryann repeated the statement to be certain she had understood it. "That means someone is staying with you. Who?"

"Cole Whitfield."

"Who is Cole Whitfield?" Almost immediately a light dawned in her eyes. "Whitfield? You don't mean the sarcastic Mr. Whitfield?"

"That is precisely the Cole Whitfield that I mean."

Maryann's mouth opened in astonishment. For several seconds, she was incapable of getting any words to come out. Finally she managed to ask, "How? What is he doing there?"

"It seems that Cole is an old family friend of Margo's husband. There was a mix-up. Margo asked me to stay at the house and her husband asked Cole."

"But when you found out...."

"It's all totally unbelievable, Maryann. I thought he was a burglar when he first walked into the house. He scared me out of my wits." Lacey went on to explain how she and Cole had come to the agreement to share the house.

"And you actually agreed, after the things you said about him?" Maryann was incredulous.

"In person, he really isn't so bad. What am I saying?" Lacey caught herself angrily. "He's worse. His alarm wakes me up in the morning. He sings in the shower. He works till all hours of the night, then is grouchy as an old bear."

"Lacey—" Maryann gave her a long, considering look "—maybe you should tell me something about this Cole Whitfield. Like, for instance, how old is he and what does he look like?"

"He's in his thirties," she admitted.

"Unmarried," Maryann inserted with certainty.

"Yes, unmarried," she nodded.

"Good-looking?"

"In a rough kind of way. He has nice blue eyes, though."

"And all you are doing is sharing the same house." Her friend eyed her skeptically. "There haven't been any 'romantic' moments between you?"

"I don't know what you mean by romantic. I sleep in my room and he sleeps in his."

"And he hasn't made a single pass at you?" Maryann took one look at Lacey's face and had her answer.

Lacey didn't try to conceal what she felt any longer. "It's all a mess. I'm half in love with him already. Lord knows he doesn't give me much encouragement."

"What happened tonight? Does he have a date with someone else? Is that why you've come here? To show him that he isn't the only pebble on the beach?"

"He doesn't have a date. He came home to have an early night." Lacey was unaware that she had referred to the beach house as home, but that was what it had become to her since she had started sharing it with Cole. "Mike was there. He'd stopped by for a beer. Cole got all hostile because he had called the office and Donna had told him Mike was working at another job site instead of explaining he had left early today. We started arguing and the whole thing became personal."

"You lost your temper and stormed out of the house," Maryann finished for her.

"Cole thinks I'm going out with Mike tonight. And Mike already has a date," Lacey explained.

"When did you find this out?"

"After I had stormed out of the house," she admitted with chagrin. Instantly her chin lifted to a defiant angle. "I couldn't go back then and endure Cole's gloating."

"So you came here."

"I didn't know where else to go." Lacey shrugged and glanced apologetically at the dark blonde girl.

"What are friends for?" Maryann smiled. "Come on. Let's fix a salad, fry some hamburgers and have some wine."

Lacey hesitated for only a second. "I'll fix the salad."

After their meal, they sat around Maryann's small living room, talking and listening to records. A little after eleven, Lacey saw Maryann stifling a yawn.

301

"I'm sorry. I forgot you have to work tomorrow morning, don't you?" Lacey remembered. "I'd better leave so you can get some sleep."

"You don't have to go," Maryann protested, rising to her feet when Lacey did.

"It's late. I think it's safe for me to go back now," she joked weakly.

"Call me and let me know what happens," her friend urged, then clicked her tongue. "I forgot. You don't have a phone out there."

"No, but I'll have lunch with you one day this next week and give you the blow-by-blow details. If there are any," she laughed. "More than likely Cole is in bed and won't have any idea what time I get in. Or care what time it is."

"You can always make a lot of noise and wake him up when you come in," Maryann suggested with a conspiring laugh.

"Cole sleeps through his alarm. I think he'd sleep through an atom-bomb explosion." Lacey started for the door. "Thanks for dinner...and the company."

"It was fun." She reached down to pick up her cat. "Wasn't it, Oscar?" The cat purred and rubbed its head against her chin.

"Good night." Lacey was smiling as she left the apartment.

Once outside in the pleasant coolness of the night air, her expression sobered. She wasn't ready to return to the beach house yet. In her car, Lacey drove aimlessly through the streets. Finally she ended up on the Virginia Beach side of the bay along the ocean front.

Disregarding the lateness of the hour, she parked her

car and strolled along the silent beach. The time she had spent with her friend had been good, but Lacey still felt depressed. Finally the cool breeze drove her back to the car and she headed homeward.

All in all not the best evening I've ever spent, but thanks to Maryann, not the worst, Lacey thought as she drove the car into the garage. She had left her watch on the bedroom dresser and the clock on the car's dash didn't work. She had no idea what time it was. She knew it was late because it had been dark for hours.

Shivering at the coolness of the night air, she hurried through the connecting door from the garage to the house entrance. Wearily she began the tedious climb up the stairs.

Three steps from the top, the back of her neck prickled in warning and she glanced up to see Cole towering above her at the head of the stairs.

His white shirt was completely unbuttoned and pulled free of the waistband of his pants to hang loosely open. There was a forbidding darkness to his gaze, his rugged male features appearing to be permanently cast in bronze.

"Where the hell have you been?" he snarled.

"That's none of your business." Lacey attempted to brush past him, but his fingers clamped themselves vise-like over her wrist to stop her.

"Do you have any idea what time it is?" Cole demanded harshly.

"No, I don't, and I don't see that it matters," she retorted.

"It happens to be nearly four o'clock in the morning," he informed her. "I want to know where you've been."

303

Lacey strained against the steel-hard grip on her wrist. "I don't have to account to you for my whereabouts. Let me go, if you please," she ordered curtly. "I'm tired."

"I'll let you go," Cole promised, "as soon as you tell me where you've been."

"I told you it's none of your business where I've been," she repeated. She was tired and ill-equipped to engage in a slanging match with Cole Whitfield.

"I know you weren't with Bowman," he snapped.

Lacey paled visibly but challenged, "Wasn't I?"

"No, you weren't," There wasn't a trace of uncertainty in his ironclad statement. "Because I went to his place to find you. Bowman told me you'd said you were in no mood for anyone's company and had left."

Silently Lacey thanked Mike for inventing a face-saving answer instead of admitting that he had had a date with some other girl that night. But it still didn't get her out of her present situation.

"And I'm still not in the mood for anyone's company—least of all yours! Now let me go!" She tried twisting her arm to free if from his grip.

But Cole used the movement to curve her arm behind her back and haul her against his chest. "I don't care whether you're in the mood for company or not. You're going to answer my questions," he ordered angrily.

"I am not!" Lacey protested vehemently.

His other hand raked through her hair, his fingers gripping the short strands to force her head back so he could see her face.

"You've been drinking, haven't you?" he accused.

"I stopped at a friend's house and had a couple of

304

glasses of wine," she answered truthfully. "Is that a crime?"

"Considering the way you drove when you left here, it borders on attempted suicide," Cole snapped. "I've called the police half a dozen times, certain you'd had an accident, especially after I discovered you weren't with Bowman."

"I didn't have an accident. I arrived safely." Tears were misting her eyes. "I seem to be more in danger of being hurt by you than in my car." And she meant that in more than one way. "Let go of my arm! You're going to break it if you keep twisting it like that."

"I hope it hurts." He forced her more fully against his rigid length. "After what you put me through to-night, you deserve to be punished."

"What I put you through?" Lacey choked in bitter laughter. "Why, you arrogant, bullheaded—"

Cole gave her no time to finish the insult. His mouth bruised her lips into silence as his arms ruthlessly mold-ed her to his body with an economy of movement. Yet the cruel kiss meant to punish ignited a bewildering response in Lacey. She had meant to struggle, to fight his embrace, but her hands were sliding inside his shirt, seeking the fiery warmth of his naked skin. Her head was whirling, throbbing painfully, confused by her reac-tion.

When Cole lifted his head, she could not open her eyes to look at him, quivering with the response his kiss had evoked. She felt his mouth and chin rubbing against the hair near her forehead.

"For God's sake, Lacey, where were you all this time?" There was a funny throb in his voice, almost like

305

pain, as his mouth moved against her hair while he spoke, roughly caressing. "I've been half out of my mind worrying that something had happened to you."

"Really?" she breathed, almost afraid to believe him.

"Yes, really." He smiled against her cheek and she felt the uneven thud of his heart beneath her hands. "Your friend, the one you had a drink with—" his arms tightened around her, demand creeping back into his voice "—was it a man or a woman?"

"It was Maryann, my girl friend," Lacey admitted, tipping her head to the side as he began nuzzling her ear.

"And I suppose you've been gossiping with her all night while I've been pacing the floor," Cole grumbled with mock anger.

"Not all the time." His hands were roaming over her bare shoulders and Lacey was shamelessly enjoying the sensations they were creating. "I left there some time past eleven."

He lifted his head, frowning, his gaze narrowing. "Where have you been since then?"

"I . . . I went for a walk on the beach."

"Alone?" Cole accused.

"Yes," she nodded, knowing it had been foolish.

"You deserve to be whipped within an inch of your life!" he stated gruffly. "You were actually walking on the beach for more than three hours?" He repeated her statement as if he still couldn't believe she had said it.

"I guess so, if that's how late it is." She couldn't bring herself to worry about the risk she had taken at this late date.

"Oh, Lacey. . . ." He sighed heavily in exasperation

306

and crushed her tightly in his arms. "I knew I shouldn't have let you walk out of that door with Bowman."

"You couldn't have stopped me," she laughed softly. "I was so mad when I left that a brick wall couldn't have stopped me. And that's all your fault."

"My fault?" Cole tucked a finger under her chin, tilting her face up and gazing at it quizzically.

"You started the whole thing," she reminded him. "If you hadn't been so rude to Mike, I would never have lost my temper."

"What was I supposed to think?" An eyebrow twisted arrogantly at her answer. "I call his office and his secretary tells me he's out on a project. But when I get here, I find him carrying you around in his arms."

"You could have given him the benefit of the doubt," she pointed out, feeling the old resentment building again, "instead of jumping to conclusions that were completely wrong and unfair."

"How can you be so sure that my conclusion wasn't right?" Cole argued complacently.

"Because Mike isn't like that." Stiffening her arms against his chest, Lacey arched away from him. "He's honest and intelligent and works as hard as you do. Yours isn't the only project he's in charge of, and the delays on yours have been caused by suppliers and labor unions, things he has no control over."

Cole's mouth thinned grimly. "There you go again, defending him!"

"Well, what am I supposed to do when he isn't around to defend himself?" She twisted completely out of his arms.

When she would have walked away, he caught her

wrist, holding it firmly. "Lacey, I don't want to argue with you." His voice was husky, its demand low.

"No?" Looking into his dark blue eyes, Lacey knew that wasn't what he really wanted. "No, you want to make love, don't you?"

His gaze searched her face with unnerving thoroughness. "Don't you?" It was less a question than a request.

Lacey's pulse hammered in instant reaction, a heady intoxication filling her senses. She felt the pliant weakening of her flesh, but her mind refused to let its rule be overthrown by physical attraction.

"No." Her answer was faintly breathless, then firmer as she repeated it. "No, I don't."

"Liar," he accused, one corner of his mouth curving into an oddly bewitching smile.

Its charm was potent and Lacey had to breathe in deeply to keep it from weaving a spell around her. It took all of her willpower to remain impassive to his subtle and powerful appeal.

"You've accused me of that more than once, Cole," she said tightly. "And you're as wrong this time as you were all of the others."

With a quick tug, she pulled her wrist free of his hold and turned away. She could feel his gaze on her, compelling her back. She had to force herself to walk calmly and unhurriedly from him and not give in to the impulse to bolt to the safety of her room.

As she closed the bedroom door behind her, reaction set in, trembling through her with a violence that had her shaking. She was dangerously attracted to him. She recognized the symptoms, the combustible mixing of their two chemistries.

Cole was aware of it, too. He probably found her an attractive and highly available woman. His desire was part of the inherent danger of sharing the same house. Lacey knew she could never accept him as a temporary lover. It was neither wise nor sane.

A tear slipped from her lashes, its moistness surprising her as it trailed down her cheek. She flicked it away with her finger and began undressing for bed with jerky, harried movements.

One tear followed another. By the time she had her pajamas on and was crawling into bed, her cheeks were damp from the confusing sadness that made her heart ache.

As she was about to switch off the bedside light, her door was pushed open. Paralyzed, her fingers remained on the switch, unable to move. Cole stood in the doorway, his masculine bulk filling the frame. The roughly planed features of his face were set in implacable lines, cast half in shadow by the uneven light streaming over him. The rich umber shade of his hair gleamed nearly black. His eyes seemed afire with purpose and smoldering desire.

A wave of intense longing washed through Lacey and she rushed to deny it.

"Cole, I'm going to bed," she declared shakily.

"Yes," he agreed with a snap. His long strides carried him into the room, all the way to her bed. "But in my bed—where you belong!"

As he reached for her, Lacey made a strangled attempt to protest before realizing that words wouldn't stop him. She grabbed for the spare pillow on the double bed and threw it at him, hoping for a few seconds to escape his hands. But he knocked it aside with a swing of his arm and succeeded in grasping her waist before she could slide out the other side of the bed.

Effortlessly he slung her over his shoulder in a fireman's carry. Her bare feet flailed the air, finding no target. Her doubled fists, however, had a ready target and she pummeled at his broad shoulders and back, screaming abusively at his caveman tactics.

"Scream a little louder," Cole taunted insensitively. "No one can hear you, and you haven't broken my eardrums yet."

"You put me down!" Lacey choked.

The door to his bedroom was ajar and he kicked it the rest of the way open to carry her in and dump her unceremoniously on his bed. Her startled cry was muffled by the pillow onto which she fell. Stunned, it took her a second to react.

Rolling onto her side, she saw Cole shrugging out of his shirt. Along with it he seemed to be shedding the thin veneer of civilization that separated man from beast. Her stomach constricted at the sight of the naked expanse of chest, powerfully muscled yet sinuously lean.

As he reached to unbuckle his belt, she recovered from that momentary pang of desire and started to finish her roll off the bed. His hand snaked out to grip her shoulder and force her back.

The mattress sagged as it took his weight. Her struggles were to no avail as his superior strength pinned her shoulders to the bed. Half lying across her as he was, the crushing weight of his chest flattened her breasts. The body heat of his flesh burned through the thin silky material of her pajamas.

Her hands strained against the rippling muscles of his upper arms, futilely trying to push him away. By turning her head far to the side, she managed to elude his searching mouth, but that didn't stop it from exploring the area of her cheek and neck she had exposed. Despite her panicked attempts to get free, a response to his rough caresses shivered through her.

"Cole, what about the ground rules?" she gasped in alarm, her heart pounding frantically against her ribs.

"To hell with the ground rules," was his terse reply.

The warmth of his breath seemed to set fire to her skin, the flames quickly spreading, her flesh a ready tinderbox to be sparked by his touch. She didn't know how to douse the fire he was starting.

"You're tired, Cole. You don't know what you're doing," she protested weakly, not certain any longer if she knew what she was doing herself, or why.

"Maybe," he agreed in a throaty murmur that caressed her spine with its gruff, soft sound. "But I'm enjoying it, whatever it is."

His fingers slid beneath her cheek, curling into the short hair near her ear. He twisted her face toward him, his mouth at last finding the softness of her lips. Hungrily he explored their sweetness, devouring their token resistance until they were moving in response to his demands.

There was a roaring in her ears and Lacey realized it was the pounding of her heartbeat she heard. When her hands curled into his shoulders to cling to him, Cole shifted his attention, nuzzling her earlobe and chuckling softly in triumph.

"And you're enjoying it, too, little strawberry girl.

Don't deny it." Lightly he nipped her skin, the tiny pain becoming exquisite pleasure.

Her surrender wasn't complete and she began a protest, "Cole...."

"Strawberry girl," he repeated, his moist mouth investigating the trembling curves of her lips. And the protest died in her throat. "Green and tart in the morning, ripely red and sweet at night."

Then his mouth was closing over hers again, his burning kiss drawing her into the vortex of his desire. Everything went spinning. Lacey felt like a wheel of fortune being spun around and around without knowing where or when she would stop, nor who would win or lose. It was a wild, dizzying merry-go-round.

His hands seemed to know exactly where to touch her and arouse her to the full pitch of sensual awareness. Boneless, she let her feminine curves be molded to fit his hard length.

Her hands slid over the steel-smooth skin of his back. She felt the pressure of his male need and the answering empty ache within her lower body.

At that instant she realized that she was losing control. She was letting herself be trapped in the whirlpool of his lust, the very thing she knew she didn't dare do.

"Don't do this, Cole, please," she whispered in aching protest, turning away from the drugging prowess of his kiss, a narcotic that was very addictive.

"Lacey, for God's sake," he muttered thickly, seeking her lips, "you know you want me to love you. I'll make you admit it."

Yes, she did want him to love her, but not just in the

312

physical sense. And his statement reaffirmed that belief. She continued her resistance.

"Do you always bully your women into submission?" She choked on the accusing demand.

Cole breathed in tightly, levering himself up on one elbow, the brilliant blue of his gaze glittering darkly over her profile. Lacey knew the advantage was hers and she couldn't weaken.

"Damn you, Lacey," he groaned finally, and rolled onto his back, dragging her with him.

His wide palm pressed her head against his bare chest, rising and falling in uneven breathing. Lacey could hear the hammering of his heart. Its beat was as erratic and aroused as her own.

She closed her eyes tightly, letting the circling steel band of his arms crush her to the comforting warmth of his chest.

He simply held her, making no further attempt to caress her or to carry out his threat to make her admit that she desired him as much as he wanted her. And she felt no fear in this embrace. The likelihood of seduction had suddenly faded.

But it was a long time before his pulse settled into a steady tempo and his breathing became relaxed and level. The contentment of lying in his arms was nearly as satisfying as his experienced lovemaking.

This warm glow and the late hour combined to make her eyelids heavy with sleep. Unwillingly she realized she had to leave the comfort of his arms, but as she started to disentangle herself from his hold, his muscles tightened, not letting her go.

"Stay here, Strawberry." His voice was husky with

313

sleep, a drowsily warm sound that she couldn't bring herself to fight.

Cole, too, was minutes away from sleep. Lacey snuggled against his body heat, assuring herself that she would stay just until he fell asleep, then she would leave. At her lack of protest, he sighed, his breath stirring the feathery shortness of her hair.

It wasn't easy staying awake. The one thing that helped was the bedroom window that was propped open. The cool breeze blowing in from the ocean and moving the curtains danced over her skin, its brisk chill just enough to keep her awake and aware of her surroundings.

At one particularly strong gust, Lacey shivered. Cole immediately shifted her from his chest, reaching down to pull the covers over both of them before nestling her against his side again. The bed then became a warm cocoon, relaxing and safe.

"Go to sleep, Strawberry," he whispered, and brushed his mouth briefly across her hair. Despite the casualness of the good-night caress, there was something intimately familiar about it.

"Yes," Lacey replied.

But of course she wouldn't really go to sleep. She was only pretending to agree. When Cole was asleep she would leave, she reminded herself.

Her lashes fluttered tiredly down and she decided to rest her eyes just for a few minutes. His arm was a heavy warm band around her waist, possessive and gentle.

CHAPTER SEVEN

THE ALARM BUZZED loudly, almost right in Lacey's ear. She struggled to open her eyes, not understanding why it should be so loud.

A heavy weight was around her waist, pressing her to the mattress. She started to push it aside, irritated by the buzz and wishing Cole would shut his alarm clock off just once in the mornings.

As her fingers touched the weight, she felt the roughness of wiry hair and discovered the weight was an arm—Cole's arm, to be precise.

Instantly she was wide awake, remembering the events of last night—or more correctly, early morning. And the hard, long shape in the bed beside her was Cole.

Careful not to disturb him, she reached out, her fingertips just able to reach the alarm switch to turn off the noisy buzz. For once she was glad that Cole slept through his alarms. It would give her a chance to slip out of bed before he awakened.

But as she tried to slide away from him, he reached for her. "Don't move, Strawberry." His voice was thick with sleep.

Lacey guessed that it was a momentary alertness and within seconds he would again be sound asleep. "Your belt buckle is poking me," she lied, to explain the reason she had moved away from him.

Cole mumbled something unintelligible and rolled onto his side. Lacey remained completely still for several minutes until she was satisfied that he had fallen asleep. Then she slid silently out of bed and tiptoed to her own room.

Dressed and with coffee made and a glass of orange juice in her hand, she walked back to Cole's room. She paused in the doorway, gazing at the soundly sleeping figure. Sighing, she remembered how late it had been last night before Cole had slept, and the previous night when he had fallen asleep on the sofa. She simply couldn't bring herself to waken him and deprive him of the sleep he needed.

Turning around, she walked back to the kitchen and put the glass of juice in the refrigerator. The morning sunlight glistened on the ocean, reflecting its light into the living room.

With a cup of coffee in hand, Lacey moved onto the balcony. She hesitated, then descended the steps to the inviting stretch of empty beach. The silence of the morning was broken only by the waves licking the shore and the occasional cry of a seagull on the wing.

Only it wasn't quite empty, she discovered as she strolled along the sand. An older woman in a sunbonnet with jeans rolled up to her calves was wandering along, intent upon the treasures washed up by the tide.

Sitting down on the sand, Lacey watched the woman for a while before the soaring acrobatics of a seagull attracted her attention. The ocean was in one of its serene moods, its surface calm.

The peace surrounding Lacey caught her in its spell. She sat quietly on the sand, not conscious of thinking about anything, her mind seemingly blank.

Time seemed to slip away, the quarter hours seeming like seconds, so swiftly did they fly. Only the growing brightness of the rising sun and the increasing warmth of its rays offered any change. The ocean and sky remained the same and the woman was still scouring the beach for shells and driftwood.

"Lacey!" Cole impatiently shouted her name, breaking off the lonely cry of a gull.

Turning slightly on the sand to look over her shoulder, she saw him standing on the balcony, naked to the waist. Even at this distance, she could see how wrinkled his trousers were after their night of being slept in. His dark hair was tousled and he was attempting to comb it into order with his fingers.

She waved to him, her heart somersaulting in reaction to the blatant virility he possessed so early in the morning. It was impossible not to feel the attraction he radiated, primitively male and powerful.

"Why didn't you wake me?" he accused. "I was supposed to be at the office an hour ago."

"I thought you needed your sleep!" Lacey cupped her hands to her mouth to shout the answer.

"The next time, don't think. Wake me up!" His answering shout sounded more like a roar.

As he turned from the railing to enter the house, she stuck her tongue out at him, more amused than angered by his grouchy behavior.

Rising, she wandered toward the water. The woman combing the sand for seashells glanced up, and a smile

317

wreathed her face, which was sun-lined despite the protective bonnet she wore.

"It's a beautiful morning, isn't it?" she commented.

"It certainly is," Lacey agreed, and paused near the woman. "Have you found very much this morning?"

"Nothing spectacular." The woman straightened from her bent position and pressed a hand to the small of her back.

"Do you collect shells?" Lacey glanced curiously at the pail slung over the woman's arm.

"Well, yes, I do," she admitted after a second's hesitation. "But my main hobby is making things with shells and other objects that I find on the beach."

"Like jewelry?" Lacey asked, noticing the string of shell beads around the woman's neck.

The woman touched the necklace with her finger. "Yes, jewelry—mostly earrings and necklaces. At the moment I'm making a picture with shells. That's why I'm collecting all of these little mauve shells," she explained, reaching into the bucket to lift out a handful of the tiny shells. "There are any number of things you can make with shells—mobiles, wind chimes, lots of things."

"Sounds fascinating," murmured Lacey with a trace of envy in her voice. Her creative talents seldom stretched to more than attempting a floral arrangement from time to time.

"It's very enjoyable," the woman stated. "And now that I've retired, it keeps me busy."

"Lacey!" Cole was calling to her again and she turned to the house in answer. He stood on the balcony, this time dressed in a tan leisure suit. "I'm leaving now. I'll see you tonight."

Lacey waved her understanding of his shouted message. After a brief salute, he walked into the house. She smiled faintly to herself, amused by the difference a morning cup of coffee and a shower could make to his disposition.

"That was thoughtful of your husband," the woman commented. "My John always lets me know when he's leaving the house, too."

"Cole isn't my husband." Lacey made the correction automatically and without thinking.

"Oh." The woman was momentarily startled by the answer. "Oh!" The second time, the word was drawn out with dawning understanding and a widened look of shock and vague disapproval at her conclusion.

Lacey went scarlet, realizing that the implication of her statement was that she and Cole were living together although unmarried. Correcting the impression would involve a long, detailed explanation of the circumstances surrounding their decision to share the house. But Lacey didn't attempt to justify their arrangement. She wasn't certain the woman would believe her anyway.

"I have some cleaning to do at the house. Have a nice day." Lacey offered, and self-consciously made her exit from the beach.

As she walked away, she heard the woman murmuring to herself, "These young people nowadays—they seem to have lost all sense of moral values!"

Lacey compressed her lips into a thin line and kept walking.

In actual fact, there was very little to do at the house, but she puttered around doing odds and ends, watering the plants, taking care of some hand washing until after noon. With a sandwich and some fruit, she lunched on the balcony, then settled into one of the lounge chairs with a book.

The sun was warm and relaxing. Its effect combined with the lack of regular sleep over the last two nights made her drowsy, and soon she was setting her book aside to take a short nap.

The next time she opened her eyes, they focused on the familiar brown leather briefcase. Immediately she looked for its owner and found Cole sitting in one of the deck chairs, his long legs stretched out in front of him and a can of beer in his hand. Dark spiky lashes screened the expression in his eyes, but he was watching her.

His mouth twitched briefly in a smile. "So you're finally going to wake up, sleepyhead. I thought for a while that you were going to sleep around the clock."

Stifling a yawn with the back of her hand, Lacey pushed herself up on an elbow, ignoring his teasing comment to ask, "What time is it?"

"Four-thirty or thereabouts." He shrugged, uninterested in the exact time although his gold watch was around his wrist, making it easily verified.

"I didn't realize I was so tired." She rubbed her eyes and covered another yawn with her hand. "How long have you been here?"

"Since shortly after two."

Which was only a little while after she had fallen asleep. "You haven't been sitting there all that time?" She blinked in disbelief.

Cole nodded. "Watching you sleep."

The grogginess was leaving rapidly and she was becoming more alert with each passing second. And she noticed the faint suggestion of weariness in his posture.

"You should have napped, too, instead of watching me," she said, sitting upright.

"Maybe," he conceded, "but I wanted to be here when you woke up."

It seemed a curious reason. "Why?"

"Because I wanted to apologize for last night."

"Oh." His statement suddenly made her uneasy, especially with that dark blue gaze watching her so intently through the narrowed slit of his lashes.

She walked to the balcony railing, wishing Cole had pretended last night had never happened rather than alluding to it on their first real meeting. At the same instant, she realized that she had escaped to the beach in the morning before he had awakened to avoid this confrontation after the events of last night.

Footsteps indicated his approach and she tensed herself, her heart beating as rapidly as a hummingbird's wings. Cole stopped directly behind her and she could feel the disturbing touch of his gaze.

"Aren't you going to accept my apology?" he questioned.

"For what?" She shrugged nervously. "Nothing happened."

"Not for lack of intention," he said in a gently mocking voice.

Lacey was flustered. All her poise was gone and she felt as skittish as a schoolgirl. What had happened to all her maturity, her confidence to handle any kind of a

321

situation? What power did Cole have to reduce her to a quivering mass of nerves?

His hands curled lightly on her shoulders to turn her around. She stared at his shirt collar, the top two buttons unfastened, giving her a glimpse of his bare chest. It was just about as unnerving as gazing into his magnetic blue eyes.

He crooked a finger under her chin to lift her head. "I knew you'd be a temptation from the first night when we made our agreement, but I thought I could handle it." He paused, frowning at the agitation darkening her brown eyes. "I was tired and irritable last night. And we'd argued over Bowman—"

"Cole, please," Lacey interrupted tightly, "I don't want to dissect all the events and emotions that led up to last night. Exposing them to daylight doesn't change anything. Don't do this to me."

"Don't do this to you?" He laughed without humor. "What about what you do to me?"

Seemingly of their own volition, his hands began lightly rubbing her shoulders and upper arms in what amounted to a circular caress, with Cole completely unconscious of what he was doing. It produced a bone-melting sensation and Lacey knew just how dangerous that was. But she seemed powerless to stop it.

"Do you know how I felt when you drove so recklessly away from here yesterday?" His voice lowered to an intimately husky pitch, vaguely fierce and demanding. "Or when I found out that you weren't with Bowman? Do you know what it was like waiting for you to come home last night?" His fingers dug briefly into her flesh. "Do you know what it's like going to bed each night

322

and imagining you in the next room in your cute little pajamas?''

She knew she was a breath away from surrendering to his attraction. "Then leave. Move out," she challenged in desperation rather than let her senses lead her down the garden path of temptation.

"And worry about you being here by yourself at the mercy of vandals and burglars?" Cole argued. "That would be going from the frying pan to the fire. I'd be trading cold showers for ulcers.''

"I suppose you want me to move out, then," she said stiffly.

"It would solve things."

"Would it?" she countered with a funny ache in her throat.

"I don't know...." Cole sighed heavily, releasing her to turn away. Raking his fingers roughly through his hair, he let his hand rest on the back of his head, rubbing the tight cords in his neck.

"Good, because I'm not moving out," she declared, even though every ounce of logic in her mind cried out that's what she should do. "If you'll excuse me—" she started for the door to the house "—I'll see what there is for dinner tonight."

"No!" Cole spur around, the savage bite in his voice stopping her. "We'll eat out tonight."

She hesitated for only a split second. "You can eat out if you want. I'll fix something here for myself."

She had refused his invitation, finding the prospect of going out with him on what would seem like a date as unsettling as staying in the house alone with him for the evening.

"Dammit, Lacey," he muttered, "I thought I'd made myself clear. I'm not letting you stay in this house alone at night. It's bad enough that you're by yourself in the daytime."

"You're not letting me!" Lacey flared at his arrogant statement.

"That's right, I'm not letting you," he repeated forcefully. "And you can argue about that for as long as you like, but either we both go or we both stay. That is the way it's going to be. If you're sensible, you'll agree to go out to dinner with me so we can get out of this house and be among some people."

Their eyes locked in a clashing, silent duel that lasted for several explosive seconds before Cole challenged, "Which is it going to be?"

There wasn't really any choice. "Give me a few minutes to change clothes," Lacey agreed grudgingly.

"Fine." The roughness hadn't completely left his tone. "We'll go somewhere for a before-dinner cocktail first," he told her.

It was only after they had left the cocktail lounge for the restaurant that the tension between them began to ease. They were seated by the hostess at a table with a view of the ocean, outside spotlights directed at the rolling whitecaps of the surf.

"What looks good to you?" Cole asked, glancing up from his menu to Lacey.

"I'm trying to decide whether to have the deviled crab or the steamed blue crab," she answered, nibbling thoughtfully at her lower lip.

"Have both," he offered as an alternative.

"Are you kidding? I'd be so full I couldn't move.

You'd have to carry me out of here," she joked, dismissing his suggestion.

"It wouldn't be the first time I've carried you somewhere," he reminded her quietly.

The way he was looking at her made her glow warm all over. She immediately stared at her menu, aware of his soft, almost silent chuckle. She closed the menu and set it on the table in front of her.

"I'll have the steamed crab," she decided quickly in an effort to divert the subject.

The waiter appeared at Cole's left. "The steamed blue crab for each of us," he ordered. "And a wine list, please."

When the waiter left, a silence ensued. Lacey nervously fingered the prongs of her fork, unable to think of any small talk, which had carried the first part of the evening. Cole reached out, covering her hand completely with his own to still its nervous fidgeting.

"I was only teasing you," he offered in apology, "when I reminded you about last night."

"I know, but it's nothing to joke about."

She glanced up and found she was unable to look away from his compelling gaze. Her heart turned over, its crazy flip-flop not helping the tingling warmth shooting up her arm from his hand.

"Well, well, well," a male voice declared mockingly from behind Lacey. "You two have finally ventured out of your little love nest!"

As Lacey tried to pull her hand free of Cole's, his fingers tightened around it, refusing to let her go. His gaze flicked to the voice.

"Hello, Vic." A bland mask slipped into place to conceal his expression.

At that moment the handsome blond-haired man stepped into Lacey's view. Cole's use of the man's name had already jogged her memory into placing the voice as that of Monica's brother.

"Hello, Cole." He nodded first to him, then turned his cynically distant smile to Lacey. "We meet again, Lacey Andrews."

"Hello, Mr. Hamilton." She returned his greeting with deliberate formality, not liking his spoiled, arrogant attitude any more now than she had at their first meeting.

"Vic," he corrected, and widened his smile, which didn't make it any warmer or more charming. "My sister has been gnashing her teeth over you all week. Really, Cole—" he turned his attention away from Lacey "—I think you could have let her down a little more gently."

"I've been letting her down gently for two years," Cole replied dryly. "It's time she realized it."

"I think she's become convinced that you'll be the master in any marriage," Vic commented absently. "Monica always has been very liberal, willing to forgive you for your little diversions—your pillow friends." He glanced pointedly at Lacey, who was bristling half in anger and half in embarrassment.

Cole's mouth twisted wryly. "Is that what Monica said?"

"She did suggest that I might pass the message on if I happened to run into you," Vic admitted smoothly.

"You've delivered it," Cole stated with apparent indifference.

326

"Now you want me to run along and leave you alone, is that it?" Vic shrugged. "Very well. Enjoy your evening."

When he had retreated out of hearing, Lacey sputtered indignantly, "Why didn't you correct him? He isn't Monica."

An eyebrow was arched mockingly. "Correct him about your being my 'pillow friend?' Would you have me deny that we've slept together?"

"You know it was perfectly innocent," she retorted.

Releasing her hand, he leaned back in his chair, studying her thoughtfully and just a little bit coolly. "You're very anxious to deny any relationship between us whenever Vic has been around. Are you attracted to him?"

"Of course not!" Lacey denied the allegation vigorously.

"The Hamiltons are very wealthy, and by some people's standards, Vic could be classified as a very handsome man. He'd be quite a catch in matrimonial circles."

"I'm sure the same could be said for Monica, couldn't it?" she argued.

"It could," he agreed. "But we aren't talking about Monica."

"I'm not talking about Vic, but maybe you should take his advice and get Monica's forgiveness. Then the two of you can get back together."

His mouth thinned. "You do enjoy starting arguments, don't you, Lacey?"

"I don't start them. You do."

"Let's end this one by dropping the subject," he suggested briskly.

327

"Gladly," Lacey agreed.

The waiter arrived with their dinner, negating the need for immediate conversation to fill the awkward silence. With good food and a glass of New York wine, the silence was soon reduced to a companionable level.

"How is the project coming?" Lacey inquired, using her knife to pry off the apron flap on the underside of the crab.

"Very well. Didn't Bowman mention that the men were making up for lost time?" Cole asked idly.

"No." With the top shell discarded, Lacey broke off the toothed claws and set them aside to free the meat from them later. "He didn't mention it at all."

"Considering the lost time that's been made up, I would have thought he would have been bragging about it." There was nothing derogatory in his comment.

"Mike doesn't brag about his work," Lacey stated. "He considers it his duty to do the best that he can. He never lets a problem become an excuse. He tries to solve it, which is why it was so unfair when you blamed him for the delays on your project."

Cole ignored the last red flag remark. "Bowman mentioned the two of you had been discussing business, so I presumed he was referring to the progress on the project. What were you talking about, or am I treading on forbidden ground with that question?" Amusement glittered faintly in the look he gave her.

Lacey hesitated, her knife poised to slice lengthwise through the center of the crab, now broken in half. "When did you ask Mike what we had been discussing?"

"When you were in your room, changing clothes to leave with him."

"And he told you we were talking about business?"

"Yes. At the time I found it very difficult to believe. There aren't many men I know, who can hold an attractive woman in their arms and talk business," Cole admitted.

"And you still find it difficult to believe, don't you?" she challenged.

"With you, I'm learning that anything is possible." The laugh lines around his eyes deepened, but his mouth didn't smile. "Were you talking business?"

"We were talking about the girl who's replaced me while I'm on vacation," she explained. "Mechanically Donna is an excellent secretary, but her personality can be very irritating."

"I've talked to her a couple of times." Cole nodded without elaborating any further.

"Then you understand what Mike has been going through this last week?" A smile teased the corners of her mouth.

"And sympathize," he added dryly. "But that doesn't explain why he was dangling you over the railing."

"Oh, that." Lacey didn't attempt to hide her smile this time. "I was teasing him. I told him I was considering handing in my notice and suggesting Donna as my replacement. He was threatening murder if I did."

"Are you thinking of quitting?"

She dug out a forkful of the exposed crab meat, shaking her head. "No, I like my job."

"What about when you get married? Will you still work?" Cole was slicing his crab, not even glancing up as he asked the question.

It was difficult to make a casual response. If anyone else had asked, she could have laughed away the question, but she was more than half in love with Cole right now. Marriage became a subject that sent quivers down her spine.

"More than likely I'd have to keep working after I married to make ends meet," she answered, self-consciously avoiding looking at Cole when she spoke.

"Would you mind?"

"No. As I said, I like my job and I don't think a lot of idle time would suit me. I like to be doing constructive and challenging things." That she could answer truthfully and without hesitation.

"What if your husband didn't want you to work? What if he wanted you at home?" Cole lifted his wine glass, flicking a glance at her over the rim.

"We'd probably have an argument. Are you one of those old-fashioned men who don't approve of working wives?" Lacey asked, suddenly curious.

"I don't mind if it's other men's wives that are working, but I'm not certain how I would react if it were my own wife." Cole smiled, and it had a devastating effect on Lacey's senses. "When we have children, I suppose I would insist she be home with them, at least when they're small."

"When the children are little, I would want to be home with them," Lacey agreed readily.

"Do you mean we've found something else we can agree on besides sharing the same house?" Cole declared with mock astonishment, a wicked glint in his indigo blue eyes. "Remarkable," he drawled, and Lacey laughed.

Their earlier disagreement over Vic and Monica Hamilton was forgotten. They seemed to find a surfeit of things to talk about without becoming embroiled in any controversy.

All too soon, it seemed, Cole was driving the car into the garage. In truth, they had lingered over dessert, then coffee, until it was nearly ten.

Concealing a sigh of regret that the evening was coming to a close, Lacey stepped out of the car, instinctively taking the door key from her purse. Both stepped forward at the same time to unlock the connecting door, bumping into each other.

"Allow me," Cole offered with a mocking inclination of his head.

"By all means," she agreed, replacing the key in her purse.

In the lower entrance hall he paused to lock the door behind him while she slowly began to climb the steps. She was reluctant to have the evening end so soon.

"Shall I—" she began.

"Let's make a pact," Cole interrupted, a step behind her on the stairs. "You don't offer to make coffee or a nightcap and I won't suggest showing you my etchings."

"All right," Lacey agreed without enthusiasm.

She knew exactly why he had said that. They were back in the house again, and its privacy and isolation invited an intimacy they were both trying to avoid.

His hand lightly took hold of her elbow, his touch disquietingly impersonal, and guided her across the living room to the hall leading to the bedrooms. As they started down the hall, Lacey wanted to protest that she

331

wasn't sleepy, but she knew it wasn't wise and kept silent.

At the closed door of her bedroom they stopped, and Lacey turned hesitantly toward him. An elemental tension crackled between them.

"Do you know this is the first time I've escorted a girl directly to her bedroom door to say good night?" Cole joked wryly.

"It's a first for me, too." Lacey tried to respond in the same vein, but her voice sounded husky and as unnerved by his nearness as she felt.

His large palm cupped the side of her face in a caress that was gentle rather than arousing. "You'd better go straight to bed," he said. "After these last couple of days, you need a good night's sleep."

Something in the way he said it made her ask, "What about you? Aren't you going to bed right away?"

"No." There was a short negative shake of his head. "I thought I'd take a walk along the beach before turning in."

"But I—" Lacey started to suggest that she might go along, but his thumb pressed her lips into silence.

"No," he refused abruptly, his gaze sliding to her mouth. "I know what I'm doing, Lacey."

Her heart was skipping beats all over the place and her brown eyes were round and luminous. She nodded briefly her agreement and anger sparkled darkly in his eyes.

"Don't be so damned meek," Cole growled. "It doesn't suit you."

"I—" Lacey started to defend her action.

"Just shut up," he interrupted, and she detected the

332

faint groan in his throat before he let his mouth replace the thumb that had been pressed against her lips.

The hard, searing kiss flamed through her as his arms crushed her against his male length. The lean warmth of his body added to the fire already raging inside her. The fierce, sensual masculinity about him, almost tangible, was irresistible to her feminine core.

Her lips parted under the bruising urgency of his mouth, permitting him to deepen the kiss with shattering expertise. She felt his tenseness, his muscles like coiled springs in an effort to keep control, while she herself had none. But she had long ago realized that in Cole's arms she lost her inhibition, and that made his touch doubly dangerous.

Abruptly he broke off the kiss, lifting his head. A muscle twitched convulsively along his powerful jaw as he stared grimly into her dazed, love-softened face. He breathed in deeply and pivoted away.

"Good night, Lacey," he ordered.

For an instant she was incapable of speech. "Good night," she answered finally, but he was already striding into the living room, not glancing back when she spoke.

Not until she heard the sliding door to the balcony open and close did she enter her bedroom. She was emotionally shaken by the feelings and sensations he had aroused. She knew she couldn't sleep so she walked to the window, gazing out at the moon casting a pale silvery light on the sand.

In seconds Cole was in her view, long strides carrying him toward the waves. His hands were thrust deep in his pockets and his attention fixed on the ground. Lacey watched him until he walked out of her sight, striding along the beach into the night.

Changing into her pajamas, she crawled into bed. She didn't attempt to close her eyes as she listened to the clock on the bedside table tick the seconds away. The hands of the clock were nearly clasped together to signal the midnight hour when she finally heard Cole enter the house.

His pace had slowed considerably as he wandered into the hallway. He stopped outside her door. When she saw the doorknob turn, she closed her eyes, feigning sleep.

Opening the door, Cole made no attempt to enter the room, but stared at her for several silent minutes before he closed the door. She heard him walk to his own room. The pounding of her heart became almost an aching pain as she turned onto her side and tried to sleep.

CHAPTER EIGHT

THE NEXT MORNING Lacey awoke early from habit. She lay in bed for several minutes listening to the sounds of Cole stirring about.

Finally she climbed out of bed, realizing that she couldn't get back to sleep and that she would have to get up sooner or later. Pulling on her housecoat, she walked into the hall.

At that moment Cole stepped out of his room softly whistling a tuneless melody. He was wearing swimming trunks, chocolate brown with tan stripes. He smiled when he saw her.

"Good morning," he greeted her cheerfully.

"You must have been up for a while," Lacey observed, her own voice still husky from sleep.

"I have. How did you know? Did I wake you?" he questioned, waiting for her and falling into step beside her.

"No, you didn't. I just guessed you'd been up because you're usually grouchy when you first wake up," she replied.

He reached out and ruffled her short hair. "You aren't exactly Miss Sunshine when you first get up in the mornings, either," he commented.

"Don't do that!" she protested, and tried to brush her hair down with the flat of her hand.

"See what I mean?" He winked, an impish light dancing in his dark blue eyes.

"I never have claimed to be Miss Sunshine," she pointed out. "Did you make coffee?"

"Not yet. I was on my way out for a morning swim before breakfast, hoping you'd be up and have it ready when I came in," he replied with engaging honesty, the mocking amusement still gleaming in his look.

"You could have fixed it and had it ready for me when I got up," she countered, unable to take offense this early in the day.

"I could have," he agreed. "Would you like to come for a swim with me? I'll wait."

"No, thanks," Lacey refused, not glancing at his lean, browned physique, which was altogether too disturbingly virile for her senses to cope with when she wasn't fully awake yet.

"Okay," he shrugged, branching away from her toward the balcony door. "I'll see you later."

He seemed to take much of the morning sunshine with him when he left. Lacey halfheartedly fixed the coffee pot and plugged it in. She took her orange juice onto the balcony, her gaze searching the waves until she found Cole. He was a strong swimmer, as she had guessed he would be. She watched him for a long time before finally reminding herself to get dressed.

Showering first, she put on shorts of tan plaid with a white boat-necked top. The coffee was perked when she returned to the kitchen. She poured a cup and wandered again to the balcony, her gaze once more drawn magnetically to the beach.

Two figures caught her attention. One was Cole

wading out of the ocean, lifting a hand in greeting to the second figure. It was the woman in the sunbonnet to whom Lacey had talked the previous morning.

She paled slightly as Cole stopped to talk to the woman searching the beach for shells. His tanned body glistened like bronze from the moistness of the water beading over his skin.

Lacey had no idea what the two were talking about, but Cole was listening with obvious attention. Once he glanced to the house, spying Lacey on the balcony.

Apprehension shivered over her skin. The woman surely wouldn't mention her impression that she and Cole were living together. Surely she wouldn't be that bold?

Soon Cole was nodding a goodbye to the woman, his long legs striding across the sands to the balcony stairs. Lacey was tempted to retreat into the house, but she forced herself to stand her ground and react calmly to his return.

"Did you have a good swim?" she asked.

"Great." His hair glistened darkly in the sunlight as he effortlessly took the steps two at a time to reach the top. "Ah, the coffee's done," he said, seeing the cup in Lacey's hand.

"I'll get you a cup," she offered quickly, finding an excuse to leave.

"It can wait." He walked to the railing near her, leaning both hands on it and gazing silently at the ocean beyond.

Then, unexpectedly, he looked at her, his gaze piercing yet with a roguish glint in it. He was so vibrant and

337

male, a bronzed statue come to life, that her breath was coming in uneven spurts.

"I just had a very intriguing conversation with that woman on the beach," he said. "A Mrs. Carlyle—she lives a few houses down. Do you know her?"

Something in the inflection of his voice told Lacey that he already knew the answer, possibly recognizing the woman from yesterday.

"I talked to her for a few minutes the other day," she admitted, "but I didn't know her name." Slightly flustered, she knew there was a tinge of pink in her cheeks. She sipped quickly at her coffee, pretending the tepid liquid was hot. "She collects shells and makes things with them, jewelry and such."

"So she told me—among other things." There was a hint of laughter in his reply, but his mockingly intent gaze did not relent an inch. "I'm curious about what you told her."

"Me?" Lacey swallowed nervously.

"You're aware that Mrs. Carlyle is under the impression that we're living together in the immoral interpretation of the phrase?" he murmured.

"I was afraid she thought that," Lacey admitted after a second's hesitation.

"What did you tell her?" he prodded, a smile playing with the corners of his mouth.

"She assumed we were married and I automatically said you weren't my husband. She drew her own conclusions from that," she explained self-consciously.

"And you didn't correct her assumption?"

"It would have been such a long drawn-out story, and she was a stranger." She shrugged and curled both

338

hands around her coffee cup. "What did she say to you?"

"I was on the receiving end of a very stern lecture." The creases deepened on either side of his mouth, his amusement at Lacey's obvious discomfort.

"Oh," was all she could think to say, and she stared at her half-empty cup of coffee.

Cole reached out and removed the cup from her hands, setting it on a deck table. Before she could protest that action, he was curving both arms around her. She pressed her hands against his chest, her fingers coming in contact with the cloud of moist dark hairs.

"She was trying to convince me that if I had any respect for you at all, I'd make an honest woman out of you." He smiled down at her, the dampness of his legs against her thighs evoking a roughly warm sensation. "And I haven't even found out how dishonest you can be."

"Cole, please!" Her throat had constricted and she had to force the words out.

He bent his head to brush his mouth over the soft curve of her jaw. The tangy ocean scent clinging to his skin assailed her senses, already turned upside down by his touch. He teased the sensitive skin of her neck, his breath dancing warm over her flesh.

"Shall I make an honest woman out of you, Lacey?" he mused playfully, not a serious note in his voice.

She quickly swallowed to ease the tightness in her throat and pushed away from his disturbing nearness. "Don't be ridiculous, Cole!" She couldn't joke about a thing like marriage.

He made no attempt to recapture her as he watched

her widen the distance between them with quick, retreating steps. Yet behind the glitter of teasing amusement, his expression seemed to be curiously guarded and alert.

"Maybe I should make a dishonest woman of you first," he said again in that same laughing tone, to indicate he was teasing.

Lacey felt light-headed and quite unable to match his bantering words. "Maybe you should have some coffee to sober you up. You've had either too much ocean or too much sun," she suggested.

"I don't want coffee now." The inflection of his answer implied he wanted something else.

The undercurrents vibrating in the air seemed to increase in voltage. Lacey paled, unsure how much more of this electrically charged atmosphere she could tolerate before succumbing to its force. She nearly jumped out of her skin when Cole moved unexpectedly.

But he swept past her, speaking abruptly. "I'll shower and dress first, then have coffee."

"I'll start breakfast," she offered, in need of something to say. She was trembling uncontrollably from the aftershocks, but Cole wasn't there to see her reaction.

Bacon was sizzling in the skillet when he entered the kitchen, wearing khaki trousers and a short-sleeved pullover top of white knit. The clinging fabric accented the width of his shoulders and molded the muscled leanness of his torso. The clean fragrance of soap mingled with the musky scent of his after-shave lotion.

Lacey couldn't help being aware of the heady combination as he helped himself to the coffee and moved to the counter near the stove. He was brimming with vitality, positively overpowering her with the force of his presence. She began turning the bacon strips to keep them from burning, aware that he was watching her intently with his disconcerting gaze.

"Do you have to stare at me like that?" she asked impatiently, not letting her own gaze wander from the frying bacon in the skillet. "It makes me feel as if I've suddenly grown two heads."

"Sorry." Offhandedly Cole made the apology and sipped at his coffee. "Do you have any plans for today?"

"Plans?" she echoed.

"Yes." A brow twisted in amusement at the darting blank look she gave him. "Are you expecting Bowman or anyone over for the day?"

"No, he didn't mention he'd be stopping by," she qualified, and added a glob of butter to the egg skillet, turning on the fire beneath it.

The bacon grease popped, splattering the back of her hand, and she jumped back from the stove with a muffled exclamation of pain. Cole immediately had a hold of her arm, practically dragging her to the sink. Turning on the cold water tap, he thrust her hand beneath the running water.

"Keep it there," he ordered.

"The bacon will burn," protested Lacey.

"I'll watch it. You just let that cold water run on that burn for a while," he ordered, moving back to the stove to rescue the bacon. Lacey did as she was told, and the stinging pain was gradually reduced to a numbness.

"How does it feel?" he asked when she turned off the water to dry her hand.

"It's fine." There was a barely discernible red mark where the hot grease had splattered on her hand.

"Aren't you going to ask me why I was wondering if you'd made any plans for today?" He broke an egg into the melted butter in the second skillet.

She hesitated. "Why?"

"I thought if you hadn't made any other arrangements, we'd drive over to the Eastern Shore for the day." He added another egg to the skillet. "How would you like your eggs cooked?"

"Over easy." Lacey answered his last question first; it was the easiest.

"What about going over to the Eastern Shore?"

"It sounds like a good idea," she agreed.

"Good," he nodded. "Have you put the bread in the toaster yet?"

"Not yet." And Lacey reached for the bread.

AN HOUR LATER their breakfast was over and the dishes washed, and they were on their way to the Eastern Shore of Virginia. Traversing the seventeen-mile-long Chesapeake Bay bridge-tunnel, Lacey watched a navy ship some distance away in the Atlantic Ocean to her right. Its silhouette moved steadily closer to the ship channel leading to the waters of Chesapeake Bay on her left.

But Lacey didn't look to her left at the warships and merchant vessels more easily viewed in the waters of the bay. The confines of the car had heightened her awareness of Cole, if that was possible.

Without glancing at him, she was conscious of everything about him, from the way his dark brown hair curled near his shirt collar to the strength of his sun-browned hands on the wheel. An inbred radar system seemed tuned strictly to his presence.

342

"Any place special you want to see when we get over there?" he asked, his gaze sliding from the road to her for a brief instant.

"No." Lacey shook her head, unable to think of a single place she particularly wanted to visit.

"Let's drive to Chincoteague," he suggested.

They were approaching the concrete island in the bay where the bridge dipped beneath the water to become the tunnel under the ship channel.

"That's nearly a hundred miles, isn't it?" She frowned, turning to study his strongly defined profile.

"About that," he agreed blandly. The cavernous tunnel swallowed them, a ribbon of lights overhead.

She glanced at her watch. "Do you realize how late it will be when we get back? You have to work tomorrow. You should have an early night."

There was a wry, upward curve of his mouth, but his gaze never left the tunnel stretching ahead of them. "Let's avoid the subject of sleep and beds, Lacey, and enjoy the day," he suggested.

Jerking her head to the front, she stared straight ahead at the sunlight beckoning at the tunnel exit. A spurt of anger flashed through her at his unnecessary comment.

His hand reached out to clasp the back of her neck. His fingers felt the taut muscles and began to massage them gently.

"Relax, Lacey," he ordered in a coaxing tone. "And stop hugging the car door. I'm not going to bite."

"Aren't you?" she retorted, already stung by the point of Cupid's arrow.

"I promise." He smiled. "No bites—not even an occasional nibble!"

343

With that his gaze slid to the exposed curve of her throat, its brushing touch as effective as a caress. Immediately he withdrew his hand and returned it to the steering wheel.

"This afternoon we're just going to be a couple taking a Sunday drive," he stated.

And Lacey felt a twinge of regret that it was to be so, regardless of how sensible it was. But it was only because he was so attractive. She managed a stiff smile of agreement to his suggestion.

The Cape Charles lighthouse poked its silhouette into the skyline, signaling that land was near. Shortly the bridge curved to an end on the jutting finger of land that was Virginia's Eastern Shore.

The modern highway carved its way up the length of the unspoiled peninsula. Lacey caught glimpses of the windswept Atlantic coast and the islands scattered out from its beaches.

It was impossible to remain immune to the charm of the landscape for long. Its beauty was tireless, entrapping her in its spell, the minutes slipping by as fast as the miles.

As they neared the Maryland border, Cole turned off the main highway, crossing the bridge to the island of Chincoteague. They traveled through the small town of the same name and on across a second bridge to Assateague Island.

Declared a national seashore, the island was the refuge for the wild Chincoteague ponies, believed to be descendants of horses from the wreck of a Spanish galleon more than four hundred years ago. On the island they ran free as their ancestors did, drinking from the freshwater pools and grazing in the nutritious salt marshes. Inbreeding over the years had stunted the horses to pony size, yet the clean-limbed, delicate conformation remained in the descendants.

To keep the herds' numbers at a level the island food supply could support, there was a roundup every year by the residents of neighboring Chincoteague Island. The sick and injured among the ponies were treated and a certain number of the new crop of foals was sold at auction.

Although there was a bridge to connect the Assateague Island refuge with Chincoteague Island, tradition demanded that the ponies swim the short distance between the two islands. The annual July event drew thousands of visitors to witness it and attend the auction.

There was no one around, though, when Cole and Lacey spied a herd of the small ponies and stopped to watch them. The pinto stallion kept a wary eye on them and they took care not to alarm him. He tolerated their presence at that distance, leaving Lacey and Cole free to watch the antics of a cavorting pair of young foals.

The approach of a second party was more than the stallion would permit to invade his domain. With his head snaking low to the ground, he began moving his mares away, nipping at the recalcitrant ones slow to obey his commands.

"They're beautiful!" Lacey breathed when the last of the ponies trotted out of sight ahead of the stallion.

"Are you glad you came?" Cole asked, smiling.

"Of course," she responded naturally, the bemused light still in her brown eyes.

"So am I," he agreed, and glanced at his watch. "We aren't likely to see any more this afternoon. I don't know about your stomach, but mine says it's been a long time since breakfast. Let's go back to Chincoteague and find a place to have dinner before starting back."

The summer sun was setting as they finally began the trek back to Virginia Beach. Its golden glow gave a serene ending to a relaxing afternoon and evening. Somewhere along the long ride, Lacey closed her eyes and forgot to open them. The next thing she was aware of was a hand gently nudging her awake.

"We're home, Strawberry," Cole's low voice came to her through the drugging mists of sleep.

Lazily raising her lashes, she focused on his bent figure, holding the car door open. She smiled at him, unaware of the curious dreamlike quality to her expression.

"Already?" she murmured.

"Yes, already," he answered dryly, his helping hand more or less forcing her out of the car.

Not fully awake, she took advantage of the support he offered, leaning heavily on him as they walked slowly to the garage entrance to the house. His arm remained around the back of her waist until they reached the top of the stairs and the living room.

"I think I'd better put some coffee on," Lacey murmured, trying to blink the sandman's dust from her eyes.

"No need to bother to make it for me." Cole moved away from her to the sofa, bending down to pick up his briefcase.

She watched him sit down and open the briefcase on his lap. "What are you doing?" she asked, frowning.

"I have some work to do," he answered without looking up.

"After all that driving?" She couldn't believe he was serious.

"It has to be done," he replied, taking out a folder and his note pad.

Within seconds, Lacey was completely shut out. She stood uncertainly in the center of the room before finally wandering out onto the balcony.

Leaning against the railing, she experienced a curiously letdown feeling. The night sky was alight with stars that seemed to stretch on as endlessly as the emptiness inside of her.

Shivering, she reentered the house. "It's getting chilly out," she commented, but the temperature inside seemed several degrees cooler after Cole's indifferent nod. "Do you have to work?" she demanded in a flash of irritation.

There was a remoteness in the blue gaze that sliced to her. "I don't happen to be on vacation, Lacey," he reminded her.

"I wish I weren't," she declared, suddenly regretting the moment she had met him.

He turned back to his papers muttering, "So do I. Then you wouldn't be here. You'd be in your own apartment where you belong."

"That's what you want, isn't it? For me to move out?" she challenged tightly, a pain squeezing her chest like a constricting band.

Again his cool, glittering blue eyes regarded her with

a level look. "I thought I'd made it plain that was what I've wanted all along."

Lacey paled slightly. "I had the impression you'd changed your mind," she retorted.

There was an unfriendly gleam of mockery in his gaze. "Because I had a desire to make love to you?" he replied. "For God's sake, Lacey, you're an attractive woman, intelligent and easy to be with, as well as having a passionate nature. Any man in my situation would want to make love to you, given the opportunity."

"I see," Lacey murmured stiffly.

If she had asked him outright whether or not he felt any serious affection toward her, she couldn't have received a more explicit answer. The passes he had made at her had been strictly that—just passes.

She was available and had been available. She should have been glad that he wasn't the unscrupulous type that would have taken advantage of her vulnerability. But the ache inside was too painful to leave room for gratitude for small favors.

"Now, if you'll excuse me, I'll get back to work." Cole shuffled his papers, bending over them again. She was being dismissed.

"By all means, go ahead," Lacey urged on a spiteful note of sarcasm. "Don't let me disturb you whatever you do," she added.

"You disturb me just by being here," he muttered almost beneath his breath, but he did not let his gaze wander from the papers in his hand.

She had the impression that he hadn't meant her to hear the remark, but there was no consolation in that.

She wanted to disturb him—emotionally, not just physically.

Turning on her heel, she walked rigidly to her bedroom and closed the door. Her eyes were hot with tears, but she didn't cry. Instead she walked to the closet and took out her nightclothes.

Lying in bed, she stared at the ceiling. Her door was shut, but the light in the hallway streamed through the narrow slit at the bottom of the door. From the living room came the whisper of papers moving against each other.

CHAPTER NINE

OUTWARDLY THE PATTERN of their lives didn't change during the next three days, but subtly it had altered.

Cole's alarm still awakened Lacey in the mornings while he slept through its buzz.

They shared orange juice and coffee together, talking with apparently teasing friendliness. But it was a forced effort to maintain the previous week's atmosphere on both parts.

As before, Cole returned late in the evening, eating elsewhere, and spent the remainder of the time engrossed in paperwork. But there were no more physical encounters, no chance contact, because neither of them was leaving anything to chance.

For Lacey, it was like a rocket countdown. Five nights to live through before her cousin Margo returned, then four, then three. Now it was Thursday and the number was down to two.

The agony of being near him was almost over, but she was afraid of what was to come. She found it almost impossible to believe that in the space of one short week a man could mess up her mind and her life the way Cole had done.

"You stupid, impulsive little fool," she scolded herself angrily as she climbed out of her car. "He never asked you to fall in love with him, so it's your own dumb fault!"

"You're talking to yourself, Lacey. That's a bad sign," Mike teased, walking up behind her. "What are you mumbling about anyway?"

Recovering from her initial surprise, Lacey shook her head. "Nothing in particular—just the world in general."

"Did I lose a few days somewhere—is this Monday and you're on your way into the office?" He glanced ahead of them at the office building housing the construction company where they both worked.

"You haven't lost any days," she assured him, attempting a smile.

"You just couldn't stay away from the place, huh?" Mike laughed.

"Something like that," Lacey agreed.

"All joking aside, what are you doing here? You should be out soaking up the sun while you have the chance." His hazel eyes began inspecting her closely, noting the way she avoided looking directly at him and the fine tension behind her carefree expression.

"I drove over to my apartment this morning to pick up the mail and make sure everything was all right there," Lacey explained, striving to appear offhand so he wouldn't guess it was her own company she particularly wanted to avoid. "Since I was in the neighborhood and it was lunchtime, I decided to stop by and have lunch with Maryann."

"I'm afraid you're out of luck," His mouth twisted ruefully. "Maryann took her lunch break early to visit the dentist. I'd buy you lunch, but I'm just coming back

351

myself." He glanced at his wristwatch. "And I have an architect due in about twenty minutes."

"That's okay." Lacey shrugged, turning back to her car. "I deserve to eat alone. I should have called Maryann from my apartment instead of driving by." She didn't want to prolong the conversation with Mike. "See you Monday if not before, then."

"Don't be late," Mike warned, waving a goodbye.

In no hurry to return to the beach house, Lacey took her time on the way back. As she passed one of the more lavish resort hotels, she studied it absently. Giving in to an impulse, a trait she had moments ago derided, she left the highway and retraced the route to the hotel.

"Go ahead and splurge," she insisted. "You ought to have more out of this vacation, Lacey Andrews, than a broken heart and memories."

Parking her car in the lot, she walked into the hotel lobby, not giving herself a second chance to consider whether she should spend so much money on a simple meal. It was her vacation and she wouldn't have another for a year.

She hesitated near the lounge, trying to decide if her spree would extend to a cocktail before lunch. The thought of sitting alone at a table for two sipping a glass of wine was too depressing, and she started toward the restaurant entrance.

"Lacey!" a male voice declared, its expression somewhere between surprise and inquiry. "My eyes didn't deceive me—it *is* you!"

Halting, Lacey turned to stare at the handsome fair-haired man striding from the lounge. Her own surprise was mingled with dismay as she recognized Monica's brother, Vic Hamilton.

"Hello, Mr. Hamilton," she greeted him coolly, hoping he would receive the message and make his greeting equally short.

He clicked his tongue in mock reproval. "Vic," he corrected smoothly, and clasped both of her unwilling hands in his. "You look as beautiful in that turquoise sundress you're wearing as you did in the pajamas of almost the same color."

There was no need for him to remind her of the circumstances surrounding their first meeting. Lacey remembered them vividly. She managed to pull one hand free, but he held the other in both of his manicured hands.

"Thank you." She smiled with artificial politeness.

"What are you doing here?" He tipped his head to the side, his smile not hiding the shrewdness in his eyes. "Don't tell me you're meeting Cole?"

"No, I'm not." Lacey had to check herself quickly to keep from snapping out the answer. "I merely stopped by for lunch."

"Alone?" Vic Hamilton lifted an inquiring brow.

"Yes, alone," Lacey answered decisively.

"I can't let you do that." His smile broadened; her answer seemed to please him. "There's nothing worse than lunching alone. Come, we'll have a drink first."

"No, thank you," she refused, trying discreetly to pull her hand free.

"If you're worried about Cole being upset because we lunched together, I wouldn't." There was something secretively amused about his look, faintly smug and

353

knowing. "Besides, why should two people occupy two tables when they can sit together at one? If you like, we'll go dutch and you can pay for your own meal."

What was it going to take to get through to this blond god that she wasn't interested, Lacey wondered impatiently. Probably no one had ever told him no before and actually meant it.

"I. . . ." she began, but the sound of Cole's laughter coming from somewhere to her left cut off her retort.

The rich, throaty chuckle was instantly recognizable. Turning at an angle, she saw his rugged male figure, wearing a summer gray suit. As always, she experienced that little catch in her breath at the sight of him. So tanned, so vital, and so blatantly masculine, Cole seemed to fill the lobby—and Lacey's senses—with his presence.

Someone was on the receiving end of that flashing smile, full of virile charm. Resisting the pull of his magnetic attraction, Lacey forced her gaze to the person standing beside him.

Her eyes widened at the sight of the green-eyed blonde clinging to his arm. It was Monica Hamilton laughing up at Cole. Everything about the woman said this was her property; and Cole was not making any denial, token or otherwise.

"You didn't know Cole was going to be here, did you?" Vic murmured.

Lacey began to tremble violently. She was unconsciously clutching Vic's hands for support, the same ones that moments ago she had been trying to pull away from.

354

"No." It was a strangled sound. "I didn't know."

"Nor that he would be with my sister Monica?" Vic continued.

Completely oblivious to the ring of satisfaction in his voice, Lacey was aware only of the constricting band that seemed wrapped around her chest. The pain was so intense she thought she would die. Any second she expected her rib cage to cave in from the unbearable pressure.

"No." Again her answer was a strangled cry.

Her hands continued to cling to him as the only solid object around. He freed one of his hands to wrap an arm around her shoulders and turn her toward the entrance to the lounge. She had the fleeting sensation of a pair of deep blue eyes narrowing on her in recognition before she was faced in another direction.

Numbed by the fierce pain, she didn't remember taking the steps that brought her to the dark corner of the lounge. The next thing she was even semiconsciously aware of was Vic gently helping her into a cushioned booth.

Imperiously he snapped his fingers for the cocktail waitress's attention and called an order, but Lacey was beyond hearing. He slid onto the seat beside her. She was trembling all over and he covered her shaking hands on the table with his own. Someone stopped at the booth, then Vic was pressing the rim of a glass against her lips.

"Drink this," he ordered, and tipped the glass.

Automatically Lacey did as she was told, coughing and choking as the liquor burned a path down her throat. Once again she could feel, but she wasn't certain

355

that she was grateful for that. Seeing Cole like that, looking so happy with Monica, left her with the feeling that she had been betrayed and used.

"Cole didn't mention to you that he's been seeing Monica, did he?" Vic observed.

Pain stabbed through her at his suggestion that this wasn't the first time. She gave him a stricken look, then lowered her head, shaking it briefly.

"No, he didn't," she admitted.

"Haven't you wondered where he's been having his evening meals?" Vic chided in a tone that reproved her blindness.

"No, I . . . ." Lacey pressed a trembling hand over her eyes. It had never occurred to her to set the record straight that she and Cole were not living together in the intimate sense of the phrase. "I thought he was stopping at a restaurant somewhere."

"He's spent the last three evenings at our house, dining with Monica," he informed her.

"I see," Lacey murmured.

She saw that she had been a fool to hold out any hope where Cole was concerned. The hand covering hers tightened protectively, squeezing a warning an instant before a tall figure blocked the light. Lacey guessed it was Cole before he spoke, her nerves sharpening to a razor edge.

"What are you doing here, Lacey?" His voice was low and tautly controlled.

Lowering her hand from her face, she looked up at him, her eyes bright with pain. The hard angles and planes of his features were set in expressionless lines, yet she sensed his anger simmering just below the surface.

356

From somewhere she found the strength to challenge him. He had no right to an explanation for her presence in this hotel.

"What most people do at a place like this," she retorted, her tone brittle. "I'm having a drink before lunch."

"Yes, Lacey took pity on me being alone and agreed to join me," volunteered Vic, and Lacey didn't deny the lie.

The muscles along Cole's jawline tightened noticeably as he flashed an accusing look at Lacey. Monica appeared at his elbow, eyeing Lacey for a brief second before smiling possessively at Cole.

"Darling, they're holding our table," she reminded him huskily.

Distracted, Cole glanced down at her. He hesitated for a fraction of a second, then his gaze pinned Lacey again, sharp and metallic blue.

"Would you join us?" he requested stiffly.

"No," she refused, lowering her pain-filled gaze to the liquor glass on the table.

Beside her, Vic shrugged. "The lady says no, Cole. And I certainly don't have any reason to try to change her mind."

"Our table," Monica prodded.

Out of her side vision, Lacey saw Cole abruptly pivot away from the booth. The rigidity of controlled anger was in his carriage as he walked from the lounge with Monica on his arm. Pain shuddered through Lacey, relief mixed with a wounding ache.

"You're in love with him, aren't you?" Vic's statement was coated with sardonic mockery.

Pale and shaken, Lacey knew she couldn't escape the truth, so she nodded a silent admission. There was a terrible unreality to the situation, as if none of it was really happening.

"You poor kid." But he sounded more amused than sorry for her. "You thought you had a chance against Monica. If you'd asked me, I could have told you it was inevitable that Cole would end up with her."

"Really?" Tears seemed to be frozen on her lashes. She flicked them away with her finger, refusing to break down, but more returned to hang like liquid icicles. She breathed in deeply, sniffling a little, but obtaining some control.

"Monica has too many things going for her," Vic told her. "Besides, Cole is just the kind of man she needs. He would have been hers two years ago if she hadn't started ordering him around and throwing childish tantrums when he wouldn't do what she wanted. Theirs has been an on-again-off-again affair ever since. You have met Cole in one of the off-again stages."

"Yes, probably," Lacey agreed tightly, not about to explain their meeting now.

"To be perfectly frank, I'm all in favor of the marriage," he went on. "With Cole for a brother-in-law, I know my father will get off my back. I haven't any business sense and I don't want anything to do with the family operations."

He slid an arm around her shoulders again. At first Lacey accepted its comfort. "I'm not cut out for the business world, and Cole is. I'm much better at consoling beautiful women like you, Lacey."

She stiffened at his words. "If you're the consolation

358

prize for losing Cole, Mr. Hamilton, I'm not interested," she declared, and removed his arm from around her shoulders. "Would you please let me out of this booth?" she requested curtly.

Vic Hamilton was not interested in consoling her, only in taking advantage of her weakness at the moment. To remain in his company would simply remind her that Cole was with Monica. At long last she realized what a fool she had made of herself by falling in love with Cole. There was no need to make a bigger fool of herself.

"Where are you going?" He appeared incredulous that she was actually rejecting him.

"I'm leaving, and 'where' is my business," she retorted.

"You don't really mean it," Vic persisted.

"I do. So if you don't want me to create a scene, you will move."

He gave her an ugly smile. "You'll be sorry for this some day. Once a girl says no to me, it's the last time she's ever asked," he threatened.

"No, Mr. Hamilton. No, no, I don't want you ever," Lacey repeated, enunciating each word.

White with anger, he slid out of the booth. "You're nothing but a stupid little secretary," he jeered. "I don't know why I bothered with you."

His spiteful words bounced off her, not leaving any marks, as she swept past him to the lobby. When she stepped outside into the sun, the tears on her lashes streamed down her cheeks.

Once she was in her car, instinct took over, making all the right turns to take her to the beach house. She drove the last two miles in a sea of tears that blinded her to the point that she could barely make out the road.

Bolting into the house, she stumbled up the stairs to sink into the nearest chair, drowning in waves of despair and self-pity. Outside a car engine roared angrily into the driveway, brakes squealing it to a halt short of the garage door. The reverberation of a car door being slammed echoed into the house.

A sixth sense warned Lacey it was Cole. She quickly wiped the tears from her face and was blowing her nose as he slammed more doors on his way into the house, climbing the stairs two at a time.

His anger was no longer suppressed, but raging freely in his every line. But Lacey was beyond being intimidated by his anger; he had already hurt her too deeply for that. She met the blue storm clouds of his gaze without flinching.

"It's a little early for you to be here, isn't it?" she suggested stiffly.

"You know damned well why I'm here!" His voice rolled like thunder across the room and Cole quickly followed it. His hands were clenched in fists at his side, muscles leaping along his jaw. "I want to know what you were doing at that hotel with Hamilton."

Lacey tilted her chin defiantly, pain hammering at her throat. "It's no concern of yours what I was doing at the hotel or with whom!"

If she had had any doubts about that statement, they had faded into nothing when she had seen him with Monica. She started to pivot away from him, but his fingers closed in an iron grip around her forearm to spin her back.

"When I ask a question, I want an answer," he growled savagely. "What were you doing at the hotel?"

"You're hurting my arm," she pointed out curtly. His punishing grip began to cut off the circulation, making her hand and wrist throb.

"A lot more is going to hurt if you don't give me a straight answer," he warned, not relaxing his hold a fraction.

"I certainly didn't go because I thought you would be there." Lacey choked out the answer, fighting the tears that were once again stinging her eyes.

"But you arranged to meet Vic Hamilton there, didn't you?" Cole accused.

"Yes, I met him there. Is that what you wanted to hear?" she cried in challenge.

He released her arm abruptly as if she had suddenly become contaminated. With fires still raging in his eyes, he looked away in angry exasperation. He let his gaze slice back to her, dissecting her into little pieces.

"I knew it was only a matter of time before Vic made a play for you, but I thought you were smart enough to know what a philanderer he is," he said with contempt. "But the combination of money and looks was too much for you, wasn't it?" He didn't wait for an answer. "How many other times have you met him before today?"

Lacey was gently massaging her arm where he had gripped her so roughly. There would be bruises in the morning where his fingers had dug into her flesh.

"It isn't any concern of yours," she declared tightly, countering with, "I've never asked you how many times you've seen Monica."

"Monica has no part in this, so just leave her out of it!" he snapped.

"Gladly!"

Lacey stalked out of the living room onto the balcony. Her fingers curled into the railing, her nails digging into the smooth painted surface. Waves of pain racked her system, leaving her shaken and trembling.

She was angry with herself because she was letting Cole tear up her emotions further when the damage he had already done was beyond repair. She used that anger as a protective shield against him when he followed her onto the balcony.

"Lacey, I want you to stay away from Vic Hamilton," he ordered. His anger was held in check by a very tight rein, capable of snapping at the slightest provocation.

"I'll do as I please where Vic Hamilton or anyone else is concerned," Lacey retorted in a low, trembling voice that was fierce in her attempt to establish an independence. "Not you, nor any man, has the right to tell me whom I may see!"

The fragile reins of his temper snapped. Her shoulders were seized and roughly shaken as if she were a rag doll. The pain ripping through her body made her as weak and limp as one.

"Do I have to shake some sense into you?" he demanded gruffly.

"I think you've already tried." Her laugh was brittle, her already rattled senses in worse shape than before.

"Then listen to me and stay away from him," he declared, gritting his teeth in determination.

With a supreme effort, Lacey pushed and twisted out

of his hold. "I don't have to listen to you!" she cried angrily, her voice ringing with the pulsing hurt inside, her nerves raw. "You don't have any right to tell me what to do or not to do! I don't tell you who you can have for friends, and you're not going to tell me!"

His smoldering gaze flashed past her for an instant. "You don't have to shout, Lacey," he reproved in a low, sharp tone.

Automatically she glanced over her shoulder, an unconscious reaction to discover what had distracted his attention. A woman wearing a sunbonnet was on the beach near the tideline. Lacey recognized her instantly. It was the Mrs. Carlyle, who regularly searched the beach for seashells, and she was staring toward the house, the ocean air undoubtedly carrying their angry voices to her.

"I will shout if I want to." But Lacey did lower her volume. "And if you don't like it, you can leave!"

"We've been through that before," Cole retorted.

"Yes, we have." Her chin quivered traitorously. "And you'll be glad to learn that you've finally won that argument. I'm leaving!"

Cole frowned, his gaze narrowing in surprise at her announcement. Lacey didn't wait to hear his response, but darted past him into the house, not slowing up until she had reached her bedroom. The decision had been made on impulse, but she knew it was the only recourse left open to her.

Gulping back sobs, she dragged her suitcases from the closet and tossed them onto the bed. She began gathering her clothes and stuffing them carelessly into the open bags, jamming them together with no thought to orderliness. She hesitated for a split second when Cole appeared in the doorway before continuing her hurried packing.

A muscle was working convulsively along his jaw. His mouth was a grim line, but there was regret flickering in the hard blue steel of his gaze.

"Lacey, I—" he began tautly.

"There's nothing left to say," she interrupted briskly, aware of his tall muscular figure filling the door frame. "I have three full days of my vacation left and I'm not going to let you ruin those for me."

Impatiently he burst out, "Dammit, Lacey, I'm not trying to ruin anything for you. I—"

"You've certainly done a first-rate job for someone who wasn't trying!" She slammed a handful of clothes into one of the cases, her voice growing thick with suppressed emotion.

"You don't understand," Cole muttered.

"Isn't it time you were going back to your office?" challenged Lacey, scooping a handful of cosmetics from the dresser and dumping them into their small case.

"Yes, it is, but first—"

She turned on him roundly, trembling from the mental anguish his presence induced. "I'm leaving! The house is yours! Isn't that what you want?"

His expression hardened, his mouth compressed into a thin line. "Yes," he snapped after a second's hesitation. "That is exactly what I want!"

In the next instant the doorway was empty. Heavy, angry strides were carrying him down the hallway. Lacey resumed her packing in a frenzied need for activity, faltering briefly when she heard the door slam below.

AN HOUR AND A HALF later, she was carrying the last of her belongings into her own apartment. Setting the bag on the floor, she collapsed into one of the chairs, burying her face in her hands.

She didn't cry; there didn't seem to be any tears inside her. She was just a big empty ache. Vital parts had been removed and she knew she would never function quite the same again.

The telephone rang. It seemed an eternity since she had heard the sound. She stared at it blankly for several rings before pushing herself out of the chair to answer it.

"Hello," she said in a tired and dispirited voice.

"Lacey?"

It was Cole. The sound of his voice seemed to slash at her heart like a knife. Lacey hung up the phone to stop the piercing hurt.

Within minutes it was ringing again. She had made up her mind not to answer it when her hand picked up the receiver of its own volition and carried it to her ear.

"Don't hang up, Lacey." The remnants of his temper were evident in his irritated tone. "I'm at my office, so I don't have time to argue. We're going to get together tonight so we can talk this thing out. I'll be free around eight-thirty. . . ."

After he had dined with Monica, Lacey realized. "Leave me alone!" she begged angrily. "Get out of my life and stay out of it! I don't want to see or hear from you again—ever!"

She slammed the receiver down, breaking the connection, but Cole was as stubborn as she was. He would call back. Trembling, Lacey picked up the telephone again, hesitated, then dialed a number.

When it was answered, she said, "Jane? This is Lacey. May I speak to Maryann?"

"Sure," was the reply. "How is your vacation?"

"Fine," Lacey lied, and her call was switched through. "Hello, Maryann?"

"Hi, Lacey," was the cheerful response. "Mike told me you stopped this noon for lunch. I only wish I'd known you were coming—it would have given me a perfect excuse to cancel my dental appointment."

"I should have called you in the morning, but I didn't think of it," Lacey replied absently.

"How are you enjoying the sun and the sand and the surf?"

"That's what I'm calling about," she began hesitantly. "I'm not at the beach house. I've moved out."

"Good heavens, what happened?" Maryann asked with instant concern.

"It's a long story." Her friend already knew part of it from the visit Lacey had made the previous Friday night. "I was wondering if I could sleep on your couch for a few nights."

"Of course," was the puzzled reply, "but I thought you were going to Richmond to visit your parents this weekend after Margo came back."

"I was, but I've changed my mind."

The thought of explaining to her parents all that had happened was too daunting, and Lacey knew she would never be able to keep it from them. They were too close. And she couldn't stay in her apartment. Cole would keep phoning and possibly even come over.

"What happened, Lacey? Did—"

"I'll tell you all about it tonight," she promised. "What time will you be getting off work?"

"I shouldn't have any trouble leaving by five, but I have to stop at the bank and the store." Maryann paused. "Why don't you stop by the office and I'll give you the key to my apartment? That way you won't have to wait for me," she suggested.

"Thanks." Lacey swallowed, her throat suddenly constricting.

"Oh, I have a motive," her friend laughed. "If I have to wait until tonight to find out what happened, I'll be insane with curiosity. When you stop by, you can give me an outline at least."

CHAPTER TEN

RETURNING TO WORK on Monday morning, Lacey hoped her job would take her mind off the dead ache of her heart. So far that hope hadn't shown much promise. She had difficulty concentrating. Typing a letter was proving to be an impossible task as her fingers constantly hit the wrong keys.

"You look as if you could use some coffee. Shall I pour you a cup?" Mike offered, pausing beside her desk to reach for her coffee mug.

"Please," Lacey sighed, then bent over her typewriter to erase her latest error.

Mike filled her cup as well as his own and set it back on her desk. "It's only ten o'clock in the morning and you look bushed. I think that's a symptom of what's known as the first-day-back-from-vacation malady," he teased as his hazel gaze made an assessing sweep of her.

"Probably," she agreed, and removed the corrected letter from the typewriter carriage to add it to the stack on her desk. "Here are the letters you wanted out this morning."

"Mmm, good," said Mike between sips of his coffee. He gathered up the pile of letters and walked to the connecting door to his private office. He paused in the doorway. "It's good to have you back, Lacey."

"Thanks." It was a weary smile that accompanied her reply, etched with strain.

As he closed the door behind him, she rested her elbows on the desk top. Her shoulders slumped as if the weight of keeping up the appearance that she was her normal self had become too heavy to maintain when no one was around to see.

With the tips of her fingers she rubbed the throbbing pressure point between her eyebrows. She blinked at the tears that unexpectedly sprang into her eyes.

The door to the main office area opened and she straightened to an erect posture. The forced smile of polite greeting she had affixed to her lips drooped as Cole walked into the office.

He looked haggard and worn, but there was a relentlessly unyielding set to his jaw. It seemed to match the determined glitter in his indigo blue eyes.

Recovering from her initial shock, Lacey reached for the phone, ringing the interoffice line to Mike. "Cole Whitfield is here to see you, Mike," she said the minute that he answered her buzz.

"What?" His stunned reaction indicated that he had not expected Cole.

Lacey's pulse skyrocketed in alarm. "I'll. . . ."

Cole reached over her desk and pushed the button to break the connection. "I'm not here to see Bowman," he stated. "It's you I want to talk to, Lacey."

Hastily she replaced the receiver and gathered the miscellaneous folders and papers from the filing basket. She rose quickly from her chair to walk to the filing cabinet, wanting distance between herself and Cole.

"Did Margo and Bob get back safely?" She tried to

make the question sound nonchalant, pretending an indifference to his presence as she pulled open a file drawer.

Cole was right behind her to push the drawer shut. Her heart began leaping like a jumping bean. Raw, aching nerves were crying out for relief.

"As a matter of fact, they did," he said tersely. "But that's not why I'm here and you know it."

The connecting office door opened and Mike stepped out, frowning bewilderedly at Cole. "I'm sorry about the confusion, Cole, but Lacey's replacement must have forgotten to leave a message that you were coming this morning. What was it you wanted to talk to me about?"

Cole flashed an impatient look at him, annoyed by the interruption. "It isn't you I'm here to see," he repeated. "I want a few words with Lacey, if you don't mind."

The latter phrase was merely a polite gesture. Lacey had the impression Cole would stay whether Mike gave his permission or not.

"We have nothing to discuss," she told him stiffly, and brushed past him to return to her desk.

"That's where you're wrong," Cole stated flatly. "We have a great deal to discuss."

"This sounds private," Mike muttered, and retreated behind his office door.

Lacey turned to call him back and came face to face with Cole. All her senses were heightened by his closeness; she was quivering in reaction to his forceful presence.

"Why don't you go away and leave me alone?" she demanded hoarsely. "Can't you see I'm working?"

"You chose the time and place. I didn't," Cole informed her. "You knew I wanted to speak to you. I've been trying all weekend to get hold of you, but you've been hiding somewhere."

"I was not hiding!" she lied, and angrily shoved the papers back into the filing basket.

"Oh?" A dark brow was raised in mocking skepticism. "What do you call it?"

"Enjoying what remained of my vacation," Lacey retorted, and started to walk away from him again.

His hand caught at the soft flesh of her upper arm to stop her. "Will you stand still?" he demanded in an exasperated breath.

His touch burned through her like a branding iron and Lacey reacted as violently as if it were, trying to wrench her arm out of his grip. Cole merely tightened his hold.

"Let me go!" she hissed, pathetically vulnerable to his touch.

Desperate, she grabbed for the first item on her desk top that could be used as a weapon. It turned out to be the stapler. She raised it to strike him, but Cole captured her wrist before she could even begin the swing.

"This is where I came in, isn't it?" The grim line of his mouth twisted wryly as she was pulled close by her struggles. "Only the other time you were trying to bash my head in with a poker."

"I hate you, Cole Whitfield!" Her voice was breaking. "You are the rudest, most arrogant—"

"You said something similar to that before, too." He pried the stapler free from the death-grip of her fingers and replaced it on the desk top. "Now, do you think we

371

can sit down and talk this out like two civilized human beings?"

Averting her head from the tantalizing nearness of his well-formed mouth, she nodded reluctantly. "Yes."

"Sit down." Cole more or less pushed her into her chair and drew a second for himself opposite hers.

"I still don't see that we have anything to talk about," she insisted stubbornly, her pulse behaving not quite as erratically as it had seconds ago in his arms.

"For starters—" the direct blue eyes studied her closely "—why didn't you tell me that you didn't go to the hotel to meet Vic Hamilton?"

"You weren't in any mood to listen to me and I didn't see why I should explain." After the defensive answer, she hesitated and asked, "How did you find out?"

"From Vic, after a little prompting," Cole answered with a half smile. "Luckily for him, he was too concerned about having his handsome face messed up, so it took only a few threats. As angry as I was, I would have beaten the truth out of him."

"It wasn't any of your business," Lacey muttered, looking away. She refused to read any implication into his personal involvement in her affairs.

"Wasn't it?" he asked quietly, his low voice rolling over her skin.

The interoffice line buzzed and she reached for the phone, grateful for the interruption. But Cole took the receiver out of her hand.

"Hold all the calls. Don't put any more through," he ordered and hung up.

"You can't do that," Lacey protested in astonishment.

"That's funny—I thought I just did," he countered with a laughing glint in his eye.

"You know what I mean," she retorted impatiently.

"But do you know what I mean?" His voice was wistfully soft and enigmatic.

Its tug on her heartstrings was more than she could bear. Agitatedly she rose from her chair, her hands clasped tightly in front of her.

"There isn't any point to this conversation," she insisted. "Everything has been said. Our little interlude, affair, whatever you want to call it, is over. You are free to go your way and I'm free to go mine."

"Is that the way you want it?" Cole sounded skeptical.

Lacey knew she had to convince him somehow that it was what she wanted, even though she knew with all her heart that it wasn't.

"Yes, that is the way I want it," she repeated stiffly. "So I don't see what there is for us to discuss."

In a fluid move, Cole was behind her, his hands settling lightly on her shoulders to turn her to face him. Lacey could find no strength to resist his undemanding touch.

"The point to this conversation is that I miss you," he said quietly. He ran his gaze over her face, and she caught her breath at the fires smoldering in his eyes. "It's been pure and simple misery since you left. You're not there in the mornings anymore to wake me up when I sleep through the alarm. No coffee, no orange juice made. I never minded before coming home to an empty house, but I do now after having you there to greet me. And in the evenings, I can't get any work done without you sitting quietly in a nearby chair."

"You make me sound as if I've become a habit." There was a painful lump in her throat, choking her.

"A very pleasurable habit that I don't want to give up," Cole responded, stroking a hand over her cheek into the silken brown of her hair.

"What are you suggesting, Cole?" Tears were misting her eyes when she met his look, doubt stealing pleasure from his words. "That we should resume our arrangement of living together, throwing out the ground rules?"

"And if I said yes, what would you say?" That glowing look in his eyes was tugging at her heart.

Lacey struggled with her pride. "I would say, thanks but no thanks. I'm not interested in taking on a lover at the present time." Just for a moment she weakened to ask, "That is what you're suggesting, isn't it?"

"In a sense, yes." His slow smile was disarming. "I want to marry you, Lacey. I want you to be my wife."

"Oh!" The tiny word escaped in an indrawn breath of surprise as she melted slightly against him. "Are you serious? What about Monica?"

"Monica?" A curious frown creased his forehead. "Why should she have anything to do with it?"

"I don't know." She was confused and uncertain about the conclusion she had previously drawn. "You dined with her all last week, didn't you?"

"At her parents' home, yes, and she was at the table, but it was her father I was meeting, not Monica," Cole explained in amusement. "Who told you I was there? Vic, I suppose."

"Yes," Lacey nodded, and sighed when his arm tightened around her waist. "He said that ever since you

374

broke your engagement with Monica, you had continued to go on seeing her."

"And you believed him," he concluded.

"I believed him. You were there at the hotel with her, having lunch. He said your relationship with her had been an on-again, off-again affair and that I had met you during one of the off-again times. It seemed logical," Lacey said, trying to defend the erroneous conclusion she had reached.

"I should have known he would make mischief of some sort," he concluded, bending his head to brush his mouth over the warmth of her skin, teasingly near her lips. Her lashes fluttered in tempo with her heart. "I have business dealings with Carter Hamilton, her father. That's the only reason I was there."

Her hands slipped nearer to the collar of his shirt. "I didn't know," she whispered. "I thought—at the hotel, you looked so happy with her. Not like the other time when you were...."

"Rude, is that the word you're looking for?" Cole finished, mockingly. "That Sunday at the beach house, Monica arrived uninvited. I saw no reason to be polite to a woman who wasn't welcome in my home. And if you had the impression I was happy to be with her at the hotel, I'm a better actor than I realized. Regardless of how it looked, I was merely being polite to the daughter of a business associate, even if she's an ugly old crow."

"Monica's beautiful," Lacey protested.

"That, my love, is in the eye of the beholder," he corrected, drawing his head back to look at her. "When are you going to stop talking so I can kiss you?"

"Now."

Her hands slid around his neck as she raised herself on tiptoes to meet his descending mouth. Joy spilled over, lighting every corner of her world.

The taste of his mouth possessively covering hers was like a sweet wine that went to her head, and Lacey felt drunk with the rapture of love returned. When the kiss ended on a reluctant note, she rested her head on his shoulder, deliriously happy in a quiet kind of way.

"You haven't said you'll marry me yet." His voice was a husky tremor.

"Haven't I?" she returned with faint surprise. Tipping her head back, she smiled at his soberly rapt expression. "I will."

"Do you have any objection to a quick elopement?"

"None." She shook her head. She lifted a hand to let her fingertips trace the forceful line of his jaw. "Why did you let me leave last Thursday? You acted as if you were glad to see me go."

"I was." He caught her hand, lightly kissing the tips of her fingers. "It was sheer torture lying in bed at nights with you in the next room. If you'd stayed those last two nights, I knew I would throw those stupid ground rules out the window. When you decided to leave, I never expected you'd disappear. It turned out to be worse not knowing where you were or who you were with."

"I stayed at a girl friend's," Lacey said in answer to his unspoken question.

"While I went quietly out of my mind," Cole added wryly.

"I'm sorry," she whispered.

"You should be," he declared with mock gruffness.

"I wasn't having an easy time of it, either, this weekend," Lacey reminded him. "I kept imagining you with Monica and wondering when I would read about your engagement in the newspapers."

"There has never been any reason for you to be jealous of Monica," Cole assured her.

"I know that...now." But she hoped she would never have to live through another weekend like that again.

The remembered pain must have been reflected in her eyes, because Cole's dark gaze became suddenly very intense. "Never forget that I love you, Lacey." He kissed her hard and fiercely, as if to drive out the painful memory so there would be room only for his love.

The interoffice door opened and Mike walked through, halting at the sight of the embracing pair. "Sorry. It was so quiet out here I thought you'd gone, Whitfield," he apologized, and started to retreat.

"There's no need to leave, Mike," said Cole. "Lacey and I were just going."

"What?" Mike frowned and Lacey stared at Cole in confusion and surprise.

"I'll have someone over to replace her in half an hour," Cole continued. "She's going to have a lot to do in the next few days. And after we're married, if she wants to be anyone's secretary, I'd rather have her be mine."

"But...." Lacey didn't know what protest she was about to make since she didn't really object to Cole's plan.

"In the meantime," Cole interrupted, "there's something I want to show her."

She forgot all about Mike and how he would get along without a secretary.

"What?" Her curiosity was aroused.

"Get your purse and I'll show you." He smiled mysteriously.

"Congratulations," Mike offered as Cole hurried Lacey out the door.

As Cole was helping her into his car, Lacey repeated her question, "What are you going to show me?"

"You'll see," was all he would say.

"Give me a hint at least," she persisted.

But his only response was an enigmatic smile as he pulled out of the parking lot into the street.

Within a short time, she realized they were driving toward Virginia Beach, crossing the Chesapeake Bay bridge-tunnel into Norfolk. When they turned onto a side road she recognized, she became thoroughly confused. It led to her cousin Margo's house.

"Why are we going to the beach house?" She frowned.

Cole reached for her hand and held it warmly in his. "Patience."

At the house, he parked the car in the driveway and turned to face her, smiling. "Would the future Mrs. Whitfield like to see her new home?"

"What?" She gave him an incredulous look and he chuckled softly.

"When Margo and Bob came back from their cruise, he told me that they were moving to Florida near his parents as soon as he could make all the arrangements here." He reached in his pocket and handed her a key. "I bought the house for us. After all the frustrating nights I'd spent here with you, I decided it was fitting that this should be our home where I can spend a million satisfying evenings with you."

"You've bought it?" Lacey stared at the key in the palm of her hand, not certain that she had really understood him.

"You did like the house, didn't you?" Cole tipped his head to the side, studying her closely, a ring of uncertainty in his voice.

"I love the house!" she declared vigorously. "I just can't believe it's really mine—ours," she corrected herself quickly.

"Believe it, honey."

A sound, somewhere between a laugh and a cry, came from her throat as she threw her arms around his neck, happiness and love bubbling from her like an eternal fountain. Cole removed the need to express herself with words. Deeds were much more enjoyable.

Her arms were locked around Cole's neck when he finally lifted his mouth from her lips. "Would it be improper to prematurely carry my bride over the threshold?"

"Why worry about whether it's proper or not?" Lacey questioned in an amused voice. "You've already carried me into your bedroom."

"So I have." He grinned and swept her up into the cradle of his arms.

The key to the front door was still clutched in her fingers. Lacey was certain Cole was going to drop her before she was able to insert it in the lock and open the door. Laughing, he carried her into the house and up the stairs, kissing her soundly as he set her on her feet. Lacey glanced around, catching back the sob in her throat.

"What's the matter?" Cole frowned curiously.

"I'm afraid this is all a dream and I'm going to wake up," she murmured. He pinched her arm. "Ouch!"

"It isn't a dream. I'm still here and you still have the key to our house in your hand," he told her, his eyes crinkling at the corners.

"I can't believe it," Lacey insisted with a shake of her head, adding a quick, "but don't pinch me again. That hurt."

"I promise not to damage the merchandise until I'm sure it's totally mine. Which reminds me, when we leave here, we'll drive to Richmond. Your parents might like to meet me before I marry their daughter."

"Good heavens!" she declared as she realized the truth of his words. "My parents have never even heard of you. I haven't written them or talked to them on the phone since I met you. What will they think?"

"They'll think that I swept you off your feet, the way every romantic lover should," he mocked.

She laughed. "Just wait until I tell Maryann."

"Who is Maryann?"

"My friend. My very best friend." Lacey made the definition a little more emphatic.

"The same one you stayed with this weekend?" Cole asked.

"Yes, the very same."

"I suppose she's the one you'll run to whenever we have an argument."

"More than likely," Lacey retorted.

"I want her name, address and telephone number so I'll know where to find you the next time you storm out of the house."

"Do you think there will be a next time?" She tipped her head to the side, finding it difficult to imagine that she could ever get that angry with him again.

"Probably," Cole sighed. "We're both pretty stubborn."

"You are more stubborn than I am," Lacey reminded him.

"You see?" He tweaked the tip of her nose. "You're already trying to start an argument."

"It seems to me a smart fellow like you might be able to figure out how to shut me up." Her brown eyes were bright with silent invitation.

"It will be very enjoyable trying," he declared before seeking her lips.

COLE WADED from the water, a bronze-skinned sea god emerging from the ocean, and love tingled over Lacey's flesh at the sight of him walking toward her, the flashing white of his smile lighting her life.

An interlocking diamond solitaire ring and gold wedding band was on the third finger of her left hand, proof that she really was his wife. Yet often in the past few days, Lacey had been overcome with the urge to pinch herself to be reassured it wasn't just a beautiful dream. Every time she looked at Cole, touched him, she fell in love with him all over again.

Reaching her side, he dropped to his knees on the sand, droplets of salt water clinging to him. For a minute he simply studied her, stretched on the sand in her metallic blue gray swimsuit.

Instantly every nerve was alert, her senses quivering at the disturbing ardor in his look. He reached for her hand, pulling her into a sitting position, then kissing her with familiar ease.

"Happy?" he murmured, raking his fingers through her short brown hair and cupping the back of her head in his hand.

"Heavenly so, if there is such a thing," Lacey answered softly, a delicious warmth spreading through her limbs.

"Even though we have to set the alarm to get up in the morning?" Cole reminded her wryly.

"Are you dreading breaking in your new secretary?" she teased.

"I don't know." The creases along the corners of his mouth deepened attractively. "I've certainly enjoyed breaking in my new wife these past few days."

"Have you?" Her lips parted, inviting his kiss.

His dark blue gaze flicked to them for a tantalizing second, a fire smoldering to life in his eyes. Then he was straightening, pulling her to her feet along with him. The kiss he gave her held a promise of more to come in a more private place than the beach.

When he turned toward the house, an arm was curved around Lacey's waist to tuck her close to his side. A woman was walking to their right, intent upon the sand at her feet. The old-fashioned sunbonnet on her head instantly identified the woman to Cole and Lacey. He stopped.

"Good afternoon, Mrs. Carlyle," he greeted her.

The woman glanced up, momentarily surprised. "Good afternoon." Her gaze took in the affectionate attitude of the pair. "I see the two of you here made up after your little spat." Despite the friendliness in her remark, there was evidence of disapproval in the tightness of her smile.

"We did," Cole admitted, adding with a dancing light in his eye, "And I took your advice, too." He held up Lacey's left hand, showing off the gold band encircling her ring finger. "I made an honest woman of her."

Immediately the woman's smile turned into a radiant beam. "I'm delighted for both of you, really I am. As much in love as the two of you are, you won't be sorry," she insisted.

"No, we won't be a bit sorry," Cole agreed, and smiled down at Lacey's upturned face.

Harlequin Celebrates

Thirty-five Years of Excellence

...and our commitment to excellence continues. Indulge in the pleasure of superb romance reading by choosing the most popular love stories in the world.

Harlequin Presents®

Exciting romance novels for the woman of today— a rare blend of passion and dramatic realism.

Harlequin Romance™

Tender, captivating stories that sweep to faraway places and delight with the magic of love.

HARLEQUIN SUPERROMANCE™

Longer, more absorbing love stories for the connoisseur of romantic fiction.

Harlequin Temptation™

Sensual and romantic stories about choices, dilemmas, resolutions, and above all, the fulfillment of love.

Harlequin American Romance™

Contemporary romances— uniquely North American in flavor and appeal.

Code: 35-1